The Rivals of
SHERLOCK
HOLMES

DOVER MYSTERY CLASSICS

The Rivals of SHERLOCK HOLMES

A Collection of Victorian-Era Detective Stories

DOVER PUBLICATIONS, INC.
Mineola, New York

Bibliographical Note

The Rivals of Sherlock Holmes: A Collection of Victorian-Era Detective Stories, first published by Dover Publications, Inc., in 2019, is a new compilation of sixteen previously published stories. See the Bibliography at the end of the book for the publication history of each story; a new Publisher's Note has been specially prepared for this edition

Library of Congress Cataloging-in-Publication Data

Title: The rivals of Sherlock Holmes.
Description: Mineola, New York : Dover Publications, Inc., 2019. | "The Rivals of Sherlock Holmes: A Collection of Victorian-Era Detective Stories, first published by Dover Publications, Inc., in 2019, is a new compilation of sixteen previously published stories. See the Bibliography at the end of the book for the publication history of each story." | Includes bibliographical references.
Identifiers: LCCN 2019017479 | ISBN 9780486838618 | ISBN 0486838617
Subjects: LCSH: Detective and mystery stories, English—19th century.
Classification: LCC PR1309.D4 R45 2019 | DDC 823/.087208—dc23
LC record available at https://lccn.loc.gov/2019017479

Manufactured in the United States by LSC Communications
83861701
www.doverpublications.com

2 4 6 8 10 9 7 5 3 1

2019

Publisher's Note

IT is hard, from a remove of more than one hundred years, to understand just how large an impact the initial appearance of Sherlock Holmes had on the literary scene. There was the world before Sherlock—drab, lackluster, somewhat boring—and after—thrilling, conspiratorial, adventuresome. With him came the true birth and codification of an exciting new genre: the detective story.

If book publishing knows how to do one thing, it is to pursue and replicate a successful formula forever. Inspired by Arthur Conan Doyle's example, a raft of imitators, some more similar than others, appeared in print over the ensuing decades. Conan Doyle had tried to kill off his creation, but was compelled to bring him back by popular demand. It would, however, be impossible to even attempt to kill off all of the sleuths that emerged in the immediate wake of the initial Holmes wave.

There is a mini-tradition of anthologies that present these other detectives at work. Perhaps the most celebrated version was compiled by Hugh Greene (a major figure in British journalism, and the brother of Graham) in the early 1970s; it led to several follow-up volumes, which ranged far and wide—even to America!—in collecting detective stories that could delight those readers already fully versed in every move that Sherlock Holmes had ever made. While the Greene editions segregated their sleuths by geography, this Dover anthology, in an attempt to present the broadest and most inclusive roster of detectives, includes stories from around the globe.

Among the most celebrated are Father Brown, the humble, intuitive creation of British author G. K. Chesterton, and the gallant Arsène Lupin, the French thief/detective that Maurice Leblanc set loose in

Paris in the early 1900s. From Australia, we hear from Fergus Hume, author of the early crime bestseller, *The Mystery of a Hansom Cab*. Over in the United States, the detective is given a spiritual spin in the person of Uncle Abner, who resolves an Appalachian crime in "The Angel of the Lord."

Closer to Holmes' territory, there is Arthur Morrison's barrister-turned-sleuth Martin Hewitt. With Hewitt, Morrison dialed back the detective's eccentricities, so that he became more of an everyman, allowing readers to more readily identify with the character. Perhaps, too, this is why these stories still read so well today. And as if being rather commonplace wasn't handicap enough, Ernest Bramah, early in the twentieth century, created the blind hero Max Carrados, whose other senses, magnified by the loss of sight, prove sharp enough to solve even the most vexing conundrums.

Less a collection of "Sherlock-like" adventures, this volume is an attempt to show the many variations Conan Doyle inspired via his immortal "consulting detective." Whether these sleuths truly rival Holmes is a question that can only be answered by making your way through this collection of stories. *The game is indeed afoot!*

Contents

The Rivals of
SHERLOCK HOLMES

The Great Ruby Robbery

Grant Allen

I.

PERSIS REMANET was an American heiress. As she justly remarked, this was a commonplace profession for a young woman nowadays; for almost everybody of late years has been an American and an heiress. A poor Californian, indeed, would be a charming novelty in London society. But London society, so far, has had to go without one.

Persis Remanet was on her way back from the Wilcoxes' ball. She was stopping, of course, with Sir Everard and Lady Maclure at their house at Hampstead. I say "of course" advisedly; because if you or I go to see New York, we have to put up at our own expense (five dollars a day, without wine or extras) at the Windsor or the Fifth Avenue; but when the pretty American comes to London (and every American girl is *ex officio* pretty, in Europe at least; I suppose they keep their ugly ones at home for domestic consumption) she is invariably the guest either of a dowager duchess or of a Royal Academician, like Sir Everard, of the first distinction. Yankees visit Europe, in fact, to see, among other things, our art and our old nobility; and by dint of native persistence they get into places that you and I could never succeed in penetrating, unless we devoted all the energies of a long and blameless life to securing an invitation.

Persis hadn't been to the Wilcoxes with Lady Maclure, however. The Maclures were too really great to know such people as the Wilcoxes, who were something tremendous in the City, but didn't buy pictures; and Academicians, you know, don't care to cultivate City people—unless they're customers. ("Patrons," the Academicians more usually call them; but I prefer the simple business word myself, as being a deal less patronizing.) So Persis had accepted an invitation from Mrs. Duncan Harrison, the wife of the well-known member for the Hackness Division of Elmetshire, to take a seat in her carriage to and from the Wilcoxes. Mrs. Harrison knew the habits and manners of American heiresses too well to offer to chaperon Persis; and indeed, Persis, as a free-born American citizen, was quite as well able to take care of herself, the wide world over, as any three ordinary married Englishwomen.

Now, Mrs. Harrison had a brother, an Irish baronet, Sir Justin O'Byrne, late of the Eighth Hussars, who had been with them to the Wilcoxes, and who accompanied them home to Hampstead on the back seat of the carriage. Sir Justin was one of those charming, ineffective, elusive Irishmen whom everybody likes and everybody disapproves of. He had been everywhere, and done everything—except to earn an honest livelihood. The total absence of rents during the sixties and seventies had never prevented his father, old Sir Terence O'Byrne, who sat so long for Connemara in the unreformed Parliament, from sending his son Justin in state to Eton, and afterwards to a fashionable college at Oxford. "He gave me the education of a gentleman," Sir Justin was wont regretfully to observe; "but he omitted to give me also the income to keep it up with."

Nevertheless, society felt O'Byrne was the sort of man who must be kept afloat somehow; and it kept him afloat accordingly in those mysterious ways that only society understands, and that you and I, who are not society, could never get to the bottom of if we tried for a century. Sir Justin himself had essayed Parliament, too, where he sat for a while behind the great Parnell without for a moment forfeiting society's regard even in those earlier days when it was held as a prime article of faith by the world that no gentleman could possibly call himself a Home-Ruler. 'Twas only one of O'Byrne's wild Irish tricks, society said, complacently, with that singular indulgence it always extends to its special favourites, and which is, in fact, the correlative of that unsparing cruelty it shows in turn to those who happen to offend against its unwritten precepts. If Sir Justin had blown up a Czar or two in a fit of political exuberance, society would only have regarded the escapade as "one of O'Byrne's eccentricities." He had also held a commission for a while in a cavalry regiment, which he left, it was understood, owing to a difference of opinion about a lady with the colonel; and he was now a gentleman-at-large on London society, supposed by those who know more about everyone than one knows about oneself, to be on the look-out for a nice girl with a little money.

Sir Justin had paid Persis a great deal of attention that particular evening; in point of fact, he had paid her a great deal of attention from the very first, whenever he met her; and on the way home from the dance he had kept his eyes fixed on Persis's face to an extent that was almost embarrassing. The pretty Californian leaned back in her place in the carriage and surveyed him languidly. She was looking her level best that night, in her pale pink dress, with the famous Remanet rubies in a cascade of red light setting off that snowy neck of hers. 'Twas a neck for a painter. Sir Justin let his eyes fall regretfully more than once on the glittering rubies. He liked and admired Persis, oh! quite immensely. Your society man who has been through seven or eight London seasons could hardly be expected to go quite so far as falling in love with any woman; his habit is rather to look about him critically among all the nice girls trotted out by their mammas for his lordly inspection, and to reflect with a faint smile that this, that, or the other one might perhaps really suit him—if it were not for—and there comes in the inevitable *But* of all human commendation. Still, Sir Justin admitted with a sigh to himself that he liked Persis ever so much; she was so fresh and original! and she talked so cleverly! As for Persis, she would have given her eyes (like every other American girl) to be made "my lady"; and she had seen no man yet, with that auxiliary title in his gift, whom she liked half so well as this delightful wild Irishman.

At the Maclures' door the carriage stopped. Sir Justin jumped out and gave his hand to Persis. You know the house well, of course; Sir Everard Maclure's; it's one of those large new artistic mansions, in red brick and old oak, on the top of the hill; and it stands a little way back from the road, discreetly retired, with a big wooden porch, very convenient for leave-taking. Sir Justin ran up the steps with Persis to ring the bell for her; he had too much of the irrepressible Irish blood in his veins to leave that pleasant task to his sister's footman. But he didn't ring it at once; at the risk of keeping Mrs. Harrison waiting outside for nothing, he stopped and talked a minute or so with the pretty American. "You looked charming to-night, Miss Remanet," he said, as she threw back her light opera wrap for a moment in the porch and displayed a single flash of that snowy neck with the famous rubies; "those stones become you so."

Persis looked at him and smiled. "You think so?" she said, a little tremulous, for even your American heiress, after all, is a woman. "Well, I'm glad you do. But it's good-bye to-night, Sir Justin, for I go next week to Paris."

Even in the gloom of the porch, just lighted by an artistic red and blue lantern in wrought iron, she could see a shade of disappointment pass quickly over his handsome face as he answered, with a little gulp, "No! you don't mean that? Oh, Miss Remanet, I'm so sorry!" Then he paused and drew back: "And yet . . . . after all," he continued, "perhaps——," and there he checked himself.

Persis looked up at him hastily. "Yet, after all, what?" she asked, with evident interest.

The young man drew an almost inaudible sigh. "Yet, after all— nothing," he answered, evasively.

"That might do for an Englishwoman," Persis put in, with American frankness, "but it won't do for me. You must tell me what you mean by it." For she reflected sagely that the happiness of two lives might depend upon those two minutes; and how foolish to throw away the chance of a man you really like (with a my-ladyship to boot), all for the sake of a pure convention!

Sir Justin leaned against the woodwork of that retiring porch. She was a beautiful girl. He had hot Irish blood. . . . Well, yes; just for once—he would say the plain truth to her.

"Miss Remanet," he began, leaning forward, and bringing his face close to hers, "Miss Remanet—Persis—shall I tell you the reason why? Because I like you so much. I almost think I love you!"

Persis felt the blood quiver in her tingling cheeks. How handsome he was—and a baronet!

"And yet you're not altogether sorry," she said, reproachfully, "that I'm going to Paris!"

"No, not altogether sorry," he answered, sticking to it; "and I'll tell you why, too, Miss Remanet. I like you very much, and I think you like me. For a week or two, I've been saying to myself, 'I really believe I *must* ask her to marry me.' The temptation's been so strong I could hardly resist it."

"And why do you want to resist it?" Persis asked, all tremulous.

Sir Justin hesitated a second; then with a perfectly natural and instinctive movement (though only a gentleman would have ventured to make it) he lifted his hand and just touched with the tips of his fingers the ruby pendants on her necklet. "*This* is why," he answered simply, and with manly frankness. "Persis, you're so rich! I never dare ask you."

"Perhaps you don't know what my answer would be," Persis murmured very low, just to preserve her own dignity.

"Oh yes, I think I do," the young man replied, gazing deeply into her dark eyes. "It isn't that; if it were only that, I wouldn't so much mind it. But I think you'd take me." There was moisture in her eye. He went on more boldly: "I know you'd take me, Persis, and that's why I don't ask you. "You're a great deal too rich, and *these* make it impossible."

"Sir Justin," Persis answered, removing his hand gently, but with the moisture growing thicker, for she really liked him, "it's most unkind of you to say so; either you oughtn't to have told me at all, or else—if you did——" She stopped short. Womanly shame overcame her.

The man leaned forward and spoke earnestly. "Oh, don't say that!" he cried, from his heart. "I couldn't bear to offend you. But I couldn't bear, either, to let you go away—well—without having ever told you. In that case you might have thought I didn't care at all for you, and was only flirting with you. But, Persis, I've cared a great deal for you—a great, great deal—and had hard work many times to prevent myself from asking you. And I'll tell you the plain reason why I haven't asked you. I'm a man about town, not much good, I'm afraid, for anybody or anything; and everybody says I'm on the look-out for an heiress—which happens not to be true; and if I married you, everybody'd say, 'Ah, there! I told you so!' Now, I wouldn't mind that for myself; I'm a man, and I could snap my fingers at them; but I'd mind it for *you*, Persis, for I'm enough in love with you to be very, very jealous, indeed, for your honour. I couldn't bear to think people should say, 'There's that pretty American girl, Persis Remanet that was, you know; she's thrown herself away upon that good-for-nothing Irishman, Justin O'Byrne, a regular fortune-hunter, who's married her for her money.' So for your sake, Persis, I'd rather not ask you; I'd rather leave you for some better man to marry."

"But *I* wouldn't," Persis cried aloud. "Oh, Sir Justin, you must believe me. You must remember——"

At that precise point, Mrs. Harrison put her head out of the carriage window and called out rather loudly:—

"Why, Justin, what's keeping you? The horses'll catch their deaths of cold; and they were clipped this morning. Come back at once, my dear boy. Besides, you know, *les convenances!*"

"All right, Nora," her brother answered; "I won't be a minute. We can't get them to answer this precious bell. I believe it don't ring! But I'll try again, anyhow." And half forgetting that his own words weren't strictly true, for he hadn't yet tried, he pressed the knob with a vengeance.

"Is that your room with the light burning, Miss Remanet?" he went on, in a fairly loud official voice, as the servant came to answer. "The one with the balcony, I mean? Quite Venetian, isn't it? Reminds one of Romeo and Juliet. But most convenient for a burglary, too! Such nice low rails! Mind you take good care of the Remanet rubies!"

"I don't want to take care of them," Persis answered, wiping her dim eyes hastily with her lace pocket-handkerchief, "if they make you feel as you say, Sir Justin. I don't mind if they go. Let the burglar take them!"

And even as she spoke, the Maclure footman, immutable, sphinx-like, opened the door for her.

II.

Persis sat long in her own room that night before she began undressing. Her head was full of Sir Justin and those mysterious hints of his. At last, however, she took her rubies off, and her pretty silk bodice. "I don't care for them at all," she thought, with a gulp, "if they keep from me the love of the man I'd like to marry."

It was late before she fell asleep; and when she did, her rest was troubled. She dreamt a great deal; in her dreams, Sir Justin, and dance music, and the rubies, and burglars were incongruously mingled. To make up for it, she slept late next morning; and Lady Maclure let her sleep on, thinking she was probably wearied out with much dancing the previous evening—as though any amount of excitement could ever weary a pretty American! About ten o'clock she woke with a start. A vague feeling oppressed her that somebody had come in during the night and stolen her rubies. She rose hastily and went to her dressing-table to look for them. The case was there all right; she opened it and looked at it. Oh, prophetic soul! the rubies were gone, and the box was empty!

Now, Persis had honestly said the night before the burglar might take her rubies if he chose, and she wouldn't mind the loss of them. But that was last night, and the rubies hadn't then as yet been taken. This morning, somehow, things seemed quite different. It would be rough on us all (especially on politicians) if we must always be bound by what we said yesterday. Persis was an American, and no American is insensible to the charms of precious stones; 'tis a savage taste which the European immigrants seem to have inherited obliquely from their Red Indian predecessors. She rushed over to the bell and rang it with feminine violence. Lady Maclure's maid answered the summons, as usual. She was a clever, demure-looking girl, this maid of Lady Maclure's; and when Persis cried to her wildly, "Send for the police at once, and tell Sir Everard my jewels are stolen!" she answered, "Yes, miss," with such sober acquiescence that Persis, who was American, and therefore a bundle of nerves, turned round and stared at her as an incomprehensible mystery. No Mahatma could have been more unmoved. She seemed quite to expect those rubies would be stolen, and to take no more notice of the incident than if Persis had told her she wanted hot water.

Lady Maclure, indeed, greatly prided herself on this cultivated imperturbability of Bertha's; she regarded it as the fine flower of English domestic service. But Persis was American, and saw things otherwise; to her, the calm repose with which Bertha answered, "Yes, miss; certainly, miss; I'll go and tell Sir Everard," seemed nothing short of exasperating.

Bertha went off with the news, closing the door quite softly; and a few minutes later Lady Maclure herself appeared in the Californian's room, to console her visitor under this severe domestic affliction. She found Persis sitting up in bed, in her pretty French dressing jacket (pale blue with *revers* of fawn colour), reading a book of verses. "Why, my dear!" Lady Maclure exclaimed, "then you've found them again, I suppose? Bertha told us you'd lost your lovely rubies!"

"So I have, dear Lady Maclure," Persis answered, wiping her eyes; "they're gone. They've been stolen. I forgot to lock my door when I came home last night, and the window was open; somebody must have come in, this way or that, and taken them. But whenever I'm in trouble, I try a dose of Browning. He's splendid for the nerves. He's so consoling, you know; he brings one to anchor."

She breakfasted in bed; she wouldn't leave the room, she declared, till the police arrived. After breakfast she rose and put on her dainty Parisian morning wrap—Americans have always such pretty bedroom things for these informal receptions—and sat up in state to await the police officer. Sir Everard himself, much disturbed that such a mishap should have happened in his house, went round in person to fetch the official. While he was gone, Lady Maclure made a thorough search of the room, but couldn't find a trace of the missing rubies.

"Are you sure you put them in the case, dear?" she asked, for the honour of the household.

And Persis answered: "Quite confident, Lady Maclure; I always put them there the moment I take them off; and when I came to look for them this morning, the case was empty."

"They were *very* valuable, I believe?" Lady Maclure said, inquiringly.

"Six thousand pounds was the figure in your money, I guess," Persis answered, ruefully. "I don't know if you call that a lot of money in England, but we do in America."

There was a moment's pause, and then Persis spoke again:—

"Lady Maclure," she said abruptly, "do you consider that maid of yours a Christian woman?"

Lady Maclure was startled. That was hardly the light in which she was accustomed to regard the lower classes.

"Well, I don't know about that," she said, slowly; "that's a great deal, you know, dear, to assert about *anybody*, especially one's maid. But I should think she was honest, quite decidedly honest."

"Well, that's the same thing, about, isn't it?" Persis answered, much relieved. "I'm glad you think that's so; for I was almost half afraid of her. She's too quiet for my taste, somehow; so silent, you know, and inscrutable."

"Oh, my dear," her hostess cried, "don't blame her for silence; that's just what I like about her. It's exactly what I chose her for. Such a nice, noiseless girl; moves about the room like a cat on tiptoe; knows her proper place, and never dreams of speaking unless she's spoken to."

"Well, you may like them that way in Europe," Persis responded frankly; "but in America, we prefer them a little bit human."

Twenty minutes later the police officer arrived. He wasn't in uniform. The inspector, feeling at once the gravity of the case, and recognizing that this was a Big Thing, in which there was glory to be won, and perhaps promotion, sent a detective at once, and advised that if possible nothing should be said to the household on the subject for the present, till the detective had taken a good look round the premises. That was useless, Sir Everard feared, for the lady's-maid knew; and the lady's-maid would be sure to go down, all agog with the news, to the servants' hall immediately. However, they might try; no harm in trying; and the sooner the detective got round to the house, of course, the better.

The detective accompanied him back—a keen-faced, close-shaven, irreproachable-looking man, like a vulgarized copy of Mr. John Morley. He was curt and business-like. His first question was, "Have the servants been told of this?"

Lady Maclure looked inquiringly across at Bertha. She herself had been sitting all the time with the bereaved Persis, to console her (with Browning) under this heavy affliction.

"No, my lady," Bertha answered, ever calm (invaluable servant, Bertha!), "I didn't mention it to anybody downstairs on purpose, thinking perhaps it might be decided to search the servants' boxes."

The detective pricked up his ears. He was engaged already in glancing casually round the room. He moved about it now, like a conjurer, with quiet steps and slow. "He doesn't get on one's nerves," Persis remarked, approvingly, in an undertone to her friend; then she added, aloud: "What's your name, please, Mr. Officer?"

The detective was lifting a lace handkerchief on the dressing-table at the side. He turned round softly. "Gregory, madam," he answered, hardly glancing at the girl, and going on with his occupation.

"The same as the powders!" Persis interposed, with a shudder. "I used to take them when I was a child. I never could bear them."

"We're useful, as remedies," the detective replied, with a quiet smile; "but nobody likes us." And he relapsed contentedly into his work once more, searching round the apartment.

"The first thing we have to do," he said, with a calm air of superiority, standing now by the window, with one hand in his pocket, "is to satisfy ourselves whether or not there has really, at all, been a robbery. We must look through the room well, and see you haven't left the rubies lying about loose somewhere. Such things often happen. We're constantly called in to investigate a case, when it's only a matter of a lady's carelessness."

At that Persis flared up. A daughter of the great republic isn't accustomed to be doubted like a mere European woman. "I'm quite sure I took them off," she said, "and put them back in the jewel case. Of that I'm just confident. There isn't a doubt possible."

Mr. Gregory redoubled his search in all likely and unlikely places. "I should say that settles the matter," he answered blandly. "Our experience is that whenever a lady's perfectly certain, beyond the possibility of doubt, she put a thing away safely, it's absolutely sure to turn up where she says she didn't put it."

Persis answered him never a word. Her manners had not that repose that stamps the caste of Vere de Vere; so, to prevent an outbreak, she took refuge in Browning.

Mr. Gregory, nothing abashed, searched the room thoroughly, up and down, without the faintest regard to Persis's feelings; he was a detective, he said, and his business was first of all to unmask crime, irrespective of circumstances. Lady Maclure stood by, meanwhile, with the imperturbable Bertha. Mr. Gregory investigated every hole and cranny, like a man who wishes to let the world see for itself he performs a disagreeable duty with unflinching thoroughness. When he had finished, he turned to Lady Maclure. "And now, if you please," he said blandly, "we'll proceed to investigate the servants' boxes."

Lady Maclure looked at her maid. "Bertha," she said, "go downstairs, and see that none of the other servants come up, meanwhile, to their bedrooms." Lady Maclure was not quite to the manner born, and had never acquired the hateful aristocratic habit of calling women servants by their surnames only.

But the detective interposed. "No, no," he said sharply. "This young woman had better stop here with Miss Remanet—strictly under her eye—till I've searched the boxes. For if I find nothing there, it may perhaps be my disagreeable duty, by-and-by, to call in a female detective to search her."

It was Lady Maclure's turn to flare up now. "Why, this is my own maid," she said, in a chilly tone, "and I've every confidence in her."

"Very sorry for that, my lady," Mr. Gregory responded, in a most official voice; "but our experience teaches us that if there's a person in the case whom nobody ever dreams of suspecting, that person's the one who has committed the robbery."

"Why, you'll be suspecting myself next!" Lady Maclure cried, with some disgust.

"Your ladyship's just the last person in the world I should think of suspecting," the detective answered, with a deferential bow—which, after his previous speech, was to say the least of it equivocal.

Persis began to get annoyed. She didn't half like the look of that girl Bertha, herself; but still, she was there as Lady Maclure's guest, and she couldn't expose her hostess to discomfort on her account.

"The girl shall *not* be searched," she put in, growing hot. "I don't care a cent whether I lose the wretched stones or not. Compared to human dignity, what are they worth? Not five minutes' consideration."

"They're worth just seven years," Mr. Gregory answered, with professional definiteness. "And as to searching, why, that's out of your hands now. This is a criminal case. I'm here to discharge a public duty."

"I don't in the least mind being searched," Bertha put in obligingly, with an air of indifference. "You can search me if you like—when you've got a warrant for it."

The detective looked up sharply; so also did Persis. This ready acquaintance with the liberty of the subject in criminal cases impressed her unfavourably. "Ah! we'll see about that," Mr. Gregory answered, with a cool smile. "Meanwhile, Lady Maclure, I'll have a look at the boxes."

III.

The search (strictly illegal) brought out nothing. Mr. Gregory returned to Persis's bedroom, disconsolate. "You can leave the room," he said to Bertha; and Bertha glided out. "I've set another man outside to keep a constant eye on her," he added in explanation.

By this time Persis had almost made her mind up as to who was the culprit; but she said nothing overt, for Lady Maclure's sake, to the detective. As for that immovable official, he began asking questions—some of them, Persis thought, almost bordering on the personal. Where had she been last night? Was she sure she had really worn the rubies? How did she come home? Was she certain she took them off? Did the maid help her undress? Who came back with her in the carriage?

To all these questions, rapidly fired off with cross-examining acuteness, Persis answered in the direct American fashion. She was sure she had the rubies on when she came home to Hampstead, because Sir Justin O'Byrne, who came back with her in his sister's carriage, had noticed them the last thing, and had told her to take care of them.

At mention of that name the detective smiled meaningly. (A meaning smile is stock-in-trade to a detective.) "Oh, Sir Justin O'Byrne!" he repeated, with quiet self-constraint. "*He* came back with you in the carriage, then? And did he sit the same side with you?"

Lady Maclure grew indignant (that was Mr. Gregory's cue). "Really, sir," she said, angrily, "if you're going to suspect gentlemen in Sir Justin's position, we shall none of us be safe from you."

"The law," Mr. Gregory replied, with an air of profound deference, "is no respecter of persons."

"But it ought to be of characters," Lady Maclure cried, warmly. "What's the good of having a blameless character, I should like to know, if—if——"

"If it doesn't allow you to commit a robbery with impunity?" the detective interposed, finishing her sentence his own way. "Well, well, that's true. That's per-fectly true—but Sir Justin's character, you see, can hardly be called blameless."

"He's a gentleman," Persis cried, with flashing eyes, turning round upon the officer; "and he's quite incapable of such a mean and despicable crime as you dare to suspect him of."

"Oh, I see," the officer answered, like one to whom a welcome ray of light breaks suddenly through a great darkness. "Sir Justin's a friend of yours! Did he come into the porch with you?"

"He did," Persis answered, flushing crimson; "and if you have the insolence to bring a charge against him——"

"Calm yourself, madam," the detective replied coolly. "I do nothing of the sort—at this stage of the proceedings. It's possible there may have been no robbery in the case at all. We must keep our minds open for the present to every possible alternative. It's—it's a delicate matter to hint at; but before we go any further—do you think, perhaps, Sir Justin may have carried the rubies away by mistake, entangled in his clothes?—say, for example, his coat-sleeve?"

It was a loophole of escape; but Persis didn't jump at it.

"He had never the opportunity," she answered, with a flash. "And I know quite well they were there on my neck when he left me, for the last thing he said to me was, looking up at this very window: 'That balcony's awfully convenient for a burglary. Mind you take good care of the Remanet rubies.' And I remembered what he'd said when I took them off last night; and that's what makes me so sure I really had them."

"*And* you slept with the window open!" the detective went on, still smiling to himself. "Well, here we have all the materials, to be sure, for a first-class mystery!"

IV.

For some days more, nothing further turned up of importance about the Great Ruby Robbery. It got into the papers, of course, as everything does nowadays, and all London was talking of it. Persis found herself quite famous as the American lady who had lost her jewels. People pointed her out in the park; people stared at her hard through their opera-glasses at the theatre. Indeed, the possession of the celebrated Remanet rubies had never made her half so conspicuous in the world as the loss of them made her. It was almost worth while losing them, Persis thought, to be so much made of as she was in society in consequence. All the world knows a young lady must be somebody when she can offer a reward of five hundred pounds for the recovery of gewgaws valued at six thousand.

Sir Justin met her in the Row one day. "Then you don't go to Paris for awhile yet—until you get them back?" he inquired very low.

And Persis answered, blushing, "No, Sir Justin; not yet; and—I'm almost glad of it."

"No, you don't mean that!" the young man cried, with perfect boyish ardour. "Well, I confess, Miss Remanet, the first thing I thought myself when I read it in *The Times* was just the very same: 'Then, after all, she won't go yet to Paris!'"

Persis looked up at him from her pony with American frankness. "And I," she said, quivering, "I found anchor in Browning. For what do you think I read?

> 'And learn to rate a true man's heart
> Far above rubies.'

The book opened at the very place; and *there* I found anchor!"

But when Sir Justin went round to his rooms that same evening his servant said to him, "A gentleman was inquiring for you here this afternoon, sir. A close-shaven gentleman. Not very prepossessin'. And it seemed to me somehow, sir, as if he was trying to pump me."

Sir Justin's face was grave. He went to his bedroom at once. He knew what that man wanted; and he turned straight to his wardrobe, looking hard at the dress coat he had worn on the eventful evening. Things may cling to a sleeve, don't you know—or be entangled in a cuff—or get casually into a pocket! Or someone may put them there.

V.

For the next ten days or so Mr. Gregory was busy, constantly busy. Without doubt, he was the most active and energetic of detectives. He carried out so fully his own official principle of suspecting everybody, from China to Peru, that at last poor Persis got fairly mazed with his web of possibilities. Nobody was safe from his cultivated and highly-trained suspicion—not Sir Everard in his studio, nor Lady Maclure in her boudoir, nor the butler in his pantry, nor Sir Justin O'Byrne in his rooms in St. James's. Mr. Gregory kept an open mind against everybody and everything. He even doubted the parrot, and had views as to the intervention of rats and terriers. Persis got rather tired at last of his perverse ingenuity; especially as she had a very shrewd idea herself who had stolen the rubies. When he suggested various doubts, however, which seemed remotely to implicate Sir Justin's honesty, the sensitive American girl "felt it go on her nerves," and refused to listen to him, though Mr. Gregory never ceased to enforce upon her, by precept and example, his own pet doctrine that the last person on earth one would be likely to suspect is always the one who turns out to have done it.

A morning or two later, Persis looked out of her window as she was dressing her hair. She dressed it herself now, though she was an American heiress, and, therefore, of course, the laziest of her kind; for she had taken an unaccountable dislike, somehow, to that quiet girl Bertha. On this particular morning, however, when Persis looked out, she saw Bertha engaged in close, and apparently very intimate, conversation with the Hampstead postman. This sight disturbed the unstable equilibrium of her equanimity not a little. Why should Bertha go to the door to the postman at all? Surely it was no part of the duty of Lady Maclure's maid to take in the letters! And why should she want to go prying into the question of who wrote to Miss Remanet? For Persis, intensely conscious herself that a note from Sir Justin lay on top of the postman's bundle—she recognized it at once, even at that distance below, by the peculiar shape of the broad rough envelope—jumped to the natural feminine conclusion that Bertha must needs be influenced by some abstruse motive of which she herself, Persis, was, to say the very least, a component element. 'Tis a human fallacy. We're all of us prone to see everything from a personal standpoint; indeed, the one quality which makes a man or woman into a possible novelist, good, bad, or indifferent, is just that special power of throwing himself or herself into a great many people's personalities alternately. And this is a power possessed on an average by not one in a thousand men or not one in ten thousand women.

Persis rang the bell violently. Bertha came up, all smiles: "Did you want anything, miss?" Persis could have choked her. "Yes," she answered plainly, taking the bull by the horns; "I want to know what you were doing down there, prying into other people's letters with the postman?"

Bertha looked up at her, ever bland; she answered at once, without a second's hesitation: "The postman's my young man, miss; and we hope before very long now to get married."

"Odious thing!" Persis thought. "A glib lie always ready on the tip of her tongue for every emergency."

But Bertha's full heart was beating violently. Beating with love and hope and deferred anxiety.

A little later in the day Persis mentioned the incident casually to Lady Maclure—mainly in order to satisfy herself that the girl had been lying. Lady Maclure, however, gave a qualified assent:—

"I *believe* she's engaged to the postman," she said. "I *think* I've heard so; though I make it a rule, you see, my dear, to know as little as I can of these people's love affairs. They're so very uninteresting. But Bertha certainly told me she wouldn't leave me to get married for an indefinite period. That was only ten days ago. She said her young man wasn't just yet in a position to make a home for her."

"Perhaps," Persis suggested grimly, "something has occurred meanwhile to better her position. Such strange things crop up. She may have come into a fortune!"

"Perhaps so," Lady Maclure replied languidly. The subject bored her. "Though, if so, it must really have been very sudden; for I think it was the morning before you lost your jewels she told me so."

Persis thought that odd, but she made no comment.

Before dinner that evening she burst suddenly into Lady Maclure's room for a minute. Bertha was dressing her lady's hair. Friends were coming to dine—among them Sir Justin. "How do these pearls go with my complexion, Lady Maclure?" Persis asked rather anxiously; for she specially wished to look her best that evening, for one of the party.

"Oh, charming!" her hostess answered, with her society smile. "Never saw anything suit you better, Persis."

"Except my poor rubies!" Persis cried rather ruefully, for coloured gewgaws are dear to the savage and the woman. "I wish I could get them back! I wonder that man Gregory hasn't succeeded in finding them."

"Oh! my dear," Lady Maclure drawled out, "you may be sure by this time they're safe at Amsterdam. That's the only place in Europe now to look for them."

"Why to Amsterdam, my lady?" Bertha interposed suddenly, with a quick side-glance at Persis.

Lady Maclure threw her head back in surprise at so unwonted an intrusion. "What do you want to know that for, child?" she asked, somewhat curtly. "Why, to be cut, of course. All the diamond-cutters in the world are concentrated in Amsterdam; and the first thing a thief does when he steals big jewels is to send them across, and have them cut in new shapes so that they can't be identified."

"I shouldn't have thought," Bertha put in, calmly, "they'd have known who to send them to."

Lady Maclure turned to her sharply. "Why, these things," she said, with a calm air of knowledge, "are always done by experienced thieves, who know the ropes well, and are in league with receivers the whole world over. But Gregory has his eye on Amsterdam, I'm sure, and we'll soon hear something."

"Yes, my lady," Bertha answered, in her acquiescent tone, and relapsed into silence.

VI.

Four days later, about nine at night, that hard-worked man, the posty on the beat, stood loitering outside Sir Everard Maclure's house, openly defying the rules of the department, in close conference with Bertha.

"Well, any news?" Bertha asked, trembling over with excitement, for she was a very different person outside with her lover from the demure and imperturbable model maid who waited on my lady.

"Why, yes," the posty answered, with a low laugh of triumph. "A letter from Amsterdam! And I think we've fixed it!"

Bertha almost flung herself upon him. "Oh, Harry!" she cried, all eagerness, "this is too good to be true! Then in just one other month we can really get married!"

There was a minute's pause, inarticulately filled up by sounds unrepresentable through the art of the type-founder. Then Harry spoke again. "It's an awful lot of money!" he said, musing. "A regular fortune! And what's more, Bertha, if it hadn't been for your cleverness we never should have got it!"

Bertha pressed his hand affectionately. Even ladies'-maids are human.

"Well, if I hadn't been so much in love with you," she answered frankly, "I don't think I could ever have had the wit to manage it. But, oh! Harry, love makes one do or try anything!"

If Persis had heard those singular words, she would have felt no doubt was any longer possible.

VII.

Next morning, at ten o'clock, a policeman came round, post haste, to Sir Everard's. He asked to see Miss Remanet. When Persis came down, in her morning wrap, he had but a brief message from headquarters to give her: "Your jewels are found, miss. Will you step round and identify them?"

Persis drove back with him, all trembling. Lady Maclure accompanied her. At the police-station they left their cab, and entered the ante-room.

A little group had assembled there. The first person Persis distinctly made out in it was Sir Justin. A great terror seized her. Gregory had so poisoned her mind by this time with suspicion of everybody and everything she came across, that she was afraid of her own shadow. But next moment she saw clearly he wasn't there as prisoner, or even as witness; merely as spectator. She acknowledged him with a hasty bow, and cast her eye round again. The next person she definitely distinguished was Bertha, as calm and cool as ever, but in the very centre of the group, occupying as it were the place of honour which naturally belongs to the prisoner on all similar occasions. Persis was not surprised at that; she had known it all along; she glanced meaningly at Gregory, who stood a little behind, looking by no means triumphant. Persis found his dejection odd; but he was a proud detective, and perhaps someone else had effected the capture!

"These are your jewels, I believe," the inspector said, holding them up; and Persis admitted it.

"This is a painful case," the inspector went on. "A very painful case. We grieve to have discovered such a clue against one of our own men; but as he owns to it himself, and intends to throw himself on the mercy of the Court, it's no use talking about it. He won't attempt to defend it; indeed, with such evidence, I think he's doing what's best and wisest."

Persis stood there, all dazed. "I—I don't understand," she cried, with a swimming brain. "Who on earth are you talking about?"

The inspector pointed mutely with one hand at Gregory; and then for the first time Persis saw he was guarded. She clapped her hand to her head. In a moment it all broke in upon her. When she had called in the police, the rubies had never been stolen at all. It was Gregory who stole them!

She understood it now, at once. The real facts came back to her. She had taken her necklet off at night, laid it carelessly down on the dressing-table (too full of Sir Justin), covered it accidentally with her lace pocket-handkerchief, and straightway forgotten all about it. Next day she missed it, and jumped at conclusions. When Gregory came, he spied the rubies askance under the corner of the handkerchief—of course, being a woman, she had naturally looked everywhere except in the place where she had laid them—and knowing it was a safe case he had quietly pocketed them before her very eyes, all unsuspected. He felt sure nobody could accuse him of a robbery which was committed before he came, and which he had himself been called in to investigate.

"The worst of it is," the inspector went on, "he had woven a very ingenious case against Sir Justin O'Byrne, whom we were on the very point of arresting to-day, if this young woman hadn't come in at the eleventh hour, in the very nick of time, and earned the reward by giving us the clue that led to the discovery and recovery of the jewels. They were brought over this morning by an Amsterdam detective."

Persis looked hard at Bertha. Bertha answered her look. "My young man was the postman, miss," she explained, quite simply; "and after what my lady said, I put him up to watch Mr. Gregory's delivery for a letter from Amsterdam. I'd suspected him from the very first; and when the letter came, we had him arrested at once, and found out from it who were the people at Amsterdam who had the rubies."

Persis gasped with astonishment. Her brain was reeling. But Gregory in the background put in one last word:—

"Well, I was right, after all," he said, with professional pride. "I told you the very last person you'd dream of suspecting was sure to be the one that actually did it."

Lady O'Byrne's rubies were very much admired at Monte Carlo last season. Mr. Gregory has found permanent employment for the next seven years at Her Majesty's quarries on the Isle of Portland. Bertha and her postman have retired to Canada with five hundred pounds to buy a farm. And everybody says Sir Justin O'Byrne has beaten the record, after all, even for Irish baronets, by making a marriage at once of money and affection.

The Absent-Minded Coterie

Robert Barr

SOME years ago I enjoyed the unique experience of pursuing a man for one crime, and getting evidence against him of another. He was innocent of the misdemeanour, the proof of which I sought, but was guilty of another most serious offence, yet he and his confederates escaped scot-free in circumstances which I now purpose to relate.

You may remember that in Rudyard Kipling's story, *Bedalia Herodsfoot*, the unfortunate woman's husband ran the risk of being arrested as a simple drunkard, at a moment when the blood of murder was upon his boots. The case of Ralph Summertrees was rather the reverse of this. The English authorities were trying to fasten upon him a crime almost as important as murder, while I was collecting evidence which proved him guilty of an action much more momentous than that of drunkenness.

The English authorities have always been good enough, when they recognise my existence at all, to look down upon me with amused condescension. If today you ask Spenser Hale, of Scotland Yard, what he thinks of Eugène Valmont, that complacent man will put on the superior smile which so well becomes him, and if you are a very intimate friend of his, he may draw down the lid of his right eye, as he replies,—

"Oh, yes, a very decent fellow, Valmont, but he's a Frenchman," as if, that said, there was no need of further inquiry.

Myself, I like the English detective very much, and if I were to be in a *mêlée* tomorrow, there is no man I would rather find beside me than Spenser Hale. In any situation where a fist that can fell an ox is desirable, my friend Hale is a useful companion, but for intellectuality, mental acumen, finesse—ah, well! I am the most modest of men, and will say nothing.

It would amuse you to see this giant come into my room during an evening, on the bluff pretence that he wishes to smoke a pipe with me. There is the same difference between this good-natured giant and

21

myself as exists between that strong black pipe of his and my delicate cigarette, which I smoke feverishly when he is present, to protect myself from the fumes of his terrible tobacco. I look with delight upon the huge man, who, with an air of the utmost good humour, and a twinkle in his eye as he thinks he is twisting me about his finger, vainly endeavours to obtain a hint regarding whatever case is perplexing him at that moment. I baffle him with the ease that an active greyhound eludes the pursuit of a heavy mastiff, then at last I say to him with a laugh,—

"Come *mon ami* Hale, tell me all about it, and I will help you if I can."

Once or twice at the beginning he shook his massive head, and replied the secret was not his. The last time he did this I assured him that what he said was quite correct, and then I related full particulars of the situation in which he found himself, excepting the names, for these he had not mentioned. I had pieced together his perplexity from scraps of conversation in his half-hour's fishing for my advice, which, of course, he could have had for the plain asking. Since that time he has not come to me except with cases he feels at liberty to reveal, and one or two complications I have happily been enabled to unravel for him.

But, staunch as Spenser Hale holds the belief that no detective service on earth can excel that centring in Scotland Yard, there is one department of activity in which even he confesses that Frenchmen are his masters, although he somewhat grudgingly qualifies his admission by adding that we in France are constantly allowed to do what is prohibited in England. I refer to the minute search of a house during the owner's absence. If you read that excellent story, entitled *The Purloined Letter,* by Edgar Allan Poe, you will find a record of the kind of thing I mean, which is better than any description I, who have so often taken part in such a search, can set down.

Now, these people among whom I live are proud of their phrase, "The Englishman's house is his castle," and into that castle even a policeman cannot penetrate without a legal warrant. This may be all very well in theory, but if you are compelled to march up to a man's house, blowing a trumpet, and rattling a snare drum, you need not be disappointed if you fail to find what you are in search of when all the legal restrictions are complied with. Of course, the English are a very excellent people, a fact to which I am always proud to bear testimony, but it must be admitted that for cold common sense the French are very much their superiors. In Paris, if I wish to obtain an incriminating document, I do not send the possessor a *carte postale* to inform him of my desire, and in this procedure the French people sanely acquiesce. I have known men who, when they go out to spend an evening on the boulevards, toss their bunch of keys to the concierge, saying,—

"If you hear the police rummaging about while I'm away, pray assist them, with an expression of my distinguished consideration."

I remember while I was chief detective in the service of the French Government being requested to call at a certain hour at the private hotel of the Minister for Foreign Affairs. It was during the time that Bismarck meditated a second attack upon my country, and I am happy to say that I was then instrumental in supplying the Secret Bureau with documents which mollified that iron man's purpose, a fact which I think entitled me to my country's gratitude, not that I ever even hinted such a claim when a succeeding ministry forgot my services. The memory of a republic, as has been said by a greater man than I, is short. However, all that has nothing to do with the incident I am about to relate. I merely mention the crisis to excuse a momentary forgetfulness on my part which in any other country might have been followed by serious results to myself. But in France—ah, we understand those things, and nothing happened.

I am the last person in the world to give myself away, as they say in the great West. I am usually the calm, collected Eugène Valmont whom nothing can perturb, but this was a time of great tension, and I had become absorbed. I was alone with the minister in his private house, and one of the papers he desired was in his bureau at the Ministry for Foreign Affairs; at least, he thought so, and said,—

"Ah, it is in my desk at the bureau. How annoying! I must send for it!"

"No, Excellency," I cried, springing up in a self-oblivion the most complete, "it is here." Touching the spring of a secret drawer, I opened it, and taking out the document he wished, handed it to him.

It was not until I met his searching look, and saw the faint smile on his lips that I realised what I had done.

"Valmont," he said quietly, "on whose behalf did you search my house?"

"Excellency," I replied in tones no less agreeable than his own, "tonight at your orders I pay a domiciliary visit to the mansion of

Baron Dumoulaine, who stands high in the estimation of the President of the French Republic. If either of those distinguished gentlemen should learn of my informal call and should ask me in whose interests I made the domiciliary visit, what is it you wish that I should reply?"

"You should reply, Valmont, that you did it in the interests of the Secret Service."

"I shall not fail to do so, Excellency, and in answer to your question just now, I had the honour of searching this mansion in the interests of the Secret Service of France."

The Minister for Foreign Affairs laughed; a hearty laugh that expressed no resentment.

"I merely wished to compliment you, Valmont, on the efficiency of your search, and the excellence of your memory. This is indeed the document which I thought was left in my office."

I wonder what Lord Lansdowne would say if Spenser Hale showed an equal familiarity with his private papers! But now that we have returned to our good friend Hale, we must not keep him waiting any longer.

★   ★   ★

I well remember the November day when I first heard of the Summertrees case, because there hung over London a fog so thick that two or three times I lost my way, and no cab was to be had at any price. The few cabmen then in the streets were leading their animals slowly along, making for their stables. It was one of those depressing London days which filled me with ennui and a yearning for my own clear city of Paris, where, if we are ever visited by a slight mist, it is at least clean, white vapour, and not this horrible London mixture saturated with suffocating carbon. The fog was too thick for any passer to read the contents bills of the newspapers plastered on the pavement, and as there were probably no races that day the newsboys were shouting what they considered the next most important event—the election of an American President. I bought a paper and thrust it into my pocket. It was late when I reached my flat, and, after dining there, which was an unusual thing for me to do, I put on my slippers, took an easy-chair before the fire, and began to read my evening journal. I was distressed to learn that the eloquent Mr. Bryan had been defeated. I knew little about the silver question, but the man's oratorical powers had appealed to me, and my sympathy was aroused because he owned many silver mines, and yet the price of the metal was so low that apparently he could not make a living through the operation of them. But, of course, the cry that he was a plutocrat, and a reputed millionaire over and over again, was bound to defeat him in a democracy where the average voter is exceedingly poor and not comfortably well-to-do as is the case with our peasants in France. I always took great interest in the affairs of the huge republic to the west, having been at some pains to inform myself accurately regarding its politics, and although, as my readers know, I seldom quote anything complimentary that is said of me, nevertheless, an American client of mine once admitted that he never knew the true inwardness—I think that was the phrase he used—of American politics until he heard me discourse upon them. But then, he added, he had been a very busy man all his life.

I had allowed my paper to slip to the floor, for in very truth the fog was penetrating even into my flat, and it was becoming difficult to read, notwithstanding the electric light. My man came in, and announced that Mr. Spenser Hale wished to see me, and, indeed, any night, but especially when there is rain or fog outside, I am more pleased to talk with a friend than to read a newspaper.

"*Mon Dieu,* my dear Monsieur Hale, it is a brave man you are to venture out in such a fog as is abroad tonight."

"Ah, Monsieur Valmont," said Hale with pride, "you cannot raise a fog like this in Paris!"

"No. There you are supreme," I admitted, rising and saluting my visitor, then offering him a chair.

"I see you are reading the latest news," he said, indicating my newspaper, "I am very glad that man Bryan is defeated. Now we shall have better times."

I waved my hand as I took my chair again. I will discuss many things with Spenser Hale, but not American politics; he does not understand them. It is a common defect of the English to suffer complete ignorance regarding the internal affairs of other countries.

"It is surely an important thing that brought you out on such a night as this. The fog must be very thick in Scotland Yard."

This delicate shaft of fancy completely missed him, and he answered stolidly,—

"It's thick all over London, and, indeed, throughout most of England."

"Yes, it is," I agreed, but he did not see that either.

Still a moment later he made a remark which, if it had come from some people I know, might have indicated a glimmer of comprehension.

"You are a very, very clever man, Monsieur Valmont, so all I need say is that the question which brought me here is the same as that on which the American election was fought. Now, to a countryman, I should be compelled to give further explanation, but to you, monsieur, that will not be necessary."

There are times when I dislike the crafty smile and partial closing of the eyes which always distinguishes Spenser Hale when he places on the table a problem which he expects will baffle me. If I said he never did baffle me, I would be wrong, of course, for sometimes the utter simplicity of the puzzles which trouble him leads me into an intricate involution entirely unnecessary in the circumstances.

I pressed my fingertips together, and gazed for a few moments at the ceiling. Hale had lit his black pipe, and my silent servant placed at his elbow the whisky and soda, then tiptoed out of the room. As the door closed my eyes came from the ceiling to the level of Hale's expansive countenance.

"Have they eluded you?" I asked quietly.

"Who?"

"The coiners."

Hale's pipe dropped from his jaw, but he managed to catch it before it reached the floor. Then he took a gulp from the tumbler.

"That was just a lucky shot," he said.

"*Parfaitement*," I replied carelessly.

"Now, own up, Valmont, wasn't it?"

I shrugged my shoulders. A man cannot contradict a guest in his own house.

"Oh, stow that!" cried Hale impolitely. He is a trifle prone to strong and even slangy expressions when puzzled. "Tell me how you guessed it."

"It is very simple, *mon ami*. The question on which the American election was fought is the price of silver, which is so low that it has ruined Mr. Bryan, and threatens to ruin all the farmers of the west who possess silver mines on their farms. Silver troubled America, ergo silver troubles Scotland Yard.

"Very well, the natural inference is that someone has stolen bars of silver. But such a theft happened three months ago, when the metal was being unloaded from a German steamer at Southampton, and my dear friend Spenser Hale ran down the thieves very cleverly as they were trying to dissolve the marks off the bars with acid. Now crimes do not run in series, like the numbers in roulette at Monte Carlo. The thieves are men of brains. They say to themselves, 'What chance is there successfully to steal bars of silver while Mr. Hale is at Scotland Yard?' Eh, my good friend?"

"Really, Valmont," said Hale, taking another sip, "sometimes you almost persuade me that you have reasoning powers."

"Thanks, comrade. Then it is not a *theft* of silver we have now to deal with. But the American election was fought on the *price* of silver. If silver had been high in cost, there would have been no silver question. So the crime that is bothering you arises through the low price of silver, and this suggests that it must be a case of illicit coinage, for there the low price of the metal comes in. You have, perhaps, found a more subtle illegitimate act going forward than heretofore. Someone is making your shillings and your half-crowns from real silver, instead of from baser metal, and yet there is a large profit which has not hitherto been possible through the high price of silver. With the old conditions you were familiar, but this new element sets at nought all your previous formulae. That is how I reasoned the matter out."

"Well, Valmont, you have hit it. I'll say that for you; you have hit it. There is a gang of expert coiners who are putting out real silver money, and making a clear shilling on the half-crown. We can find no trace of the coiners, but we know the man who is shoving the stuff."

"That ought to be sufficient," I suggested.

"Yes, it should, but it hasn't proved so up to date. Now I came tonight to see if you would do one of your French tricks for us, right on the quiet."

"What French trick, Monsieur Spenser Hale?" I inquired with some asperity, forgetting for the moment that the man invariably became impolite when he grew excited.

"No offence intended," said this blundering officer, who really is a good-natured fellow, but always puts his foot in it, and then apologises. "I want someone to go through a man's house without a search warrant, spot the evidence, let me know, and then we'll rush the place before he has time to hide his tracks."

"Who is this man, and where does he live?"

"His name is Ralph Summertrees, and he lives in a very natty little bijou residence, as the advertisements call it, situated in no less a fashionable street than Park Lane."

"I see. What has aroused your suspicions against him?"

"Well, you know, that's an expensive district to live in; it takes a bit of money to do the trick. This Summertrees has no ostensible business, yet every Friday he goes to the United Capital Bank in Piccadilly, and deposits a bag of swag, usually all silver coin."

"Yes, and this money?"

"This money, so far as we can learn, contains a good many of these new pieces which never saw the British Mint."

"It's not all the new coinage, then?"

"Oh, no, he's a bit too artful for that. You see, a man can go round London, his pockets filled with new coinage five-shilling pieces, buy this, that, and the other, and come home with his change in legitimate coins of the realm—half-crowns, florins, shillings, sixpences, and all that."

"I see. Then why don't you nab him one day when his pockets are stuffed with illegitimate five-shilling pieces?"

"That could be done, of course, and I've thought of it, but you see, we want to land the whole gang. Once we arrested him, without knowing where the money came from, the real coiners would take flight."

"How do you know he is not the real coiner himself?"

Now poor Hale is as easy to read as a book. He hesitated before answering this question, and looked confused as a culprit caught in some dishonest act.

"You need not be afraid to tell me," I said soothingly after a pause. "You have had one of your men in Mr. Summertrees' house, and so learned that he is not the coiner. But your man has not succeeded in getting you evidence to incriminate other people."

"You've about hit it again, Monsieur Valmont. One of my men has been Summertrees' butler for two weeks, but, as you say, he has found no evidence."

"Is he still butler?"

"Yes."

"Now tell me how far you have got. You know that Summertrees deposits a bag of coin every Friday in the Piccadilly bank, and I suppose the bank has allowed you to examine one or two of the bags."

"Yes, sir, they have, but, you see, banks are very difficult to treat with. They don't like detectives bothering round, and whilst they do not stand out against the law, still they never answer any more questions than they're asked, and Mr. Summertrees has been a good customer at the United Capital for many years."

"Haven't you found out where the money comes from?"

"Yes, we have; it is brought there night after night by a man who looks like a respectable city clerk, and he puts it into a large safe, of which he holds the key, this safe being on the ground floor, in the dining-room."

"Haven't you followed the clerk?"

"Yes. He sleeps in the Park Lane house every night, and goes up in the morning to an old curiosity shop in Tottenham Court Road, where he stays all day, returning with his bag of money in the evening."

"Why don't you arrest and question him?"

"Well, Monsieur Valmont, there is just the same objection to his arrest as to that of Summertrees himself. We could easily arrest both, but we have not the slightest evidence against either of them, and then, although we put the go-betweens in clink, the worst criminals of the lot would escape."

"Nothing suspicious about the old curiosity shop?"

"No. It appears to be perfectly regular."

"This game has been going on under your noses for how long?"

"For about six weeks."

"Is Summertrees a married man?"

"No."

"Are there any women servants in the house?"

"No, except that three charwomen come in every morning to do up the rooms."

"Of what is his household comprised?"

"There is the butler, then the valet, and last, the French cook."

"Ah," cried I, "the French cook! This case interests me. So Summertrees has succeeded in completely disconcerting your man? Has he prevented him going from top to bottom of the house?"

"Oh no, he has rather assisted him than otherwise. On one occasion he went to the safe, took out the money, had Podgers—that's my chap's name—help him to count it, and then actually sent Podgers to the bank with the bag of coin."

"And Podgers has been all over the place?"

"Yes."

"Saw no signs of a coining establishment?"

"No. It is absolutely impossible that any coining can be done there. Besides, as I tell you, that respectable clerk brings him the money."

"I suppose you want me to take Podgers' position?"

"Well, Monsieur Valmont, to tell you the truth, I would rather you didn't. Podgers has done everything a man can do, but I thought if you got into the house, Podgers assisting, you might go through it night after night at your leisure."

"I see. That's just a little dangerous in England. I think I should prefer to assure myself the legitimate standing of being the amiable Podgers' successor. You say that Summertrees has no business?"

"Well, sir, not what you might call a business. He is by the way of being an author, but I don't count that any business."

"Oh, an author, is he? When does he do his writing?"

"He locks himself up most of the day in his study."

"Does he come out for lunch?"

"No; he lights a little spirit lamp inside, Podgers tells me, and makes himself a cup of coffee, which he takes with a sandwich or two."

"That's rather frugal fare for Park Lane."

"Yes, Monsieur Valmont, it is, but he makes it up in the evening, when he has a long dinner with all them foreign kickshaws you people like, done by his French cook."

"Sensible man! Well, Hale, I see I shall look forward with pleasure to making the acquaintance of Mr. Summertrees. Is there any restriction on the going and coming of your man Podgers?"

"None in the least. He can get away either night or day."

"Very good, friend Hale, bring him here tomorrow, as soon as our author locks himself up in his study, or rather, I should say, as soon as the respectable clerk leaves for Tottenham Court Road, which I should guess, as you put it, is about half an hour after his master turns the key of the room in which he writes."

"You are quite right in that guess, Valmont. How did you hit it?"

"Merely a surmise, Hale. There is a good deal of oddity about that Park Lane house, so it doesn't surprise me in the least that the master gets to work earlier in the morning than the man. I have also a suspicion that Ralph Summertrees knows perfectly well what the estimable Podgers is there for."

"What makes you think that?"

"I can give no reason except that my opinion of the acuteness of Summertrees has been gradually rising all the while you were speaking, and at the same time my estimate of Podgers' craft has been as steadily declining. However, bring the man here tomorrow, that I may ask him a few questions."

★   ★   ★

Next day, about eleven o'clock, the ponderous Podgers, hat in hand, followed his chief into my room. His broad, impassive, immobile smooth face gave him rather more the air of a genuine butler than I had expected, and this appearance, of course, was enhanced by his livery. His replies to my questions were those of a well-trained servant who will not say too much unless it is made worth his while. All in all, Podgers exceeded my expectations, and really my friend Hale had some justification for regarding him, as he evidently did, a triumph in his line.

"Sit down, Mr. Hale, and you, Podgers."

The man disregarded my invitation, standing like a statue until his chief made a motion; then he dropped into a chair. The English are great on discipline.

"Now, Mr. Hale, I must first congratulate you on the make-up of Podgers. It is excellent. You depend less on artificial assistance than we do in France, and in that I think you are right."

"Oh, we know a bit over here, Monsieur Valmont," said Hale, with pardonable pride.

"Now then, Podgers, I want to ask you about this clerk. What time does he arrive in the evening?"

"At prompt six, sir."

"Does he ring, or let himself in with a latchkey?"

"With a latchkey, sir."

"How does he carry the money?"

"In a little locked leather satchel, sir, flung over his shoulder."

"Does he go direct to the dining-room?"

"Yes, sir."

"Have you seen him unlock the safe and put in the money?"

"Yes, sir."

"Does the safe unlock with a word or a key?"

"With a key, sir. It's one of the old-fashioned kind."

"Then the clerk unlocks his leather money bag?"

"Yes, sir."

"That's three keys used within as many minutes. Are they separate or in a bunch?"

"In a bunch, sir."

"Did you ever see your master with this bunch of keys?"

"No, sir."

"You saw him open the safe once, I am told?"

"Yes, sir."

"Did he use a separate key, or one of a bunch?"

Podgers slowly scratched his head, then said,—

"I don't just remember, sir."

"Ah, Podgers, you are neglecting the big things in that house. Sure you can't remember?"

"No, sir."

"Once the money is in and the safe locked up, what does the clerk do?"

"Goes to his room, sir."

"Where is this room?"

"On the third floor, sir."

"Where do you sleep?"

"On the fourth floor with the rest of the servants, sir."

"Where does the master sleep?"

"On the second floor, adjoining his study."

"The house consists of four stories and a basement, does it?"

"Yes, sir."

"I have somehow arrived at the suspicion that it is a very narrow house. Is that true?"

"Yes, sir."

"Does the clerk ever dine with your master?"

"No, sir. The clerk don't eat in the house at all, sir."

"Does he go away before breakfast?"

"No, sir."

"No one takes breakfast to his room?"

"No, sir."

"What time does he leave the house?"

"At ten o'clock, sir."

"When is breakfast served?"

"At nine o'clock, sir."

"At what hour does your master retire to his study?"

"At half-past nine, sir."

"Locks the door on the inside?"

"Yes, sir."

"Never rings for anything during the day?"

"Not that I know of, sir."

"What sort of a man is he?"

Here Podgers was on familiar ground, and he rattled off a description minute in every particular.

"What I meant was, Podgers, is he silent, or talkative, or does he get angry? Does he seem furtive, suspicious, anxious, terrorised, calm, excitable, or what?"

"Well, sir, he is by way of being very quiet, never has much to say for himself; never saw him angry, or excited."

"Now, Podgers, you've been at Park Lane for a fortnight or more. You are a sharp, alert, observant man. What happens there that strikes you as unusual?"

"Well, I can't exactly say, sir," replied Podgers, looking rather help-lessly from his chief to myself, and back again.

"Your professional duties have often compelled you to enact the part of butler before, otherwise you wouldn't do it so well. Isn't that the case."

Podgers did not reply, but glanced at his chief. This was evidently a question pertaining to the service, which a subordinate was not allowed to answer. However, Hale said at once,—

"Certainly. Podgers has been in dozens of places."

"Well, Podgers, just call to mind some of the other households where you have been employed, and tell me any particulars in which Mr. Summertrees' establishment differs from them."

Podgers pondered a long time.

"Well, sir, he do stick to writing pretty close."

"Ah, that's his profession, you see, Podgers. Hard at it from half-past nine till towards seven, I imagine?"

"Yes, sir."

"Anything else, Podgers? No matter how trivial."

"Well, sir, he's fond of reading too; leastways, he's fond of newspapers."

"When does he read?"

"I've never seen him read 'em, sir; indeed, so far as I can tell, I never knew the papers to be opened, but he takes them all in, sir."

"What, all the morning papers?"

"Yes, sir, and all the evening papers too."

"Where are the morning papers placed?"

"On the table in his study, sir."

"And the evening papers?"

"Well, sir, when the evening papers come, the study is locked. They are put on a side table in the dining-room, and he takes them upstairs with him to his study."

This has happened every day since you've been there?"

"Yes, sir."

"You reported that very striking fact to your chief, of course?"

"No, sir, I don't think I did," said Podgers, confused.

"You should have done so. Mr. Hale would have known how to make the most of a point so vital."

"Oh, come now, Valmont," interrupted Hale, "you're chaffing us. Plenty of people take in all the papers!"

"I think not. Even clubs and hotels subscribe to the leading journals only. You said *all*, I think, Podgers?"

"Well, *nearly* all, sir."

"But which is it? There's a vast difference."

"He takes a good many, sir."

"How many?"

"I don't just know, sir."

"That's easily found out, Valmont," cried Hale, with some impatience, "if you think it really important."

"I think it so important that I'm going back with Podgers myself. You can take me into the house, I suppose, when you return?"

"Oh, yes, sir."

"Coming back to these newspapers for a moment, Podgers. What is done with them?"

"They are sold to the ragman, sir, once a week."

"Who takes them from the study?"

"I do, sir."

"Do they appear to have been read very carefully?"

"Well, no, sir; leastways, some of them seem never to have been opened, or else folded up very carefully again."

"Did you notice that extracts have been clipped from any of them?"

"No, sir."

"Does Mr. Summertrees keep a scrapbook?"

"Not that I know of, sir."

"Oh, the case is perfectly plain," said I, leaning back in my chair, and regarding the puzzled Hale with that cherubic expression of self-satisfaction which I know is so annoying to him.

"*What's* perfectly plain?" he demanded, more gruffly perhaps than etiquette would have sanctioned.

"Summertrees is no coiner, nor is he linked with any band of coiners."

"What is he, then?"

"Ah, that opens another avenue of enquiry. For all I know to the contrary, he may be the most honest of men. On the surface it would appear that he is a reasonably industrious tradesman in Tottenham Court Road, who is anxious that there should be no visible connection between a plebian employment and so aristocratic a residence as that in Park Lane."

At this point Spenser Hale gave expression to one of those rare flashes of reason which are always an astonishment to his friends.

"That is nonsense, Monsieur Valmont," he said, "the man who is ashamed of the connection between his business and his house is one who is trying to get into Society, or else the women of his family are trying it, as is usually the case. Now Summertrees has no family. He himself goes

nowhere, gives no entertainments, and accepts no invitations. He belongs
to no club, therefore to say that he is ashamed of his connection with the
Tottenham Court Road shop is absurd. He is concealing the connection
for some other reason that will bear looking into."

"My dear Hale, the goddess of Wisdom herself could not have made
a more sensible series of remarks. Now, *mon ami*, do you want my
assistance, or have you enough to go on with?"

"Enough to go on with? We have nothing more than we had when
I called on you last night."

"Last night, my dear Hale, you supposed this man was in league with
coiners. Today you know he is not."

"I know you *say* he is not."

I shrugged my shoulders, and raised my eyebrows, smiling at him.

"It is the same thing, Monsieur Hale."

"Well, of all the conceited—" and the good Hale could get no
further.

"If you wish my assistance, it is yours."

"Very good. Not to put too fine a point upon it, I do."

"In that case, my dear Podgers, you will return to the residence of our
friend Summertrees, and get together for me in a bundle all of yesterday's morning and evening papers, that were delivered to the house.
Can you do that, or are they mixed up in a heap in the coal cellar?"

"I can do it, sir. I have instructions to place each day's papers in a
pile by itself in case they should be wanted again. There is always one
week's supply in the cellar, and we sell the papers of the week before
to the rag men."

"Excellent. Well, take the risk of abstracting one day's journals, and
have them ready for me. I will call upon you at half-past three o'clock
exactly, and then I want you to take me upstairs to the clerk's bedroom
in the third story, which I suppose is not locked during the daytime?"

"No, sir, it is not."

With this the patient Podgers took his departure. Spenser Hale rose
when his assistant left.

"Anything further I can do?" he asked.

"Yes; give me the address of the shop in Tottenham Court Road.
Do you happen to have about you one of those new five-shilling pieces
which you believe to be illegally coined?"

He opened his pocket-book, took out the bit of white metal, and handed it to me.

"I'm going to pass this off before evening," I said, putting it in my pocket, "and I hope none of your men will arrest me."

"That's all right," laughed Hale as he took his leave.

At half-past three Podgers was waiting for me, and opened the front door as I came up the steps, thus saving me the necessity of ringing. The house seemed strangely quiet. The French cook was evidently down in the basement, and we had probably all the upper part to ourselves, unless Summertrees was in his study, which I doubted. Podgers led me directly upstairs to the clerk's room on the third floor, walking on tiptoe, with an elephantine air of silence and secrecy combined, which struck me as unnecessary.

"I will make an examination of this room," I said. "Kindly wait for me down by the door of the study."

The bedroom proved to be of respectable size when one considers the smallness of the house. The bed was all nicely made up, and there were two chairs in the room, but the usual washstand and swing-mirror were not visible. However, seeing a curtain at the farther end of the room, I drew it aside, and found, as I expected, a fixed lavatory in an alcove of perhaps four feet deep by five in width. As the room was about fifteen feet wide, this left two-thirds of the space unaccounted for. A moment later, I opened a door which exhibited a closet filled with clothes hanging on hooks. This left a space of five feet between the clothes closet and the lavatory. I thought at first that the entrance to the secret stairway must have issued from the lavatory, but examining the boards closely, although they sounded hollow to the knuckles, they were quite evidently plain matchboarding, and not a concealed door. The entrance to the stairway, therefore, must issue from the clothes closet. The right hand wall proved similar to the matchboarding of the lavatory as far as the casual eye or touch was concerned, but I saw at once it was a door. The latch turned out to be somewhat ingeniously operated by one of the hooks which held a pair of old trousers. I found that the hook, if pressed upward, allowed the door to swing outward, over the stairhead. Descending to the second floor, a similar latch let me in to a similar clothes closet in the room beneath. The two rooms were identical in size, one directly above the other, the only difference being that the lower room door gave into the study, instead of into the hall, as was the case with the upper chamber.

The study was extremely neat, either not much used, or the abode of a very methodical man. There was nothing on the table except a pile of that morning's papers. I walked to the farther end, turned the key in the lock, and came out upon the astonished Podgers.

"Well, I'm blowed!" exclaimed he.

"Quite so," I rejoined, "you've been tiptoeing past an empty room for the last two weeks. Now, if you'll come with me, Podgers, I'll show you how the trick is done."

When he entered the study, I locked the door once more, and led the assumed butler, still tiptoeing through force of habit, up the stair into the top bedroom, and so out again, leaving everything exactly as we found it. We went down the main stair to the front hall, and there Podgers had my parcel of papers all neatly wrapped up. This bundle I carried to my flat, gave one of my assistants some instructions, and left him at work on the papers.

★   ★   ★

I took a cab to the foot of Tottenham Court Road, and walked up that street till I came to J. Simpson's old curiosity shop. After gazing at the well-filled windows for some time, I stepped aside, having selected a little iron crucifix displayed behind the pane; the work of some ancient craftsman.

I knew at once from Podgers's description that I was waited upon by the veritable respectable clerk who brought the bag of money each night to Park Lane, and who I was certain was no other than Ralph Summertrees himself.

There was nothing in his manner differing from that of any other quiet salesman. The price of the crucifix proved to be seven-and-six, and I threw down a sovereign to pay for it.

"Do you mind the change being all in silver, sir?" he asked, and I answered without any eagerness, although the question aroused a suspicion that had begun to be allayed,—

"Not in the least."

He gave me half-a-crown, three two-shilling pieces, and four separate shillings, all the coins being well-worn silver of the realm, the undoubted inartistic product of the reputable British Mint. This seemed to dispose of the theory that he was palming off illegitimate money. He asked me if I were interested in any particular branch of antiquity, and I replied that my curiosity was merely general, and exceedingly amateurish, whereupon he invited me to look around. This I proceeded to do, while he resumed the addressing and stamping of some wrapped-up pamphlets which I surmised to be copies of his catalogue.

He made no attempt either to watch me or to press his wares upon me. I selected at random a little ink-stand, and asked its price. It was two shillings, he said, whereupon I produced my fraudulent five-shilling piece. He took it, gave me the change without comment, and the last doubt about his connection with coiners flickered from my mind.

At this moment a young man came in, who, I saw at once, was not a customer. He walked briskly to the farther end of the shop, and disappeared behind a partition which had one pane of glass in it that gave an outlook towards the front door.

"Excuse me a moment," said the shopkeeper, and he followed the young man into the private office.

As I examined the curious heterogeneous collection of things for sale, I heard the clink of coins being poured out on the lid of a desk or an uncovered table, and the murmur of voices floated out to me. I was now near the entrance of the shop, and by a sleight-of-hand trick, keeping the corner of my eye on the glass pane of the private office, I removed the key of the front door without a sound, and took an impression of it in wax, returning the key to its place unobserved. At this moment another young man came in, and walked straight past me into the private office. I heard him say,—

"Oh, I beg pardon, Mr. Simpson. How are you, Rogers?"

"Hallo, Macpherson," saluted Rogers, who then came out, bidding good-night to Mr. Simpson, and departed whistling down the street, but not before he had repeated his phrase to another young man entering, to whom he gave the name of Tyrrel.

I noted these three names in my mind. Two others came in together, but I was compelled to content myself with memorising their features, for I did not learn their names. These men were evidently collectors, for I heard the rattle of money in every case; yet here was a small shop, doing apparently very little business, for I had been within it for more than half an hour, and yet remained the only customer. If credit were given, one collector would certainly have been sufficient, yet five had come in, and had poured their contributions into the pile Summertrees was to take home with him that night.

I determined to secure one of the pamphlets which the man had been addressing. They were piled on a shelf behind the counter, but I had no difficulty in reaching across and taking the one on top, which I slipped into my pocket. When the fifth young man went down the street Summertrees himself emerged, and this time he carried in his hand the well-filled locked leather satchel, with the straps dangling, It was now approaching half-past five, and I saw he was eager to close up and get away.

"Anything else you fancy, sir?" he asked me.

"No, or rather yes and no. You have a very interesting collection here, but it's getting so dark I can hardly see."

"I close at half-past five, sir."

"Ah, in that case," I said, consulting my watch, "I shall be pleased to call some other time."

"Thank you, sir," replied Summertrees quietly, and with that I took my leave.

From the corner of an alley on the other side of the street I saw him put up the shutters with his own hands, then he emerged with overcoat on, and the money satchel slung across his shoulder. He locked the door, tested it with his knuckles, and walked down the street, carrying under one arm the pamphlets he had been addressing. I followed him some distance, saw him drop the pamphlets into the box at the first post office he passed, and walk rapidly towards his house in Park Lane.

When I returned to my flat and called in my assistant, he said,—

"After putting to one side the regular advertisements of pills, soap, and what not, here is the only one common to all the newspapers, morning and evening alike. The advertisements are not identical, sir, but they have two points of similarity, or perhaps I should say three. They all profess to furnish a cure for absent-mindedness; they all ask that the applicant's chief hobby shall be stated, and they all bear the same address: Dr. Willoughby, in Tottenham Court Road."

"Thank you," said I, as he placed the scissored advertisements before me.

I read several of the announcements. They were all small, and perhaps that is why I had never noticed one of them in the newspapers, for certainly they were odd enough. Some asked for lists of absent-minded men, with the hobbies of each, and for these lists, prizes of from one shilling to six were offered. In other clippings Dr. Willoughby professed to be able to cure absent-mindedness. There were no fees, and no treatment, but a pamphlet would be sent, which, if it did not benefit the receiver, could do no harm. The doctor was unable to meet patients personally, nor could he enter into correspondence with them. The address was the same as that of the old curiosity shop in Tottenham Court Road. At this juncture I pulled the pamphlet from my pocket, and saw it was entitled *Christian Science and Absent-Mindedness,* by Dr. Stamford Willoughby, and at the end of the article was the statement contained in the advertisements, that Dr Willoughby would neither see patients nor hold any correspondence with them.

I drew a sheet of paper towards me, wrote to Dr. Willoughby alleging that I was a very absent-minded man, and would be glad of his pamphlet, adding that my special hobby was the collecting of first editions. I then signed myself, "Alport Webster, Imperial Flats, London, W."

I may here explain that it is often necessary for me to see people under some other name than the well-known appellation of Eugène Valmont. There are two doors to my flat, and on one of these is painted, "Eugène Valmont"; on the other there is a receptacle, into which can be slipped a sliding panel bearing any *nom de guerre* I choose. The same device is arranged on the ground floor, where the names of all the occupants of the building appear on the right-hand wall.

I sealed, addressed, and stamped my letter, then told my man to put out the name of Alport Webster, and if I did not happen to be in when anyone called upon that mythical person, he was to make an appointment for me.

It was nearly six o'clock next afternoon when the card of Angus Macpherson was brought in to Mr. Alport Webster. I recognised the young man at once as the second who had entered the little shop carrying his tribute to Mr. Simpson the day before. He held three volumes under his arm, and spoke in such a pleasant, insinuating sort of way, that I knew at once he was an adept in his profession of canvasser.

"Will you be seated, Mr. Macpherson? In what can I serve you?"

He placed the three volumes, backs upward, on my table.

"Are you interested at all in first editions, Mr. Webster?"

"It is the one thing I am interested in," I replied; "but unfortunately they often run into a lot of money."

"That is true," said Macpherson sympathetically, "and I have here three books, one of which is an exemplification of what you say. This one costs a hundred pounds. The last copy that was sold by auction in London brought a hundred and twenty-three pounds. This next one is forty pounds, and the third ten pounds. At these prices I am certain you could not duplicate three such treasures in any book shop in Britain."

I examined them critically, and saw at once that what he said was true. He was still standing on the opposite side of the table.

"Please take a chair, Mr. Macpherson. Do you mean to say you go round London with a hundred and fifty pounds worth of goods under your arm in this careless way?"

The young man laughed.

"I run very little risk, Mr. Webster. I don't suppose anyone I meet imagines for a moment there is more under my arm than perhaps a trio of volumes I have picked up in the fourpenny box to take home with me."

I lingered over the volume for which he asked a hundred pounds, then said, looking across at him:—

"How came you to be possessed of this book, for instance?"

He turned upon me a fine, open countenance, and answered without hesitation in the frankest possible manner,—

"I am not in actual possession of it, Mr. Webster. I am by way of being a connoisseur in rare and valuable books myself, although, of course, I have little money with which to indulge in the collection of them. I am acquainted, however, with the lovers of desirable books in different quarters of London. These three volumes, for instance, are from the library of a private gentleman in the West End. I have sold many books to him, and he knows I am trustworthy. He wishes to dispose of them at something under their real value, and has kindly allowed me to conduct the negotiation. I make it my business to find out those who are interested in rare books, and by such trading I add considerably to my income."

"How, for instance, did you learn that I was a bibliophile?"

Mr. Macpherson laughed genially.

"Well, Mr. Webster, I must confess that I chanced it. I do that very often. I take a flat like this, and send in my card to the name on the door. If I am invited in, I ask the occupant the question I asked you just now: 'Are you interested in rare editions?' If he says no, I simply beg pardon and retire. If he says yes, then I show my wares."

"I see," said I, nodding. What a glib young liar he was, with that innocent face of his, and yet my next question brought forth the truth.

"As this is the first time you have called upon me, Mr. Macpherson, you have no objection to my making some further inquiry, I suppose. Would you mind telling me the name of the owner of these books in the West End?"

"His name is Mr. Ralph Summertrees, of Park Lane."

"Of Park Lane? Ah, indeed."

"I shall be glad to leave the books with you, Mr. Webster, and if you care to make an appointment with Mr. Summertrees, I am sure he will not object to say a word in my favour."

"Oh, I do not in the least doubt it, and should not think of troubling the gentleman."

"I was going to tell you," went on the young man, "that I have a friend, a capitalist, who, in a way, is my supporter; for, as I said, I have little money of my own. I find it is often inconvenient for people to pay down any considerable sum. When, however, I strike a bargain, my capitalist buys the book, and I make an arrangement with my customer to pay a certain amount each week, and so even a large purchase is not felt, as I make the instalments small enough to suit my client."

"You are employed during the day, I take it?"

"Yes, I am a clerk in the City."

Again we were in the blissful realms of fiction!

"Suppose I take this book at ten pounds, what instalment should I have to pay each week?"

"Oh, what you like, sir. Would five shillings be too much?"

"I think not."

"Very well, sir, if you pay me five shillings now, I will leave the book with you, and shall have pleasure in calling this day week for the next instalment."

I put my hand into my pocket, and drew out two half-crowns, which I passed over to him.

"Do I need to sign any form or undertaking to pay the rest?"

The young man laughed cordially.

"Oh, no, sir, there is no formality necessary. You see, sir, this is largely a labour of love with me, although I don't deny I have my eye on the future. I am getting together what I hope will be a very valuable connection with gentlemen like yourself who are fond of books, and I trust some day that I may be able to resign my place with the insurance company and set up a choice little business of my own, where my knowledge of values in literature will prove useful."

And then, after making a note in a little book he took from his pocket, he bade me a most graceful good-bye and departed, leaving me cogitating over what it all meant.

Next morning two articles were handed to me. The first came by post and was a pamphlet on *Christian Science and Absent-Mindedness*, exactly similar to the one I had taken away from the old curiosity shop; the second was a small key made from my wax impression that would fit the front door of the same shop—a key fashioned by an excellent anarchist friend of mine in an obscure street near Holborn.

That night at ten o'clock I was inside the old curiosity shop, with a small storage battery in my pocket, and a little electric glow-lamp at my buttonhole, a most useful instrument for either burglar or detective.

I had expected to find the books of the establishment in a safe, which, if it was similar to the one in Park Lane, I was prepared to open with the false keys in my possession or to take an impression of the keyhole and trust to my anarchist friend for the rest. But to my amazement I discovered all the papers pertaining to the concern in a desk which was not even locked. The books, three in number, were the ordinary day book, journal, and ledger referring to the shop; book-keeping of the older fashion; but in a portfolio lay half a dozen foolscap sheets, headed "Mr. Rogers's List", "Mr. Macpherson's", "Mr. Tyrrel's", the names I had already learned, and three others. These lists contained in the first column, names; in the second column, addresses; in the third, sums of money; and then in the small, square places following were amounts ranging from two-and-sixpence to a pound. At the bottom of Mr. Macpherson's list was the name Alport Webster, Imperial Flats, £10; then in the small, square place, five shillings. These six sheets, each headed by a canvasser's name, were evidently the record of current collections, and the innocence of the whole thing was so apparent that if it were not for my fixed rule never to believe that I am at the bottom of any case until I have come on something suspicious, I would have gone out empty-handed as I came in.

The six sheets were loose in a thin portfolio, but standing on a shelf above the desk were a number of fat volumes, one of which I took down, and saw that it contained similar lists running back several years. I noticed on Mr. Macpherson's current list the name of Lord Semptam, an eccentric old nobleman whom I knew slightly. Then turning to the list immediately before the current one the name was still there; I traced it back through list after list until I found the first entry, which was no less than three years previous, and there Lord Semptam was down for a piece of furniture costing fifty pounds, and on that account he had paid a pound a week for more than three years, totalling a hundred and seventy pounds at the least, and instantly the glorious simplicity of the scheme dawned upon me, and I became so interested in the swindle that I lit the gas, fearing my little lamp would be exhausted before my investigation ended, for it promised to be a long one.

In several instances the intended victim proved shrewder than old Simpson had counted upon, and the word "Settled" had been written on the line carrying the name when the exact number of instalments was paid. But as these shrewd persons dropped out, others took their places, and Simpson's dependence on their absent-mindedness seemed to be justified in nine cases out of ten. His collectors were collecting long after the debt had been paid. In Lord Semptam's case, the payment had evidently become chronic, and the old man was giving away his pound a week to the suave Macpherson two years after his debt had been liquidated.

From the big volume I detached the loose leaf, dated 1893, which recorded Lord Semptam's purchase of a carved table for fifty pounds, and on which he had been paying a pound a week from that time to the date of which I am writing, which was November, 1896. This single document taken from the file of three years previous, was not likely to be missed, as would have been the case if I had selected a current sheet. I nevertheless made a copy of the names and addresses of Macpherson's present clients; then, carefully placing everything exactly as I had found it, I extinguished the gas, and went out of the shop, locking the door behind me. With the 1893 sheet in my pocket I resolved to prepare a pleasant little surprise for my suave friend Macpherson when he called to get his next instalment of five shillings.

Late as was the hour when I reached Trafalgar Square, I could not deprive myself of the felicity of calling on Mr. Spenser Hale, who I knew was then on duty. He never appeared at his best during office hours, because officialism stiffened his stalwart frame. Mentally he was impressed with the importance of his position, and added to this he was not then allowed to smoke his big, black pipe and terrible tobacco. He received me with the curtness I had been taught to expect when I inflicted myself upon him at his office. He greeted me abruptly with,—

"I say, Valmont, how long do you expect to be on this job?"

"What job?" I asked mildly.

"Oh, you know what I mean: the Summertrees affair."

"Oh, *that!*" I exclaimed, with surprise. "The Summertrees case is already completed, of course. If I had known you were in a hurry, I should have finished up everything yesterday, but as you and Podgers, and I don't know how many more, have been at it sixteen or seventeen days, if not longer, I thought I might venture to take as many hours, as I am working entirely alone. You said nothing about haste, you know."

"Oh, come now, Valmont, that's a bit thick. Do you mean to say you have already got evidence against the man?"

"Evidence absolute and complete."

"Then who are the coiners?"

"My most estimable friend, how often have I told you not to jump at conclusions? I informed you when you first spoke to me about the matter that Summertrees was neither a coiner nor a confederate of coiners. I secured evidence sufficient to convict him of quite another offence, which is probably unique in the annals of crime. I have penetrated the mystery of the shop, and discovered the reason for all those suspicious actions which quite properly set you on his trail. Now I wish you to come to my flat next Wednesday night at a quarter to six, prepared to make an arrest."

"I must know who I am to arrest, and on what counts."

"Quite so, *mon ami* Hale; I did not say you were to make an arrest, but merely warned you to be prepared. If you have time now to listen to the disclosures, I am quite at your service. I promise you there are some original features in the case. If, however, the present moment is inopportune, drop in on me at your convenience, previously telephoning so that you may know whether I am there or not, and thus your valuable time will not be expended purposelessly."

With this I presented to him my most courteous bow, and although his mystified expression hinted a suspicion that he thought I was chaffing him, as he would call it, official dignity dissolved somewhat, and he intimated his desire to hear all about it then and there. I had succeeded in arousing my friend Hale's curiosity. He listened to the evidence with perplexed brow, and at last ejaculated he would be blessed.

"This young man," I said, in conclusion, "will call upon me at six on Wednesday afternoon, to receive his second five shillings. I propose that you, in your uniform, shall be seated there with me to receive him, and I am anxious to study Mr. Macpherson's countenance when he realises he has walked in to confront a policeman. If you will then allow me to cross-examine him for a few moments, not after the manner of Scotland Yard, with a warning lest he incriminate himself, but in the free and easy fashion we adopt in Paris, I shall afterwards turn the case over to you to be dealt with at your discretion."

"You have a wonderful flow of language, Monsieur Valmont," was the officer's tribute to me. "I shall be on hand at a quarter to six on Wednesday."

"Meanwhile," said I, "kindly say nothing of this to anyone. We must arrange a complete surprise for Macpherson. That is essential. Please make no move in the matter at all until Wednesday night."

Spenser Hale, much impressed, nodded acquiescence, and I took a polite leave of him.

★   ★   ★

The question of lighting is an important one in a room such as mine, and electricity offers a good deal of scope to the ingenious. Of this fact I have taken full advantage. I can manipulate the lighting of my room so that any particular spot is bathed in brilliancy, while the rest of the space remains in comparative gloom, and I arranged the lamps so that the full force of their rays impinged against the door that Wednesday evening, while I sat on one side of the table in semi-darkness and Hale sat on the other, with a light beating down on him from above which gave him the odd, sculptured look of a living statue of Justice, stern and triumphant. Anyone entering the room would first be dazzled by the light, and next would see the gigantic form of Hale in the full uniform of his order.

When Angus Macpherson was shown into this room he was quite visibly taken aback, and paused abruptly on the threshold, his gaze riveted on the huge policeman. I think his first purpose was to turn and run, but the door closed behind him, and he doubtless heard, as we all did, the sound of the bolt being thrust in its place, thus locking him in.

"I—I beg your pardon," he stammered, "I expected to meet Mr. Webster."

As he said this, I pressed the button under my table, and was instantly enshrouded with light. A sickly smile overspread the countenance of Macpherson as he caught sight of me, and he made a very creditable attempt to carry off the situation with nonchalance.

"Oh, there you are, Mr. Webster; I did not notice you at first."

It was a tense moment. I spoke slowly and impressively.

"Sir, perhaps you are not unacquainted with the name of Eugène Valmont."

He replied brazenly,—

"I am sorry to say, sir, I never heard of the gentleman before."

At this came a most inopportune "Haw-haw" from that blockhead Spenser Hale, completely spoiling the dramatic situation I had elaborated with such thought and care. It is little wonder the English possess no drama, for they show scant appreciation of the sensational moments in life.

"Haw-haw," brayed Spenser Hale, and at once reduced the emotional atmosphere to a fog of commonplace. However, what is a man to do? He must handle the tools with which it pleases Providence to provide him. I ignored Hale's untimely laughter.

"Sit down, sir," I said to Macpherson, and he obeyed.

"You have called on Lord Semptam this week," I continued sternly.

"Yes, sir."

"And collected a pound from him?"

"Yes, sir."

"In October, 1893, you sold Lord Semptam a carved antique table for fifty pounds?"

"Quite right, sir."

"When you were here last week you gave me Ralph Summertrees as the name of a gentleman living in Park Lane. You knew at the time that this man was your employer?"

Macpherson was now looking fixedly at me, and on this occasion made no reply. I went on calmly:—

"You also knew that Summertrees, of Park Lane, was identical with Simpson, of Tottenham Court Road?"

"Well, sir," said Macpherson, "I don't exactly see what you're driving at, but it's quite usual for a man to carry on a business under an assumed name. There is nothing illegal about that."

"We will come to the illegality in a moment, Mr. Macpherson. You, and Rogers, and Tyrrel, and three others, are confederates of this man Simpson."

"We are in his employ; yes, sir, but no more confederates than clerks usually are."

"I think, Mr. Macpherson, I have said enough to show you that the game is, what you call, up. You are now in the presence of Mr. Spenser Hale, from Scotland Yard, who is waiting to hear your confession."

Here the stupid Hale broke in with his—

"And remember, sir, that anything you say will be—"

"Excuse me, Mr. Hale," I interrupted hastily, "I shall turn over the case to you in a very few moments, but I ask you to remember our compact, and to leave it for the present entirely in my hands. Now, Mr. Macpherson, I want your confession, and I want it at once."

"Confession? Confederates?" protested Macpherson with admirably simulated surprise. "I must say you use extraordinary terms, Mr.— Mr.—What did you say the name was?"

"Haw-haw," roared Hale. "His name is Monsieur Valmont."

"I implore you, Mr. Hale, to leave this man to me for a very few moments. Now, Macpherson, what have you to say in your defence?"

"Where nothing criminal has been alleged, Monsieur Valmont, I see no necessity for defence. If you wish me to admit that somehow you have acquired a number of details regarding our business, I am perfectly willing to do so, and to subscribe to their accuracy. If you will be good enough to let me know of what you complain, I shall endeavour to make the point clear to you if I can. There has evidently been some misapprehension, but for the life of me, without further explanation, I am as much in a fog as I was on my way coming here, for it is getting a little thick outside."

Macpherson certainly was conducting himself with great discretion, and presented, quite unconsciously, a much more diplomatic figure than my friend, Spenser Hale, sitting stiffly opposite me. His tone was one of mild expostulation, mitigated by the intimation that all misunderstanding speedily would be cleared away. To outward view he offered a perfect picture of innocence, neither protesting too much nor too little. I had, however, another surprise in store for him, a trump card, as it were, and I played it down on the table.

"There!" I cried with vim, "have you ever seen that sheet before?"

He glanced at it without offering to take it in his hand.

"Oh, yes," he said, "that has been abstracted from our file. It is what I call my visiting list."

"Come, come, sir," I cried sternly, "you refuse to confess, but I warn you we know all about it. You never heard of Dr. Willoughby, I suppose?"

"Yes, he is the author of the silly pamphlet on Christian Science."

"You are in the right, Mr. Macpherson; on Christian Science and Absent-Mindedness."

"Possibly. I haven't read it for a long while."

"Have you ever met this learned doctor, Mr. Macpherson?"

"Oh, yes. Dr. Willoughby is the pen-name of Mr. Summertrees. He believes in Christian Science and that sort of thing, and writes about it."

"Ah, really. We are getting your confession bit by bit, Mr. Macpherson. I think it would be better to be quite frank with us."

"I was just going to make the same suggestion to you, Monsieur Valmont. If you will tell me in a few words exactly what is your charge against either Mr. Summertrees or myself, I will know then what to say."

"We charge you, sir, with obtaining money under false pretences, which is a crime that has landed more than one distinguished financier in prison."

Spenser Hale shook his fat forefinger at me, and said,—

"Tut, tut, Valmont; we mustn't threaten, we mustn't threaten, you know;" but I went on without heeding him.

"Take for instance, Lord Semptam. You sold him a table for fifty pounds, on the instalment plan. He was to pay a pound a week, and in less than a year the debt was liquidated. But he is an absent-minded man, as all your clients are. That is why you came to me. I had answered the bogus Willoughby's advertisement. And so you kept on collecting and collecting for something more than three years. Now do you understand the charge?"

Mr. Macpherson's head during this accusation was held slightly inclined to one side. At first his face was clouded by the most clever imitation of anxious concentration of mind I had ever seen, and this was gradually cleared away by the dawn of awakening perception. When I had finished, an ingratiating smile hovered about his lips.

"Really, you know," he said, "that is rather a capital scheme. The absent-minded league, as one might call them. Most ingenious. Summertrees, if he had any sense of humour, which he hasn't, would be rather taken by the idea that his innocent fad for Christian Science had led him to be suspected of obtaining money under false pretences. But, really, there are no pretensions about the matter at all. As I understand it, I simply call and receive the money through the forgetfulness of the persons on my list, but where I think you would have both Summertrees and myself, if there was anything in your audacious theory, would be an indictment for conspiracy. Still, I quite see how the mistake arises. You have jumped to the conclusion that we sold nothing to Lord Semptam except that carved table three years ago. I have pleasure in pointing out to you that his lordship is a frequent customer of ours, and has had many things from us at one time or another. Sometimes he is in our debt; sometimes we are in his. We keep a sort of running contract with him by which he pays us a pound a week. He and several other customers deal on the same plan, and in return for an income that we can count upon, they get the first offer of anything in which they are supposed to be interested. As I have told you, we call these sheets in the office our visiting lists, but to make the visiting lists complete you need what we term our encyclopaedia. We call it that because it is in so many volumes; a volume for each year, running back I don't know how long. You will notice little figures here from time to time above the amount stated on this visiting list. These figures refer to the page of the encyclopaedia for the current year, and on that page is noted the new sale, and the amount of it, as it might be set down, say, in a ledger."

"That is a very entertaining explanation, Mr. Macpherson. I suppose this encyclopaedia, as you call it, is in the shop at Tottenham Court Road?"

"Oh, no, sir. Each volume of the encyclopaedia is self-locking. These books contain the real secret of our business, and they are kept in the safe at Mr. Summertrees' house in Park Lane. Take Lord Semptam's account, for instance. You will find in faint figures under a certain date, 102. If you turn to page 102 of the encyclopaedia for that year, you will then see a list of what Lord Semptam has bought, and the prices he was charged for them. It is really a very simple matter. If you will allow me to use your telephone for a moment, I will ask Mr. Summertrees, who has not yet begun dinner, to bring with him here the volume for 1893, and, within a quarter of an hour, you will be perfectly satisfied that everything is quite legitimate."

I confess that the young man's naturalness and confidence staggered me, the more so as I saw by the sarcastic smile on Hale's lips that he did not believe a single word spoken. A portable telephone stood on the table, and as Macpherson finished his explanation, he reached over and drew it towards him. Then Spenser Hale interfered.

"Excuse *me*," he said, "I'll do the telephoning. What is the call number of Mr. Summertrees?"

"140 Hyde Park."

Hale at once called up Central, and presently was answered from Park Lane. We heard him say,—

"Is this the residence of Mr. Summertrees? Oh, is that you, Podgers? Is Mr. Summertrees in? Very well. This is Hale. I am in Valmont's flat—Imperial Flats—you know. Yes, where you went with me the other day. Very well, go to Mr. Summertrees, and say to him that Mr. Macpherson wants the encyclopaedia for 1893. Do you get that? Yes, encyclopaedia. Oh, he'll understand what it is. Mr. Macpherson. No, don't mention my name at all. Just say Mr. Macpherson wants the encyclopaedia for the year 1893, and that you are to bring it. Yes, you may tell him that Mr. Macpherson is at Imperial Flats, but don't mention my name at all. Exactly. As soon as he gives you the book, get into a cab, and come here as quickly as possible with it. If Summertrees doesn't want to let the book go, then tell him to come with you. If he won't do that, place him under arrest, and bring both him and the book here. All right. Be as quick as you can; we're waiting."

Macpherson made no protest against Hale's use of the telephone; he merely sat back in his chair with a resigned expression on his face which, if painted on canvas, might have been entitled "The Falsely Accused." When Hale rang off, Macpherson said,—

"Of course you know your own business best, but if your man arrests Summertrees, he will make you the laughing-stock of London. There is such a thing as unjustifiable arrest, as well as getting money under false pretences, and Mr. Summertrees is not the man to forgive an insult. And then, if you will allow me to say so, the more I think over your absent-minded theory, the more absolutely grotesque it seems, and if the case ever gets into the newspapers, I am sure, Mr. Hale, you'll experience an uncomfortable half-hour with your chiefs at Scotland Yard."

"I'll take the risk of that, thank you," said Hale stubbornly.

"Am I to consider myself under arrest?" inquired the young man.

"No, sir."

"Then, if you will pardon me, I shall withdraw. Mr. Summertrees will show you everything you wish to see in his books, and can explain his business much more capably than I, because he knows more about it; therefore, gentlemen, I bid you good-night."

"No you don't. Not just yet awhile," exclaimed Hale, rising to his feet simultaneously with the young man.

"Then I *am* under arrest," protested Macpherson.

"You're not going to leave this room until Podgers brings that book."

"Oh, very well," and he sat down again.

And now, as talking is dry work, I set out something to drink, a box of cigars, and a box of cigarettes. Hale mixed his favourite brew, but Macpherson, shunning the wine of his country, contented himself with a glass of plain mineral water, and lit a cigarette. Then he awoke my high regard by saying pleasantly as if nothing had happened,—

"While we are waiting, Monsieur Valmont, may I remind you that you owe me five shillings?"

I laughed, took the coin from my pocket, and paid him, whereupon he thanked me.

"Are you connected with Scotland Yard, Monsieur Valmont?" asked Macpherson, with the air of a man trying to make conversation to bridge over a tedious interval; but before I could reply, Hale blurted out,—

"Not likely!"

"You have no official standing as a detective, then, Monsieur Valmont?"

"None whatever," I replied quickly, thus getting in my oar ahead of Hale.

"This is a loss to our country," pursued this admirable young man, with evident sincerity.

I began to see I could make a good deal of so clever a fellow if he came under my tuition.

"The blunders of our police," he went on, "are something deplorable. If they would but take lessons in strategy, say, from France, their unpleasant duties would be so much more acceptably performed, with much less discomfort to their victims."

"France," snorted Hale in derision, "why, they call a man guilty there until he's proven innocent."

"Yes, Mr. Hale, and the same seems to be the case in Imperial Flats. You have quite made up your mind that Mr. Summertrees is guilty, and will not be content until he proves his innocence. I venture to predict that you will hear from him before long in a manner that may astonish you."

Hale grunted and looked at his watch. The minutes passed very slowly as we sat there smoking, and at last even I began to get uneasy. Macpherson, seeing our anxiety, said that when he came in the fog was almost as thick as it had been the week before, and that there might be some difficulty in getting a cab. Just as he was speaking the door was unlocked from the outside, and Podgers entered, bearing a thick volume in his hand. This he gave to his superior, who turned over its pages in amazement, and then looked at the back, crying,—

"*Encyclopaedia of Sport*, 1893! What sort of a joke is this, Mr. Macpherson?"

There was a pained look on Mr. Macpherson's face as he reached forward and took the book. He said with a sigh,—

"If you had allowed me to telephone, Mr. Hale, I should have made it perfectly plain to Summertrees what was wanted. I might have known this mistake was liable to occur. There is an increasing demand for out-of-date books of sport, and no doubt Mr. Summertrees thought this was what I meant. There is nothing for it but to send your man back to Park Lane and tell Mr. Summertrees that what we want is the locked volume of accounts for 1893, which we call the encyclopaedia. Allow me to write an order that will bring it. Oh, I'll show you what I have written before your man takes it," he said, as Hale stood ready to look over his shoulder.

On my notepaper he dashed off a request such as he had outlined, and handed it to Hale, who read it and gave it to Podgers.

"Take that to Summertrees, and get back as quickly as possible. Have you a cab at the door?"

"Yes, sir."

"Is it foggy outside?"

"Not so much, sir, as it was an hour ago. No difficulty about the traffic now, sir."

"Very well, get back as soon as you can."

Podgers saluted, and left with the book under his arm. Again the door was locked, and again we sat smoking in silence until the stillness was broken by the tinkle of the telephone. Hale put the receiver to his ear.

"Yes, this is the Imperial Flats. Yes. Valmont. Oh, yes; Macpherson is here. What? Out of what? Can't hear you. Out of print. What, the encyclopaedia's out of print? Who is that speaking? Dr. Willoughby; thanks."

Macpherson rose as if he would go to the telephone, but instead (and he acted so quietly that I did not notice what he was doing until the thing was done), he picked up the sheet which he called his visiting list, and walking quite without haste, held it in the glowing coals of the fireplace until it disappeared in a flash of flame up the chimney. I sprang to my feet indignant, but too late to make even a motion outwards saving the sheet. Macpherson regarded us both with that self-deprecatory smile which had several times lighted up his face.

"How dared you burn that sheet?" I demanded.

"Because, Monsieur Valmont, it did not belong to you; because you do not belong to Scotland Yard; because you stole it; because you had no right to it; and because you have no official standing in this country. If it had been in Mr. Hale's possession I should not have dared, as you put it, to destroy the sheet, but as this sheet was abstracted from my master's premises by you, an entirely unauthorised person, whom he would have been justified in shooting dead if he had found you house-breaking and you had resisted him on his discovery, I took the liberty of destroying the document. I have always held that these sheets should not have been kept, for, as has been the case, if they fell under the scrutiny of so intelligent a person as Eugène Valmont, improper inferences might have been drawn. Mr. Summertrees, however, persisted in keeping them, but made this concession, that if I ever telegraphed him or telephoned him the word 'Encyclopaedia', he would at once burn these records, and he, on his part, was to telegraph or telephone to me 'The *Encyclopaedia* is out of print,' whereupon I would know that he had succeeded.

"Now, gentlemen, open this door, which will save me the trouble of forcing it. Either put me formally under arrest, or cease to restrict my liberty. I am very much obliged to Mr. Hale for telephoning, and I have made no protest to so gallant a host as Monsieur Valmont is, because of the locked door. However, the farce is now terminated. The proceedings I have sat through were entirely illegal, and if you will pardon me, Mr. Hale, they have been a little too French to go down here in old England, or to make a report in the newspapers that would be quite satisfactory to your chiefs. I demand either my formal arrest, or the unlocking of that door."

In silence I pressed a button, and my man threw open the door. Macpherson walked to the threshold, paused, and looked back at Spenser Hale, who sat there silent as a sphinx.

"Good-evening, Mr. Hale."

There being no reply, he turned to me with the same ingratiating smile,—

"Good-evening, Monsieur Eugène Valmont," he said, "I shall give myself the pleasure of calling next Wednesday at six for my five shillings."

The Lenton Croft Robberies

Arthur Morrison

THOSE who retain any memory of the great law cases of fifteen or twenty years back will remember, at least, the title of that extraordinary will case, "Bartley *v*. Bartley and others," which occupied the Probate Court for some weeks on end, and caused an amount of public interest rarely accorded to any but the cases considered in the other division of the same court. The case itself was noted for the large quantity of remarkable and unusual evidence presented by the plaintiff's side—evidence that took the other party completely by surprise, and overthrew their case like a house of cards. The affair will, perhaps, be more readily recalled as the occasion of the sudden rise to eminence, in their profession, of Messrs. Crellan, Hunt, and Crellan, solicitors for the plaintiff—a result due entirely to the wonderful ability shown in this case of building up, apparently out of nothing, a smashing weight of irresistible evidence. That the firm has since maintained—indeed, enhanced—the position it then won for itself, need scarcely be said here; its name is familiar to everybody. But there are not many of the outside public who know that the credit of the whole performance was primarily due to a young clerk in the employ of Messrs. Crellan, who had been given charge of the seemingly desperate task of collecting evidence in the case.

This Mr. Martin Hewitt had, however, full credit and reward for his exploit from his firm and from their client, and more than one other firm of lawyers engaged in contentious work made good offers to entice Hewitt to change his employers. Instead of this, however, he determined to work independently for the future, having conceived the idea of making a regular business of doing, on behalf of such clients as might retain him, similar work to that he had just done, with such conspicuous success, for Messrs. Crellan, Hunt, and Crellan. This was the beginning of the private detective business of Martin Hewitt, and his action at that time has been completely justified by the brilliant professional successes he has since achieved.

57

His business has always been conducted in the most private manner, and he has always declined the help of professional assistants, preferring to carry out, himself, such of the many investigations offered him as he could manage. He has always maintained that he has never lost by this policy, since the chance of his refusing a case begets competition for his services, and his fees rise by a natural process. At the same time, no man could know better how to employ casual assistance at the right time.

Some curiosity has been expressed as to Mr. Martin Hewitt's system, and as he himself always consistently maintains that he has no system beyond a judicious use of ordinary faculties, I intend setting forth in detail a few of the more interesting of his cases, in order that the public may judge for itself if I am right in estimating Mr. Hewitt's "ordinary faculties" as faculties very extraordinary indeed. He is not a man who has made many friendships (this, probably, for professional reasons), notwithstanding his genial and companionable manners. I myself first made his acquaintance as a result of an accident resulting in a fire at the old house in which Hewitt's office was situated, and in an upper floor of which I occupied bachelor chambers. I was able to help in saving a quantity of extremely important papers relating to his business, and, while repairs were being made, allowed him to lock them in an old wall-safe in one of my rooms, which the fire had scarcely damaged.

The acquaintance thus begun has lasted many years, and has become a rather close friendship. I have even accompanied Hewitt on some of his expeditions, and, in a humble way, helped him. Such of the cases, however, as I personally saw nothing of I have put into narrative form from the particulars given me.

"I consider you, Brett," he said, addressing me, "the most remarkable journalist alive. Not because you're particularly clever, you know; because, between ourselves, I hope you'll admit you're not; but because you have known something of me and my doings for some years, and have never yet been guilty of giving away any of my little business secrets you may have become acquainted with. I'm afraid you're not so enterprising a journalist as some, Brett. But now, since you ask, you shall write something—if you think it worth while."

This he said, as he said most things, with a cheery, chaffing good-nature that would have been, perhaps, surprising to a stranger who thought of him only as a grim and mysterious discoverer of secrets and crimes. Indeed, the man had always as little of the aspect of the conventional detective as may be imagined. Nobody could appear more cordial or less observant in manner, although there was to be seen a certain sharpness of the eye—which might, after all, only be the twinkle of good-humor.

I *did* think it worth while to write something of Martin Hewitt's investigations, and a description of one of his adventures follows.

★ ★ ★

At the head of the first flight of a dingy staircase leading up from an ever-open portal in a street by the Strand stood a door, the dusty ground-glass upper panel of which carried in its centre the single word "Hewitt," while at its right-hand lower corner, in smaller letters, "Clerk's Office" appeared. On a morning when the clerks in the ground-floor offices had barely hung up their hats, a short, well-dressed young man, wearing spectacles, hastening to open the dusty door, ran into the arms of another man who suddenly issued from it.

"I beg pardon," the first said. "Is this Hewitt's Detective Agency Office?"

"Yes, I believe you will find it so," the other replied. He was a stoutish, clean-shaven man, of middle height, and of a cheerful, round countenance. "You'd better speak to the clerk."

In the little outer office the visitor was met by a sharp lad with inky fingers, who presented him with a pen and a printed slip. The printed slip having been filled with the visitor's name and present business, and conveyed through an inner door, the lad reappeared with an invitation to the private office. There, behind a writing-table, sat the stoutish man himself, who had only just advised an appeal to the clerk.

"Good morning, Mr. Lloyd—Mr. Vernon Lloyd," he said, affably, looking again at the slip. "You'll excuse my care to start even with my visitors—I must, you know. You come from Sir James Norris, I see."

"Yes; I am his secretary. I have only to ask you to go straight to Lenton Croft at once, if you can, on very important business. Sir James would have wired, but had not your precise address. Can you go by the next train? Eleven-thirty is the first available from Paddington."

"Quite possibly. Do you know anything of the business?"

"It is a case of a robbery in the house, or, rather, I fancy, of several robberies. Jewellery has been stolen from rooms occupied by visitors to the Croft. The first case occurred some months ago—nearly a year ago, in fact. Last night there was another. But I think you had better get the details on the spot; Sir James has told me to telegraph if you are coming, so that he may meet you himself at the station; and I must hurry, as his drive to the station will be rather a long one. Then I take it you will go, Mr. Hewitt? Twyford is the station."

"Yes, I shall come, and by the eleven-thirty. Are you going by that train yourself?"

"No, I have several things to attend to now I am in town. Good morning; I shall wire at once."

Mr. Martin Hewitt locked the drawer of his table and sent his clerk for a cab.

At Twyford Station Sir James Norris was waiting with a dog-cart. Sir James was a tall, florid man of fifty or thereabout, known away from home as something of a county historian, and nearer his own parts as a great supporter of the hunt, and a gentleman much troubled with poachers. As soon as he and Hewitt had found one another, the baronet hurried the detective into his dog-cart. "We've something over seven miles to drive," he said, "and I can tell you all about this wretched business as we go. That is why I came for you myself, and alone."

Hewitt nodded.

"I have sent for you, as Lloyd probably told you, because of a robbery at my place last evening. It appears, as far as I can guess, to be one of three by the same hand, or by the same gang. Late yesterday afternoon——"

"Pardon me, Sir James," Hewitt interrupted, "but I think I must ask you to begin at the first robbery and tell me the whole tale in proper order. It makes things clearer, and sets them in their proper shape."

"Very well. Eleven months ago, or thereabout, I had rather a large party of visitors, and among them Colonel Heath and Mrs. Heath—the lady being a relative of my own late wife. Colonel Heath has not been long retired, you know—used to be political resident in an Indian native State. Mrs. Heath had rather a good stock of jewellery of one sort and another, about the most valuable piece being a bracelet set with a particularly fine pearl—quite an exceptional pearl, in fact—that had been one of a heap of presents from the Maharajah of his State when Heath left India.

"It was a very noticeable bracelet, the gold setting being a mere feath-erweight piece of native filigree work—almost too fragile to trust on the wrist—and the pearl being, as I have said, of a size and quality not often seen. Well, Heath and his wife arrived late one evening, and after lunch the following day, most of the men being off by themselves—shooting, I think—my daughter, my sister (who is very often down here), and Mrs. Heath took it into their heads to go walking—fern-hunting, and so on. My sister was rather long dressing, and while they waited, my daughter went into Mrs. Heath's room, where Mrs. Heath turned over all her treasures to show her—as women do, you know. When my sister was at last ready they came straight away, leaving the things littering about the room rather than stay longer to pack them up. The bracelet, with other things, was on the dressing-table then."

"One moment. As to the door?"

"They locked it. As they came away my daughter suggested turning the key, as we had one or two new servants about."

"And the window?"

"That they left open, as I was going to tell you. Well, they went on their walk and came back, with Lloyd (whom they had met somewhere) carry-ing their ferns for them. It was dusk and almost dinner time. Mrs. Heath went straight to her room, and—the bracelet was gone."

"Was the room disturbed?"

"Not a bit. Everything was precisely where it had been left, except the bracelet. The door hadn't been tampered with, but of course the window was open, as I have told you."

"You called the police, of course?"

"Yes, and had a man from Scotland Yard down in the morning. He seemed a pretty smart fellow, and the first thing he noticed on the dressing-table, within an inch or two of where the bracelet had been, was a match, which had been lit and thrown down. Now, nobody about the house had had occasion to use a match in that room that day, and, if they had, certainly wouldn't have thrown it on the cover of the dressing-table. So that, presuming the thief to have used that match, the robbery must have been committed when the room was getting dark—immediately before Mrs. Heath returned, in fact. The thief had evidently struck the match, passed it hurriedly over the various trinkets lying about, and taken the most valuable."

"Nothing else was even moved?"

"Nothing at all. Then the thief must have escaped by the window, although it was not quite clear how. The walking party approached the house with a full view of the window, but saw nothing, although the robbery must have been actually taking place a moment or two before they turned up.

"There was no water-pipe within any practicable distance of the window. But a ladder usually kept in the stable-yard was found lying along the edge of the lawn. The gardener explained, however, that he had put the ladder there after using it himself early in the afternoon."

"Of course, it might easily have been used again after that and put back."

"Just what the Scotland Yard man said. He was pretty sharp, too, on the gardener, but very soon decided that he knew nothing of it. No stranger had been seen in the neighbourhood, nor had passed the lodge gates. Besides, as the detective said, it scarcely seemed the work of a stranger. A stranger could scarcely have known enough to go straight to the room where a lady—only arrived the day before—had left a valuable jewel, and away again without being seen. So all the people about the house were suspected in turn. The servants offered, in a body, to have their boxes searched, and this was done; everything was turned over, from the butler's to the new kitchenmaid's. I don't know that I should have had this carried quite so far if I had been the loser myself, but it was my guest, and I was in such a horrible position. Well, there's little more to be said about that, unfortunately. Nothing came of it all, and the thing's as great a mystery now as ever. I believe the Scotland Yard man got as far as suspecting *me* before he gave it up altogether, but give it up he did in the end. I think that's all I know about the first robbery. Is it clear?"

"Oh, yes; I shall probably want to ask a few questions when I have seen the place, but they can wait. What next?"

"Well," Sir James pursued, "the next was a very trumpery affair, that I should have forgotten all about, probably, if it hadn't been for one circumstance. Even now I hardly think it could have been the work of the same hand. Four months or thereabout after Mrs. Heath's disaster— in February of this year, in fact—Mrs. Armitage, a young widow, who had been a schoolfellow of my daughter's, stayed with us for a week or so. The girls don't trouble about the London season, you know, and I have no town house, so they were glad to have their old friend here for a little in the dull time. Mrs. Armitage is a very active young lady, and was scarcely in the house half an hour before she arranged a drive in a pony-cart with Eva—my daughter—to look up old people in the village that she used to know before she was married. So they set off in the afternoon, and made such a round of it that they were late for dinner. Mrs. Armitage had a small plain gold brooch—not at all valuable, you know; two or three pounds, I suppose—which she used to pin up a cloak or anything of that sort. Before she went out she stuck this in the pincushion on her dressing-table, and left a ring—rather a good one, I believe—lying close by."

"This," asked Hewitt, "was not in the room that Mrs. Heath had occupied, I take it?"

"No; this was in another part of the building. Well, the brooch went—taken, evidently, by someone in a deuce of a hurry, for when Mrs. Armitage got back to her room, there was the pincushion with a little tear in it, where the brooch had been simply snatched off. But the curious thing was that the ring—worth a dozen of the brooch—was left where it had been put. Mrs. Armitage didn't remember whether or not she had locked the door herself, although she found it locked when she returned; but my niece, who was indoors all the time, went and tried it once—because she remembered that a gasfitter was at work on the landing near by—and found it safely locked. The gasfitter, whom we didn't know at the time, but who since seems to be quite an honest fellow, was ready to swear that nobody but my niece had been to the door while he was in sight of it—which was almost all the time. As to the window, the sash-line had broken that very morning, and Mrs. Armitage had propped open the bottom half about eight or ten inches with a brush; and when she returned, that brush, sash and all, were exactly as she had left them. Now, I scarcely need tell *you* what an awkward job it must have been for anybody to get noiselessly in at that unsupported window; and how unlikely he would have been to replace it, with the brush, exactly as he found it."

"Just so. I suppose the brooch was really gone? I mean, there was no chance of Mrs. Armitage having mislaid it?"

"Oh, none at all. There was a most careful search."

"Then, as to getting in at the window, would it have been easy?"

"Well, yes," Sir James replied; "yes, perhaps it would. It is a first-floor window, and it looks over the roof and skylight of the billiard-room. I built the billiard-room myself—built it out from a smoking-room just at this corner. It would be easy enough to get at the window from the billiard-room roof. But, then," he added, "that couldn't have been the way. Somebody or other was in the billiard-room the whole time, and nobody could have got over the roof (which is nearly all skylight) without being seen and heard. I was there myself for an hour or two, taking a little practice."

"Well, was anything done?"

"Strict inquiry was made among the servants, of course, but nothing came of it. It was such a small matter that Mrs. Armitage wouldn't hear of my calling in the police or anything of that sort, although I felt pretty certain that there must be a dishonest servant about somewhere. A servant might take a plain brooch, you know, who would feel afraid of a valuable ring, the loss of which would be made a greater matter of."

"Well, yes—perhaps so, in the case of an inexperienced thief, who also would be likely to snatch up whatever she took in a hurry. But I'm doubtful. What made you connect these two robberies together?"

"Nothing whatever—for some months. They seemed quite of a different sort. But scarcely more than a month ago I met Mrs. Armitage at Brighton, and we talked, among other things, of the previous robbery—that of Mrs. Heath's bracelet. I described the circumstances pretty minutely, and when I mentioned the match found on the table she said, 'How strange! Why, *my* thief left a match on the dressing-table when he took my poor little brooch!'"

Hewitt nodded. "Yes," he said. "A spent match, of course?"

"Yes, of course, a spent match. She noticed it lying close by the pincushion, but threw it away without mentioning the circumstance. Still, it seemed rather curious to me that a match should be lit and dropped, in each case, on the dressing-cover an inch from where the article was taken. I mentioned it to Lloyd when I got back, and he agreed that it seemed significant."

"Scarcely," said Hewitt, shaking his head. "Scarcely, so far, to be called significant, although worth following up. Everybody uses matches in the dark, you know."

"Well, at any rate, the coincidence appealed to me so far that it struck me it might be worth while to describe the brooch to the police in order that they could trace it if it had been pawned. They had tried that, of course, over the bracelet, without any result, but I fancied the shot might be worth making, and might possibly lead us on the track of the more serious robbery."

"Quite so. It was the right thing to do. Well?"

"Well, they found it. A woman had pawned it in London—at a shop in Chelsea. But that was some time before, and the pawnbroker had clean forgotten all about the woman's appearance. The name and address she gave were false. So that was the end of that business."

"Had any of your servants left you between the time the brooch was lost and the date of the pawnticket?"

"No."

"Were all your servants at home on the day the brooch was pawned?"

"Oh, yes. I made that inquiry myself."

"Very good. What next?"

"Yesterday—and this is what made me send for you. My late wife's sister came here last Tuesday, and we gave her the room from which Mrs. Heath lost her bracelet. She had with her a very old-fashioned brooch, containing a miniature of her father, and set, in front, with three very fine brilliants and a few smaller stones. Here we are, though, at the Croft; I'll tell you the rest indoors."

Hewitt laid his hand on the baronet's arm. "Don't pull up, Sir James," he said. "Drive a little further. I should like to have a general idea of the whole case before we go in."

"Very good." Sir James Norris straightened the horse's head again and went on. "Late yesterday afternoon, as my sister-in-law was changing her dress, she left her room for a moment to speak to my daughter in her room, almost adjoining. She was gone no more than three minutes, or five at most, but on her return the brooch, which had been left on the table, had gone. Now, the window was shut fast, and had not been tampered with. Of course, the door was open, but so was my daughter's, and anybody walking near must have been heard. But the strangest circumstance, and one that almost makes me wonder whether I have been awake to-day or not, was that there lay *a used match* on the very spot, as nearly as possible, where the brooch had been—and it was broad daylight!"

Hewitt rubbed his nose and looked thoughtfully before him. "Um—curious, certainly," he said. "Anything else?"

"Nothing more than you shall see for yourself. I have had the room locked and watched till you could examine it. My sister-in-law had heard of your name, and suggested that you should be called in; so, of course, I did exactly as she wanted. That she should have lost that brooch, of all things, in my house, is most unfortunate; you see, there was some small difference about the thing between my late wife and her sister when their mother died and left it. It's almost worse than the Heath's bracelet business, and altogether I'm not pleased with things, I can assure you. See what a position it is for me! Here are three ladies in the space of one year, robbed one after another in this mysterious fashion in my house, and I can't find the thief. It's horrible! People will be afraid to come near the place. And I can do nothing!"

"Ah, well—we'll see. Perhaps we had better turn back now. By-the-bye, were you thinking of having any alterations or additions made to your house?"

"No. What makes you ask?"

"I think you might at least consider the question of painting and decorating, Sir James—or, say, putting up another coach-house, or something. Because I should like to be (to the servants) the architect—or the builder, if you please—come to look round. You haven't told any of them about this business?"

"Not a word. Nobody knows but my relatives and Lloyd. I took every precaution myself, at once. As to your little disguise, be the architect, by all means, and do as you please. If you can only find this thief and put an end to this horrible state of affairs, you'll do me the greatest service I've ever asked for—and as to your fee, I'll gladly make it whatever is usual, and three hundred in addition."

Martin Hewitt bowed. "You're very generous, Sir James, and you may be sure I'll do what I can. As a professional man, of course, a good fee always stimulates my interest, although this case of yours certainly seems interesting enough by itself."

"Most extraordinary! Don't you think so? Here are three persons, all ladies, all in my house, two even in the same room, each successively robbed of a piece of jewellery, each from a dressing-table, and a used match left behind in every case. All in the most difficult—one would say impossible—circumstances for a thief, and yet there is no clue!"

"Well, we won't say that just yet, Sir James; we must see. And we must guard against any undue predisposition to consider the robberies in a lump. Here we are at the lodge gate again. Is that your gardener—the man who left the ladder by the lawn on the first occasion you spoke of?" Mr. Hewitt nodded in the direction of a man who was clipping a box border.

"Yes; will you ask him anything?"

"No, no; at any rate, not now. Remember the building alterations. I think, if there is no objection, I will look first at the room that the lady—Mrs.——?" Hewitt looked up, inquiringly.

"My sister-in-law? Mrs. Cazenove. Oh, yes, you shall come to her room at once."

"Thank you. And I think Mrs. Cazenove had better be there."

They alighted; and a boy from the lodge led the horse and dog-cart away.

Mrs. Cazenove was a thin and faded, but quick and energetic, lady of middle age. She bent her head very slightly on learning Martin Hewitt's name, and said: "I must thank you, Mr. Hewitt, for your very prompt attention. I need scarcely say that any help you can afford in tracing the thief who has my property—whoever it may be—will make me most grateful. My room is quite ready for you to examine."

The room was on the second floor—the top floor at that part of the building. Some slight confusion of small articles of dress was observable in parts of the room.

"This, I take it," inquired Hewitt, "is exactly as it was at the time the brooch was missed?"

"Precisely," Mrs. Cazenove answered. "I have used another room, and put myself to some other inconveniences, to avoid any disturbance."

Hewitt stood before the dressing-table. "Then this is the used match," he observed, "exactly where it was found?"

"Yes."

"Where was the brooch?"

"I should say almost on the very same spot. Certainly no more than a very few inches away."

Hewitt examined the match closely. "It is burnt very little," he remarked. "It would appear to have gone out at once. Could you hear it struck?"

"I heard nothing whatever; absolutely nothing."

"If you will step into Miss Norris's room now for a moment," Hewitt suggested, "we will try an experiment. Tell me if you hear matches struck, and how many. Where is the match-stand?"

The match-stand proved to be empty, but matches were found in Miss Norris's room, and the test was made. Each striking could be heard distinctly, even with one of the doors pushed to.

"Both your own door and Miss Norris's were open, I understand; the window shut and fastened inside as it is now, and nothing but the brooch was disturbed?"

"Yes, that was so."

"Thank you, Mrs. Cazenove. I don't think I need trouble you any further just at present. I think, Sir James," Hewitt added, turning to the baronet, who was standing by the door—"I think we will see the other room and take a walk outside the house, if you please. I suppose, by-the-bye, that there is no getting at the matches left behind on the first and second occasions?"

"No," Sir James answered. "Certainly not here. The Scotland Yard man may have kept his."

The room that Mrs. Armitage had occupied presented no peculiar feature. A few feet below the window the roof of the billiard-room was visible, consisting largely of skylight. Hewitt glanced casually about the walls, ascertained that the furniture and hangings had not been materially changed since the second robbery, and expressed his desire to see the windows from the outside. Before leaving the room, however, he wished to know the names of any persons who were known to have been about the house on the occasions of all three robberies.

"Just carry your mind back, Sir James," he said. "Begin with yourself, for instance. Where were you at these times?"

"When Mrs. Heath lost her bracelet I was in Tagley Wood all the afternoon. When Mrs. Armitage was robbed, I believe I was some-where about the place most of the time she was out. Yesterday I was down at the farm." Sir James's face broadened. "I don't know whether you call those suspicious movements?" he added, and laughed.

"Not at all; I only asked you so that, remembering your own move-ments, you might the better recall those of the rest of the household.

Was anybody, to your knowledge—*anybody,* mind—in the house on all three occasions?"

"Well, you know, it's quite impossible to answer for all the servants. You'll only get that by direct questioning—I can't possibly remember things of that sort. As to the family and visitors—why, you don't suspect any of them, do you?"

"I don't suspect a soul, Sir James," Hewitt answered, beaming genially, "not a soul. You see, I *can't* suspect people till I know something about where they were. It's quite possible there will be independent evidence enough as it is, but you must help me if you can. The visitors, now. Was there any visitor here each time—or even on the first and last occasions only?"

"No—not one. And my own sister, perhaps you will be pleased to know, was only there at the time of the first robbery."

"Just so. And your daughter, as I have gathered, was clearly absent from the spot each time—indeed, was in company with the party robbed. Your niece, now?"

"Why, hang it all, Mr. Hewitt, I can't talk of my niece as a suspected criminal. The poor girl's under my protection, and I really can't allow——"

Hewitt raised his hand and shook his head deprecatingly.

"My dear sir, haven't I said that I don't suspect a soul? *Do* let me know how the people were distributed, as nearly as possible. Let me see. It was your niece, I think, who found that Mrs. Armitage's door was locked—this door in fact—on the day she lost her brooch?"

"Yes, it was."

"Just so—at the time when Mrs. Armitage, herself, had forgotten whether she locked it or not. And yesterday—was she out then?"

"No, I think not. Indeed, she goes out very little—her health is usually bad. She was indoors, too, at the time of the Heath robbery, since you ask. But come, now, I don't like this. It's ridiculous to suppose that *she* knows anything of it."

"I don't suppose it, as I have said. I am only asking for information. That is all your resident family, I take it, and you know nothing of anybody else's movements—except, perhaps, Mr. Lloyd's?"

"Lloyd? Well, you know yourself that he was out with the ladies when the first robbery took place. As to the others, I don't remember.

Yesterday he was probably in his room, writing. I think that acquits *him*, eh?" Sir James looked quizzically into the broad face of the affable detective, who smiled and replied:—

"Oh, of course, nobody can be in two places at once, else what would become of the *alibi* as an institution? But as I have said, I am only setting my facts in order. Now, you see, we get down to the servants—unless some stranger is the party wanted. Shall we go outside now?"

Lenton Croft was a large, desultory sort of house, nowhere more than three floors high, and mostly only two. It had been added to bit by bit till it zig-zagged about its site, as Sir James Norris expressed it, "like a game of dominoes." Hewitt scrutinized its external features carefully as they strolled round, and stopped some little while before the windows of the two bedrooms he had just seen from the inside. Presently they approached the stables and coach-house, where a groom was washing the wheels of the dog-cart.

"Do you mind my smoking?" Hewitt asked Sir James. "Perhaps you will take a cigar yourself—they are not so bad, I think. I will ask your man for a light."

Sir James felt for his own match-box, but Hewitt had gone, and was lighting his cigar with a match from a box handed him by the groom. A smart little terrier was trotting about by the coach-house, and Hewitt stooped to rub its head. Then he made some observation about the dog, which enlisted the groom's interest, and was soon absorbed in a chat with the man. Sir James, waiting a little way off, tapped the stones rather impatiently with his foot, and presently moved away.

For full a quarter of an hour Hewitt chatted with the groom, and when at last he came away and overtook Sir James, that gentleman was about re-entering the house.

"I beg your pardon, Sir James," Hewitt said, "for leaving you in that unceremonious fashion to talk to your groom, but a dog, Sir James—a good dog—will draw me anywhere."

"Oh," replied Sir James, shortly.

"There is one other thing," Hewitt went on, disregarding the other's curtness, "that I should like to know: There are two windows directly below that of the room occupied yesterday by Mrs. Cazenove—one on each floor. What rooms do they light?"

"That on the ground floor is the morning-room; the other is Mr. Lloyd's—my secretary. A sort of study or sitting-room."

"Now, you will see at once, Sir James," Hewitt pursued, with an affable determination to win the baronet back to good humour, "you will see at once that if a ladder had been used in Mrs. Heath's case, anybody looking from either of these rooms would have seen it."

"Of course. The Scotland Yard man questioned everybody as to that, but nobody seemed to have been in either of the rooms when the thing occurred; at any rate, nobody saw anything."

"Still, I think I should like to look out of those windows myself; it will, at least, give me an idea of what *was* in view and what was not, if anybody had been there."

Sir James Norris led the way to the morning-room. As they reached the door, a young lady, carrying a book and walking very languidly, came out. Hewitt stepped aside to let her pass, and afterwards said, interrogatively: "Miss Norris—your daughter, Sir James?"

"No, my niece. Do you want to ask her anything? Dora, my dear," Sir James added, following her in the corridor, "this is Mr. Hewitt, who is investigating these wretched robberies for me. I think he would like to hear if you remember anything happening at any of the three times."

The lady bowed slightly, and said in a plaintive drawl: "I, uncle? Really, I don't remember anything; nothing at all."

"You found Mrs. Armitage's door locked, I believe," asked Hewitt, "when you tried it, on the afternoon when she lost her brooch?"

"Oh, yes; I believe it was locked. Yes, it was."

"Had the key been left in?"

"The key? Oh, no! I think not; no."

"Do you remember anything out of the common happening—anything whatever, no matter how trivial—on the day Mrs. Heath lost her bracelet?"

"No, really I don't. I can't remember at all."

"Nor yesterday?"

"No, nothing. I don't remember anything."

"Thank you," said Hewitt, hastily; "thank you. Now the morning-room, Sir James."

In the morning-room Hewitt stayed but a few seconds, doing little more than casually glance out of the windows. In the room above he took a little longer time. It was a comfortable room, but with rather effeminate indications about its contents. Little pieces of draped silk-work hung about the furniture, and Japanese silk fans decorated the mantelpiece. Near the window was a cage containing a grey parrot, and the writing-table was decorated with two vases of flowers.

"Lloyd makes himself pretty comfortable, eh?" Sir James observed. "But it isn't likely anybody would be here while he was out, at the time that bracelet went."

"No," replied Hewitt, meditatively. "No, I suppose not."

He stared thoughtfully out of the window, and then, still deep in thought, rattled at the wires of the cage with a quill tooth-pick and played a moment with the parrot. Then looking up at the window again, he said: "That is Mr. Lloyd, isn't it, coming back in a fly?"

"Yes, I think so. Is there anything else you would care to see here?"

"No, thank you," Hewitt replied; "I don't think there is."

They went down to the smoking-room, and Sir James went away to speak to his secretary. When he returned, Hewitt said, quietly, "I think, Sir James—I *think* that I shall be able to give you your thief presently."

"What! Have you a clue? Who do you think? I began to believe you were hopelessly stumped."

"Well, yes. I have rather a good clue, although I can't tell you much about it just yet. But it is so good a clue that I should like to know now whether you are determined to prosecute, when you have the criminal?"

"Why, bless me, of course," Sir James replied, with surprise. "It doesn't rest with me, you know—the property belongs to my friends. And even if *they* were disposed to let the thing slide, I shouldn't allow it—I couldn't, after they had been robbed in my house."

"Of course, of course. Then, if I can, I should like to send a message to Twyford by somebody perfectly trustworthy—not a servant. Could anybody go?"

"Well, there's Lloyd, although he's only just back from his journey. But if it's important, he'll go."

"It is important. The fact is, we must have a policeman or two here this evening, and I'd like Mr. Lloyd to fetch them without telling anybody else."

Sir James rang, and, in response to his message, Mr. Lloyd appeared. While Sir James gave his secretary his instructions, Hewitt strolled to the door of the smoking-room, and intercepted the latter as he came out.

"I'm sorry to give you this trouble, Mr. Lloyd," he said, "but I must stay here myself for a little, and somebody who can be trusted must go. Will you just bring back a police-constable with you?—or rather two—two would be better. That is all that is wanted. You won't let the servants know, will you? Of course, there will be a female searcher at the Twyford police-station? Ah—of course. Well, you needn't bring her, you know. That sort of thing is done at the station." And chatting thus confidentially, Martin Hewitt saw him off.

When Hewitt returned to the smoking-room Sir James said, suddenly, "Why, bless my soul, Mr. Hewitt, we haven't fed you! I'm awfully sorry. We came in rather late for lunch, you know, and this business has bothered me so, I clean forgot everything else. There's no dinner till seven, so you'd better let me give you something now. I'm really sorry. Come along."

"Thank you, Sir James," Hewitt replied; "I won't take much. A few biscuits, perhaps, or something of that sort. And, by-the-bye, if you don't mind, I rather think I should like to take it alone. The fact is, I want to go over this case thoroughly by myself. Can you put me in a room?"

"Any room you like. Where will you go? The dining-room's rather large, but there's my study, that's pretty snug, or——"

"Perhaps I can go into Mr. Lloyd's room for half an hour or so—I don't think he'll mind, and it's pretty comfortable."

"Certainly, if you'd like. I'll tell them to send you whatever they've got.

"Thank you very much. Perhaps they'll also send me a lump of sugar and a walnut—it's—it's just a little fad of mine."

"A—what? A lump of sugar and a walnut?" Sir James stopped for a moment, with his hand on the bell-rope. "Oh, certainly, if you'd like it; certainly," he added, and stared after this detective of curious tastes as he left the room.

When the vehicle, bringing back the secretary and the policemen, drew up on the drive, Martin Hewitt left the room on the first floor and proceeded downstairs. On the landing he met Sir James Norris and

Mrs. Cazenove, who stared with astonishment on perceiving that the detective carried in his hand the parrot-cage.

"I think our business is about brought to a head now," Hewitt remarked, on the stairs. "Here are the police-officers from Twyford." The men were standing in the hall with Mr. Lloyd, who, on catching sight of the cage in Hewitt's hand, paled suddenly.

"This is the person who will be charged, I think," Hewitt pursued, addressing the officers, and indicating Lloyd with his finger.

"What, Lloyd?" gasped Sir James, aghast. "No—not Lloyd—nonsense!"

"He doesn't seem to think it nonsense himself, does he?" Hewitt placidly observed. Lloyd had sunk on a chair, and, grey of face, was staring blindly at the man he had run against at the office door that morning. His lips moved in spasms, but there was no sound. The wilted flower fell from his button-hole to the floor, but he did not move.

"This is his accomplice," Hewitt went on, placing the parrot and cage on the hall table, "though I doubt whether there will be any use in charging *him*. Eh, Polly?"

The parrot put its head aside and chuckled. "Hullo, Polly!" it quietly gurgled. "Come along!"

Sir James Norris was hopelessly bewildered. "Lloyd—Lloyd—" he said, under his breath, "Lloyd—and that!"

"This was his little messenger, his useful Mercury," Hewitt explained, tapping the cage complacently; "in fact, the actual lifter. Hold him up."

The last remark referred to the wretched Lloyd, who had fallen forward with something between a sob and a loud sigh. The policemen took him by the arms and propped him in his chair.

"System?" said Hewitt, with a shrug of the shoulders an hour or two after, in Sir James's study. "I can't say I have a system. I call it nothing but common-sense and a sharp pair of eyes. Nobody using these could help taking the right road in this case. I began at the match, just as the Scotland Yard man did, but I had the advantage of taking a line through three cases. To begin with, it was plain that that match, being left there in daylight, in Mrs. Cazenove's room, could not have been used to light the table-top, in the full glare of the window; therefore it had been used for some other purpose—*what* purpose I could not, at the moment, guess. Habitual thieves, you know, often have curious superstitions, and some will never take anything without leaving something behind—a pebble or a piece of coal, or something like that—in the premises they have been robbing. It seemed at first extremely likely that this was a case of that kind. The match had clearly been *brought in*—because when I asked for matches there were none in the stand—not even an empty box; and the room had not been disturbed. Also the match probably had not been struck there, nothing having been heard, although, of course, a mistake in this matter was just possible. This match then, it was fair to assume, had been lit somewhere else and blown out immediately—I remarked at the time that it was very little burnt. Plainly it could not have been treated thus for nothing, and the only possible object would have been to prevent it igniting accidentally. Following on this it became obvious that the match was used, for whatever purpose, not *as* a match, but merely as a convenient splinter of wood.

"So far so good. But on examining the match very closely I observed—as you can see for yourself—certain rather sharp indentations in the wood. They are very small, you see, and scarcely visible, except upon narrow inspection; but there they are, and their positions are regular. See—there are two on each side, each opposite the corresponding mark of the other pair. The match, in fact, would seem to have been gripped in some fairly sharp instrument, holding it at two points above, and two below—an instrument, as it may at once strike you, not unlike the beak of a bird.

"Now, here was an idea. What living creature but a bird could possibly have entered Mrs. Heath's window without a ladder—supposing no ladder to have been used—or could have got into Mrs. Armitage's window without lifting the sash higher than the eight or ten inches it was already open? Plainly, nothing. Further, it is significant that only *one* article was stolen at a time, although others were about. A human being could have carried any reasonable number, but a bird could only take one at a time. But why should a bird carry a match in its beak? Certainly it must have been trained to do that for a purpose, and a little consideration made that purpose pretty clear. A noisy, chattering bird would probably betray itself at once. Therefore it must be trained to keep quiet both while going for and coming away with its plunder. What readier or more probably effectual way than, while teaching it to carry without dropping, to teach it also to keep quiet while carrying? The one thing would practically cover the other.

"I thought at once, of course, of a jackdaw or a magpie—these birds' thievish reputations made the guess natural. But the marks on the match were much too wide apart to have been made by the beak of either. I conjectured, therefore, that it must be a raven. So that when we arrived near the coach-house I seized the opportunity of a little chat with your groom on the subject of dogs and pets in general, and ascertained that there was no tame raven in the place. I also, incidentally, by getting a light from the coach-house box of matches, ascertained that the match found was of the sort generally used about the establishment— the large, thick, red-topped English match. But I further found that Mr. Lloyd had a parrot which was a most intelligent pet, and had been trained into comparative quietness—for a parrot. Also, I learnt that more than once the groom had met Mr. Lloyd carrying his parrot under his coat—it having, as its owner explained, learnt the trick of opening its cage-door, and escaping.

"I said nothing, of course, to you of all this, because I had as yet nothing but a train of argument and no results. I got to Lloyd's room as soon as possible. My chief object in going there was achieved when I played with the parrot, and induced it to bite a quill tooth-pick.

"When you left me in the smoking-room I compared the quill and the match very carefully, and found that the marks corresponded exactly. After this I felt very little doubt indeed. The fact of Lloyd having met the ladies walking before dark on the day of the first robbery proved nothing, because, since it was clear that the match had *not* been used to procure a light, the robbery might as easily have taken place in daylight as not—must have so taken place, in fact, if my conjectures were right. That they were right I felt no doubt. There could be no other explanation.

"When Mrs. Heath left her window open and her door shut, anybody climbing upon the open sash of Lloyd's high window could have put the bird upon the sill above. The match placed in the bird's beak for the purpose I have indicated and struck first, in case by accident it should ignite by rubbing against something and startle the bird—this match would, of course, be dropped just where the object to be removed was taken up; as you know, in every case the match was found almost upon the spot where the missing article had been left— scarcely a likely triple coincidence, had the match been used by a human thief. This would have been done as soon after the ladies had left as possible, and there would then have been plenty of time for Lloyd to hurry out and meet them before dark—especially plenty of time to meet them *coming back,* as they must have been, since they were carrying their ferns. The match was an article well chosen for its purpose, as being a not altogether unlikely thing to find on a dressing-table, and, if noticed, likely to lead to the wrong conclusions adopted by the official detective.

"In Mrs. Armitage's case, the taking of an inferior brooch and the leaving of a more valuable ring pointed clearly either to the operator being a fool or unable to distinguish values, and certainly, from other indications, the thief seemed no fool. The door was locked, and the gasfitter, so to speak, on guard, and the window was only eight or ten inches open and propped with a brush. A human thief entering the window would have disturbed this arrangement, and would scarcely risk discovery by attempting to replace it, especially a thief in so great a hurry as to snatch the brooch up without unfastening the pin. The bird could pass through the opening as it was, and *would have* to tear the pincushion to pull the brooch off—probably holding the cushion down with its claw the while.

"Now, in yesterday's case we had an alteration of conditions. The window was shut and fastened, but the door was open—but only left for a few minutes, during which time no sound was heard either of coming or going. Was it not possible, then, that the thief was *already* in the room, in hiding, while Mrs. Cazenove was there, and seized its first opportunity on her temporary absence? The room is full of draperies, hangings, and what-not, allowing of plenty of concealment for a bird, and a bird could leave the place noiselessly and quickly. That the whole scheme was strange mattered not at all. Robberies presenting such unaccountable features must have been effected by strange means of one sort or another. There was no improbability—consider how many hundreds of examples of infinitely higher degrees of bird-training are exhibited in the London streets every week for coppers.

"So that, on the whole, I felt pretty sure of my ground. But before taking any definite steps, I resolved to see if Polly could not be persuaded to exhibit his accomplishments to an indulgent stranger. For that purpose I contrived to send Lloyd away again and have a quiet hour alone with his bird. A piece of sugar, as everybody knows, is a good parrot bribe; but a walnut, split in half, is a better—especially if the bird be used to it; so I got you to furnish me with both. Polly was shy at first, but I generally get along very well with pets, and a little perseverance soon led to a complete private performance for my benefit. Polly would take the match, mute as wax, jump on the table, pick up the brightest thing he could see, in a great hurry, leave the match behind, and scuttle away round the room; but at first wouldn't give up the plunder to *me*. It was enough. I also took the liberty, as you know, of a general look round, and discovered that little collection of Brummagem rings and trinkets that you have just seen—used in Polly's education, no doubt. When we sent Lloyd away it struck me that he might as well be usefully employed as not, so I got him to fetch the police—deluding him a little, I fear, by talking about the servants and a female searcher. There will be no trouble about evidence—he'll confess; of that I'm sure. I know the sort of man. But I doubt if you'll get Mrs. Cazenove's brooch back. You see, he has been to London to-day, and by this time the swag is probably broken up."

Sir James listened to Hewitt's explanation with many expressions of assent and some of surprise. When it was over he smoked a few whiffs and then said: "But Mrs. Armitage's brooch was pawned; and by a woman."

"Exactly. I expect our friend Lloyd was rather disgusted at his small luck—probably gave the brooch to some female connection in London, and she realized on it. Such persons don't always trouble to give a correct address."

The two smoked in silence for a few minutes, and then Hewitt continued: "I don't expect our friend has had an easy job altogether with that bird. His successes at most have only been three, and I suspect he had many failures and not a few anxious moments that we know nothing of. I should judge as much merely from what the groom told me of frequently meeting Lloyd with his parrot. But the plan was not a bad one—not at all. Even if the bird had been caught in the act, it would only have been 'That mischievous parrot!' you see. And his master would only have been looking for him."

The Murder at Troyte's Hill

Catherine L. Pirkis

GRIFFITHS, of the Newcastle Constabulary, has the case in hand," said Mr. Dyer; "those Newcastle men are keen-witted, shrewd fellows, and very jealous of outside interference. They only sent to me under protest, as it were, because they wanted your sharp wits at work inside the house."

"I suppose throughout I am to work with Griffiths, not with you?" said Miss Brooke.

"Yes; when I have given you in outline the facts of the case, I simply have nothing more to do with it, and you must depend on Griffiths for any assistance of any sort that you may require."

Here, with a swing, Mr. Dyer opened his big ledger and turned rapidly over its leaves till he came to the heading "Troyte's Hill" and the date "September 6th."

"I'm all attention," said Loveday, leaning back in her chair in the attitude of a listener.

"The murdered man," resumed Mr. Dyer, "is a certain Alexander Henderson—usually known as old Sandy—lodge-keeper to Mr. Craven, of Troyte's Hill, Cumberland. The lodge consists merely of two rooms on the ground floor, a bedroom and a sitting-room; these Sandy occupied alone, having neither kith nor kin of any degree. On the morning of September 6th, some children going up to the house with milk from the farm, noticed that Sandy's bed-room window stood wide open. Curiosity prompted them to peep in; and then, to their horror, they saw old Sandy, in his night-shirt, lying dead on the floor, as if he had fallen backwards from the window. They raised an alarm; and on examination, it was found that death had ensued from a heavy blow on the temple, given either by a strong fist or some blunt instrument. The room, on being entered, presented a curious appearance. It was as if a herd of monkeys had been turned into it and allowed to work their impish will. Not an article of furniture remained in its place: the bed-clothes had been rolled into a bundle and stuffed into the chimney; the bedstead—a small iron one—lay on its side; the one chair in the room stood on the top of the table; fender and fire-irons lay across the wash-stand, whose basin was to be found in a farther comer, holding bolster and pillow. The clock stood on its head in the middle of the mantel-piece; and the small vases and ornaments, which flanked it on either side, were walking, as it were, in a straight line towards the door. The old man's clothes had been rolled into a ball and thrown on the top of a high cupboard in which he kept his savings and whatever valuables he had. This cupboard, however, had not been meddled with, and its contents remained intact, so it was evident that robbery was not the motive for the crime. At the inquest, subsequently held, a verdict of 'willful murder' against some person or persons unknown was returned. The local police are diligently investigating the affair, but, as yet, no arrests have been made. The opinion that at present prevails in the neighbourhood is that the crime has been perpetrated by some lunatic, escaped or otherwise and enquiries are being made at the local asylums as to missing or lately released inmates. Griffiths, however, tells me that his suspicions set in another direction."

"Did anything of importance transpire at the inquest?"

"Nothing specially important. Mr. Craven broke down in giving his evidence when he alluded to the confidential relations that had always subsisted between Sandy and himself, and spoke of the last time that he had seen him alive. The evidence of the butler, and one or two of the female servants, seems clear enough, and they let fall something of a hint that Sandy was not altogether a favourite among them, on account of the overbearing manner in which he used his influence with his master. Young Mr. Craven, a youth of about nineteen, home from Oxford for the long vacation, was not present at the inquest; a doctor's certificate was put in stating that he was suffering from typhoid fever, and could not leave his bed without risk to his life. Now this young man is a thor-oughly bad sort, and as much a gentleman-blackleg as it is possible for such a young fellow to be. It seems to Griffiths that there is something suspicious about this illness of his. He came back from Oxford on the verge of delirium tremens, pulled round from that, and then suddenly, on the day after the murder, Mrs. Craven rings the bell, announces that he has developed typhoid fever and orders a doctor to be sent for."

"What sort of man is Mr. Craven senior?"

"He seems to be a quiet old fellow, a scholar and learned philologist. Neither his neighbours nor his family see much of him; he almost lives in his study, writing a treatise, in seven or eight volumes, on comparative philology. He is not a rich man. Troyte's Hill, though it carries position in the county, is not a paying property, and Mr. Craven is unable to keep it up properly. I am told he has had to cut down expenses in all directions in order to send his son to college, and his daughter from first to last has been entirely educated by her mother. Mr. Craven was originally intended for the church, but for some reason or other, when his college career came to an end, he did not present himself for ordination—went out to Natal instead, where he obtained some civil appointment and where he remained for about fifteen years. Henderson was his servant during the latter portion of his Oxford career, and must have been greatly respected by him, for although the remuneration derived from his appointment at Natal was small, he paid Sandy a regular yearly allowance out of it. When, about ten years ago, he succeeded to Troyte's Hill, on the death of his elder brother, and returned home with his family, Sandy was immediately installed as lodge-keeper, and at so high a rate of pay that the butler's wages were cut down to meet it."

"Ah, that wouldn't improve the butler's feelings towards him," ejaculated Loveday.

Mr. Dyer went on: "But, in spite of his high wages, he doesn't appear to have troubled much about his duties as lodge-keeper, for they were performed, as a rule, by the gardener's boy, while he took his meals and passed his time at the house, and, speaking generally, put his finger into every pie. You know the old adage respecting the servant of twenty-one years' standing: 'Seven years my servant, seven years my equal, seven years my master.' Well, it appears to have held good in the case of Mr. Craven and Sandy. The old gentleman, absorbed in his philological studies, evidently let the reins slip through his fingers, and Sandy seems to have taken easy possession of them The servants frequently had to go to him for orders, and he carried things, as a rule, with a high hand."

"Did Mrs. Craven never have a word to say on the matter?"

"I've not heard much about her. She seems to be a quiet sort of person. She is a Scotch missionary's daughter; perhaps she spends her time working for the Cape mission and that sort of thing."

"And young Mr. Craven: did he knock under to Sandy's rule?"

"Ah, now you're hitting the bull's eye and we come to Griffiths' theory. The young man and Sandy appear to have been at loggerheads ever since the Cravens took possession of Troyte's Hill. As a schoolboy Master Harry defied Sandy and threatened him with his hunting-crop; and subsequently, as a young man, has used strenuous endeavours to put the old servant in his place. On the day before the murder, Griffiths says, there was a terrible scene between the two, in which the young gentleman, in the presence of several witnesses, made use of strong language and threatened the old man's life. Now, Miss Brooke, I have told you all the circumstances of the case so far as I know them. For fuller particulars I must refer you to Griffiths. He, no doubt, will meet you at Grenfell—the nearest station to Troyte's Hill, and tell you in what capacity he has procured for you an entrance into the house. By-the-way, he has wired to me this morning that he hopes you will be able to save the Scotch express to-night."

Loveday expressed her readiness to comply with Mr. Griffiths' wishes.

"I shall be glad," said Mr. Dyer, as he shook hands with her at the office door, "to see you immediately on your return—that, however, I suppose, will not be yet awhile. This promises, I fancy, to be a longish affair?" This was said interrogatively.

"I haven't the least idea on the matter," answered Loveday. "I start on my work without theory of any sort—in fact, I may say, with my mind a perfect blank."

And anyone who had caught a glimpse of her blank, expressionless features, as she said this, would have taken her at her word.

Grenfell, the nearest post-town to Troyte's Hill, is a fairly busy, populous little town–looking south towards the black country, and northwards to low, barren hills. Pre-eminent among these stands Troyte's Hill, famed in the old days as a border keep, and possibly at a still earlier date as a Druid stronghold.

At a small inn at Grenfell, dignified by the title of "The Station Hotel," Mr. Griffiths, of the Newcastle constabulary, met Loveday and still further initiated her into the mysteries of the Troyte's Hill murder.

"A little of the first excitement has subsided," he said, after preliminary greetings had been exchanged; "but still the wildest rumours are flying about and repeated as solemnly as if they were Gospel truths. My chief here and my colleagues generally adhere to their first conviction, that the criminal is some suddenly crazed tramp or else an escaped lunatic, and they are confident that sooner or later we shall come upon his traces. Their theory is that Sandy, hearing some strange noise at the Park Gates, put his head out of the window to ascertain the cause and immediately had his death blow dealt him; then they suppose that the lunatic scrambled into the room through the window and exhausted his frenzy by turning things generally upside down. They refuse altogether to share my suspicions respecting young Mr. Craven."

Mr. Griffiths was a tall, thin-featured man, with iron-grey hair, but so close to his head that it refused to do anything but stand on end. This gave a somewhat comic expression to the upper portion of his face and clashed oddly with the melancholy look that his mouth habitually wore.

"I have made all smooth for you at Troyte's Hill," he presently went on. "Mr. Craven is not wealthy enough to allow himself the luxury of a family lawyer, so he occasionally employs the services of Messrs. Wells and Sugden, lawyers in this place, and who, as it happens, have, off and on, done a good deal of business for me. It was through them I heard that Mr. Craven was anxious to secure the assistance of an amanuensis. I immediately offered your services, stating that you were a friend of mine, a lady of impoverished means, who would gladly undertake the duties for the munificent sum of a guinea a month, with board and lodging. The old gentleman at once jumped at the offer, and is anxious for you to be at Troyte's Hill at once."

Loveday expressed her satisfaction with the programme that Mr. Griffiths had sketched for her, then she had a few questions to ask.

"Tell me," she said, "what led you, in the first instance, to suspect young Mr. Craven of the crime?"

"The footing on which he and Sandy stood towards each other, and the terrible scene that occurred between them only the day before the murder," answered Griffiths, promptly. "Nothing of this, however, was elicited at the inquest, where a very fair face was put on Sandy's relations with the whole of the Craven family. I have subsequently unearthed a good deal respecting the private life of Mr. Harry Craven, and, among other things, I have found out that on the night of the murder he left the house shortly after ten o'clock, and no one, so far as I have been able to ascertain, knows at what hour he returned. Now I must draw your attention, Miss Brooke, to the fact that at the inquest the medical evidence went to prove that the murder had been committed between ten and eleven at night."

"Do you surmise, then, that the murder was a planned thing on the part of this young man?"

"I do. I believe that he wandered about the grounds until Sandy shut himself in for the night, then aroused him by some outside noise, and, when the old man looked out to ascertain the cause, dealt him a blow with a bludgeon or loaded stick, that caused his death."

"A cold-blooded crime that, for a boy of nineteen?"

"Yes. He's a good-loking, gentlemanly youngster, too, with manners as mild as milk, but from all accounts is as full of wickedness as an egg is full of meat. Now, to come to another point–if, in connection with these ugly facts, you take into consideration the suddenness of his illness, I think you'll admit that it bears a suspicious appearance and might reasonably give rise to the surmise that it was a plant on his part, in order to get out of the inquest."

"Who is the doctor attending him?"

"A man called Waters; not much of a practitioner, from all accounts, and no doubt he feels himself highly honoured in being summoned to Troyte's Hill. The Cravens, it seems, have no family doctor. Mrs. Craven, with her missionary experience, is half a doctor herself, and never calls in one except in a serious emergency."

"The certificate was in order, I suppose?"

"Undoubtedly. And, as if to give colour to the gravity of the case, Mrs. Craven sent a message down to the servants, that if any of them were afraid of the infection they could at once go to their homes. Several of the maids, I believe, took advantage of her permission, and packed their boxes. Miss Craven, who is a delicate girl, was sent away with her maid to stay with friends at Newcastle, and Mrs. Craven isolated herself with her patient in one of the disused wings of the house."

"Has anyone ascertained whether Miss Craven arrived at her destination at Newcastle?"

Griffiths drew his brows together in thought.

"I did not see any necessity for such a thing," he answered. "I don't quite follow you. What do you mean to imply?"

"Oh, nothing. I don't suppose it matters much: it might have been interesting as a side-issue." She broke off for a moment, then added:

"Now tell me a little about the butler, the man whose wages were cut down to increase Sandy's pay."

"Old John Hales? He's a thoroughly worthy, respectable man; he was butler for five or six years to Mr. Craven's brother, when he was master of Troyte's Hill, and then took duty under this Mr. Craven. There's no ground for suspicion in that quarter. Hales's exclamation when he heard of the murder is quite enough to stamp him as an innocent man: 'Serve the old idiot right,' he cried: 'I couldn't pump up a tear for him if I tried for a month of Sundays!' Now I take it, Miss Brooke, a guilty man wouldn't dare make such a speech as that!"

"You think not?"

Griffiths stared at her. "I'm a little disappointed in her," he thought. "I'm afraid her powers have been slightly exaggerated if she can't see such a straight-forward thing as that."

Aloud he said, a little sharply, "Well, I don't stand alone in my thinking. No one yet has breathed a word against Hales, and if they did, I've no doubt he could prove an *alibi* without any trouble, for he lives in the house, and everyone has a good word for him."

"I suppose Sandy's lodge has been put into order by this time?"

"Yes; after the inquest, and when all possible evidence had been taken, everything was put straight."

"At the inquest it was stated that no marks of footsteps could be traced in any direction?"

"The long drought we've had would render such a thing impossible, let alone the feet that Sandy's lodge stands right on the graveled drive, without flower-beds or grass borders of any sort around it. But look here, Miss Brooke, don't you be wasting your time over the lodge and its surroundings. Every iota of fact on that matter has been gone through over and over again by me and my chief. What we want you to do is to go straight into the house and concentrate attention on Master Harry's sick-room, and find out what's going on there. What he did outside the house on the night of the 6th, I've no doubt I shall be able to find out for myself. Now, Miss Brooke, you've asked me no end of questions, to which I have replied as fully as it was in my power to do; will you be good enough to answer one question that I wish to put, as straightforwardly as I have answered yours? You have had fullest particulars given you of the condition of Sandy's room when the police entered it on the morning after the murder. No doubt, at the present moment, you can see it all in your mind's eye— the bedstead on its side, the clock on its head, the bed-clothes half-way up the chimney, the little vases and ornaments walking in a straight line towards the door?"

Loveday bowed her head.

"Very well, Now will you be good enough to tell me what this scene of confusion recalls to your mind before anything else?"

"The room of an unpopular Oxford freshman after a raid upon it by undergrads," answered Loveday promptly.

Mr. Griffiths rubbed his hands.

"Quite so!" he ejaculated. "I see, after all, we are one at heart in this matter, in spite of a little surface disagreement of ideas. Depend upon it, by-and-bye, like the engineers tunneling from different quarters under the Alps, we shall meet at the same point and shake hands. By-the-way, I have arranged for daily communication between us through the post-boy who takes the letters to Troyte's Hill. He is trustworthy, and any letter you give him for me will find its way into my hands within the hour."

It was about three o'clock in the afternoon when Loveday drove in through the park gates of Troyte's Hill, past the lodge where old Sandy had met with his death It was a pretty little cottage, covered with Virginia creeper and wild honeysuckle, and showing no outward sign of the tragedy that had been enacted within.

The park and pleasure-grounds of Troyte's Hill were extensive, and the house itself was a somewhat imposing red brick structure, built, possibly, at the time when Dutch William's taste had grown popular in the country. Its frontage presented a somewhat forlorn appearance, its centre windows—a square of eight—alone seeming to show signs of occupation. With the exception of two windows at the extreme end of the bedroom floor of the north wing, where, possibly, the invalid and his mother were located, and two windows at the extreme end of the ground floor of the south wing, which Loveday ascertained subsequently were those of Mr. Craven's study, not a single window in either wing owned blind or curtain. The wings were extensive, and it was easy to understand that at the extreme end of the one the fever patient would be isolated from the rest of the household, and that at the extreme end of the other Mr. Craven could secure the quiet and freedom from interruption which, no doubt, were essential to the due prosecution of his philological studies.

Alike on the house and ill-kept grounds were present the stamp of the smallness of the income of the master and owner of the place. The terrace, which ran the length of the house in front, and on to which every window on the ground floor opened, was miserably out of repair: not a lintel or door-post, window-ledge or balcony but what seemed to cry aloud for the touch of the painter. "Pity me! I have seen better days," Loveday could fancy written as a legend across the redbrick porch that gave entrance to the old house.

The butler, John Hales, admitted Loveday, shouldered her portmanteau and told her he would show her to her room He was a tall, powerfully-built man, with a ruddy face and dogged expression of countenance. It was easy to understand that, off and on, there must have been many a sharp encounter between him and old Sandy. He treated Loveday in an easy, familiar fashion, evidently considering that an amanuensis took much the same rank as a nursery governess—that is to say, a little below a lady's maid and a little above a house-maid.

"We're short of hands, just now," he said, in broad Cumberland dialect, as he led the way up the wide stair case. "Some of the lasses downstairs took fright at the fever and went home. Cook and I are single-handed, for Moggie, the only maid left, has been told off to wait on Madam and Master Harry. I hope you're not afeared of fever?"

Loveday explained that she was not, and asked if the room at the extreme end of the north wing was the one assigned to "Madam and Master Harry."

"Yes," said the man; "it's convenient for sick nursing; there's a flight of stairs runs straight down from it to the kitchen quarters. We put all Madam wants at the foot of those stairs and Moggie herself never enters the sick-room. I take it you'll not be seeing Madam for many a day, yet awhile."

"When shall I see Mr. Craven? At dinner to-night?"

"That's what naebody could say," answered Hales. "He may not come out of his study till past midnight; sometimes he sits there till two or three in the morning. Shouldn't advise you to wait till he wants his dinner—better have a cup of tea and a chop sent up to you. Madam never waits for him at any meal."

As he finished speaking he deposited the portmanteau outside one of the many doors opening into the gallery.

"This is Miss Craven's room," he went on; "cook and me thought you'd better have it, as it would want less getting ready than the other rooms, and work is work when there are so few hands to do it. Oh, my stars! I do declare there is cook putting it straight for you now." The last sentence was added as the opened door laid bare to view, the cook, with a duster in her hand, polishing a mirror; the bed had been made, it is true, but otherwise the room must have been much as Miss Craven left it, after a hurried packing up.

To the surprise of the two servants Loveday took the matter very lightly.

"I have a special talent for arranging rooms and would prefer getting this one straight for myself," she said. "Now, if you will go and get ready that chop and cup of tea we were talking about just now, I shall think it much kinder than if you stayed here doing what I can so easily do for myself."

When, however, the cook and butler had departed in company, Loveday showed no disposition to exercise the "special talent" of which she had boasted.

She first carefully turned the key in the lock and then proceeded to make a thorough and minute investigation of every corner of the room. Not an article of furniture, not an ornament or toilet accessory, but what was lifted from its place and carefully scrutinized. Even the ashes in the grate, the debris of the last fire made there, were raked over and well looked through.

This careful investigation of Miss Craven's late surroundings occupied in all about three quarters of an hour, and Loveday, with her hat in her hand, descended the stairs to see Hales crossing the hall to the dining-room with the promised cup of tea and chop.

In silence and solitude she partook of the simple repast in a dining-hall that could with ease have banqueted a hundred and fifty guests.

"Now for the grounds before it gets dark," she said to herself, as she noted that already the outside shadows were beginning to slant.

The dining-hall was at the back of the house; and here, as in the front, the windows, reaching to the ground, presented easy means of egress. The flower-garden was on this side of the house and sloped downhill to a pretty stretch of well-wooded country.

Loveday did not linger here even to admire, but passed at once round the south corner of the house to the windows which she had ascertained, by a careless question to the butler, were those of Mr. Craven's study.

Very cautiously she drew near them, for the blinds were up, the curtains drawn back. A side glance, however, relieved her apprehensions, for it showed her the occupant of the room, seated in an easy-chair, with his back to the windows. From the length of his outstretched limbs he was evidently a tall man. His hair was silvery and curly, the lower part of his face was hidden from her view by the chair, but she could see one hand was pressed tightly across his eyes and brows. The whole attitude was that of a man absorbed in deep thought. The room was comfortably furnished, but presented an appearance of disorder from the books and manuscripts scattered in all directions. A whole pile of torn fragments of foolscap sheets, overflowing from a waste-paper basket beside the writing-table, seemed to proclaim the fact that the scholar had of late grown weary of, or else dissatisfied with his work, and had condemned it freely.

Although Loveday stood looking in at this window for over five minutes, not the faintest sign of life did that tall, reclining figure give, and it would have been as easy to believe him locked in sleep as in thought.

From here she turned her steps in the direction of Sandy's lodge. As Griffiths had said, it was graveled up to its doorstep. The blinds were closely drawn, and it presented the ordinary appearance of a disused cottage.

A narrow path beneath over-arching boughs of cherry-laurel and arbutus, immediately facing the lodge, caught her eye, and down this she at once turned her footsteps.

This path led, with many a wind and turn, through a belt of shrubbery that skirted the frontage of Mr. Craven's grounds, and eventually, after much zig-zagging, ended in close proximity to the stables. As Loveday entered it, she seemed literally to leave daylight behind her.

"I feel as if I were following the course of a circuitous mind," she said to herself as the shadows closed around her. "I could not fancy

Sir Isaac Newton or Bacon planning or delighting in such a wind-about-alley as this!"

The path showed greyly in front of her out of the dimness. On and on she followed it; here and there the roots of the old laurels, struggling out of the ground, threatened to trip her up. Her eyes, however, had now grown accustomed to the half-gloom, and not a detail of her surroundings escaped her as she went along.

A bird flew from out the thicket on her right hand with a startled cry. A dainty little frog leaped out of her way into the shriveled leaves lying below the laurels. Following the movements of this frog, her eye was caught by something black and solid among those leaves. What was it? A bundle—a shiny black coat? Loveday knelt down, and using her hands to assist her eyes, found that they came into contact with the dead, stiffened body of a beautiful black retriever. She parted, as well as she was able, the tower boughs of the evergreens, and minutely examined the poor animal. Its eyes were still open, though glazed and bleared, and its death had, undoubtedly, been caused by the blow of some blunt, heavy instrument, for on one side its skull was almost battered in.

"Exactly the death that was dealt to Sandy," she thought, as she groped hither and thither beneath the trees in hopes of lighting upon the weapon of destruction.

She searched until increasing darkness warned her that search was useless. Then, still following the zig-zagging path, she made her way out by the stables and thence back to the house.

She went to bed that night without having spoken to a soul beyond the cook and butler. The next morning, however, Mr. Craven introduced himself to her across the breakfast-table. He was a man of really handsome personal appearance, with a fine carriage of the head and shoulders, and eyes that had a forlorn, appealing look in them. He entered the room with an air of great energy, apologized to Loveday for the absence of his wife, and for his own remissness in not being in the way to receive her on the previous day. Then he bade her make herself at home at the breakfast-table, and expressed his delight in having found a coadjutor in his work.

"I hope you understand what a great—a stupendous work it is?" he added, as he sank into a chair. "It is a work that will leave its impress upon thought in all the ages to come. Only a man who has studied comparative philology as I have for the past thirty years, could gauge the magnitude of the task I have set myself."

With the last remark, his energy seemed spent, and he sank back in his chair, covering his eyes with his hand in precisely the same attitude as that in which Loveday had seen him over-night, and utterly oblivious of the fact that breakfast was before him and a stranger-guest seated at table. The butler entered with another dish. "Better go on with your breakfast," he whispered to Loveday, "he may sit like that for another hour."

He placed his dish in front of his master.

"Captain hasn't come back yet, sir," he said, making an effort to arouse him from his reverie.

"Eh, what?" said Mr. Craven, for a moment lifting his hand from his eyes.

"Captain, sir—the black retriever," repeated the man.

The pathetic look in Mr. Craven's eyes deepened.

"Ah, poor Captain!" he murmured; "the best dog I ever had."

Then he again sank back in his chair, putting his hand to his forehead.

The butler made one more effort to arouse him.

"Madam sent you down a newspaper, sir, that she thought you would like to see," he shouted almost into his master's ear, and at the same time laid the morning's paper on the table beside his plate.

"Confound you! leave it there," said Mr. Craven irritably. "Fools! dolts that you all are! With your trivialities and interruptions you are sending me out of the world with my work undone!"

And again he sank back in his chair, closed his eyes and became lost to his surroundings.

Loveday went on with her breakfast. She changed her place at table to one on Mr. Craven's right hand, so that the newspaper sent down for his perusal lay between his plate and hers. It was folded into an oblong shape, as if it were wished to direct attention to a certain portion of a certain column.

A clock in a corner of the room struck the hour with a loud, resonant stroke. Mr. Craven gave a start and rubbed his eyes.

"Eh, what's this?" he said. "What meal are we at?" He looked around with a bewildered air. "Eh!—who are you?" he went on, staring hard at Loveday. "What are you doing here? Where's Nina?—Where's Harry?"

Loveday began to explain, and gradually recollection seemed to come back to him.

"Ah, yes, yes," he said. "I remember; you've come to assist me with my great work. You promised, you know, to help me out of the hole I've got into. Very enthusiastic, I remember they said you were, on certain abstruse points in comparative philology. Now, Miss—Miss—I've forgotten your name—tell me a little of what you know about the elemental sounds of speech that are common to all languages. Now, to how many would you reduce those elemental sounds—to six, eight, nine? No, we won't discuss the matter here, the cups and saucers distract me. Come into my den at the other end of the house; we'll have perfect quiet there."

And utterly ignoring the fact that he had not as yet broken his fast, he rose from the table, seized Loveday by the wrist, and led her out of the room and down the long corridor that led through the south wing to his study.

But seated in that study his energy once more speedily exhausted itself.

He placed Loveday in a comfortable chair at his writing-table, consulted her taste as to pens, and spread a sheet of foolscap before her. Then he settled himself in his easy-chair, with his back to the light, as if he were about to dictate folios to her.

In a loud, distinct voice he repeated the title of his learned work, then its sub-division, then the number and heading of the chapter that was at present engaging his attention Then he put his hand to his head. "It's the elemental sounds that are my stumbling-block," he said. "Now, how on earth is it possible to get a notion of a sound of agony that is not in part a sound of terror? or a sound of surprise that is not in part a sound of either joy or sorrow?"

With this his energies were spent, and although Loveday remained seated in that study from early morning till daylight began to fade, she had not ten sentences to show for her day's work as amanuensis.

Loveday in all spent only two clear days at Troyte's Hill.

On the evening of the first of those days Detective Griffiths received, through the trustworthy post-boy, the following brief note from her:

"I have found out that Hales owed Sandy close upon a hundred pounds, which he had borrowed at various times. I don't know whether you will think this fact of any importance.—L. B."

Mr. Griffiths repeated the last sentence blankly. "If Harry Craven were put upon his defence, his counsel, I take it, would consider the fact of first importance," he muttered. And for the remainder of that day Mr. Griffiths went about his work in a perturbed state of mind, doubtful whether to hold or to let go his theory concerning Harry Craven's guilt.

The next morning there came another brief note from Loveday which ran thus:

"As a matter of collateral interest, find out if a person, calling himself Harold Cousins, sailed two days ago from London Docks for Natal in the *Bonnie Dundee?*"

To this missive Loveday received, in reply, the following somewhat lengthy dispatch:

"I do not quite see the drift of your last note, but have wired to our agents in London to carry out its suggestion On my part, I have important news to communicate. I have found out what Harry Craven's business out of doors was on the night of the murder, and at my instance a warrant has been issued for his arrest. This warrant it will be my duty to serve on him in the course of to-day. Things are beginning to look very black against him, and I am convinced his illness is all a sham. I have seen Waters, the man who is supposed to be attending him, and have driven him into a corner and made him admit that he has only seen young Craven once—on the first day of his illness—and that he gave his certificate entirely on the strength of what Mrs. Craven told him of her son's condition On the occasion of this, his first and only visit, the lady, it seems, also told him that it would not be necessary for him to continue his attendance, as she quite felt herself competent to treat the case, having had so much experience in fever cases among the blacks at Natal.

"As I left Waters's house, after eliciting this important information, I was accosted by a man who keeps a low-class inn in the place, McQueen by name. He said that he wished to speak to me on a matter of importance. To make a long story short, this McQueen stated that on the night of the sixth, shortly after eleven o'clock, Harry Craven came to his house, bringing with him a valuable piece of plate—a handsome epergne—and requested him to lend him a hundred pounds on it, as he hadn't a penny in his pocket. McQueen complied with his request to the extent of ten sovereigns, and now, in a fit of nervous terror, comes to me to confess himself a receiver of stolen goods and play the honest man! He says he noticed that the young gentleman was very much agitated as he made the request, and he also begged him to mention his visit to no one. Now, I am curious to learn how Master Harry will get over the fact that he passed the lodge at the hour at which the murder was most probably committed; or how he will get out of the dilemma of having repassed the lodge on his way back to the house, and not noticed the wide-open window with the full moon shining down on it?

"Another word! Keep out of the way when I arrive at the house, somewhere between two and three in the afternoon, to serve the warrant. I do not wish your professional capacity to get wind, for you will most likely yet be of some use to us in the house.

Loveday read this note, seated at Mr. Craven's writing-table, with the old gentleman himself reclining motionless beside her in his easy-chair. A little smile played about the corners of her mouth as she read over again the words—"for you will most likely yet be of some use to us in the house."

Loveday's second day in Mr. Craven's study promised to be as unfruitful as the first. For fully an hour after she had received Griffiths' note, she sat at the writing-table with her pen in her hand, ready to transcribe Mr. Craven's inspirations. Beyond, however, the phrase, muttered with closed eyes—"It's all here, in my brain, but I can't put it into words"—not a half-syllable escaped his lips.

At the end of that hour the sound of footsteps on the outside gravel made her turn her head towards the window. It was Griffiths approaching with two constables. She heard the hall door opened to admit them, but, beyond that, not a sound reached her ear, and she realized how fully she was cut off from communication with the rest of the household at the farther end of this unoccupied wing.

Mr. Craven, still reclining in his semi-trance, evidently had not the faintest suspicion that so important an event as the arrest of his only son on a charge of murder was about to be enacted in the house.

Meantime, Griffiths and his constables had mounted the stairs leading to the north wing, and were being guided through the corridors to the sick-room by the flying figure of Moggie, the maid.

"Hoot, mistress!" cried the girl, "here are three men coming up the stairs—policemen, every one of them—will ye come and ask them what they be wanting?"

Outside the door of the sick-room stood Mrs. Craven—a tall, sharp-featured woman with sandy hair going rapidly grey.

"What is the meaning of this? What is your business here?" she said haughtily, addressing Griffiths, who headed the party.

Griffiths respectfully explained what his business was, and requested her to stand on one side that he might enter her son's room.

"This is my daughter's room; satisfy yourself of the fact," said the lady, throwing back the door as she spoke.

And Griffiths and his confrères entered, to find pretty Miss Craven, looking very white and scared, seated beside a fire in a long flowing robe de chambre.

Griffiths departed in haste and confusion, without the chance of a professional talk with Loveday. That afternoon saw him telegraphing wildly in all directions, and dispatching messengers in all quarters. Finally he spent over an hour drawing up an elaborate report to his chief at Newcastle, assuring him of the identity of one, Harold Cousins, who had sailed in the *Bonnie Dundee* for Natal, with Harry Craven, of Troyte's Hill, and advising that the police authorities in that far-away district should be immediately communicated with.

The ink had not dried on the pen with which this report was written before a note, in Loveday's writing, was put into his hand.

Loveday evidently had had some difficulty in finding a messenger for this note, for it was brought by a gardener's boy, who informed Griffiths that the lady had said he would receive a gold sovereign if he delivered the letter all right.

Griffiths paid the boy and dismissed him, and then proceeded to read Loveday's communication.

It was written hurriedly in pencil, and ran as follows:

"Things are getting critical here. Directly you receive this, come up to the house with two of your men, and post yourselves anywhere in the grounds where you can see and not be seen. There will be no difficulty in this, for it will be dark by the time you are able to get there. I am not sure whether I shall want your aid to-night, but you had better keep in the grounds until morning, in case of need; and above all, never once lose sight of the study windows." (This was underscored.) "If I put a lamp with a green shade in one of those windows, do not lose a moment in entering by that window, which I will contrive to keep unlocked."

Detective Griffiths rubbed his forehead—rubbed his eyes, as he finished reading this.

"Well, I daresay it's all right," he said, "but I'm bothered, that's all, and for the life of me I can't see one step of the way she is going."

He looked at his watch: the hands pointed to a quarter past six. The short September day was drawing rapidly to a close. A good five miles lay between him and Troyte's Hill—there was evidently not a moment to lose.

At the very moment that Griffiths, with his two constables, were once more starting along the Grenfell High Road behind the best horse they could procure, Mr. Craven was rousing himself from his long slumber, and beginning to look around him. That slumber, however, though long, had not been a peaceful one, and it was sundry of the old gentleman's muttered exclamations, as he had started uneasily in his sleep, that had caused Loveday to open, and then to creep out of the room to dispatch, her hurried note.

What effect the occurrence of the morning had had upon the household generally, Loveday, in her isolated corner of the house, had no means of ascertaining. She only noted that when Hales brought in her tea, as he did precisely at five o'clock, he wore a particularly ill-tempered expression of countenance, and she heard him mutter, as he set down the tea-tray with a clatter, something about being a respectable man, and not used to such "goings on."

It was not until nearly an hour and a half after this that Mr. Craven had awakened with a sudden start, and, looking wildly around him, had questioned Loveday who had entered the room.

Loveday explained that the butler had brought in lunch at one, and tea at five, but that since then no one had come in.

"Now that's false," said Mr. Craven, in a sharp, unnatural sort of voice; "I saw him sneaking round the room, the whining, canting hypocrite, and you must have seen him, too! Didn't you hear him say, in his squeaky old voice: 'Master, I knows your secret—'" He broke off abruptly, looking wildly round. "Eh, what's this?" he cried. "No, no, I'm all wrong—Sandy is dead and buried—they held an inquest on him, and we all praised him up as if he were a saint."

"He must have been a bad man, that old Sandy," said Loveday sympathetically.

"You're right! you're right!" cried Mr. Craven, springing up excitedly from his chair and seizing her by the hand. "If ever a man deserved his death, he did. For thirty years he held that rod over my head, and then—ah where was I?"

He put his hand to his head and again sank, as if exhausted, into his chair.

"I suppose it was some early indiscretion of yours at college that he knew of?" said Loveday, eager to get at as much of the truth as possible while the mood for confidence held sway in the feeble brain.

"That was it! I was fool enough to marry a disreputable girl—a barmaid in the town—and Sandy was present at the wedding, and then—"
Here his eyes closed again and his mutterings became incoherent.

For ten minutes he lay back in his chair, muttering thus; "A yelp—a groan," were the only words Loveday could distinguish among those mutterings, then suddenly, slowly and distinctly, he said, as if answering some plainly-put question: "A good blow with the hammer and the thing was done."

"I should like amazingly to see that hammer," said Loveday, "do you keep it anywhere at hand?"

His eyes opened with a wild, cunning look in them.

"Who's talking about a hammer? I did not say I had one. If anyone says I did it with a hammer, they're telling a lie."

"Oh, you've spoken to me about the hammer two or three times," said Loveday calmly; "the one that killed your dog, Captain, and I should like to see it, that's all."

The took of cunning died out of the old man's eye—"Ah, poor Captain! splendid dog that! Well, now, where were we? Where did we leave off? Ah, I remember, it was the elemental sounds of speech that bothered me so that night. Were you here then? Ah, no! I remember. I had been trying all day to assimilate a dog's yelp of pain to a human groan, and I couldn't do it. The idea haunted me—followed me about wherever I went. If they were both elemental sounds, they must have something in common, but the link between them I could not find;

then it occurred to me, would a well-bred, well-trained dog like my Captain in the stables, there, at the moment of death give an unmitigated currish yelp; would there not be something of a human note in his death-cry? The thing was worth putting to the test. If I could hand down in my treatise a fragment of fact on the matter, it would be worth a dozen dogs' lives, so I went out into the moonfight—ah, but you know all about it—now, don't you?"

"Yes. Poor Captain! did he yelp or groan?"

"Why, he gave one loud, long, hideous yelp, just as if he had been a common cur. I might just as well have let him alone; it only set that other brute opening his window and spying out on me, and saying in his cracked old voice: 'Master, what are you doing out here at this time of night?' "

Again he sank back in his chair, muttering incoherently with half-closed eyes.

Loveday let him alone for a minute or so; then she had another question to ask.

"And that other brute—did he yelp or groan when you dealt him his blow?"

"What, old Sandy—the brute? he fell back—Ah, I remember, you said you would like to see the hammer that stopped his babbling old tongue—now didn't you?"

He rose a little unsteadily from his chair, and seemed to drag his long limbs with an effort across the room to a cabinet at the farther end. Opening a drawer in this cabinet, he produced, from amidst some specimens of strata and fossils, a large-sized geological hammer.

He brandished it for a moment over his head, then paused with his finger on his lip.

"Hush!" he said, "we shall have the fools creeping in to peep at us if we don't take care." And to Loveday's horror he suddenly made for the door, turned the key in the lock, withdrew it and put it into his pocket.

She looked at the clock; the hands pointed to half-past seven. Had Griffiths received her note at the proper time, and were the men now in the grounds? She could only pray that they were.

"The light is too strong for my eyes," she said, and rising from her chair, she lifted the green-shaded lamp and placed it on a table that stood at the window.

"No, no, that won't do," said Mr. Craven; "that would show every-one outside what we're doing in here." He crossed to the window as he spoke and removed the lamp thence to the mantelpiece.

Loveday could only hope that in the few seconds it had remained in the window it had caught the eye of the outside watchers.

The old man beckoned to Loveday to come near and examine his deadly weapon. "Give it a good swing round," he said, suiting the action to the word, "and down it comes with a splendid crash." He brought the hammer round within an inch of Loveday's forehead.

She started back.

"Ha, ha," he laughed harshly and unnaturally, with the light of mad-ness dancing in his eyes now; "did I frighten you? I wonder what sort of sound you would make if I were to give you a little tap just there." Here he lightly touched her forehead with the hammer. "Elemental, of course, it would be, and—"

Loveday steadied her nerves with difficulty. Locked in with this lunatic, her only chance lay in gaining time for the detectives to reach the house and enter through the window.

"Wait a minute," she said, striving to divert his attention; "you have not yet told me what sort of an elemental sound old Sandy made when he fell. If you'll give me pen and ink, I'll write down a full account of it all, and you can incorporate it afterwards in your treatise."

For a moment a look of real pleasure flitted across the old man's face, then it faded. "The brute fell back dead without a sound," he answered; "it was all for nothing, that night's work; yet not altogether for nothing. No, I don't mind owning I would do it all over again to get the wild thrill of joy at my heart that I had when I looked down into that old man's dead face and felt myself free at last! Free at last!" his voice rang out excitedly-once more he brought his hammer round with an ugly swing.

"For a moment I was a young man again; I leaped into his room—the moon was shining full in through the window—I thought of my old college days, and the fun we used to have at Pembroke—topsy turvey I turned everything—" He broke off abruptly, and drew a step nearer to Loveday. "The pity of it all was," he said, suddenly dropping from his high, excited tone to a low, pathetic one, "that he fell without a sound of any sort." Here he drew another step nearer. "I wonder—" he said, then broke off again, and came close to Loveday's side. "It has only this moment occurred to me," he said, now with his lips close to Loveday's ear, "that a woman, in her death agony, would be much more likely to give utterance to an elemental sound than a man."

He raised his hammer, and Loveday fled to the window, and was lifted from the outside by three pairs of strong arms.

"I thought I was conducting my very last case—I never had such a narrow escape before!" said Loveday, as she stood talking with Mr. Griffiths on the Grenfell platform, awaiting the train to carry her back to London. "It seems strange that no one before suspected the old gentleman's sanity—I suppose, however, people were so used to his eccentricities that they did not notice how they had deepened into positive lunacy. His cunning evidently stood him in good stead at the inquest."

"It is possible" said Griffiths thoughtfully, "that he did not absolutely cross the very slender line that divided eccentricity from madness until after the murder. The excitement consequent upon the discovery of the crime may just have pushed him over the border. Now, Miss Brooke, we have exactly ten minutes before your train comes in. I should feel greatly obliged to you if you would explain one or two things that have a professional interest for me."

"With pleasure," said Loveday. "Put your questions in categorical order and I will answer them."

"Well, then, in the first place, what suggested to your mind the old man's guilt?"

"The relations that subsisted between him and Sandy seemed to me to savour too much of fear on the one side and power on the other. Also the income paid to Sandy during Mr. Craven's absence in Natal bore, to my mind, an unpleasant resemblance to hush-money."

"Poor wretched being! And I hear that, after all, the woman he married in his wild young days died soon afterwards of drink. I have no doubt, however, that Sandy sedulously kept up the fiction of her existence, even after his master's second marriage. Now for another question: how was it you knew that Miss Craven had taken her brother's place in the sick-room?"

"On the evening of my arrival I discovered a rather long lock of fair hair in the unswept fireplace of my room, which, as it happened, was usually occupied by Miss Craven. It at once occurred to me that the young lady had been cutting off her hair and that there must be some powerful motive to induce such a sacrifice. The suspicious circumstances attending her brother's illness soon supplied me with such a motive."

"Ah! that typhoid fever business was very cleverly done. Not a servant in the house, I verily believe, but who thought Master Harry was upstairs, ill in bed, and Miss Craven away at her friends' in Newcastle. The young fellow must have got a clear start off within an hour of the murder. His sister, sent away the next day to Newcastle, dismissed her maid there, I hear, on the plea of no accommodation at her friends' house—sent the girl to her own home for a holiday and herself returned to Troyte's Hill in the middle of the night, having walked the five miles from Grenfell. No doubt her mother admitted her through one of those easily-opened front windows, cut her hair and put her to bed to personate her brother without delay. With Miss Craven's strong likeness to Master Harry, and in a darkened room, it is easy to understand that the eyes of a doctor, personally unacquainted with the family, might easily be deceived. Now, Miss Brooke, you must admit that with all this elaborate chicanery and double dealing going on, it was only natural that my suspicions should set in strongly in that quarter."

"I read it all in another light, you see," said Loveday. "It seemed to me that the mother, knowing her son's evil proclivities, believed in his guilt, in spite, possibly, of his assertions of innocence. The son, most likely, on his way back to the house after pledging the family plate, had met old Mr. Craven with the hammer in his hand. Seeing, no doubt, how impossible it would be for him to clear himself without incriminating his father, he preferred flight to Natal to giving evidence at the inquest."

"Now about his alias?" said Mr. Griffiths briskly, for the train was at that moment steaming into the station "How did you know that Harold Cousins was identical with Harry Craven, and had sailed in the *Bonnie Dundee?*"

"Oh, that was easy enough," said Loveday, as she stepped into the train; "a newspaper sent down to Mr. Craven by his wife, was folded so as to direct his attention to the shipping list. In it I saw that the *Bonnie Dundee* had sailed two days previously for Natal. Now it was only natural to connect Natal with Mrs. Craven, who had passed the greater part of her life there; and it was easy to understand her wish to get her scapegrace son among her early friends. The alias under which he sailed came readily enough to light. I found it scribbled all over one of Mr. Craven's writing pads in his study; evidently it had been drummed into his ears by his wife as his son's alias, and the old gentleman had taken this method of fixing it in his memory. We'll hope that the young fellow, under his new name, will make a new reputation for himself—at any rate, he'll have a better chance of doing so with the ocean between him and his evil companions. Now it's good-bye, I think."

"No," said Mr. Griffiths; "it's au revoir, for you'll have to come back again for the assizes, and give the evidence that will shut old Mr. Craven in an asylum for the rest of his life."

The Ninescore Mystery

Baroness Orczy

I.

WELL, you know, some say she is the daughter of a duke, others that she was born in the gutter, and that the handle has been soldered on to her name in order to give her style and influence.

I could say a lot, of course, but "my lips are sealed," as the poets say. All through her successful career at the Yard she honoured me with her friendship and confidence, but when she took me in partnership, as it were, she made me promise that I would never breathe a word of her private life, and this I swore on my Bible oath—"wish I may die," and all the rest of it.

Yes, we always called her "my lady," from the moment that she was put at the head of our section; and the chief called her "Lady Molly" in our presence. We of the Female Department are dreadfully snubbed by the men, though don't tell me that women have not ten times as much intuition as the blundering and sterner sex; my firm belief is that we shouldn't have half so many undetected crimes if some of the so-called mysteries were put to the test of feminine investigation.

Do you suppose for a moment, for instance, that the truth about that extraordinary case at Ninescore would ever have come to light if the men alone had had the handling of it? Would any man have taken so bold a risk as Lady Molly did when——But I am anticipating.

Let me go back to that memorable morning when she came into my room in a wild state of agitation.

"The chief says I may go down to Ninescore if I like, Mary," she said in a Voice all a-quiver with excitement.

"You!" I ejaculated. "What for?"

"What for—what for?" she repeated eagerly. "Mary, don't you understand? It is the chance I have been waiting for—the chance of a lifetime? They are all desperate about the case up at the Yard; the public is furious, and columns of sarcastic letters appear in the daily press. None of our men know what to do; they are at their wits' end, and so this morning I went to the chief——"

"Yes?" I queried eagerly, for she had suddenly ceased speaking.

"Well, never mind now how I did it—I will tell you all about it on the way, for we have just got time to catch the 11 a.m. down to Canterbury. The chief says I may go, and that I may take whom I like with me. He suggested one of the men, but somehow I feel that this is woman's work, and I'd rather have you, Mary, than anyone. We will go over the preliminaries of the case together in the train, as I don't suppose that you have got them at your fingers' ends yet, and you have only just got time to put a few things together and meet me at Charing Cross booking-office in time for that 11.0 sharp."

She was off before I could ask her any more questions, and anyhow I was too flabbergasted to say much. A murder case in the hands of the Female Department! Such a thing had been unheard of until now. But I was all excitement, too, and you may be sure I was at the station in good time.

Fortunately Lady Molly and I had a carriage to ourselves. It was a non-stop run to Canterbury, so we had plenty of time before us, and I was longing to know all about this case, you bet, since I was to have the honour of helping Lady Molly in it.

The murder of Mary Nicholls had actually been committed at Ash Court, a fine old mansion which stands in the village of Ninescore. The Court is surrounded by magnificently timbered grounds, the most fascinating portion of which is an island in the midst of a small pond, which is spanned by a tiny rustic bridge. The island is called "The Wilderness," and is at the furthermost end of the grounds, out of sight and earshot of the mansion itself. It was in this charming spot, on the edge of the pond, that the body of a girl was found on the 5th of February last.

I will spare you the horrible details of this gruesome discovery. Suffice it to say for the present that the unfortunate woman was lying on her face, with the lower portion of her body on the small grass-covered embankment, and her head, arms, and shoulders sunk in the slime of the stagnant water just below.

It was Timothy Coleman, one of the under-gardeners at Ash Court, who first made this appalling discovery. He had crossed the rustic bridge and traversed the little island in its entirety, when he noticed something blue lying half in and half out of the water beyond. Timothy is a stolid, unemotional kind of yokel, and, once having ascertained that the object was a woman's body in a blue dress with white facings, he quietly stooped and tried to lift it out of the mud.

But here even his stolidity gave way at the terrible sight which was revealed before him. That the woman—whoever she might be—had been brutally murdered was obvious, her dress in front being stained with blood; but what was so awful that it even turned old Timothy sick with horror, was that, owing to the head, arms and shoulders having apparently been in the slime for some time, they were in an advanced state of decomposition.

Well, whatever was necessary was immediately done, of course. Coleman went to get assistance from the lodge, and soon the police were on the scene and had removed the unfortunate victim's remains to the small local police-station.

Ninescore is a sleepy, out-of-the-way village, situated some seven miles from Canterbury and four from Sandwich. Soon everyone in the place had heard that a terrible murder had been committed in the village, and all the details were already freely discussed at the Green Man.

To begin with, everyone said that though the body itself might be practically unrecognisable, the bright blue serge dress with the white facings was unmistakable, as were the pearl and ruby ring and the red leather purse found by Inspector Meisures close to the murdered woman's hand.

Within two hours of Timothy Coleman's gruesome find the identity of the unfortunate victim was firmly established as that of Mary Nicholls, who lived with her sister Susan at 2, Elm Cottages, in Nine-score Lane, almost opposite Ash Court. It was also known that when the police called at that address they found the place locked and apparently uninhabited.

Mrs. Hooker, who lived at No. 1 next door, explained to Inspector Meisures that Susan and Mary Nicholls had left home about a fortnight ago, and that she had not seen them since.

"It'll be a fortnight to-morrow," she said. "I was just inside my own front door a-calling to the cat to come in. It was past seven o'clock, and as dark a night as ever you did see. You could hardly see your 'and afore your eyes, and there was a nasty damp drizzle comin' from every-where. Susan and Mary come out of their cottage; I couldn't rightly see Susan, but I 'eard Mary's voice quite distinck. She says: 'We'll have to 'urry,' says she. I, thinkin' they might be goin' to do some shoppin' in the village, calls out to them that I'd just 'eard the church clock strike seven, and that bein' Thursday, and early closin', they'd find all the shops shut at Ninescore. But they took no notice, and walked off towards the village, and that's the last I ever seed o' them two."

Further questioning among the village folk brought forth many curi-ous details. It seems that Mary Nicholls was a very flighty young woman, about whom there had already been quite a good deal of scan-dal, whilst Susan, on the other hand—who was very sober and steady in her conduct—had chafed considerably under her younger sister's questionable reputation, and, according to Mrs. Hooker, many were the bitter quarrels which occurred between the two girls. These quar-rels, it seems, had been especially violent within the last year whenever Mr. Lionel Lydgate called at the cottage. He was a London gentleman, it appears—a young man about town, it afterwards transpired—but he frequently stayed at Canterbury, where he had some friends, and on those occasions he would come over to Ninescore in his smart dogcart and take Mary out for drives.

Mr. Lydgate is brother to Lord Edbrooke, the multi-millionaire, who was the recipient of birthday honours last year. His lordship resides at Edbrooke Castle, but he and his brother Lionel had rented Ash Court once or twice, as both were keen golfers and Sandwich Links are very close by. Lord Edbrooke, I may add, is a married man. Mr. Lionel Lydgate, on the other hand, is just engaged to Miss Marbury, daughter of one of the canons of Canterbury.

No wonder, therefore, that Susan Nicholls strongly objected to her sister's name being still coupled with that of a young man far above her in station, who, moreover, was about to marry a young lady in his own rank of life.

But Mary seemed not to care. She was a young woman who only liked fun and pleasure, and she shrugged her shoulders at public opin-ion, even though there were ugly rumours anent the parentage of a little baby girl whom she herself had placed under the care of

Mrs. Williams, a widow who lived in a somewhat isolated cottage on the Canterbury road. Mary had told Mrs. Williams that the father of the child, who was her own brother, had died very suddenly, leaving the little one on her and Susan's hands; and, as they couldn't look after it properly, they wished Mrs. Williams to have charge of it. To this the latter readily agreed.

The sum for the keep of the infant was decided upon, and thereafter Mary Nicholls had come every week to see the little girl, and always brought the money with her.

Inspector Meisures called on Mrs. Williams, and certainly the worthy widow had a very startling sequel to relate to the above story.

"A fortnight to-morrow," explained Mrs. Williams to the inspector, "a little after seven o'clock, Mary Nicholls come runnin' into my cottage. It was an awful night, pitch dark and a nasty drizzle. Mary says to me she's in a great hurry; she is goin' up to London by a train from Canterbury and wants to say good-bye to the child. She seemed terribly excited, and her clothes were very wet. I brings baby to her, and she kisses it rather wild-like and says to me: 'You'll take great care of her, Mrs. Williams,' she says; 'I may be gone some time.' Then she puts baby down and gives me £2, the child's keep for eight weeks."

After which, it appears, Mary once more said "good-bye" and ran out of the cottage, Mrs. Williams going as far as the front door with her. The night was very dark, and she couldn't see if Mary was alone or not, until presently she heard her voice saying tearfully: "I had to kiss baby——" then the voice died out in the distance "on the way to Canterbury," Mrs. Williams said most emphatically.

So far, you see, Inspector Meisures was able to fix the departure of the two sisters Nicholls from Ninescore on the night of January 23rd. Obviously they left their cottage about seven, went to Mrs. Williams, where Susan remained outside while Mary went in to say good-bye to the child.

After that all traces of them seem to have vanished. Whether they did go to Canterbury, and caught the last up train, at what station they alighted, or when poor Mary came back, could not at present be discovered.

According to the medical officer, the unfortunate girl must have been dead twelve or thirteen days at the very least, as, though the stagnant water may have accelerated decomposition, the head could not have got into such an advanced state much under a fortnight.

At Canterbury station neither the booking-clerk nor the porters could throw any light upon the subject. Canterbury West is a busy station, and scores of passengers buy tickets and go through the barriers every day. It was impossible, therefore, to give any positive information about two young women who may or may not have travelled by the last up train on Saturday, January 23rd—that is, a fortnight before.

One thing only was certain—whether Susan went to Canterbury and travelled by that up train or not, alone or with her sister—Mary had undoubtedly come back to Ninescore either the same night or the following day, since Timothy Coleman found her half-decomposed remains in the grounds of Ash Court a fortnight later.

Had she come back to meet her lover, or what? And where was Susan now?

From the first, therefore, you see, there was a great element of mystery about the whole case, and it was only natural that the local police should feel that, unless something more definite came out at the inquest, they would like to have the assistance of some of the fellows at the Yard.

So the preliminary notes were sent up to London, and some of them drifted into our hands. Lady Molly was deeply interested in it from the first, and my firm belief is that she simply worried the chief into allowing her to go down to Ninescore and see what she could do.

2

At first it was understood that Lady Molly should only go down to Canterbury after the inquest, if the local police still felt that they were in want of assistance from London. But nothing was further from my lady's intentions than to wait until then.

"I was not going to miss the first act of a romantic drama," she said to me just as our train steamed into Canterbury station. "Pick up your bag, Mary. We're going to tramp it to Ninescore—two lady artists on a sketching tour, remember—and we'll find lodgings in the village, I dare say."

We had some lunch in Canterbury, and then we started to walk the six and a half miles to Ninescore, carrying our bags. We put up at one of the cottages, where the legend "Apartments for single respectable lady or gentleman" had hospitably invited us to enter, and at eight o'clock the next morning we found our way to the local police-station, where the inquest was to take place. Such a funny little place, you know—just a cottage converted for official use—and the small room packed to its utmost holding capacity. The entire able-bodied population of the neighbourhood had, I verily believe, congregated in these ten cubic yards of stuffy atmosphere.

Inspector Meisures, apprised by the chief of our arrival, had reserved two good places for us well in sight of witnesses, coroner and jury. The room was insupportably close, but I assure you that neither Lady Molly nor I thought much about our comfort then. We were terribly interested.

From the outset the case seemed; as it were, to wrap itself more and more in its mantle of impenetrable mystery. There was precious little in the way of clues, only that awful intuition, that dark unspoken suspicion with regard to one particular man's guilt, which one could feel hovering in the minds of all those present.

Neither the police nor Timothy Coleman had anything to add to what was already known. The ring and purse were produced, also the dress worn by the murdered woman. All were sworn to by several witnesses as having been the property of Mary Nicholls.

Timothy, on being closely questioned, said that, in his opinion, the girl's body had been pushed into the mud, as the head was absolutely embedded in it, and he didn't see how she could have fallen like that.

Medical evidence was repeated; it was as uncertain—as vague—as before. Owing to the state of the head and neck it was impossible to ascertain by what means the death blow had been dealt. The doctor repeated his statement that the unfortunate girl must have been dead quite a fortnight. The body was discovered on February 5th—a fortnight before that would have been on or about January 23rd.

The caretaker who lived at the lodge at Ash Court could also throw but little light on the mysterious event. Neither he nor any member of his family had seen or heard anything to arouse their suspicions.

Against that he explained that "The Wilderness," where the murder was committed, is situated some 200 yards from the lodge, with the mansion and flower garden lying between. Replying to a question put to him by a juryman, he said that that portion of the grounds is only divided off from Ninescore Lane by a low, brick wall, which has a door in it, opening into the lane almost opposite Elm Cottages. He added that the mansion had been empty for over a year, and that he succeeded the last man, who died, about twelve months ago. Mr. Lydgate had not been down for golf since witness had been in charge.

It would be useless to recapitulate all that the various witnesses had already told the police, and were now prepared to swear to. The private life of the two sisters Nicholls was gone into at full length, as much, at least, as was publicly known. But you know what village folk are, except when there is a bit of scandal and gossip, they know precious little of one another's inner lives.

The two girls appeared to be very comfortably off. Mary was always smartly dressed; and the baby girl, whom she had placed in Mrs. Williams's charge, had plenty of good and expensive clothes, whilst her keep, 5s. a week, was paid with unfailing regularity. What seemed certain, however, was that they did not get on well together, that Susan violently objected to Mary's association with Mr. Lydgate, and that recently she had spoken to the vicar asking him to try to persuade her sister to go away from Ninescore altogether, so as to break entirely with the past. The Reverend Octavius Ludlow, Vicar of Ninescore, seems thereupon to have had a little talk with Mary on the subject, suggesting that she should accept a good situation in London.

"But," continued the reverend gentleman, "I didn't make much impression on her. All she replied to me was that she certainly need never go into service, as she had a good income of her own, and could obtain £5,000 or more quite easily at any time if she chose."

"Did you mention Mr. Lydgate's name to her at all?" asked the coroner.

"Yes, I did," said the vicar, after a slight hesitation.

"Well, what was her attitude then?"

"I am afraid she laughed," replied the Reverend Octavius, primly, "and said very picturesquely, if somewhat ungrammatically, that 'some folks didn't know what they was talkin' about.'"

All very indefinite, you see. Nothing to get hold of, no motive suggested—beyond a very vague suspicion, perhaps, of blackmail—to account for a brutal crime. I must not, however, forget to tell you the two other facts which came to light in the course of this extraordinary inquest. Though, at the time, these facts seemed of wonderful moment for the elucidation of the mystery, they only helped ultimately to plunge the whole case into darkness still more impenetrable than before.

I am alluding, firstly, to the deposition of James Franklin, a carter in the employ of one of the local farmers. He stated that about half-past six on that same Saturday night, January 23rd, he was walking along Ninescore Lane leading his horse and cart, as the night was indeed pitch dark. Just as he came somewhere near Elm Cottages he heard a man's voice saying in a kind of hoarse whisper:

"Open the door, can't you? It's as dark as blazes!"

Then a pause, after which the same voice added:

"Mary, where the dickens are you?" Whereupon a girl's voice replied: "All right, I'm coming."

James Franklin heard nothing more after that, nor did he see anyone in the gloom.

With the stolidity peculiar to the Kentish peasantry, he thought no more of this until the day when he heard that Mary Nicholls had been murdered; then he voluntarily came forward and told his story to the police. Now, when he was closely questioned, he was quite unable to say whether these voices proceeded from that side of the lane where stand Elm Cottages or from the other side, which is edged by the low, brick wall.

Finally, Inspector Meisures, who really showed an extraordinary sense of what was dramatic, here produced a document which he had reserved for the last. This was a piece of paper which he had found in the red leather purse already mentioned, and which at first had not been thought very important, as the writing was identified by several people as that of the deceased, and consisted merely of a series of dates and hours scribbled in pencil on a scrap of notepaper. But suddenly these dates had assumed a weird and terrible significance: two of them, at least—December 26th and January 1st followed by "10 a.m."—were days on which Mr. Lydgate came over to Ninescore and took Mary for drives. One or two witnesses swore to this positively. Both dates had been local meets of the harriers, to which other folk from the village had gone, and Mary had openly said afterwards how much she had enjoyed these.

The other dates (there were six altogether) were more or less vague. One Mrs. Hooker remembered as being coincident with a day Mary Nicholls had spent away from home; but the last date, scribbled in the same handwriting, was January 23rd, and below it the hour—6 p.m.

The coroner now adjourned the inquest. An explanation from Mr. Lionel Lydgate had become imperative.

3

Public excitement had by how reached a very high pitch; it was no longer a case of mere local interest. The country inns all round the immediate neighbourhood were packed with visitors from London, artists, journalists, dramatists, and actor-managers, whilst the hotels and fly-proprietors of Canterbury were doing a roaring trade.

Certain facts and one vivid picture stood out clearly before the thoughtful mind in the midst of a chaos of conflicting and irrelevant evidence: the picture was that of the two women tramping in the wet and pitch dark night towards Canterbury. Beyond that everything was a blur.

When did Mary Nicholls come back to Ninescore, and why?

To keep an appointment made with Lionel Lydgate, it was openly whispered; but that appointment—if the rough notes were interpreted rightly—was for the very day on which she and her sister went away from home. A man's voice called to her at half-past six certainly, and she replied to it. Franklin, the carter, heard her; but half an hour afterwards Mrs. Hooker heard her voice when she left home with her sister, and she visited Mrs. Williams after that.

The only theory compatible with all this was, of course, that Mary merely accompanied Susan part of the way to Canterbury, then went back to meet her lover, who enticed her into the deserted grounds of Ash Court, and there murdered her.

The motive was not far to seek. Mr. Lionel Lydgate, about to marry, wished to silence for ever a voice that threatened to be unpleasantly persistent in its demands for money and in its threats of scandal.

But there was one great argument against that theory—the disappearance of Susan Nicholls. She had been extensively advertised for. The murder of her sister was published broadcast in every newspaper in the United Kingdom—she could not be ignorant of it. And, above all, she hated Mr. Lydgate. Why did she not come and add the weight of her testimony against him if, indeed, he was guilty?

And if Mr. Lydgate was innocent, then where was the criminal? And why had Susan Nicholls disappeared?

Why? why? why?

Well, the next day would show. Mr. Lionel Lydgate had been cited by the police to give evidence at the adjourned inquest.

Good-looking, very athletic, and obviously frightfully upset and nervous, he entered the little courtroom, accompanied by his solicitor, just before the coroner and jury took their seats.

He looked keenly at Lady Molly as he sat down, and from the expression of his face I guessed that he was much puzzled to know who she was.

He was the first witness called. Manfully and clearly he gave a concise account of his association with the deceased.

"She was pretty and amusing," he said. "I liked to take her out when I was in the neighbourhood; it was no trouble to me. There was no harm in her, whatever the village gossips might say. I know she had been in trouble, as they say, but that had nothing to do with me. It wasn't for me to be hard on a girl, and I fancy that she has been very badly treated by some scoundrel."

Here he was hard pressed by the coroner, who wished him to explain what he meant. But Mr. Lydgate turned obstinate, and to every leading question he replied stolidly and very emphatically:

"I don't know who it was. It had nothing to do with me, but I was sorry for the girl because of everyone turning against her, including her sister, and I tried to give her a little pleasure when I could."

That was all right. Very sympathetically told. The public quite liked this pleasing specimen of English cricket-, golf- and football-loving manhood. Subsequently Mr. Lydgate admitted meeting Mary on December 26th and January 1st, but he swore most emphatically that that was the last he ever saw of her.

"But the 23rd of January," here insinuated the coroner; "you made an appointment with the deceased then?"

"Certainly not," he replied.

"But you met her on that day?"

"Most emphatically no," he replied quietly. "I went down to
Edbrooke Castle, my brother's place in Lincolnshire, on the 20th of last
month, and only got back to town about three days ago."

"You swear to that, Mr. Lydgate?" asked the coroner.

"I do, indeed, and there are a score of witnesses to bear me out. The
family, the house-party, the servants."

He tried to dominate his own excitement. I suppose, poor man, he
had only just realised that certain horrible suspicions had been resting
upon him. His solicitor pacified him, and presently he sat down, whilst
I must say that everyone there present was relieved at the thought that
the handsome young athlete was not a murderer, after all. To look
at him it certainly seemed preposterous.

But then, of course, there was the deadlock, and as there were no
more witnesses to be heard, no new facts to elucidate, the jury returned
the usual verdict against some person or persons unknown; and we, the
keenly interested spectators, were left to face the problem—Who murdered Mary Nicholls, and where was her sister Susan?

4

After the verdict we found our way back to our lodgings. Lady Molly
tramped along silently, with that deep furrow between her brows
which I knew meant that she was deep in thought.

"Now we'll have some tea," I said, with a sigh of relief, as soon as
we entered the cottage door.

"No, you won't," replied my lady, dryly. "I am going to write out a
telegram, and we'll go straight on to Canterbury and send it from there."

"To Canterbury!" I gasped. "Two hours' walk at least, for I don't
suppose we can get a trap, and it is past three o'clock. Why not send
your telegram from Ninescore?"

"Mary, you are stupid," was all the reply I got.

She wrote out two telegrams—one of which was at least three dozen
words long—and, once more calling to me to come along, we set out
for Canterbury.

I was tea-less, cross, and puzzled. Lady Molly was alert, cheerful, and
irritatingly active.

We reached the first telegraph office a little before five. My lady sent the telegram without condescending to tell me anything of its destination or contents; then she took me to the Castle Hotel and graciously offered me tea.

"May I be allowed to inquire whether you propose tramping back to Ninescore to-night?" I asked with a slight touch of sarcasm, as I really felt put out.

"No, Mary," she replied, quietly munching a bit of Sally Lunn; "I have engaged a couple of rooms at this hotel and wired the chief that any message will find us here to-morrow morning."

After that there was nothing for it but quietude, patience, and finally supper and bed.

The next morning my lady walked into my room before I had finished dressing. She had a newspaper in her hand, and threw it down on the bed as she said calmly:

"It was in the evening paper all right last night. I think we shall be in time."

No use asking her what "it" meant. It was easier to pick up the paper, which I did. It was a late edition of one of the leading London evening shockers, and at once the front page, with its startling headline, attracted my attention:

THE NINESCORE MYSTERY

MARY NICHOLLS'S BABY DYING

Then, below that, a short paragraph:—

"We regret to learn that the little baby daughter of the unfortunate girl who was murdered recently at Ash Court, Ninescore, Kent, under such terrible and mysterious circumstances, is very seriously ill at the cottage of Mrs. Williams, in whose charge she is. The local doctor who visited her to-day declares that she cannot last more than a few hours. At the time of going to press the nature of the child's complaint was not known to our special representative at Ninescore."

"What does this mean?" I gasped.

But before she could reply there was a knock at the door.

"A telegram for Miss Granard," said the voice of the hall-porter.

"Quick, Mary," said Lady Molly, eagerly. "I told the chief and also Meisures to wire here and to you."

The telegram turned out to have come from Ninescore, and was signed "Meisures." Lady Molly read it out aloud:

> "Mary Nicholls arrived here this morning. Detained her at station. Come at once."

"Mary Nicholls! I don't understand," was all I could contrive to say. But she only replied:

"I knew it! I knew it! Oh, Mary, what a wonderful thing is human nature, and how I thank Heaven that gave me a knowledge of it!"

She made me get dressed all in a hurry, and then we swallowed some breakfast hastily whilst a fly was being got for us. I had, perforce, to satisfy my curiosity from my own inner consciousness. Lady Molly was too absorbed to take any notice of me. Evidently the chief knew what she had done and approved of it: the telegram from Meisures pointed to that.

My lady had suddenly become a personality. Dressed very quietly, and in a smart close-fitting hat, she looked years older than her age, owing also to the seriousness of her mien.

The fly took us to Ninescore fairly quickly. At the little police-station we found Meisures awaiting us. He had Elliott and Pegram from the Yard with him. They had obviously got their orders, for all three of them were mighty deferential.

"The woman is Mary Nicholls, right enough," said Meisures, as Lady Molly brushed quickly past him, "the woman who was supposed to have been murdered. It's that silly bogus paragraph about the infant brought her out of her hiding-place. I wonder how it got in," he added blandly; "the child is well enough."

"I wonder," said Lady Molly, whilst a smile—the first I had seen that morning—lit up her pretty face.

"I suppose the other sister will turn up too, presently," rejoined Elliott. "Pretty lot of trouble we shall have now. If Mary Nicholls is alive and kickin', who was murdered at Ash Court, say I?"

"I wonder," said Lady Molly, with the same charming smile.

Then she went in to see Mary Nicholls.

The Reverend Octavius Ludlow was sitting beside the girl, who seemed in great distress, for she was crying bitterly.

Lady Molly asked Elliott and the others to remain in the passage whilst she herself went into the room, I following behind her.

When the door was shut, she went up to Mary Nicholls, and assuming a hard and severe manner, she said:

"Well, you have at last made up your mind, have you, Nicholls? I suppose you know that we have applied for a warrant for your arrest?"

The woman gave a shriek which unmistakably was one of fear.

"My arrest?" she gasped. "What for?"

"The murder of your sister Susan."

" 'Twasn't me!" she said quickly.

"Then Susan *is* dead?" retorted Lady Molly, quietly.

Mary saw that she had betrayed herself. She gave Lady Molly a look of agonised horror, then turned as white as a sheet and would have fallen had not the Reverend Octavius Ludlow gently led her to a chair.

"It wasn't me," she repeated, with a heart-broken sob.

"That will be for you to prove," said Lady Molly dryly. "The child cannot now, of course, remain with Mrs. Williams; she will be removed to the workhouse, and——"

"No, that she shan't be," said the mother excitedly. "She shan't be, I tell you. The workhouse, indeed," she added in a paroxysm of hysterical tears, "and her father a lord!"

The reverend gentleman and I gasped in astonishment; but Lady Molly had worked up to this climax so ingeniously that it was obvious she had guessed it all along, and had merely led Mary Nicholls on in order to get this admission from her.

How well she had known human nature in pitting the child against the sweetheart! Mary Nicholls was ready enough to hide herself, to part from her child even for a while, in order to save the man she had once loved from the consequences of his crime; but when she heard that her child was dying, she no longer could bear to leave it among strangers, and when Lady Molly taunted her with the workhouse, she exclaimed in her maternal pride:

"The workhouse! And her father a lord!"

Driven into a corner, she confessed the whole truth.

Lord Edbrooke, then Mr. Lydgate, was the father of her child. Knowing this, her sister Susan had, for over a year now, systematically blackmailed the unfortunate man—not altogether, it seems, without Mary's connivance. In January last she got him to come down to Ninescore under the distinct promise that Mary would meet him and hand over to him the letters she had received from him, as well as the ring he had given her, in exchange for the sum of £5,000.

The meeting-place was arranged, but at the last moment Mary was afraid to go in the dark. Susan, nothing daunted, but anxious about her own reputation in case she should be seen talking to a man so late at night, put on Mary's dress, took the ring and the letters, also her sister's purse, and went to meet Lord Edbrooke.

What happened at that interview no one will ever know. It ended with the murder of the blackmailer. I suppose the fact that Susan had, in a measure, begun by impersonating her sister, gave the murderer the first thought of confusing the identity of his victim by the horrible device of burying the body in the slimy mud. Anyway, he almost did succeed in hoodwinking the police, and would have done so entirely but for Lady Molly's strange intuition in the matter.

After his crime he ran instinctively to Mary's cottage. He had to make a clean breast of it to her, as, without her help, he was a doomed man.

So he persuaded her to go away from home and to leave no clue or trace of herself or her sister in Ninescore. With the help of money which he would give her, she could begin life anew somewhere else, and no doubt he deluded the unfortunate girl with promises that her child should be restored to her very soon.

Thus he enticed Mary Nicholls away, who would have been the great and all-important witness against him the moment his crime was discovered. A girl of Mary's type and class instinctively obeys the man she has once loved, the man who is the father of her child. She consented to disappear and to allow all the world to believe that she had been murdered by some unknown miscreant.

Then the murderer quietly returned to his luxurious home at Edbrooke Castle, unsuspected. No one had thought of mentioning his name in connection with that of Mary Nicholls. In the days when he used to come down to Ash Court he was Mr. Lydgate, and, when he became a peer, sleepy, out-of-the-way Ninescore ceased to think of him.

Perhaps Mr. Lionel Lydgate knew all about his brother's association with the village girl. From his attitude at the inquest I should say he did, but of course he would not betray his own brother unless forced to do so.

Now, of course, the whole aspect of the case was changed: the veil of mystery had been torn asunder owing to the insight, the marvellous intuition, of a woman who, in my opinion, is the most wonderful psychologist of her time.

You know the sequel. Our fellows at the Yard, aided by the local police, took their lead from Lady Molly, and began their investigations of Lord Edbrooke's movements on or about the 23rd of January.

Even their preliminary inquiries revealed the fact that his lordship had left Edbrooke Castle on the 21st. He went up to town, saying to his wife and household that he was called away on business, and not even taking his valet with him. He put up at the Langham Hotel.

But here police investigations came to an abrupt ending. Lord Edbrooke evidently got wind of them. Anyway, the day after Lady Molly so cleverly enticed Mary Nicholls out of her hiding-place, and surprised her into an admission of the truth, the unfortunate man threw himself in front of the express train at Grantham railway station, and was instantly killed. Human justice cannot reach him now!

But don't tell me that a man would have thought of that bogus paragraph, or of the taunt which stung the motherly pride of the village girl to the quick, and thus wrung from her an admission which no amount of male ingenuity would ever have obtained.

The Hammer of God

G. K. Chesterton

THE little village of Bohun Beacon was perched on a hill so steep that the tall spire of its church seemed only like the peak of a small mountain. At the foot of the church stood a smithy, generally red with fires and always littered with hammers and scraps of iron; opposite to this, over a rude cross of cobbled paths, was "The Blue Boar," the only inn of the place. It was upon this crossway, in the lifting of a leaden and silver daybreak, that two brothers met in the street and spoke; though one was beginning the day and the other finishing it. The Rev. and Hon. Wilfred Bohun was very devout, and was making his way to some austere exercises of prayer or contemplation at dawn. Colonel the Hon. Norman Bohun, his elder brother, was by no means devout, and was sitting in evening dress on the bench outside "The Blue Boar," drinking what the philosophic observer was free to regard either as his last glass on Tuesday or his first on Wednesday. The colonel was not particular.

The Bohuns were one of the very few aristocratic families really dating from the Middle Ages, and their pennon had actually seen Palestine. But it is a great mistake to suppose that such houses stand high in chivalric tradition. Few except the poor preserve traditions. Aristocrats live not in traditions but in fashions. The Bohuns had been Mohocks under Queen Anne and Mashers under Queen Victoria. But like more than one of the really ancient houses, they had rotted in the last two centuries into mere drunkards and dandy degenerates, till there had even come a whisper of insanity. Certainly there was something hardly human about the colonel's wolfish pursuit of pleasure, and his chronic resolution not to go home till morning had a touch of the hideous clarity of insomnia. He was a tall, fine animal, elderly, but with hair still startlingly yellow. He would have looked merely blonde and leonine, but his blue eyes were sunk so deep in his face that they looked black. They were a little too close together. He had very long yellow moustaches; on each side of them a fold or furrow from nostril to jaw, so that a sneer seemed cut into his face. Over his evening clothes he wore a curious pale yellow coat that looked more like a very light dressing gown than an overcoat, and on the back of his head was stuck an extraordinary broad-brimmed hat of a bright green colour, evidently some oriental curiosity caught up at random. He was proud of appearing in such incongruous attires—proud of the fact that he always made them look congruous.

His brother the curate had also the yellow hair and the elegance, but he was buttoned up to the chin in black, and his face was clean-shaven, cultivated, and a little nervous. He seemed to live for nothing but his religion; but there were some who said (notably the blacksmith, who was a Presbyterian) that it was a love of Gothic architecture rather than of God, and that his haunting of the church like a ghost was only another and purer turn of the almost morbid thirst for beauty which sent his brother raging after women and wine. This charge was doubtful, while the man's practical piety was indubitable. Indeed, the charge was mostly an ignorant misunderstanding of the love of solitude and secret prayer, and was founded on his being often found kneeling, not before the altar, but in peculiar places, in the crypts or gallery, or even in the belfry. He was at the moment about to enter the church through the yard of the smithy, but stopped and frowned a little as he saw his brother's cavernous eyes staring in the same direction. On the hypothesis that the colonel was interested in the church he did not waste any speculations. There only remained the blacksmith's shop, and though the blacksmith was a Puritan and none of his people, Wilfred Bohun had heard some scandals about a beautiful and rather celebrated wife. He flung a suspicious look across the shed, and the colonel stood up laughing to speak to him.

"Good morning, Wilfred," he said. "Like a good landlord I am watching sleeplessly over my people. I am going to call on the blacksmith."

Wilfred looked at the ground, and said: "The blacksmith is out. He is over at Greenford."

"I know," answered the other with silent laughter; "that is why I am calling on him."

"Norman," said the cleric, with his eye on a pebble in the road, "are you ever afraid of thunderbolts?"

"What do you mean? "asked the colonel. "Is your hobby meteorology?"

"I mean," said Wilfred, without looking up, "do you ever think that God might strike you in the street?"

"I beg your pardon," said the colonel; "I see your hobby is folk-lore."

"I know your hobby is blasphemy," retorted the religious man, stung in the one live place of his nature. "But if you do not fear God, you have good reason to fear man."

The elder raised his eyebrows politely. "Fear man?" he said.

"Barnes the blacksmith is the biggest and strongest man for forty miles round," said the clergyman sternly. "I know you are no coward or weakling, but he could throw you over the wall."

This struck home, being true, and the lowering line by mouth and nostril darkened and deepened. For a moment he stood with the heavy sneer on his face. But in an instant Colonel Bohun had recovered his own cruel good humour and laughed, showing two dog-like front teeth under his yellow moustache. "In that case, my dear Wilfred," he said quite carelessly, "it was wise for the last of the Bohuns to come out partially in armour."

And he took off the queer round hat covered with green, showing that it was lined within with steel. Wilfred recognised it indeed as a light Japanese or Chinese helmet torn down from a trophy that hung in the old family hall.

"It was the first hat to hand," explained his brother airily; "always the nearest hat—and the nearest woman."

"The blacksmith is away at Greenford," said Wilfred quietly; "the time of his return is unsettled."

And with that he turned and went into the church with bowed head, crossing himself like one who wishes to be quit of an unclean spirit. He was anxious to forget such grossness in the cool twilight of his tall Gothic cloisters; but on that morning it was fated that his still round of religious exercises should be everywhere arrested by small shocks. As he entered the church, hitherto always empty at that hour, a kneeling figure rose hastily to its feet and came towards the full daylight of the doorway. When the curate saw it he stood still with surprise. For the early worshipper was none other than the village idiot, a nephew of the blacksmith, one who neither would nor could care for the church or for anything else. He was always called "Mad Joe," and seemed to have no other name; he was a dark, strong, slouching lad, with a heavy white face, dark straight hair, and a mouth always open. As he passed the priest, his moon-calf countenance gave no hint of what he had been doing or thinking of. He had never been known to pray before. What sort of prayers was he saying now? Extraordinary prayers surely.

Wilfred Bohun stood rooted to the spot long enough to see the idiot go out into the sunshine, and even to see his dissolute brother hail him with a sort of avuncular jocularity. The last thing he saw was the colonel throwing pennies at the open mouth of Joe, with the serious appearance of trying to hit it.

This ugly sunlight picture of the stupidity and cruelty of the earth sent the ascetic finally to his prayers for purification and new thoughts. He went up to a pew in the gallery, which brought him under a coloured window which he loved and always quieted his spirit; a blue window with an angel carrying lilies. There he began to think less about the half-wit, with his livid face and mouth like a fish. He began to think less of his evil brother, pacing like a lean lion in his horrible hunger. He sank deeper and deeper into those cold and sweet colours of silver blossoms and sapphire sky.

In this place half an hour afterwards he was found by Gibbs, the village cobbler, who had been sent for him in some haste. He got to his feet with promptitude, for he knew that no small matter would have brought Gibbs into such a place at all. The cobbler was, as in many villages, an atheist, and his appearance in church was a shade more extraordinary than Mad Joe's. It was a morning of theological enigmas.

"What is it?" asked Wilfred Bohun rather stiffly, but putting out a trembling hand for his hat.

The atheist spoke in a tone that, coming from him, was quite startlingly respectful, and even, as it were, huskily sympathetic.

"You must excuse me, sir," he said in a hoarse whisper, "but we didn't think it right not to let you know at once. I'm afraid a rather dreadful thing has happened, sir. I'm afraid your brother—"

Wilfred clenched his frail hands. "What devilry has he done now?" he cried in involuntary passion.

"Why, sir," said the cobbler, coughing, "I'm afraid he's done nothing, and won't do anything. I'm afraid he's done for. You had really better come down, sir."

The curate followed the cobbler down a short winding stair which brought them out at an entrance rather higher than the street. Bohun saw the tragedy in one glance, flat underneath him like a plan. In the yard of the smithy were standing five or six men mostly in black, one in an inspector's uniform. They included the doctor, the Presbyterian minister, and the priest from the Roman Catholic chapel, to which the blacksmith's wife belonged. The latter was speaking to her, indeed, very rapidly, in an undertone, as she, a magnificent woman with red-gold hair, was sobbing blindly on a bench. Between these two groups, and just clear of the main heap of hammers, lay a man in evening dress, spread-eagled and flat on his face. From the height above Wilfred could have sworn to every item of his costume and appearance, down to the Bohun rings upon his fingers; but the skull was only a hideous splash, like a star of blackness and blood.

Wilfred Bohun gave but one glance, and ran down the steps into the yard. The doctor, who was the family physician, saluted him, but he scarcely took any notice. He could only stammer out: "My brother is dead. What does it mean? What is this horrible mystery?" There was an unhappy silence; and then the cobbler, the most outspoken man present, answered: "Plenty of horror, sir," he said; "but not much mystery."

"What do you mean?" asked Wilfred, with a white face.

"It's plain enough," answered Gibbs. "There is only one man for forty miles round that could have struck such a blow as that, and he's the man that had most reason to."

"We must not prejudge anything," put in the doctor, a tall, black-bearded man, rather nervously; "but it is competent for me to corroborate what Mr. Gibbs says about the nature of the blow, sir; it is an incredible blow. Mr. Gibbs says that only one man in this district could have done it. I should have said myself that nobody could have done it."

A shudder of superstition went through the slight figure of the curate. "I can hardly understand," he said.

"Mr. Bohun," said the doctor in a low voice, "metaphors literally fail me. It is inadequate to say that the skull was smashed to bits like an eggshell. Fragments of bone were driven into the body and the ground like bullets into a mud wall. It was the hand of a giant."

He was silent a moment, looking grimly through his glasses; then he added: "The thing has one advantage—that it clears most people of suspicion at one stroke. If you or I or any normally made man in the country were accused of this crime, we should be acquitted as an infant would be acquitted of stealing the Nelson column."

"That's what I say," repeated the cobbler obstinately; "there's only one man that could have done it, and he's the man that would have done it. Where's Simeon Barnes, the blacksmith?"

"He's over at Greenford," faltered the curate.

"More likely over in France," muttered the cobbler.

"No; he is in neither of those places," said a small and colourless voice, which came from the little Roman priest who had joined the group. "As a matter of fact, he is coming up the road at this moment."

The little priest was not an interesting man to look at, having stubbly brown hair and a round and stolid face. But if he had been as splendid as Apollo no one would have looked at him at that moment. Everyone turned round and peered at the pathway which wound across the plain below, along which was indeed walking, at his own huge stride and with a hammer on his shoulder, Simeon the smith. He was a bony and gigantic man, with deep, dark, sinister eyes and a dark chin beard. He was walking and talking quietly with two other men; and though he was never specially cheerful, he seemed quite at his ease.

"My God!" cried the atheistic cobbler, "and there's the hammer he did it with."

"No," said the inspector, a sensible-looking man with a sandy moustache, speaking for the first time. "There's the hammer he did it with over there by the church wall. We have left it and the body exactly as they are."

All glanced round and the short priest went across and looked down in silence at the tool where it lay. It was one of the smallest and the lightest of the hammers, and would not have caught the eye among the rest; but on the iron edge of it were blood and yellow hair.

After a silence the short priest spoke without looking up, and there was a new note in his dull voice. "Mr. Gibbs was hardly right," he said, "in saying that there is no mystery. There is at least the mystery of why so big a man should attempt so big a blow with so little a hammer."

"Oh, never mind that," cried Gibbs, in a fever. "What are we to do with Simeon Barnes?"

"Leave him alone," said the priest quietly. "He is coming here of himself. I know those two men with him. They are very good fellows from Greenford, and they have come over about the Presbyterian chapel."

Even as he spoke the tall smith swung round the corner of the church, and strode into his own yard. Then he stood there quite still, and the hammer fell from his hand. The inspector, who had preserved impenetrable propriety, immediately went up to him.

"I won't ask you, Mr. Barnes," he said, "whether you know anything about what has happened here. You are not bound to say. I hope you don't know, and that you will be able to prove it. But I must go through the form of arresting you in the King's name for the murder of Colonel Norman Bohun."

"You are not bound to say anything," said the cobbler in officious excitement. "They've got to prove everything. They haven't proved yet that it is Colonel Bohun, with the head all smashed up like that."

"That won't wash," said the doctor aside to the priest. "That's out of the detective stories. I was the colonel's medical man, and I knew his body better than he did. He had very fine hands, but quite peculiar ones. The second and third fingers were the same length. Oh, that's the colonel right enough."

As he glanced at the brained corpse upon the ground the iron eyes of the motionless blacksmith followed them and rested there also.

"Is Colonel Bohun dead?" said the smith quite calmly. "Then he's damned."

"Don't say anything! Oh, don't say anything," cried the atheist cobbler, dancing about in an ecstasy of admiration of the English legal system. For no man is such a legalist as the good Secularist.

The blacksmith turned on him over his shoulder the august face of a fanatic.

"It's well for you infidels to dodge like foxes because the world's law favours you," he said; "but God guards His own in His pocket, as you shall see this day."

Then he pointed to the colonel and said: "When did this dog die in his sins?"

"Moderate your language," said the doctor.

"Moderate the Bible's language, and I'll moderate mine. When did he die?"

"I saw him alive at six o'clock this morning," stammered Wilfred Bohun.

"God is good," said the smith. "Mr. Inspector, I have not the slightest objection to being arrested. It is you who may object to arresting me. I don't mind leaving the court without a stain on my character. You do mind perhaps leaving the court with a bad set-back in your career."

The solid inspector for the first time looked at the blacksmith with a lively eye; as did everybody else, except the short, strange priest, who was still looking down at the little hammer that had dealt the dreadful blow.

"There are two men standing outside this shop," went on the blacksmith with ponderous lucidity, "good tradesmen in Greenford whom you all know, who will swear that they saw me from before midnight till daybreak and long after in the committee-room of our Revival Mission, which sits all night, we save souls so fast. In Greenford itself twenty people could swear to me for all that time. If I were a heathen, Mr. Inspector, I would let you walk on to your downfall. But as a Christian man I feel bound to give you your chance, and ask you whether you will hear my alibi now or in court."

The inspector seemed for the first time disturbed, and said, "Of course I should be glad to clear you altogether now."

The smith walked out of his yard with the same long and easy stride, and returned to his two friends from Greenford, who were indeed friends of nearly everyone present. Each of them said a few words which no one ever thought of disbelieving. When they had spoken, the innocence of Simeon stood up as solid as the great church above them.

One of those silences struck the group which are more strange and insufferable than any speech. Madly, in order to make conversation, the curate said to the Catholic priest:

"You seem very much interested in that hammer, Father Brown."

"Yes, I am," said Father Brown; "why is it such a small hammer?"

The doctor swung round on him.

"By George, that's true," he cried; "who would use a little hammer with ten larger hammers lying about?"

Then he lowered his voice in the curate's ear and said: "Only the kind of person that can't lift a large hammer. It is not a question of force or courage between the sexes. It's a question of lifting power in the shoulders. A bold woman could commit ten murders with a light hammer and never turn a hair. She could not kill a beetle with a heavy one."

Wilfred Bohun was staring at him with a sort of hypnotised horror, while Father Brown listened with his head a little on one side, really interested and attentive. The doctor went on with more hissing emphasis:

"Why do these idiots always assume that the only person who hates the wife's lover is the wife's husband? Nine times out of ten the person who most hates the wife's lover is the wife. Who knows what insolence or treachery he had shown her—look there?"

He made a momentary gesture towards the red-haired woman on the bench. She had lifted her head at last and the tears were drying on her splendid face. But the eyes were fixed on the corpse with an electric glare that had in it something of idiocy.

The Rev. Wilfred Bohun made a limp gesture as if waving away all desire to know; but Father Brown, dusting off his sleeve some ashes blown from the furnace, spoke in his indifferent way.

"You are like so many doctors," he said; "your mental science is really suggestive. It is your physical science that is utterly impossible. I agree that the woman wants to kill the co-respondent much more than the petitioner does. And I agree that a woman will always pick up a small hammer instead of a big one. But the difficulty is one of physical impossibility. No woman ever born could have smashed a man's skull out flat like that." Then he added reflectively, after a pause: "These people haven't grasped the whole of it. The man was actually wearing an iron helmet, and the blow scattered it like broken glass. Look at that woman. Look at her arms."

Silence held them all up again, and then the doctor said rather sulkily: "Well, I may be wrong; there are objections to everything. But I stick to the main point. No man but an idiot would pick up that little hammer if he could use a big hammer."

With that the lean and quivering hands of Wilfred Bohun went up to his head and seemed to clutch his scanty yellow hair. After an instant they dropped, and he cried: "That was the word I wanted; you have said the word."

Then he continued, mastering his discomposure: "The words you said were, 'No man but an idiot would pick up the small hammer.'"

"Yes," said the doctor. "Well?"

"Well," said the curate, "no man but an idiot did." The rest stared at him with eyes arrested and riveted, and he went on in a febrile and feminine agitation.

"I am a priest," he cried unsteadily, "and a priest should be no shedder of blood. I—I mean that he should bring no one to the gallows. And I thank God that I see the criminal clearly now—because he is a criminal who cannot be brought to the gallows."

"You will not denounce him?" inquired the doctor.

"He would not be hanged if I did denounce him," answered Wilfred with a wild but curiously happy smile. "When I went into the church this morning I found a madman praying there—that poor Joe, who has been wrong all his life. God knows what he prayed; but with such strange folk it is not incredible to suppose that their prayers are all upside down. Very likely a lunatic would pray before killing a man. When I last saw poor Joe he was with my brother. My brother was mocking him."

"By Jove!" cried the doctor, "this is talking at last. But how do you explain——"

The Rev. Wilfred was almost trembling with the excitement of his own glimpse of the truth. "Don't you see; don't you see," he cried feverishly; "that is the only theory that covers both the queer things, that answers both the riddles. The two riddles are the little hammer and the big blow. The smith might have struck the big blow, but would not have chosen the little hammer. His wife would have chosen the little hammer, but she could not have struck the big blow. But the madman might have done both. As for the little hammer—why, he was mad and might have picked up anything. And for the big blow, have you never heard, doctor, that a maniac in his paroxysm may have the strength of ten men?"

The doctor drew a deep breath and then said, "By golly, I believe you've got it."

Father Brown had fixed his eyes on the speaker so long and steadily as to prove that his large grey, ox-like eyes were not quite so insignificant as the rest of his face. When silence had fallen he said with marked respect: "Mr. Bohun, yours is the only theory yet propounded which holds water every way and is essentially unassailable. I think, therefore, that you deserve to be told, on my positive knowledge, that it is not the true one." And with that the old little man walked away and stared again at the hammer.

"That fellow seems to know more than he ought to," whispered the doctor peevishly to Wilfred. "Those popish priests are deucedly sly."

"No, no," said Bohun, with a sort of wild fatigue. "It was the lunatic. It was the lunatic."

The group of the two clerics and the doctor had fallen away from the more official group containing the inspector and the man he had arrested. Now, however, that their own party had broken up, they heard voices from the others. The priest looked up quietly and then looked down again as he heard the blacksmith say in a loud voice:

"I hope I've convinced you, Mr. Inspector. I'm a strong man, as you say, but I couldn't have flung my hammer bang here from Greenford. My hammer hasn't got wings that it should come flying half a mile over hedges and fields."

The inspector laughed amicably and said: "No, I think you can be considered out of it, though it's one of the rummiest coincidences I ever saw. I can only ask you to give us all the assistance you can in finding a man as big and strong as yourself. By George! you might be useful, if only to hold him! I suppose you yourself have no guess at the man?"

"I may have a guess," said the pale smith, "but it is not at a man." Then, seeing the scared eyes turn towards his wife on the bench, he put his huge hand on her shoulder and said: "Nor a woman either."

"What do you mean?" asked the inspector jocularly. "You don't think cows use hammers, do you?"

"I think no thing of flesh held that hammer," said the blacksmith in a stifled voice; "mortally speaking, I think the man died alone."

Wilfred made a sudden forward movement and peered at him with burning eyes.

"Do you mean to say, Barnes," came the sharp voice of the cobbler, "that the hammer jumped up of itself and knocked the man down?"

"Oh, you gentlemen may stare and snigger," cried Simeon; "you clergymen who tell us on Sunday in what a stillness the Lord smote

Sennacherib. I believe that One who walks invisible in every house defended the honour of mine, and laid the defiler dead before the door of it. I believe the force in that blow was just the force there is in earthquakes, and no force less."

Wilfred said, with a voice utterly undescribable: "I told Norman myself to beware of the thunderbolt."

"That agent is outside my jurisdiction," said the inspector with a slight smile.

"You are not outside His," answered the smith; "see you to it," and, turning his broad back, he went into the house.

The shaken Wilfred was led away by Father Brown, who had an easy and friendly way with him. "Let us get out of this horrid place, Mr. Bohun," he said. "May I look inside your church? I hear it's one of the oldest in England. We take some interest, you know," he added with a comical grimace, "in old English churches."

Wilfred Bohun did not smile, for humour was never his strong point. But he nodded rather eagerly, being only too ready to explain the Gothic splendours to someone more likely to be sympathetic than the Presbyterian blacksmith or the atheist cobbler.

"By all means," he said; "let us go in at this side." And he led the way into the high side entrance at the top of the flight of steps. Father Brown was mounting the first step to follow him when he felt a hand on his shoulder, and turned to behold the dark, thin figure of the doctor, his face darker yet with suspicion.

"Sir," said the physician harshly, "you appear to know some secrets in this black business. May I ask if you are going to keep them to yourself?"

"Why, doctor," answered the priest, smiling quite pleasantly, "there is one very good reason why a man of my trade should keep things to himself when he is not sure of them, and that is that it is so constantly his duty to keep them to himself when he is sure of them. But if you think I have been discourteously reticent with you or anyone, I will go to the extreme limit of my custom. I will give you two very large hints."

"Well, sir?" said the doctor gloomily.

"First," said Father Brown quietly, "the thing is quite in your own province. It is a matter of physical science. The blacksmith is mistaken, not perhaps in saying that the blow was divine, but certainly in saying that it came by a miracle. It was no miracle, doctor, except in so far as man is himself a miracle, with his strange and wicked and yet half-heroic heart. The force that smashed that skull was a force well known to scientists—one of the most frequently debated of the laws of nature."

The doctor, who was looking at him with frowning intentness, only said: "And the other hint?"

"The other hint is this," said the priest. "Do you remember the blacksmith, though he believes in miracles, talking scornfully of the impossible fairy tale that his hammer had wings and flew half a mile across country?"

"Yes," said the doctor, "I remember that."

"Well," added Father Brown, with a broad smile, "that fairy tale was the nearest thing to the real truth that has been said to-day." And with that he turned his back and stumped up the steps after the curate.

The Reverend Wilfred, who had been waiting for him, pale and impatient, as if this little delay were the last straw for his nerves, led him immediately to his favourite corner of the church, that part of the gallery closest to the carved roof and lit by the wonderful window with the angel. The little Latin priest explored and admired everything exhaustively, talking cheerfully but in a low voice all the time. When in the course of his investigation he found the side exit and the winding stair down which Wilfred had rushed to find his brother dead, Father Brown ran not down but up, with the agility of a monkey, and his clear voice came from an outer platform above.

"Come up here, Mr. Bohun," he called. "The air will do you good."

Bohun followed him, and came out on a kind of stone gallery or balcony outside the building, from which one could see the illimitable plain in which their small hill stood, wooded away to the purple horizon and dotted with villages and farms. Clear and square, but quite small beneath them, was the blacksmith's yard, where the inspector still stood taking notes and the corpse still lay like a smashed fly.

"Might be the map of the world, mightn't it?" said Father Brown.

"Yes," said Bohun very gravely, and nodded his head.

Immediately beneath and about them the lines of the Gothic building plunged outwards into the void with a sickening swiftness akin to suicide. There is that element of Titan energy in the architecture of the Middle Ages that, from whatever aspect it be seen, it always seems to be rushing away, like the strong back of some maddened horse. This church was hewn out of ancient and silent stone, bearded with old fungoids and stained with the nests of birds. And yet, when they saw it from below, it sprang like a fountain at the stars; and when they saw it, as now, from above, it poured like a cataract into a voiceless pit. For these two men on the tower were left alone with the most terrible aspect of the Gothic; the monstrous foreshortening and disproportion, the dizzy perspectives, the glimpses of great things small and small things great; a topsy-turvydom of stone in the mid-air. Details of stone, enormous by their proximity, were relieved against a pattern of fields and farms, pygmy in their distance. A carved bird or beast at a corner seemed like some vast walking or flying dragon wasting the pastures and villages below. The whole atmosphere was dizzy and dangerous, as if men were upheld in air amid the gyrating wings of colossal genii; and the whole of that old church, as tall and rich as a cathedral, seemed to sit upon the sunlit country like a cloudburst.

"I think there is something rather dangerous about standing on these high places even to pray," said Father Brown. "Heights were made to be looked at, not to be looked from."

"Do you mean that one may fall over," asked Wilfred.

"I mean that one's soul may fall if one's body doesn't," said the other priest.

"I scarcely understand you," remarked Bohun indistinctly.

"Look at that blacksmith, for instance," went on Father Brown calmly; "a good man, but not a Christian—hard, imperious, unforgiving. Well, his Scotch religion was made up by men who prayed on hills and high crags, and learnt to look down on the world more than to look up at heaven. Humility is the mother of giants. One sees great things from the valley; only small things from the peak."

"But he—he didn't do it," said Bohun tremulously.

"No," said the other in an odd voice; "we know he didn't do it."

After a moment he resumed, looking tranquilly out over the plain with his pale grey eyes. "I knew a man," he said, "who began by worshipping with others before the altar, but who grew fond of high and lonely places to pray from, corners or niches in the belfry or the spire. And once in one of those dizzy places, where the whole world seemed to turn under him like a wheel, his brain turned also, and he fancied he was God. So that though he was a good man, he committed a great crime."

Wilfred's face was turned away, but his bony hands turned blue and white as they tightened on the parapet of stone.

"He thought it was given to *him* to judge the world and strike down the sinner. He would never have had such a thought if he had been kneeling with other men upon a floor. But he saw all men walking about like insects. He saw one especially strutting just below him, insolent and evident by a bright green hat—a poisonous insect."

Rooks cawed round the corners of the belfry; but there was no other sound till Father Brown went on.

"This also tempted him, that he had in his hand one of the most awful engines of nature; I mean gravitation, that mad and quickening rush by which all earth's creatures fly back to her heart when released. See, the inspector is strutting just below us in the smithy. If I were to toss a pebble over this parapet it would be something like a bullet by the time it struck him. If I were to drop a hammer—even a small hammer——"

Wilfred Bohun threw one leg over the parapet, and Father Brown had him in a minute by the collar.

"Not by that door," he said quite gently; "that door leads to hell."

Bohun staggered back against the wall, and stared at him with frightful eyes.

"How do you know all this? "he cried. "Are you a devil?"

"I am a man," answered Father Brown gravely; "and therefore have all devils in my heart. Listen to me," he said after a short pause. "I know what you did—at least, I can guess the great part of it. When you left your brother you were racked with no unrighteous rage, to the extent even that you snatched up a small hammer, half inclined to kill him with his foulness on his mouth. Recoiling, you thrust it under your buttoned coat instead, and rushed into the church. You pray wildly in many places, under the angel window, upon the platform above, and a higher platform still, from which you could see the colonel's Eastern hat like the back of a green beetle crawling about. Then something snapped in your soul, and you let God's thunderbolt fall."

Wilfred put a weak hand to his head, and asked in a low voice: "How did you know that his hat looked like a green beetle?"

"Oh, that," said the other with the shadow of a smile, "that was common sense. But hear me further. I say I know all this; but no one else shall know it. The next step is for you; I shall take no more steps; I will seal this with the seal of confession. If you ask me why, there are many reasons, and only one that concerns you. I leave things to you because you have not yet gone very far wrong, as assassins go. You did not help to fix the crime on the smith when it was easy; or on his wife, when that was easy. You tried to fix it on the imbecile because you knew that he could not suffer. That was one of the gleams that it is my business to find in assassins. And now come down into the village, and go your own way as free as the wind; for I have said my last word."

They went down the winding stairs in utter silence, and came out into the sunlight by the smithy. Wilfred Bohun carefully unlatched the wooden gate of the yard, and going up to the inspector, said: "I wish to give myself up; I have killed my brother."

The Problem of the Stolen Rubens

Jacques Futrelle

MATTHEW KALE made fifty million dollars out of axle grease, after which he began to patronize the high arts. It was simple enough: he had the money, and Europe had the old masters. His method of buying was simplicity itself. There were five thousand square yards, more or less, in the huge gallery of his marble mansion which were to be covered, so he bought five thousand yards, more or less, of art. Some of it was good, some of it fair, and much of it bad. The chief picture of the collection was a Rubens, which he had picked up in Rome for fifty thousand dollars.

Soon after acquiring his collection, Kale decided to make certain alterations in the vast room where the pictures hung. They were all taken down and stored in the ball room, equally vast, with their faces toward the wall. Meanwhile Kale and his family took refuge in a nearby hotel.

It was at this hotel that Kale met Jules de Lesseps. De Lesseps was distinctly French, the sort of Frenchman whose conversation resembles callisthenics. He was nervous, quick, and agile, and he told Kale in confidence that he was not only a painter himself, he was a connoisseur in the high arts. Pompous in the pride of possession, Kale went to a good deal of trouble to exhibit his private collection for de Lesseps's delectation. It happened in the ball room, and the true artist's delight shone in the Frenchman's eyes as he handled the pieces which were good. Some of the others made him smile, but it was an inoffensive sort of smile.

With his own hands Kale lifted the precious Rubens and held it before the Frenchman's eyes. It was a Madonna and Child, one of those wonderful creations which have endured through the years with all the sparkle and color beauty of their pristine days. Kale seemed disappointed because de Lesseps was not particularly enthusiastic about the picture.

"Why, it's a Rubens!" he exclaimed.

137

"Yes, I see," replied de Lesseps.

"It cost me fifty thousand dollars."

"It is perhaps worth more than that," and the Frenchman shrugged his shoulders as he turned away.

Kale looked at him in chagrin. Could it be that de Lesseps did not understand that it was a Rubens, and that Rubens was a painter? Or was it that he had failed to hear him say that it cost him fifty thousand dollars? Kale was accustomed to seeing people bob their heads and open their eyes when he said fifty thousand dollars; therefore, "Don't you like it?" he asked.

"Very much indeed," replied de Lesseps; "but I have seen it before. I saw it in Rome just a week or so before you purchased it."

"They rummaged on through the pictures, and at last a Whistler turned up for their inspection. It was one of the famous Thames series, a water color. De Lesseps' face radiated excitement, and several times he glanced from the water color to the Rubens, as if mentally comparing the exquisitely penciled and colored modern work with the bold, masterly technic of the old.

Kale misunderstood the silence. "I don't think much of this one, myself," he explained apologetically. "It's a Whistler, and all that, and it cost me five thousand dollars, and I sort of had to have it, but still it isn't just the kind of thing that I like. What do you think of it?"

"I think it is perfectly wonderful," replied the Frenchman enthusiastically. "It is the essence, the superlative of modern work. I wonder if it would be possible," and he turned to face Kale, "for me to make a copy of that? I have some slight skill in painting myself, and dare say I could make a fairly creditable copy of it."

Kale was flattered. He was more and more impressed each moment with the picture. "Why, certainly," he replied. "I will have it sent up to the hotel, and you can—"

"No, no, no!" interrupted de Lesseps quickly. "I wouldn't care to accept the responsibility of having the picture in my charge. There is always the danger of fire. But if you would give me permission to come here—this room is large and airy and light, and besides it is quiet—"

"Just as you like," said Kale magnanimously. "I merely thought the other way would be most convenient for you."

De Lesseps drew near, and laid one hand on the millionaire's arm. "My dear friend," he said earnestly, "if these pictures were ray pictures, I shouldn't try to accommodate anybody where they were concerned. I dare say the collection as it stands cost you——"

"Six hundred and eighty-seven thousand dollars," volunteered Kale proudly.

"And surely they must be well protected here in your house during your absence?"

"There are about twenty servants in the house while the workmen are making the alterations," said Kale, "and three of them don't do anything but watch this room. No one can go in or out except by the door we entered—the others are locked and barred—and then only with my permission, or a written order from me. No, sir, nobody can get away with anything in this room."

"Excellent—excellent!" said de Lesseps admiringly. He smiled a little bit. "I am afraid I did not give you credit for being the far-sighted business man that you are." He turned and glanced over the collection of pictures abstractedly. "A clever thief, though," he ventured, "might cut a valuable painting, for instance the Rubens, out of the frame, roll it up, conceal it under his coat and escape."

Kale laughed pleasantly and shook his head.

It was a couple of days later at the hotel that de Lesseps brought up the subject of copying the Whistler. He was profuse in his thanks when Kale volunteered to accompany him to the mansion and witness the preliminary stages of the work. They paused at the ballroom door.

"Jennings," said Kale to the liveried servant there, "this is Mr. de Lesseps. He is to come and go as he likes. He is going to do some work in the ballroom here. See that he isn't disturbed."

De Lesseps noticed the Rubens leaning carelessly against some other pictures, with the holy face of the Madonna toward them. "Really, Mr. Kale," he protested, "that picture is too valuable to be left about like that. If you will let your servants bring me some canvas, I shall wrap it and place it up on the table here off the floor. Suppose there were mice here?"

Kale thanked him. The necessary orders were given, and finally the picture was carefully wrapped and placed beyond harm's reach, whereupon de Lesseps adjusted himself, paper, easel, stool and all, and began his work of copying. There Kale left him.

Three days later Kale just happened to drop in, and found the artist still at his labor.

"I just dropped by," he explained, "to see how the work in the gallery was coming along. It will be finished in another week. I hope I am not disturbing you."

"Not at all," said de Lesseps. "I have nearly finished. See how I am getting along?" He turned the easel toward Kale.

The millionaire gazed from that toward the original which stood on a chair near by, and frank admiration for the artist's efforts was in his eyes. "Why, it's fine!" he exclaimed. "It's just as good as the other one, and I bet you don't want any five thousand dollars for it, eh?"

That was all that was said about it at the time. Kale wandered about the house for an hour or so, then dropped into the ballroom where the artist was just getting his paraphernalia together, and they walked back to the hotel. The artist carried under one arm his copy of the Whistler, loosely rolled up.

Another week passed and the workman who had been engaged in refinishing and decorating the gallery had gone. De Lesseps volunteered to assist in the work of rehanging the pictures, and Kale gladly turned the matter over to him. It was in the afternoon of the day this work began that de Lesseps, chatting pleasantly with Kale, ripped loose the canvas which enshrouded the precious Rubens. Then he paused with an exclamation of dismay. The picture was gone; the frame which had held it was empty. A thin strip of canvas around the inside edge showed that a sharp penknife had been used to cut out the painting.

All of these facts came to the attention of Professor Augustus S. F. X. Van Dusen—The Thinking Machine. This was a day or so after Kale had rushed into Detective Mallory's office at police headquarters, with the statement that his Rubens had been stolen. He banged his fist down on the detective's desk and roared at him.

"It cost me fifty thousand dollars!" he declared violently. "Why don't you do something? What are you sitting there staring at me for?"

"Don't excite yourself, Mr. Kale," the detective advised. "I will put my men at work right now to recover the—the—What is a Rubens, anyway?"

"It's a picture!" bellowed Mr. Kale. "A piece of canvas with some paint on it, and it cost me fifty thousand dollars—don't you forget that!"

So the police machinery was set in motion to recover the painting. And in time the matter fell under the watchful eye of Hutchinson Hatch, reporter. He learned the facts preceding the disappearance of the picture, and then called on de Lesseps. He found the artist in a state of excitement bordering on hysteria; an intimation from the reporter of the object of his visit caused de Lesseps to burst into words.

"*Mon dieu!* It is outrageous!" he exclaimed. "What can I do? I was the only one in the room for several days. I was the one who took such pains to protect the picture. And now it is gone! The loss is irreparable. What can I do?"

Hatch didn't have any very definite idea as to just what he could do, so he let him go on. "As I understand it, Mr. de Lesseps," he interrupted at last, "no one else was in the room, except you and Mr. Kale, all the time you were there?"

"No one else."

"And I think Mr. Kale said that you were making a copy of some famous water color, weren't you?"

"Yes, a Thames scene. By Whistler," was the reply. "That is it, hanging over the mantel."

Hatch glanced at the picture admiringly. It was an exquisite copy, and showed the deft touch of a man who was himself an artist of great ability.

De Lesseps read the admiration in his face. "It is not bad," he said modestly. "I studied with Carolus Duran."

With all else that was known, and this little additional information, which seemed of no particular value to the reporter, the entire matter was laid before The Thinking Machine. That distinguished man listened from beginning to end without comment.

"Who had access to the room?" he asked finally.

"That is what the police are working on now," was the reply. "There are a couple of dozen servants in the house, and I suppose in spite of Kale's rigid orders there was a certain laxity in their enforcement."

"Of course that makes it more difficult," said The Thinking Machine in the perpetually irritated voice which was so distinctly a part of himself. "Perhaps it would be best for us to go to Mr. Kale's home and personally investigate."

Kale received them with the reserve which all rich men show in the presence of representatives of the press. He stared frankly and somewhat curiously at the diminutive figure of the scientist, who explained the object of their visit.

"I guess you fellows can't do anything with them," the millionaire assured them. "I've got some regular detectives on it."

"Is Mr. Mallory here now?" asked The Thinking Machine curtly.

"Yes, he is upstairs in the servants quarters."

"May we see the room from which the picture was taken?" inquired the scientist with a suave intonation which Hatch knew well.

Kale granted the permission with a wave of his hand and ushered them into the ballroom, where the pictures had been stored. From the relative center of the room The Thinking Machine surveyed it all. The windows were high. Half a dozen doors leading out into the hallways, to the conservatory, and quiet nooks of the mansion offered innumerable possibilities of access. After this one long comprehensive squint, The Thinking Machine went over and picked up the frame from which the Rubens had been cut. For a long time he examined it. Kale's impatience was painfully evident. Finally the scientist turned to him.

"How well do you know Mr. de Lesseps?" he asked.

"I've known him only for a month or so. Why?"

"Did he bring you letters of introduction, or did you meet him casually?"

Kale regarded him with evident displeasure. "My own personal affairs have nothing whatever to do with this matter," he said pointedly. "Mr. de Lesseps is a gentleman of integrity and certainly he is the last whom I would suspect of any connection with the disappearance of the picture."

"That is usually the case," remarked The Thinking Machine tartly. He turned to Hatch. "Just how good a copy was that he made of the Whistler picture?" he asked.

"I have never seen the original," Hatch replied, "but the workmanship was superb. Perhaps Mr. Kale wouldn't object to our seeing—"

"Oh, of course not," said Kale resignedly. "Come in. It's in the gallery."

Hatch submitted the picture to a careful scrutiny. "I should say that the copy is well nigh perfect," was his verdict. "Of course, in its absence, I couldn't say exactly, but it is certainly a superb piece of work."

The curtains of a wide door almost in front of them were thrown aside suddenly, and Detective Mallory entered. He carried something in his hand, but at the sight of them, concealed it behind himself. Unrepressed triumph was in his face.

"Ah, professor, we meet often, don't we?" he said.

"This reporter here and his friend seem to be trying to drag de Lesseps into this affair somehow," Kale complained to the detective. "I don't want anything like that to happen. He is liable to go out and print anything. They always do."

The Thinking Machine glared at him unwaveringly straight in the eye for an instant, then extended his hand toward Mallory. "Where did you find it?" he asked.

"Sorry to disappoint you, professor," said the detective sarcastically, "but this is the time when you were a little late," and he produced the object which he held behind him. "Here is your picture, Mr. Kale."

Kale gasped a little in relief and astonishment, and held up the canvas with both hands to examine it. "Fine!" he told the detective. "I'll see that you don't lose anything by this. Why, that thing cost me fifty thousand dollars!" Kale didn't seem able to get over that.

The Thinking Machine leaned forward to squint at the upper right hand corner of the canvas. "Where did you find it?" he asked again.

"Rolled up tight and concealed in the bottom of a trunk in the room of one of the servants," explained Mallory. "The servant's name is Jennings. He is now under arrest."

"Jennings!" exclaimed Kale. "Why, he has been with me for years."

"Did he confess?" asked the scientist imperturbably.

"Of course not," said Mallory. "He says some of the other servants must have put it there."

The Thinking Machine nodded at Hatch. "I think perhaps that is all," he remarked. "I congratulate you, Mr. Mallory, upon bringing the matter to such a quick and satisfactory conclusion."

Ten minutes later they left the house and caught a car for the scientist's home. Hatch was a little chagrined at the unexpected termination of the affair, and was thoughtfully silent for a time.

"Mallory does occasionally show a gleam of human intelligence, doesn't he?" he said at last, quizzically.

"Not that I ever noticed," remarked the scientist.

"But he found the picture," Hatch insisted.

"Of course he found it. It was put there for him to find."

"Put there for him to find," repeated the reporter. "Didn't Jennings steal it?"

"If he did, he's a fool."

"Well, if he didn't steal it, who put it there?"

"De Lesseps."

"De Lesseps!" echoed Hatch. "Why the deuce did he steal a fifty-thousand dollar picture and put it in a servant's trunk to be found?"

The Thinking Machine twisted around in his seat and squinted at him oddly for a moment. "At times, Mr. Hatch, I am absolutely amazed at your stupidity," he said frankly. "I can understand it in a man like Mallory, but I have always given you credit for being an astute, quick-witted man."

Hatch smiled at the reproach. It was not the first time he had heard of it. But nothing bearing on the problem in hand was said until they reached The Thinking Machine's apartments.

"The only real question in my mind, Mr. Hatch," said the scientist then, "is whether or not I should take the trouble to restore Mr. Kale's picture at all. He is perfectly satisfied, and will probably never know the difference. So—"

Suddenly Hatch saw something. "Great Scott!" he exclaimed. "Do you mean that the picture that Mallory found was—"

"A copy of the original," finished The Thinking Machine. "Personally I know nothing whatever about art, therefore, I could not say from observation that it is a copy, but I know it from the logic of the thing. When the original was cut from the frame, the knife swerved a little at the upper right hand corner. The canvas remaining in the frame told me that. The picture that Mr. Mallory found did not correspond in this detail with the canvas in the frame The conclusion is obvious."

"And de Lesseps has the original?"

"De Lesseps has the original. How did he get it? In any one of a dozen ways. He might have rolled it up and stuck it under his coat. He might have had a confederate, but I don't think that any ordinary method of theft would have appealed to him. I am giving him credit for being clever, as I must when we review the whole case—

"For instance, he asked for permission to copy the Whistler, which you saw was the same size as the Rubens. It was granted. He copied it practically under guard, always with the chance that Mr. Kale himself would drop in. It took him three days to copy it, so he says. He was alone in the room all that time. He knew that Mr. Kale had not the faintest idea of art. Taking advantage of that, what would have been simpler than to have copied the Rubens in oil? He could have removed it from the frame immediately after he canvassed it over, and kept it in a position near him where it could be quickly covered if he was interrupted. Remember, the picture is worth fifty thousand dollars, therefore was worth the trouble.

"De Lesseps is an artist—we know that—and dealing with a man who knew nothing whatever of art, he had no fears. We may suppose his idea all along was to use the copy of the Rubens as a sort of decoy after he got away with the original. You saw that Mallory didn't know the difference and it was safe for de Lesseps to suppose that Mr. Kale wouldn't, either. His only danger until he could get away gracefully was of some critic or connoisseur, perhaps, seeing the copy. His boldness we see readily in the fact that he permitted himself to discover the theft, that he discovered it after he had volunteered to assist Mr. Kale in the general work of re-hanging the pictures in the gallery. Just how he put the picture in Jenning's trunk, I don't happen to know. We can imagine many ways—" He lay back in his chair for a minute without speaking, eyes steadily turned upward, fingers placed precisely tip to tip.

"The only thing remaining is to go get the picture. It is in de Lesseps's room now—you told me that—and so we know it is safe. I dare say he knows that if he tried to run away, it would inevitably put him under suspicion."

"But how did he take the picture from the Kale home?" asked Hatch.

"He took it with him probably under his arm the day he left the house with Mr. Kale," was the astonishing reply.

Hatch stared at him in amazement. After a moment the scientist rose and passed into the adjoining room, and the telephone bell there jingled. When he joined Hatch again, he picked up his hat and they went out together.

De Lesseps was in when their cards went up, and received them. They conversed of the case generally for ten minutes, while the scientist's eyes were turned inquiringly here and there about the room. At last there came a knock on the door.

"It is Detective Mallory, Mr. Hatch," remarked The Thinking Machine. "Open the door for him."

De Lesseps seemed startled for just one instant, then quickly recovered. Mallory's eyes were full of questions when he entered.

"I should like, Mr. Mallory," began The Thinking Machine quietly, "to call your attention to this copy of Mr. Kale's picture by Whistler—over the mantel here. Isn't it excellent? You have seen the original?"

Mallory grunted. De Lesseps's face, instead of expressing appreciation at the compliment, blanched suddenly, and his hands closed tightly. Again he recovered himself and smiled.

"The beauty of this picture lies not only in its faithfulness to the original," the scientist went on, "but also in the fact that it was painted under extraordinary circumstances. For instance, I don't know if you know, Mr. Mallory, that it is possible so to combine glue and putty and a few other commonplace things into a paste which would effectively blot out an oil painting and offer at the same time an excellent surface for water-color work."

There was a moment's pause, during which the three men stared at him silently—with singularly conflicting emotions depicted on their faces.

"This water color—this copy of Whistler," continued the scientist evenly, "is painted on such a paste as I have described. That paste in turn covers the original Rubens picture. It can be removed with water without damage to the picture, which is in oil, so that instead of a copy of the Whistler painting, we have an original by Rubens, worth fifty thousand dollars. That is true; isn't it, Mr. de Lesseps?"

There was no reply to the question—none was needed. It was an hour later, after de Lesseps was safely in his cell, that Hatch called up The Thinking Machine on the telephone and asked one question.

"How did you know that the water color was painted over the Rubens?"

"Because it was the only absolutely safe way in which the Rubens could be hopelessly lost to those who were looking for it, and at the same time perfectly preserved," was the answer. "I told you de Lesseps was a clever man, and a little logic did the rest. Two and two always makes four, Mr. Hatch, not sometimes, but all the time."

The Duchess of Wiltshire's Diamonds

Guy Boothby

TO the reflective mind the rapidity with which the inhabitants of the world's greatest city seize upon a new name or idea and familiarise themselves with it, can scarcely prove otherwise than astonishing. As an illustration of my meaning let me take the case of Klimo—the now famous private detective, who has won for himself the right to be considered as great as Lecocq, or even the late lamented Sherlock Holmes.

Up to a certain morning London had never even heard his name, nor had it the remotest notion as to who or what he might be. It was as sublimely ignorant and careless on the subject as the inhabitants of Kamtchatka or Peru. Within twenty-four hours, however, the whole aspect of the case was changed. The man, woman, or child who had not seen his posters, or heard his name, was counted an ignoramus unworthy of intercourse with human beings.

Princes became familiar with it as their trains tore them to Windsor to luncheon with the Queen; the nobility noticed and commented upon it as they drove about the town: merchants, and business men generally, read it as they made their ways by omnibus or Underground to their various shops and counting-houses; street boys called each other by it as a nickname; Music Hall Artistes introduced it into their patter, while it was even rumoured that the Stock Exchange itself had paused in the full flood tide of business to manufacture a riddle on the subject.

That Klimo made his profession pay him well was certain, first from the fact that his advertisements must have cost a good round sum, and, second, because he had taken a mansion in Belverton Street, Park Lane, next door to Porchester House, where, to the dismay of that aristocratic neighbourhood, he advertised that he was prepared to receive and be consulted by his clients. The invitation was responded to with alacrity, and from that day forward, between the hours of twelve and two, the pavement upon the north side of the street was lined with carriages, every one containing some person desirous of testing the great man's skill.

I must here explain that I have narrated all this in order to show the state of affairs existing in Belverton Street and Park Lane when Simon Carne arrived, or was supposed to arrive in England. If my memory serves me correctly, it was on Wednesday, the 3rd of May, that the Earl of Amberley drove to Victoria to meet and welcome the man whose acquaintance he had made in India under such peculiar circumstances, and under the spell of whose fascination he and his family had fallen so completely.

Reaching the station, his lordship descended from his carriage, and made his way to the platform set apart for the reception of the Continental express. He walked with a jaunty air, and seemed to be on the best of terms with himself and the world in general. How little he suspected the existence of the noose into which he was so innocently running his head!

As if out of compliment to his arrival, the train put in an appearance within a few moments of his reaching the platform. He immediately placed himself in such a position that he could make sure of seeing the man he wanted, and waited patiently until he should come in sight. Carne, however, was not among the first batch, indeed, the majority of passengers had passed before his lordship caught sight of him.

One thing was very certain, however great the crush might have been, it would have been difficult to mistake Carne's figure. The man's infirmity and the peculiar beauty of his face rendered him easily recognisable. Possibly, after his long sojourn in India, he found the morning cold, for he wore a long fur coat, the collar of which he had turned up round his ears, thus making a fitting frame for his delicate face. On seeing Lord Amberley he hastened forward to greet him.

"This is most kind and friendly of you," he said as he shook the other by the hand. "A fine day and Lord Amberley to meet me. One could scarcely imagine a better welcome."

As he spoke, one of his Indian servants approached and salaamed before him. He gave him an order, and received an answer in Hindustani, whereupon he turned again to Lord Amberley.

"You may imagine how anxious I am to see my new dwelling," he said. "My servant tells me that my carriage is here, so may I hope that you will drive back with me and see for yourself how I am likely to be lodged."

"I shall be delighted," said Lord Amberley, who was longing for the opportunity, and they accordingly went out into the station yard together to discover a brougham, drawn by two magnificent horses, and with Nur Ali, in all the glory of white raiment and crested turban, on the box, waiting to receive them. His lordship dismissed his Victoria, and when Jowur Singh had taken his place beside his fellow servant upon the box, the carriage rolled out of the station yard in the direction of Hyde Park.

"I trust her ladyship is quite well," said Simon Carne politely, as they turned into Gloucester Place.

"Excellently well, thank you," replied his lordship. "She bade me welcome you to England in her name as well as my own, and I was to say that she is looking forward to seeing you."

"She is most kind, and I shall do myself the honour of calling upon her as soon as circumstances will permit," answered Carne. "I beg you will convey my best thanks to her for her thought of me."

While these polite speeches were passing between them they were rapidly approaching a large hoarding on which was displayed a poster setting forth the name of the now famous detective, Klimo.

Simon Carne, leaning forward, studied it, and when they had passed, turned to his friend again.

"At Victoria and on all the hoardings we meet I see an enormous placard, bearing the word 'Klimo.' Pray, what does it mean?"

His lordship laughed.

'You are asking a question which, a month ago, was on the lips of nine out of every ten Londoners. It is only within the last fortnight that we have learned who and what 'Klimo' is."

"And pray what is he?"

"Well, the explanation is very simple. He is neither more nor less than a remarkably astute private detective, who has succeeded in attracting notice in such a way that half London has been induced to patronise him. I have had no dealings with the man myself. But a friend of mine, Lord Orpington, has been the victim of a most audacious burglary, and, the police having failed to solve the mystery, he has called Klimo in. We shall therefore see what he can do before many days are past. But, there, I expect you will soon know more about him than any of us."

"Indeed! And why?"

"For the simple reason that he has taken No. 1, Belverton Terrace, the house adjoining your own, and sees his clients there."

Simon Carne pursed up his lips, and appeared to be considering something.

"I trust he will not prove a nuisance," he said at last. "The agents who found me the house should have acquainted me with the fact. Private detectives, on however large a scale, scarcely strike one as the most desirable of neighbours—particularly for a man who is so fond of quiet as myself."

At this moment they were approaching their destination. As the carriage passed Belverton Street and pulled up, Lord Amberley pointed to a long line of vehicles standing before the detective's door.

"You can see for yourself something of the business he does," he said. "Those are the carriages of his clients, and it is probable that twice as many have arrived on foot."

"I shall certainly speak to the agent on the subject," said Carne, with a shadow of annoyance upon his face. "I consider the fact of this man's being so close to me a serious drawback to the house."

Jowur Singh here descended from the box and opened the door in order that his master and his guest might alight, while portly Ram Gafur, the butler, came down the steps and salaamed before them with Oriental obsequiousness. Carne greeted his domestics with kindly condescension, and then, accompanied by the ex- Viceroy, entered his new abode.

"I think you may congratulate yourself upon having secured one of the most desirable residences in London," said his lordship ten minutes or so later, when they had explored the principal rooms.

"I am very glad to hear you say so," said Carne. "I trust your lordship will remember that you will always be welcome in the house as long as I am its owner."

"It is very kind of you to say so," returned Lord Amberley warmly. "I shall look forward to some months of pleasant intercourse. And now I must be going. To-morrow, perhaps, if you have nothing better to do, you will give us the pleasure of your company at dinner. Your fame has already gone abroad, and we shall ask one or two nice people to meet you, including my brother and sister-in-law. Lord and Lady

Gelpington, Lord and Lady Orpington, and my cousin, the Duchess of Wiltshire, whose interest in China and Indian Art, as perhaps you know, is only second to your own."

"I shall be most glad to come."

"We may count on seeing you in Eaton Square, then, at eight o'clock?"

"If I am alive you may be sure I shall be there. Must you really go? Then good-bye, and many thanks for meeting me."

His lordship having left the house Simon Carne went upstairs to his dressing room, which it was to be noticed he found without inquiry, and rang the electric bell, beside the fireplace, three times. While he was waiting for it to be answered he stood looking out of the window at the long line of carriages in the street below.

"Everything is progressing admirably," he said to himself. "Amberley does not suspect any more than the world in general. As a proof he asks me to dinner to-morrow evening to meet his brother and sister-in-law, two of his particular friends, and above all Her Grace of Wiltshire. Of course I shall go, and when I bid Her Grace good-bye it will be strange if I am not one step nearer the interest on Liz's money."

At this moment the door opened, and his valet, the grave and respectable Belton, entered the room. Carne turned to greet him impatiently.

"Come, come, Belton," he said, "we must be quick. It is twenty minutes to twelve and if we don't hurry, the folk next door will become impatient. Have you succeeded in doing what I spoke to you about last night?"

"I have done everything, sir."

"I am glad to hear it. Now lock that door and let us get to work. You can let me have your news while I am dressing."

Opening one side of a massive wardrobe that completely filled one end of the room, Belton took from it a number of garments. They included a well worn velvet coat, a baggy pair of trousers—so old that only a notorious pauper or a millionaire could have afforded to wear them—a flannel waistcoat, a Gladstone collar, a soft silk tie, and a pair of embroidered carpet slippers upon which no old clothes man in the most reckless way of business in Petticoat Lane would have advanced a single halfpenny. Into these he assisted his master to change.

"Now give me the wig, and unfasten the straps of this hump," said Carne, as the other placed the garments just referred to upon a neighbouring chair.

Belton did as he was ordered, and then there happened a thing the like of which no one would have believed. Having unbuckled a strap on either shoulder, and slipped his hand beneath the waistcoat, he withdrew a large *papier-maché* hump, which he carried away and carefully placed in a drawer of the bureau. Relieved of his burden, Simon Carne stood up as straight and well-made a man as any in Her Majesty's dominions. The malformation, for which so many, including the Earl and Countess of Amberley, had often pitied him, was nothing but a hoax intended to produce an effect which would permit him additional facilities of disguise.

The hump discarded, and the grey wig fitted carefully to his head in such a manner that not even a pinch of his own curly locks could be seen beneath it, he adorned his cheeks with a pair of *crêpe*-hair whiskers, donned the flannel vest and the velvet coat previously mentioned, slipped his feet into the carpet slippers, placed a pair of smoked glasses upon his nose, and declared himself ready to proceed about his business. The man who would have known him for Simon Carne would have been as astute as, well, shall we say, as the private detective— Klimo himself.

"It's on the stroke of twelve," he said, as he gave a final glance at himself in the pier-glass above the dressing-table, and arranged his tie to his satisfaction. "Should anyone call, instruct Ram Gafur to tell them that I have gone out on business, and shall not be back until three o'clock."

"Very good, sir."

"Now undo the door and let me go in." Thus commanded, Belton went across to the large wardrobe which, as I have already said, covered the whole of one side of the room, and opened the middle door. Two or three garments were seen inside suspended on pegs, and these he removed, at the same time pushing towards the right the panel at the rear. When this was done a large aperture in the wall between the two houses was disclosed. Through this door Carne passed drawing it behind him.

In No. 1, Belverton Terrace, the house occupied by the detective, whose presence in the street Carne seemed to find so objectionable, the entrance thus constructed was covered by the peculiar kind of confessional box in which Klimo invariably sat to receive his clients, the rearmost panels of which opened in the same fashion as those in the wardrobe in the dressing-room. These being pulled aside, he had but to draw them to again after him, take his seat, ring the electric bell to inform his housekeeper that he was ready, and then welcome his clients as quickly as they cared to come.

Punctually at two o'clock the interviews ceased, and Klimo, having reaped an excellent harvest of fees, returned to Porchester House to become Simon Carne once more.

Possibly it was due to the fact that the Earl and Countess of Amberley were brimming over with his praise, it may have been the rumour that he was worth as many millions as you have fingers upon your hand that did it; one thing, however, was self evident, within twenty-four hours of the noble Earl's meeting him at Victoria Station, Simon Carne was the talk, not only of fashionable, but also of unfashionable, London.

That his household were, with one exception, natives of India, that he had paid a rental for Porchester House which ran into five figures, that he was the greatest living authority upon China and Indian art generally, and that he had come over to England in search of a wife, were among the smallest of the *canards* set afloat concerning him.

During dinner next evening Carne put forth every effort to please. He was placed on the right hand of his hostess and next to the Duchess of Wiltshire. To the latter he paid particular attention, and to such good purpose that when the ladies returned to the drawing-room afterwards Her Grace was full of his praises. They had discussed china of all sorts, Carne had promised her a specimen which she had longed for all her life, but had never been able to obtain, and in return she had promised to show him the quaintly carved Indian casket in which the famous necklace, of which he had, of course, heard, spent most of its time. She would be wearing the jewels in question at her own ball in a week's time, she informed him, and if he would care to see the case when it came from her bankers on that day, she would be only too pleased to show it to him.

As Simon Carne drove home in his luxurious brougham afterwards, he smiled to himself as he thought of the success which was attending his first endeavour. Two of the guests, who were stewards of the

Jockey Club, had heard with delight his idea of purchasing a horse in order to have an interest in the Derby. While another, on hearing that he desired to become the possessor of a yacht, had offered to propose him for the R.C.Y.C. To crown it all, however, and much better than all, the Duchess of Wiltshire had promised to show him her famous diamonds.

"By this time next week," he said to himself, "Liz's interest should be considerably closer. But satisfactory as my progress has been hitherto it is difficult to see how I am to get possession of the stones. From what I have been able to discover they are only brought from the bank on the day the Duchess intends to wear them, and they are taken back by His Grace the morning following.

"While she has got them on her person it would be manifestly impossible to get them from her. And as, when she takes them off, they are returned to their box and placed in a safe, constructed in the wall of the bedroom adjoining, and which for the occasion is occupied by the butler and one of the under footmen, the only key being in the possession of the Duke himself, it would be equally foolish to hope to appropriate them. In what manner therefore I am to become their possessor passes my comprehension. However, one thing is certain, obtained they must be, and the attempt must be made on the night of the ball if possible. In the meantime I'll set my wits to work upon a plan."

Next day Simon Carne was the recipient of an invitation to the ball in question, and two days later he called upon the Duchess of Wiltshire at her residence in Belgrave Square with a plan prepared. He also took with him the small vase he had promised her four nights before. She received him most graciously, and their talk fell at once into the usual channel. Having examined her collection and charmed her by means of one or two judicious criticisms, he asked permission to include photographs of certain of her treasures in his forthcoming book, then little by little he skilfully guided the conversation on to the subject of jewels.

"Since we are discussing gems, Mr. Carne," she said, "perhaps it would interest you to see my famous necklace. By good fortune I have it in the house now, for the reason that an alteration is being made to one of the clasps by my jewellers."

"I should like to see it immensely," answered Carne. "At one time and another I have had the good fortune to examine the jewels of the

leading Indian Princes, and I should like to be able to say that I had
seen the famous Wiltshire necklace."

"Then you shall certainly have that honour," she answered with a
smile. "If you will ring that bell I will send for it."

Carne rang the bell as requested, and when the butler entered he was
given the key of the safe and ordered to bring the case to the
drawing-room.

"We must not keep it very long," she observed while the man was
absent. "It is to be returned to the bank in an hour's time."

"I am indeed fortunate," Carne replied, and turned to the description of some curious Indian wood carving, of which he was making a
special feature in his book. As he explained, he had collected his illustrations from the doors of Indian temples, from the gateways of palaces,
from old brass work, and even from carved chairs and boxes he had
picked up in all sorts of odd corners. Her Grace was most interested.

"How strange that you should have mentioned it," she said. "If
carved boxes have any interest for you, it is possible my jewel case itself
may be of use to you. As I think I told you during Lady Amberley's
dinner, it came from Benares, and has carved upon it the portraits of
nearly every god in the Hindu Pantheon."

"You raise my curiosity to fever heat," said Carne.

A few moments later the servant returned, bringing with him a
wooden box, about sixteen inches long, by twelve wide, and eight
deep, which he placed upon a table beside his mistress, after which he
retired.

"This is the case to which I have just been referring," said the Duchess, placing her hand on the article in question. "If you glance at it you
will see how exquisitely it is carved."

Concealing his eagerness with an effort, Simon Carne drew his chair
up to the table, and examined the box.

It was with justice she had described it as a work of art. What the
wood was of which it was constructed Carne was unable to tell. It was
dark and heavy, and, though it was not teak, closely resembled it. It
was literally covered with quaint carving, and of its kind was a unique
work of art.

"It is most curious and beautiful," said Carne when he had finished
his examination. "In all my experience I can safely say I have never seen

its equal. If you will permit me I should very much like to include a description and an illustration of it in my book."

"Of course you may do so; I shall be only too delighted," answered Her Grace. "If it will help you in your work I shall be glad to lend it to you for a few hours in order that you may have the illustration made."

This was exactly what Carne had been waiting for, and he accepted the offer with alacrity.

"Very well, then," she said. "On the day of my ball, when it will be brought from the bank again, I will take the necklace out and send the case to you. I must make one proviso however, and that is that you let me have it back the same day."

"I will certainly promise to do that," replied Carne.

"And now let us look inside," said his hostess.

Choosing a key from a bunch she carried in her pocket, she unlocked the casket, and lifted the lid. Accustomed as Carne had all his life been to the sight of gems, what he saw before him then almost took his breath away. The inside of the box, both sides and bottom, was quilted with the softest Russia leather, and on this luxurious couch reposed the famous necklace. The fire of the stones when the light caught them was sufficient to dazzle the eyes, so fierce was it.

As Carne could see, every gem was perfect of its kind, and there were no fewer than three hundred of them. The setting was a fine example of the jeweller's art, and last, but not least, the value of the whole affair was fifty thousand pounds, a mere fleabite to the man who had given it to his wife, but a fortune to any humbler person.

"And now that you have seen my property, what do you think of it?" asked the Duchess as she watched her visitor's face.

"It is very beautiful," he answered, "and I do not wonder that you are proud of it. Yes, the diamonds are very fine, but I think it is their abiding place that fascinates me more. Have you any objection to my measuring it?"

"Pray do so, if it is likely to be of any assistance to you," replied Her Grace.

Carne thereupon produced a small ivory rule, ran it over the box, and the figures he thus obtained he jotted down in his pocket book.

Ten minutes later, when the case had been returned to the safe, he thanked the Duchess for her kindness and took his departure, promising to call in person for the empty case on the morning of the ball.

Reaching home he passed into his study, and, seating himself at his writing table, pulled a sheet of note paper towards him and began to sketch, as well as he could remember it, the box he had seen. Then he leant back in his chair and closed his eyes.

"I have cracked a good many hard nuts in my time," he said reflectively, "but never one that seemed so difficult at first sight as this. As far as I see at present, the case stands as follows: the box will be brought from the bank where it usually reposes to Wiltshire House on the morning of the dance. I shall be allowed to have possession of it, without the stones of course, for a period possibly extending from eleven o'clock in the morning to four or five, at any rate not later than seven, in the evening. After the ball the necklace will be returned to it, when it will be locked up in the safe, over which the butler and a footman will mount guard.

"To get into the room during the night is not only too risky, but physically out of the question; while to rob Her Grace of her treasure during the progress of the dance would be equally impossible. The Duke fetches the casket and takes it back to the bank himself, so that to all intents and purposes I am almost as far off the solution as ever."

Half-an-hour went by and found him still seated at his desk, staring at the drawing on the paper, then an hour. The traffic of the streets rolled past the house unheeded. Finally Jowur Singh announced his carriage, and, feeling that an idea might come to him with a change of scene, he set off for a drive in the park.

By this time his elegant mail phaeton, with its magnificent horses and Indian servant on the seat behind, was as well-known as Her Majesty's state equipage, and attracted almost as much attention. To-day, however, the fashionable world noticed that Simon Carne looked preoccupied. He was still working out his problem, but so far without much success. Suddenly something, no one will ever be able to say what, put an idea into his head. The notion was no sooner born in his brain than he left the park and drove quickly home. Ten minutes had scarcely elapsed before he was back in his study again, and had ordered that Wajib Baksh should be sent to him.

When the man he wanted put in an appearance, Carne handed him the paper upon which he had made the drawing of the jewel case.

"Look at that," he said, "and tell me what thou seest there."

"I see a box," answered the man, who by this time was well accustomed to his master's ways.

"As thou say'st, it is a box," said Carne. "The wood is heavy and thick though what wood it is I do not know. The measurements are upon the paper below. Within, both the sides and bottom are quilted with soft leather as I have also shown. Think now, Wajib Baksh, for in this case thou wilt need to have all thy wits about thee. Tell me is it in thy power, oh most cunning of all craftsmen, to insert such extra sides within this box that they, being held by a spring, shall lie so snug as not to be noticeable to the ordinary eye? Can it be so arranged that, when the box is locked, they shall fall flat upon the bottom thus covering and holding fast what lies beneath them, and yet making the box appear to the eye as if it were empty. Is it possible for thee to do such a thing?"

Wajib Baksh did not reply for a few moments. His instinct told him what his master wanted, and he was not disposed to answer hastily, for he also saw that his reputation as the most cunning craftsman in India was at stake.

"If the Heaven-born will permit me the night for thought," he said at last, "I will come to him when he rises from his bed and tell him what I can do, and he can then give his orders as it pleases him."

"Very good," said Carne. "Then tomorrow morning I shall expect thy report. Let the work be good and there will be many rupees for thee to touch in return. As to the lock and the way it shall act, let that be the concern of Hiram Singh."

Wajib Baksh salaamed and withdrew, and Simon Carne for the time being dismissed the matter from his mind.

Next morning, while he was dressing, Belton reported that the two artificers desired an interview with him. He ordered them to be admitted, and forthwith they entered the room. It was noticeable that Wajib Baksh carried in his hand a heavy box, which, upon Carne's motioning him to do so, he placed upon the table.

"Have ye thought over the matter?" he asked, seeing that the men waited for him to speak.

"We have thought of it," replied Hiram Singh, who always acted as spokesman for the pair. "If the Presence will deign to look he will see that we have made a box of the size and shape such as he drew upon the paper."

"Yes, it is certainly a good copy," said Carne condescendingly, after he had examined it.

Wajib Baksh showed his white teeth in appreciation of the compliment, and Hiram Singh drew closer to the table.

"And now, if the Sahib will open it, he will in his wisdom be able to tell if it resembles the other that he has in his mind."

Carne opened the box as requested, and discovered that the interior was an exact counterfeit of the Duchess of Wiltshire's jewel case, even to the extent of the quilted leather lining which had been the other's principal feature. He admitted that the likeness was all that could be desired.

"As he is satisfied," said Hiram Singh, "it may be that the Protector of the Poor will deign to try an experiment with it. See, here is a comb. Let it be placed in the box, so—now he will see what he will see."

The broad, silver-backed comb, lying upon his dressing-table, was placed on the bottom of the box, the lid was closed, and the key turned in the lock. The case being securely fastened, Hiram Singh laid it before his master.

"I am to open it, I suppose?" said Carne, taking the key and replacing it in the lock.

"If my master pleases," replied the other.

Carne accordingly turned it in the lock, and, having done so, raised the lid and looked inside. His astonishment was complete. To all intents and purposes the box was empty. The comb was not to be seen, and yet the quilted sides and bottom were, to all appearances, just the same as when he had first looked inside.

"This is most wonderful," he said. And indeed it was as clever a conjuring trick as any he had ever seen.

"Nay, it is very simple," Wajib Baksh replied. "The Heaven-born told me that there must be no risk of detection."

He took the box in his own hands and, running his nails down the centre of the quilting, dividing the false bottom into two pieces; these he lifted out, revealing the comb lying upon the real bottom beneath.

"The sides, as my lord will see," said Hiram Singh, taking a step forward, "are held in their appointed places by these two springs. Thus, when the key is turned the springs relax, and the sides are driven by others into their places on the bottom, where the seams in the quilting

mask the join. There is but one disadvantage. It is as follows: When the
pieces which form the bottom are lifted out in order that my lord may
get at whatever lies concealed beneath, the springs must of necessity
stand revealed. However, to anyone who knows sufficient of the working of the box to lift out the false bottom, it will be an easy matter to
withdraw the springs and conceal them about his person."

"As you say that is an easy matter," said Carne, "and I shall not be
likely to forget. Now one other question. Presuming I am in a position
to put the real box into your hands for say eight hours, do you think that
in that time you can fit it up so that detection will be impossible?"

"Assuredly, my lord," replied Hiram Singh with conviction. "There
is but the lock and the fitting of the springs to be done. Three hours at
most would suffice for that."

"I am pleased with you," said Carne. "As a proof of my satisfaction,
when the work is finished you will each receive five hundred rupees.
Now you can go."

According to his promise, ten o'clock on the Friday following found
him in his hansom driving towards Belgrave Square. He was a little
anxious, though the casual observer would scarcely have been able to
tell it. The magnitude of the stake for which he was playing was
enough to try the nerve of even such a past master in his profession as
Simon Carne.

Arriving at the house he discovered some workmen erecting an
awning across the foot-way in preparation for the ball that was to take
place at night. It was not long, however, before he found himself in the
boudoir, reminding Her Grace of her promise to permit him an opportunity of making a drawing of the famous jewel case. The Duchess was
naturally busy, and within a quarter of an hour he was on his way home
with the box placed on the seat of the carriage beside him.

"Now," he said, as he patted it good-humouredly, "if only the notion
worked out by Hiram Singh and Wajib Baksh holds good, the famous
Wiltshire diamonds will become my property before very many hours
are passed. By this time to-morrow, I suppose London will be all agog
concerning the burglary."

On reaching his house he left his carriage and himself carried the box
into his study. Once there he rang his bell and ordered Hiram Singh

and Wajib Baksh to be sent to him. When they arrived he showed them the box upon which they were to exercise their ingenuity.

"Bring your tools in here," he said, "and do the work under my own eyes. You have but nine hours before you, so you must make the most of them."

The men went for their implements, and as soon as they were ready set to work. All through the day they were kept hard at it, with the result that by five o'clock the alterations had been effected and the case stood ready. By the time Carne returned from his afternoon drive in the Park it was quite prepared for the part it was to play in his scheme. Having praised the men, he turned them out and locked the door, then went across the room and unlocked a drawer in his writing table. From it he took a flat leather jewel case which he opened. It contained a necklace of counterfeit diamonds, if anything a little larger than the one he intended to try to obtain. He had purchased it that morning in the Burlington Arcade for the purpose of testing the apparatus his servants had made, and this he now proceeded to do.

Laying it carefully upon the bottom he closed the lid and turned the key. When he opened it again the necklace was gone, and even though he knew the secret he could not for the life of him see where the false bottom began and ended. After that he reset the trap and tossed the necklace carelessly in. To his delight it acted as well as on the previous occasion. He could scarcely contain his satisfaction. His conscience was sufficiently elastic to give him no trouble. To him it was scarcely a robbery he was planning, but an artistic trial of skill, in which he pitted his wits and cunning against the forces of society in general.

At half-past seven he dined and afterwards smoked a meditative cigar over the evening paper in the billiard room. The invitations to the ball were for ten o'clock, and at nine-thirty he went to his dressing-room.

"Make me tidy as quickly as you can," he said to Belton when the latter appeared, "and while you are doing so listen to my final instructions.

"To-night, as you know, I am endeavouring to secure the Duchess of Wiltshire's necklace. Tomorrow morning all London will resound with the hubbub, and I have been making my plans in such a way as to arrange that Klimo shall be the first person consulted. When the messenger calls, if call he does, see that the old woman

next door bids him tell the Duke to come personally at twelve
o'clock. Do you understand?"

"Perfectly, sir."

"Very good. Now give me the jewel case, and let me be on. You
need not sit up for me."

Precisely as the clocks in the neighbourhood were striking ten
Simon Carne reached Belgrave Square, and, as he hoped, found himself
the first guest.

His hostess and her husband received him in the ante-room of the
drawing-room.

"I come laden with a thousand apologies," he said as he took Her
Grace's hand, and bent over it with that ceremonious politeness which
was one of the man's chief characteristics. "I am most unconscionably
early, I know, but I hastened here in order that I might personally
return the jewel case you so kindly lent me. I must trust to your gen-
erosity to forgive me. The drawings took longer than I expected."

"Please do not apologise," answered Her Grace. "It is very kind of
you to have brought the case yourself. I hope the illustrations have
proved successful. I shall look forward to seeing them as soon as they
are ready. But I am keeping you holding the box. One of my servants
will take it to my room."

She called a footman to her and bade him take the box and place it
upon her dressing-table.

"Before it goes I must let you see that I have not damaged it either
externally or internally," said Carne with a laugh. "It is such a valuable
case that I should never forgive myself if it had even received a scratch
during the time it has been in my possession."

So saying he lifted the lid and allowed her to look inside. To all
appearance it was exactly the same as when she had lent it to him earlier
in the day.

"You have been most careful," she said. And then, with an air of
banter, she continued: "If you desire it I shall be pleased to give you a
certificate to that effect."

They jested in this fashion for a few moments after the servant's
departure, during which time Carne promised to call upon her the following morning at eleven o'clock, and to bring with him the illustrations he had made and a queer little piece of china he had had the good

fortune to pick up in a dealer's shop the previous afternoon. By this time fashionable London was making its way up the grand staircase, and with its appearance further conversation became impossible.

Shortly after midnight Carne bade his hostess good night and slipped away. He was perfectly satisfied with his evening's entertainment, and if the key of the jewel case were not turned before the jewels were placed in it, he was convinced they would become his property. It speaks well for his strength of nerve when I record the fact that on going to bed his slumbers were as peaceful and untroubled as those of a little child.

Breakfast was scarcely over next morning before a hansom drew up at his front door and Lord Amberley alighted. He was ushered into Carne's presence forthwith, and on seeing that the latter was surprised at his early visit, hastened to explain.

"My dear fellow," he said as he took possession of the chair the other offered him, "I have come round to see you on most important business. As I told you last night at the dance, when you so kindly asked me to come and see the steam yacht you have purchased, I had an appointment with Wiltshire at half-past nine this morning. On reaching Belgrave Square, I found the whole house in confusion. Servants were running hither and thither with scared faces, the butler was on the borders of lunacy, the Duchess was well-nigh hysterical in her boudoir, while her husband was in his study vowing vengeance against all the world."

"You alarm me," said Carne, lighting a cigarette with a hand that was as steady as a rock. "What on earth has happened?"

"I think I might safely allow you fifty guesses and then wager a hundred pounds you'd not hit the mark; and yet in a certain measure it concerns you."

"Concerns me? Good gracious. What have I done to bring all this about?"

"Pray do not look so alarmed," said Amberley. "Personally you have done nothing. Indeed, on second thoughts, I don't know that I am right in saying that it concerns you at all. The fact of the matter is, Carne, a burglary took place last night at Wiltshire House, *and the famous necklace has disappeared.*"

"Good Heavens! You don't say so?"

"But I do. The circumstances of the case are as follows: When my cousin retired to her room last night after the ball, she unclasped the necklace, and, in her husband's presence, placed it carefully in her jewel case, which she locked. That having been done, Wiltshire took the box to the room which contained the safe, and himself placed it there, locking the iron door with his own key. The room was occupied that night, according to custom, by the butler and one of the footmen, both of whom have been in the family since they were boys.

"Next morning, after breakfast, the Duke unlocked the safe and took out the box, intending to convey it to the Bank as usual. Before leaving, however, he placed it on his study-table and went upstairs to speak to his wife. He cannot remember exactly how long he was absent, but he feels convinced that he was not gone more than a quarter of an hour at the very utmost.

"Their conversation finished, she accompanied him downstairs, where she saw him take up the case to carry it to his carriage. Before he left the house, however, she said: 'I suppose you have looked to see that the necklace is all right?' 'How could I do so?' was his reply. 'You know you possess the only key that will fit it.'

"She felt in her pockets, but to her surprise the key was not there."

"If I were a detective I should say that that is a point to be remembered," said Carne with a smile. "Pray, where did she find her keys?"

"Upon her dressing-table," said Amberley. "Though she has not the slightest recollection of leaving them there."

"Well, when she had procured the keys, what happened?"

"Why, they opened the box, and to their astonishment and dismay, *found it empty. The jewels were gone!*"

"Good gracious. What a terrible loss! It seems almost impossible that it can be true. And pray, what did they do?"

"At first they stood staring into the empty box, hardly believing the evidence of their own eyes. Stare how they would, however, they could not bring them back. The jewels had without doubt disappeared, but when and where the robbery had taken place it was impossible to say. After that they had up all the servants and questioned them, but the result was what they might have foreseen, no one from the butler to the kitchen-maid could throw any light upon the subject. To this minute it remains as great a mystery as when they first discovered it."

"I am more concerned than I can tell you," said Carne. "How thankful I ought to be that I returned the case to Her Grace last night. But in thinking of myself I am forgetting to ask what has brought you to me. If I can be of any assistance I hope you will command me."

"Well, I'll tell you why I have come," replied Lord Amberley. "Naturally they are most anxious to have the mystery solved and the jewels recovered as soon as possible. Wiltshire wanted to send to Scotland Yard there and then, but his wife and I eventually persuaded him to consult Klimo. As you know, if the police authorities are called in first he refuses the business altogether. Now, we thought, as you are his next door neighbour, you might possibly be able to assist us."

"You may be very sure, my lord, I will do everything that lies in my power. Let us go in and see him at once."

As he spoke he rose and threw what remained of his cigarette into the fireplace. His visitor having imitated his example, they procured their hats and walked round from Park Lane into Belverton Street to bring up at No. 1. After they had rung the bell the door was opened to them by the old woman who invariably received the detective's clients.

"Is Mr. Klimo at home?" asked Carne. "And, if so, can we see him?"

The old lady was a little deaf, and the question had to be repeated before she could be made to understand what was wanted. As soon, however, as she realised their desire she informed them that her master was absent from town, but would be back as usual at twelve o'clock to meet his clients.

"What on earth's to be done?" said the Earl, looking at his companion in dismay. "I am afraid I can't come back again, as I have a most important appointment at that hour."

"Do you think you could intrust the business to me?" asked Carne. "If so, I will make a point of seeing him at twelve o'clock, and could call at Wiltshire House afterwards and tell the Duke what I have done."

"That's very good of you," replied Amberley. "If you are sure it would not put you to too much trouble, that would be quite the best thing to be done."

"I will do it with pleasure," Carne replied. "I feel it my duty to help in whatever way I can."

"You are very kind," said the other. "Then, as I understand it, you are to call upon Klimo at twelve o'clock, and afterwards to let my cousins know what you have succeeded in doing. I only hope he will help us to secure the thief. We are having too many of these burglaries just now. I must catch this hansom and be off. Goodbye, and many thanks."

"Goodbye," said Carne, and shook him by the hand.

The hansom having rolled away, Carne retraced his steps to his own abode.

"It is really very strange," he muttered as he walked along, "how often chance condescends to lend her assistance to my little schemes. The mere fact that His Grace left the box unwatched in his study for a quarter of an hour may serve to throw the police off on quite another scent. I am also glad that they decided to open the case in the house, for if it had gone to the bankers' and had been placed in the strong room unexamined, I should never have been able to get possession of the jewels at all."

Three hours later he drove to Wiltshire House and saw the Duke. The Duchess was far too much upset by the catastrophe to see anyone.

"This is really most kind of you, Mr. Carne," said His Grace when the other had supplied an elaborate account of his interview with Klimo. "We are extremely indebted to you. I am sorry he cannot come before ten o'clock to-night, and that he makes this stipulation of my seeing him alone, for I must confess I should like to have had someone else present to ask any questions that might escape me. But if that's his usual hour and custom, well, we must abide by it, that's all. I hope he will do some good, for this is the greatest calamity that has ever befallen me. As I told you just now, it has made my wife quite ill. She is confined to her bedroom and quite hysterical."

"You do not suspect anyone, I suppose," inquired Carne.

"Not a soul," the other answered. "The thing is such a mystery that we do not know what to think. I feel convinced, however, that my servants are as innocent as I am. Nothing will ever make me think them otherwise. I wish I could catch the fellow, that's all. I'd make him suffer for the trick he's played me."

Carne offered an appropriate reply, and after a little further conversation upon the subject, bade the irate nobleman goodbye and left the house. From Belgrave Square he drove to one of the clubs of which he had been elected a member, in search of Lord Orpington, with whom he had promised to lunch, and afterwards took him to a ship-builder's yard near Greenwich in order to show him the steam yacht he had lately purchased.

It was close upon dinner time before he returned to his own residence. He brought Lord Orpington with him, and they dined in state together. At nine the latter bade him good-bye, and at ten Carne retired to his dressing-room and rang for Belton.

"What have you to report," he asked, "with regard to what I bade you do in Belgrave Square?"

"I followed your instructions to the letter," Belton replied. "Yesterday morning I wrote to Messrs. Horniblow and Jimson, the house agents in Piccadilly, in the name of Colonel Braithwaite, and asked for an order to view the residence to the right of Wiltshire House. I asked that the order might be sent direct to the house, where the Colonel would get it upon his arrival. This letter I posted myself in Basingstoke, as you desired me to do.

"At nine o'clock yesterday morning I dressed myself as much like an elderly army officer as possible, and took a cab to Belgrave Square. The caretaker, an old fellow of close upon seventy years of age, admitted me immediately upon hearing my name, and proposed that he should show me over the house. This, however, I told him was quite unnecessary, backing my speech with a present of half-a-crown, whereupon he returned to his breakfast perfectly satisfied, while I wandered about the house at my own leisure.

"Reaching the same floor as that upon which is situated the room in which the Duke's safe is kept, I discovered that your supposition was quite correct, and that it would be possible for a man, by opening the window, to make his way along the coping from one house to the other, without being seen. I made certain that there was no one in the bedroom in which the butler slept, and then arranged the long telescope walking stick you gave me, and fixed one of my boots to it by means of the screw in the end. With this I was able to make a regular succession of footsteps in the dust along the ledge, between one window and the other.

"That done, I went downstairs again, bade the caretaker good morning, and got into my cab. From Belgrave Square I drove to the shop of the pawnbroker whom you told me you had discovered was out of town. His assistant inquired my business and was anxious to do what he could for me. I told him, however, that I must see his master personally as it was about the sale of some diamonds I had had left me. I pretended to be annoyed that he was not at home, and muttered to myself, so that the man could hear, something about its meaning a journey to Amsterdam.

"Then I limped out of the shop, paid off my cab, and, walking down a bystreet, removed my moustache, and altered my appearance by taking off my great coat and muffler. A few streets further on I purchased a bowler hat in place of the old-fashioned topper I had hitherto been wearing, and then took a cab from Piccadilly and came home."

"You have fulfilled my instructions admirably," said Carne. "And if the business comes off, as I expect it will, you shall receive your usual percentage. Now I must be turned into Klimo and be off to Belgrave Square to put His Grace of Wiltshire upon the track of this burglar."

Before he retired to rest that night Simon Carne took something, wrapped in a red silk handkerchief, from the capacious pocket of the coat Klimo had been wearing a few moments before. Having unrolled the covering, he held up to the light the magnificent necklace which for so many years had been the joy and pride of the ducal house of Wiltshire. The electric light played upon it, and touched it with a thousand different hues.

"Where so many have failed," he said to himself, as he wrapped it in the handkerchief again and locked it in his safe, "it is pleasant to be able to congratulate oneself on having succeeded. It is without its equal, and I don't think I shall be overstepping the mark if I say that I think when she receives it Liz will be glad she lent me the money."

Next morning all London was astonished by the news that the famous Wiltshire diamonds had been stolen, and a few hours later Carne learnt from an evening paper that the detectives who had taken up the case, upon the supposed retirement from it of Klimo, were still completely at fault.

That evening he was to entertain several friends to dinner. They included Lord Amberley, Lord Orpington, and a prominent member of the Privy Council. Lord Amberley arrived late, but filled to overflowing with importance. His friends noticed his state, and questioned him.

"Well, gentlemen," he answered, as he took up a commanding position upon the drawing-room hearth-rug, "I am in a position to inform you that Klimo has reported upon the case, and the upshot of it is that the Wiltshire Diamond Mystery is a mystery no longer."

"What do you mean?" asked the others in a chorus.

"I mean that he sent in his report to Wiltshire this afternoon, as arranged. From what he said the other night, after being alone in the room with the empty jewel case and a magnifying glass for two minutes or so, he was in a position to describe the *modus operandi,* and what is more to put the police on the scent of the burglar."

"And how was it worked?" asked Carne.

"From the empty house next door," replied the other. "On the morning of the burglary a man, purporting to be a retired army officer, called with an order to view, got the caretaker out of the way, clambered along to Wiltshire House by means of the parapet outside, reached the room during the time the servants were at breakfast, opened the safe, and abstracted the jewels."

"But how did Klimo find all this out?" asked Lord Orpington.

"By his own inimitable cleverness," replied Lord Amberley. "At any rate it has been proved that he was correct. The man did make his way from next door, and the police have since discovered that an individual, answering to the description given, visited a pawnbroker's shop in the city about an hour later and stated that he had diamonds to sell."

"If that is so it turns out to be a very simple mystery after all," said Lord Orpington as they began their meal.

"Thanks to the ingenuity of the cleverest detective in the world," remarked Amberley.

"In that case here's a good health to Klimo," said the Privy Councillor, raising his glass.

"I will join you in that," said Simon Carne. "Here's a very good health to Klimo and his connection with the Duchess of Wiltshire's diamonds. May he always be equally successful!"

"Hear, hear to that," replied his guests.

The Green-Stone God and the Stockbroker

Fergus Hume

AS a rule, the average detective gets twice the credit he deserves. I am not talking of the novelist's miracle-monger, but of the flesh and blood reality who is liable to err, and who frequently proves such liability. You can take it as certain that a detective who sets down a clean run and no hitch as entirely due to his astucity, is young in years, and still younger in experience. Older men, who have been bamboozled a hundred times by the craft of criminality, recognize the influence of Chance to make or mar. There you have it! Nine times out of ten, Chance does more in clinching a case than all the dexterity and mother-wit of the man in charge. The exception must be engineered by an infallible apostle. Such a one is unknown to me—out of print.

This opinion, based rather on collective experience than on any one episode, can be substantiated by several incontrovertible facts. In this instance, one will suffice. Therefore, I take the Brixton case to illustrate Chance as a factor in human affairs. Had it not been for that Maori fetish—but such rather ends than begins the story, therefore it were wise to dismiss it for the moment. Yet that piece of green-stone hanged—a person mentioned hereafter.

When Mr. and Mrs. Paul Vincent set up housekeeping at Ulster Lodge they were regarded as decided acquisitions to Brixton society. She, pretty and musical; he, smart in looks, moderately well off, and an excellent tennis-player. Their progenitors, his father and her mother (both since deceased), had lived a life of undoubted middle-class respectability. The halo thereof still environed their children, who were, in consequence of such inherited grace and their own individualisms, much sought after by genteel Brixtonians. Moreover, this popular couple were devoted to each other, and even after three years of marriage they posed still as lovers. This was as it should be, and by admiring friends and relations the Vincents were regarded as paragons of matrimonial perfection. Vincent was a stockbroker; therefore he passed most of his time in the City.

Judge, then, of the commotion, when pretty Mrs. Vincent was discovered in the study, stabbed to the heart. So aimless a crime were scarce imaginable. She had many friends, no known enemies, yet she came to this tragic end. Closer examination revealed that the escritoire had been broken into, and Mr. Vincent declared himself the poorer by two hundred pounds. Primarily, therefore, robbery was the sole object, but, by reason of Mrs. Vincent's interference, the thief had been converted into a murderer.

So excellently had the assassin chosen his time, that such choice argued a close acquaintance with the domestic economy of Ulster Lodge. The husband was detained in town till midnight; the servants (cook and housemaid), on leave to attend wedding festivities, were absent till eleven o'clock. Mrs. Vincent therefore was absolutely alone in the house for six hours, during which period the crime had been committed. The servants discovered the body of their unfortunate mistress, and raised the alarm at once. Later on Vincent arrived, to find his wife dead, his house in possession of the police, and the two servants in hysterics. For that night nothing could be done, but at dawn a move was made towards elucidating the mystery. At this point I come into the story.

Instructed at nine o'clock to take charge of the case, by ten I was on the spot noting details and collecting evidence. Beyond removal of the body nothing had been disturbed, and the study was in precisely the same condition as when the crime was discovered. I examined carefully the apartment, and afterwards interrogated the cook, the housemaid, and, lastly, the master of the house. The result gave me slight hope of securing the assassin.

The room (a fair-sized one, looking out on to a lawn between house and road) was furnished in cheap bachelor fashion. An old-fashioned desk placed at right angles to the window, a round table reaching nigh the sill, two armchairs, three of the ordinary cane-seated kind, and on the mantelpiece an arrangement of pipes, pistols, boxing-gloves, and foils. One of these latter was missing.

A single glimpse showed how terrible a struggle had taken place before the murderer had overpowered his victim. The tablecloth lay disorderly on the floor, two of the lighter chairs were overturned, and the desk, with several drawers open, was hacked about considerably. No key was in the door-lock which faced the escritoire, and the window-snick was fastened securely.

Further search resulted in the following discoveries:—

1. A hatchet used for chopping wood (found near the desk).
2. A foil with the button broken off (lying under the table).
3. A green-stone idol (edged under the fender).

The cook (defiantly courageous by reason of brandy) declared that she had left the house at four o'clock on the previous day, and had returned close on eleven. The back door (to her surprise) was open. With the housemaid she went to inform her mistress of this fact, and found the body lying midway between door and fireplace. At once she called in the police. Her master and mistress were a most attached couple, and (so far as she knew) they had no enemies.

Similar evidence was obtained from the housemaid, with the additional information that the hatchet belonged to the wood-shed. The other rooms were undisturbed.

Poor young Vincent was so broken down by the tragedy that he could hardly answer my questions with calmness. Sympathizing with his natural grief, I interrogated him as delicately as was possible, and I am bound to admit that he replied with remarkable promptitude and clearness.

"What do you know of this unhappy affair?" I asked, when we were alone in the drawing-room. He refused to stay in the study, as was surely natural under the circumstances.

"Absolutely nothing," he replied. "I went to the City yesterday at ten in the morning, and, as I had business to do, I wired my wife I would not return till midnight. She was full of health and spirits when I last saw her, but now——" Incapable of further speech he made a gesture of despair. Then, after a pause, he added, "Have you any theory on the subject?"

"Judging from the wrecked condition of the desk I should say robbery——"

"Robbery?" he interrupted, changing colour. "Yes, that was the motive. I had two hundred pounds locked up in the desk."

"In gold or notes?"

"The latter. Four fifties. Bank of England."

"You are sure they are missing?"

"Yes. The drawer in which they were placed is smashed to pieces."

"Did any one know you had placed two hundred pounds therein?"

"No! Save my wife, and yet—ah!" he said, breaking off abruptly, "that is impossible."

"What is impossible?"

"I will tell you when I hear your theory."

"You got that notion out of novels of the shilling sort," I answered dryly; "every detective doesn't theorize on the instant. I haven't any particular theory that I know of. Whosoever committed this crime must have known your wife was alone in the house, and that there was two hundred pounds locked up in that desk. Did you mention these two facts to any one?"

Vincent pulled his moustache in some embarrassment. I guessed by the action that he had been indiscreet.

"I don't wish to get an innocent person into trouble," he said at length, "but I did mention it—to a man called Roy."

"For what reason?"

"It is a bit of a story. I lost two hundred to a friend at cards, and drew four fifties to pay him. He went out of town, so I locked up the money in my desk for safety. Last night Roy came to me at the club, much agitated, and asked me to loan him a hundred. Said it meant ruin else. I offered him a cheque, but he wanted cash. I then told him I had left two hundred at home, so, at the moment, I could not lay my hand on it. He asked if he could not go to Brixton for it, but I said the house was empty, and——"

"But it wasn't empty," I interrupted.

"I believed it would be! I knew the servants were going to that wedding, and I thought my wife, instead of spending a lonely evening, would call on some friend."

"Well, and after you told Roy that the house was empty?"

"He went away, looking awfully cut up, and swore he must have the money at any price. But it is quite impossible he could have anything to do with this."

"I don't know. You told him where the money was, and that the house was unprotected, as you thought. What was more probable than that he should have come down with the intention of stealing the money? If so, what follows? Entering by the back door, he takes the hatchet from the wood-shed to open the desk. Your wife, hearing a noise, discovers him in the study. In a state of frenzy, he snatches a foil from the mantelpiece and kills her, then decamps with the money. There is your theory, and a mighty bad one—for Roy."

"You don't intend to arrest him?" asked Vincent quickly.

"Not on insufficient evidence! If he committed the crime and stole the money it is certain that, sooner or later, he will change the notes. Now, if I had the numbers——"

"Here are the numbers," said Vincent, producing his pocket-book. "I always take the numbers of such large notes. But surely," he added, as I copied them down—"surely you don't think Roy guilty?"

"I don't know. I should like to know his movements on that night."

"I cannot tell you. He saw me at the Chestnut Club about seven o'clock, and left immediately afterwards. I kept my business appointment, went to the Alhambra, and then returned home."

"Give me Roy's address, and describe his personal appearance."

"He is a medical student, and lodges at No.—, Gower Street. Tall, fair-haired—a good-looking young fellow."

"And his dress last night?"

"He wore evening dress, concealed by a fawn-coloured overcoat."

I duly noted these particulars, and I was about to take my leave, when I recollected the green-stone idol. It was so strange an object to find in prosaic Brixton that I could not help thinking it must have come there by accident.

"By the way, Mr. Vincent," said I, producing the monstrosity, "is this green-stone god your property?"

"I never saw it before," replied he, taking it in his hand. "Is it—ah!" he added, dropping the idol, "there is blood on it!"

"'Tis the blood of your wife, sir! If it does not belong to you, it does to the murderer. From the position in which this was found I fancy it slipped out of his breast-pocket as he stood over his victim. As you see, it is stained with blood. He must have lost his presence of mind, else he would not have left behind so damning a piece of evidence. This idol, sir, will hang the assassin of Mrs. Vincent!"

"I hope so; but, unless you are sure of Roy, do not mar his life by accusing him of this crime."

"I certainly should not arrest him without sufficient proof," I answered promptly, and so took my departure.

Vincent showed up very well in this preliminary conversation. Much as he desired to punish the criminal, yet he was unwilling to subject Roy to possibly unfounded suspicions. Had I not forced the club episode out of him I doubt whether he would have told it. As it was, the information gave me the necessary clue. Roy alone knew that the notes were in the escritoire, and imagined (owing to the mistake of Vincent) that the house was empty. Determined to have the money at any price (his own words), he intended but robbery, till the unexpected appearance of Mrs. Vincent merged the lesser in the greater crime.

My first step was to advise the Bank that four fifty-pound notes, numbered so and so, were stolen, and that the thief or his deputy would probably change them within a reasonable period. I did not say a word about the crime, and kept all special details out of the newspapers; for as the murderer would probably read up the reports, so as to shape his course by the action of the police, I judged it wiser that he should know as little as possible. Those minute press notices do more harm than good. They gratify the morbid appetite of the public, and put the criminal on his guard. Thereby the police work in the dark, but he— thanks to the posting up of special reporters—knows the doings of the law, and baffles it accordingly.

The green-stone idol worried me considerably. I wanted to know how it had got into the study of Ulster Lodge. When I knew that, I could nail my man. But there was considerable difficulty to overcome before such knowledge was available. Now a curiosity of this kind is not a common object in this country. A man who owns one must have come from New Zealand, or have obtained it from a New Zealand friend. He could not have picked it up in London. If he did, he would not carry it constantly about with him. It was therefore my idea that the murderer had received the idol from a friend on the day of the crime. That friend, to possess such an idol, must have been in communication with New Zealand. The chain of thought is somewhat complicated, but it began with curiosity about the idol, and ended in my looking up the list of steamers going to the Antipodes. Then I carried out a little design which need not be mentioned at this moment. In due time it will fit in with the hanging of Mrs. Vincent's assassin. Meanwhile, I followed up the clue of the bank-notes, and left the green-stone idol to evolve its own destiny. Thus I had two strings to my bow.

The crime was committed on the twentieth of June, and on the twenty-third two fifty-pound notes, with numbers corresponding to those stolen, were paid into the Bank of England. I was astonished at the little care exercised by the criminal in concealing his crime, but still more so when I learned that the money had been banked by a very respectable solicitor. Furnished with the address, I called on this gentleman. Mr. Maudsley received me politely, and he had no hesitation in telling me how the notes had come into his possession. I did not state my primary reason for the inquiry.

"I hope there is no trouble about these notes," said he, when I explained my errand. "I have had sufficient already."

"Indeed, Mr. Maudsley, and in what way?"

For answer he touched the bell, and when it was answered, "Ask Mr. Ford to step this way," he said. Then, turning to me, "I must reveal what I had hoped to keep secret, but I trust the revelation will remain with yourself."

"That is as I may decide after hearing it. I am a detective, Mr. Maudsley, and, you may be sure, I do not make these inquiries out of idle curiosity."

Before he could reply, a slender, weak-looking young man, nervously excited, entered the room. This was Mr. Ford, and he looked from me to Maudsley with some apprehension.

"This gentleman," said his employer, not unkindly, "comes from Scotland Yard about the money you paid me two days ago."

"It is all right, I hope?" stammered Ford, turning red and pale and red again.

"Where did you get the money?" I asked, parrying this question.

"From my sister."

I started when I heard this answer, and with good reason. My inquiries about Roy had revealed that he was in love with a hospital nurse whose name was Clara Ford. Without doubt she had obtained the

notes from Roy, after he had stolen them from Ulster Lodge. But why
the necessity of the robbery?

"Why did you get a hundred pounds from your sister?" I asked
Ford.

He did not answer, but looked appealingly at Maudsley. That gentleman interposed.

"We must make a clean breast of it, Ford," he said, with a sigh;
"if you have committed a second crime to conceal the first, I cannot
help you. This time matters are not at my discretion."

"I have committed no crime," said Ford desperately, turning to me.
"Sir, I may as well admit that I embezzled one hundred pounds from
Mr. Maudsley to pay a gambling debt. He kindly and most generously
consented to overlook the delinquency if I replaced the money. Not
having it myself I asked my sister. She, a poor hospital nurse, had
not the amount. Yet, as non-payment meant ruin to me, she asked a
Mr. Julian Roy to help her. He at once agreed to do so, and gave her
two fifty-pound notes. She handed them to me, and I gave them to
Mr. Maudsley, who paid them into the bank."

This, then, was the reason of Roy's remark. He did not refer to his
own ruin, but to that of Ford. To save this unhappy man, and for love
of the sister, he had committed the crime. I did not need to see Clara
Ford, but at once made up my mind to arrest Roy. The case was perfectly clear, and I was fully justified in taking this course. Meanwhile I
made Maudsley and his clerk promise silence, as I did not wish Roy to
be put on his guard by Miss Ford, through her brother.

"Gentlemen," I said, after a few moments' pause, "I cannot at present explain my reasons for asking these questions, as it would take too
long, and I have no time to lose. Keep silent about this interview till
to-morrow, and by that time you shall know all."

"Has Ford got into fresh trouble?" asked Maudsley anxiously.

"No, but some one else has."

"My sister," began Ford faintly, when I interrupted him at once.

"Your sister is all right, Mr. Ford. Pray trust in my discretion; no
harm shall come to her or to you, if I can help it—but, above all, be
silent."

This they readily promised, and I returned to Scotland Yard, quite
satisfied that Roy would get no warning. The evidence was so clear that

I could not doubt the guilt of Roy. Else how had he come in possession of the notes? Already there was sufficient proof to hang him, yet I hoped to clinch the certainty by proving his ownership of the green-stone idol. It did not belong to Vincent, or to his dead wife, yet some one must have brought it into the study. Why not Roy, who, to all appearances, had committed the crime, the more so as the image was splashed with the victim's blood? There was no difficulty in obtaining a warrant, and with this I went off to Gower Street.

Roy loudly protested his innocence. He denied all knowledge of the crime and of the idol. I expected the denial, but I was astonished at the defence he put forth. It was very ingenious, but so manifestly absurd that it did not shake my belief in his guilt. I let him talk himself out—which perhaps was wrong—but he would not be silent, and then I took him off in a cab.

"I swear I did not commit the crime," he said passionately; "no one was more astonished than I at the news of Mrs. Vincent's death."

"Yet you were at Ulster Lodge on the night in question?"

"I admit it," he replied frankly; "were I guilty I would not do so. But I was there at the request of Vincent."

"I must remind you that all you say now will be used in evidence against you."

"I don't care! I must defend myself. I asked Vincent for a hundred pounds, and——"

"Of course you did, to give to Miss Ford."

"How do you know that?" he asked sharply.

"From her brother, through Maudsley. He paid the notes supplied by you into the bank. If you wanted to conceal your crime you should not have been so reckless."

"I have committed no crime," retorted Roy fiercely. "I obtained the money from Vincent, at the request of Miss Ford, to save her brother from being convicted for embezzlement."

"Vincent denies that he gave you the money!"

"Then he lies. I asked him at the Chestnut Club for one hundred pounds. He had not that much on him, but said that two hundred were in his desk at home. As it was imperative that I should have the money on the night, I asked him to let me go down for it."

"And he refused!"

"He did not. He consented, and gave me a note to Mrs. Vincent, instructing her to hand me over a hundred pounds. I went to Brixton, got the money in two fifties, and gave them to Miss Ford. When I left Ulster Lodge, between eight and nine, Mrs. Vincent was in perfect health, and quite happy."

"An ingenious defence," said I doubtfully, "but Vincent absolutely denies that he gave you the money."

Roy stared hard at me to see if I were joking. Evidently the attitude of Vincent puzzled him greatly.

"That is ridiculous," said he quietly; "he wrote a note to his wife instructing her to hand me the money."

"Where is that note?"

"I gave it to Mrs. Vincent."

"It cannot be found," I answered; "if such a note were in her possession it would now be in mine."

"Don't you believe me?"

"How can I against the evidence of those notes and the denial of Vincent?"

"But he surely does not deny that he gave me the money?"

"He does."

"He must be mad," said Roy, in dismay; "one of my best friends, and to tell so great a falsehood. Why, if——"

"You had better be silent," I said, weary of this foolish talk; "if what you say is true, Vincent will exonerate you from complicity in the crime. If things occurred as you say, there is no sense in his denial."

This latter remark was made to stop the torrent of his speech. It was not my business to listen to incriminating declarations, or to ingenious defences. All that sort of thing is for judge and jury; therefore I ended the conversation as above, and marched off my prisoner. Whether the birds of the air carry news I do not know, but they must have been busy on this occasion, for next morning every newspaper in London was congratulating me on my clever capture of the supposed murderer. Some detectives would have been gratified by this public laudation—I was not. Roy's passionate protestations of innocence made me feel uneasy, and I doubted whether, after all, I had the right man under lock and key. Yet the evidence was strong against him. He admitted having been with Mrs. Vincent on the fatal night, he admitted possession of two fifty-pound notes. His only defence was the letter of the stockbroker, and this was missing—if, indeed, it had ever been written.

Vincent was terribly upset by the arrest of Roy. He liked the young man and he had believed in his innocence so far as was possible. But in the face of such strong evidence, he was forced to believe him guilty: yet he blamed himself severely that he had not lent the money, and so averted the catastrophe.

"I had no idea that the matter was of such moment," he said to me, "else I would have gone down to Brixton myself and have given him the money. Then his frenzy would have spared my wife, and himself a death on the scaffold."

"What do you think of his defence?"

"It is wholly untrue. I did not write a note, nor did I tell him to go to Brixton. Why should I, when I fully believed no one was in the house?"

"It was a pity you did not go home, Mr. Vincent, instead of to the Alhambra."

"It was a mistake," he assented, "but I had no idea Roy would attempt the robbery. Besides, I was under engagement to go to the theatre with my friend Dr. Monson."

"Do you think that idol belongs to Roy?"

"I can't say, I never saw it in his possession. Why?"

"Because I firmly believe that if Roy had not the idol in his pocket on that fatal night he is innocent. Oh, you look astonished, but the man who murdered your wife owns that idol."

The morning after this conversation a lady called at Scotland Yard, and asked to see me concerning the Brixton case. Fortunately, I was then in the neighbourhood, and, guessing who she was, I afforded her the interview she sought. When all left the room she raised her veil, and I saw before me a noble-looking woman, somewhat resembling Mr. Maudsley's clerk. Yet, by some contradiction of nature, her face was the more virile of the two.

"You are Miss Ford?" I said, guessing her identity.

"I am Clara Ford," she answered quietly. "I have come to see you about Mr. Roy."

"I am afraid nothing can be done to save him."

"Something must be done," she said passionately. "We are engaged to be married, and all a woman can do to save her lover I will do. Do you believe him to be guilty?"

"In the face of such evidence, Miss Ford——"

"I don't care what evidence is against him," she retorted; "he is as innocent of the crime as I am. Do you think that a man fresh from the committal of a crime would place the money won by that crime in the hands of the woman he professes to love? I tell you he is innocent."

"Mr. Vincent doesn't think so."

"Mr. Vincent!" said Miss Ford, with scornful emphasis. "Oh, yes! I quite believe *he* would think Julian guilty."

"Surely not if it were possible to think otherwise! He is, or rather was, a staunch friend to Mr. Roy."

"So staunch that he tried to break off the match between us. Listen to me, sir. I have told no one before, but I tell you now. Mr. Vincent is a villain. He pretended to be the friend of Julian, and yet he dared to make proposals to me—dishonourable proposals, for which I could have struck him. He, a married man, a pretended friend, wished me to leave Julian and fly with him."

"Surely you are mistaken, Miss Ford. Mr. Vincent was most devoted to his wife."

"He did not care at all for his wife," she replied steadily. "He was in love with me. To save Julian annoyance I did not tell him of the insults offered to me by Mr. Vincent. Now that Julian is in trouble by an unfortunate mistake, Mr. Vincent is delighted."

"It is impossible. I assure you Vincent is very sorry to——"

"You do not believe me," she said, interrupting. "Very well, I shall give you proof of the truth. Come to my brother's rooms in Blooms-bury. I shall send for Mr. Vincent, and if you are concealed you shall hear from his own lips how glad he is that my lover and his wife are removed from the path of his dishonourable passion."

"I will come, Miss Ford, but I think you are mistaken in Vincent."

"You shall see," she replied coldly. Then, with a sudden change of tone, "Is there no way of saving Julian? I am sure that he is innocent. Appearances are against him, but it was not he who committed the crime. Is there no way—no way?"

Moved by her earnest appeal, I produced the green-stone idol, and told her all I had done in connection with it. She listened eagerly, and readily grasped at the hope thus held out to her of saving Roy. "When in possession of all the facts she considered in silence for some two minutes. At the end of that time she drew down her veil and prepared to take her departure.

"Come to my brother's rooms in Alfred Place, near Tottenham Court Road," said she, holding out her hand. "I promise you that there you shall see Mr. Vincent in his true character. Good-bye till Monday at three o'clock."

From the colour in her face and the bright light in her eye, I guessed that she had some scheme in her head for the saving of Roy. I think myself clever, but after that interview at Alfred Place I declare I am but a fool compared to this woman. She put two and two together, ferreted out unguessed-of evidence, and finally produced the most wonderful result. "When she left me at this moment the green-stone idol was in her pocket. With that she hoped to prove the innocence of her lover and the guilt of another person. It was the cleverest thing I ever saw in my life.

The inquest on the body of Mrs. Vincent resulted in a verdict of wilful murder against some person or persons unknown. Then she was buried, and all London waited for the trial of Roy. He was brought up charged with the crime, reserved his defence, and in due course he was committed for trial. Meantime I called on Miss Ford at the appointed time, and found her alone.

"Mr. Vincent will be here shortly," she said calmly. "I see Julian is committed for trial."

"And he has reserved his defence."

"I shall defend him," said she, with a strange look in her face; "I am not afraid for him now. He saved my unhappy brother. I shall save him."

"Have you discovered anything?"

"I have discovered a good deal. Hush! That is Mr. Vincent," she added, as a cab drew up to the door. "Hide yourself behind this curtain, and do not appear until I give you the signal."

Wondering what she was about to do, I concealed myself as directed. The next moment Vincent was in the room, and then ensued one of the strangest of scenes. She received him coldly, and motioned him to a seat. Vincent was nervous, but she might have been of stone, so little emotion did she display.

"I have sent for you, Mr. Vincent," she said, "to ask for your help in releasing Julian."

"How can I help you?" he answered, in amazement—"willingly would I do so, but it is out of my power."

"I don't think it is!"

"I assure you, Clara," he began eagerly, when she cut him short.

"Yes, call me Clara! Say that you love me! Lie, like all men, and yet refuse to do what I wish."

"I am not going to help Julian to marry you," declared he sullenly. "You know that I love you—I love you dearly, I wish to marry you——"

"Is not that declaration rather soon after the death of your wife?"

"My wife is gone, poor soul, let her rest."

"Yet you loved her?"

"I never loved her," he said, rising to his feet. "I love you! From the first moment I saw you I loved you. My wife is dead! Julian Roy is in prison on a charge of murdering her. With these obstacles removed there is no reason why we should not marry."

"If I marry you," she said slowly, "will you help Julian to refute this charge?"

"I cannot! The evidence is too strong against him!"

"You know that he is innocent, Mr. Vincent."

"I do not! I believe that he murdered my wife."

"You believe that he murdered your wife," she reiterated, coming a step nearer and holding out the green-stone idol—"do you believe that he dropped this in the study when his hand struck the fatal blow?"

"I don't know!" he said, coolly glancing at the idol; "I never saw it before."

"Think again, Mr. Vincent—think again. Who was it that went to the Alhambra at eight o'clock with Dr. Monson, and met there the captain of a New Zealand steamer with whom he was acquainted?"

"It was I," said Vincent defiantly; "and what of that?"

"This!" she said in a loud voice. "This captain gave you the green-stone idol at the Alhambra, and you placed it in your breast-pocket. Shortly afterwards you followed to Brixton the man whose death you had plotted. You repaired to your house, killed your unhappy wife, who received you in all innocence, took the balance of the money, hacked the desk, and then dropped by accident this idol which convicts you of the crime."

During this speech she advanced step by step towards the wretched man, who, pale and anguished, retreated before her fury. He came right to my hiding-place, and almost fell into my arms. I had heard enough to convince me of his guilt, and the next moment I was struggling with him.

"It is a lie! a lie!" he said hoarsely, trying to escape.

"It is true!" said I, pinning him down. "From my soul I believe you to be guilty."

During the fight his pocket-book fell on the floor, and the papers therein were scattered. Miss Ford picked up one spotted with blood.

"The proof!" she said, holding it before us. "The proof that Julian spoke the truth. There is the letter written by you which authorized your unhappy wife to give him one hundred pounds."

Vincent saw that all was against him, and gave in without further struggles, like the craven he was.

"Fate is too strong for me," he said, when I snapped the handcuffs on his wrists. "I admit the crime. It was for love of you that I did it. I hated my wife, who was drag on me, and I hated Roy, who loved you. In one sweep thought to rid myself of both. His application for the money put the chance into my hand. I went to Brixton, found that my wife had given the money as directed, and then I killed her with the foil snatched from the wall. I smashed the desk and overturned the chair, to favour the idea of the robbery, and then I left the house. Driving to a higher station than Brixton, I caught a train and was speedily back at the Alhambra. Monson never suspected my absence, thinking I was in a different corner of the house. I had thus an *alibi* ready. Had it not been for that letter, which I was fool enough to keep, and that infernal idol that dropped out of my pocket, I should have hanged Roy and married you. As it turns out, the idea has betrayed me. And now, sir," he added, turning to me, "you had better take me to gaol."

I did so there and then. After the legal formalities were gone through Julian Roy was released, and ultimately married Miss Ford. Vincent was hanged, as he well deserved to be, for so cowardly a crime. My reward was the green-stone god, which I keep as a memento of a very curious case. Some weeks later Miss Ford told me the way in which she had laid the trap.

"When you revealed your suspicions about the idol," she said, "I was convinced that Vincent had something to do with the crime. You mentioned Dr. Monson as having been with him at the Alhambra. He is one of the doctors at the hospital in which I am employed. I asked him about the idol, and showed it to him. He remembered it being given to Vincent by the captain of the *Kaitangata*. The curious look of the thing had impressed itself on his memory. On hearing this I went to the docks and I saw the captain. He recognized the idol, and remembered giving it to Vincent. From what you told me I guessed the way in which the plot had been carried out, so I spoke to Vincent as you heard. Most of it was guesswork, and only when I saw that letter was I absolutely sure of his guilt. It was due to the green-stone god."

So I think, but to chance also. But for the accident of the idol dropping out of Vincent's pocket, Roy would have been hanged for a crime of which he was innocent. Therefore do I say that in nine cases out of ten chance does more to clinch a case than all the dexterity of the man in charge.

Cinderella's Slipper

Hugh C. Weir

R AYMOND RENNICK might have been going to his wedding instead of to his—death.

Spick and span in a new spring suit, he paused just outside the broad, arched gates of the Duffield estate and drew his silver cigarette case from his pocket. A self-satisfied smile flashed across his face as he struck a match and inhaled the fragrant odor of the tobacco. It was good tobacco, very good tobacco—And Senator Duffield's private secretary was something of a judge!

For a moment Rennick lingered. It was a day to banish uncomfortable thoughts, to smooth the rough edges of a man's problems—and burdens. As the secretary glanced up at the soft blue sky, the reflection swept his mind that his own future was as free from clouds. It was a pleasing reflection. Perhaps the cigarette, perhaps the day helped to deepen it as he swung almost jauntily up the winding driveway toward the square, white house commanding the terraced lawn beyond.

Just ahead of him a maple tree, standing alone, rustled gaily in its spring foliage like a woman calling attention to her new finery. It was all so fresh and beautiful and innocent! Rennick felt a tingling thrill in his blood. Unconsciously he tossed away his cigarette. He reached the rustling maple and passed it. . . .

From behind the gnarled trunk, a shadow darted. A figure sprang at his shoulders, with the long blade of a dagger awkwardly poised. There was a flash of steel in the sunlight. . . .

It was perhaps ten minutes later that they found him. He had fallen face downward at the edge of the driveway, with his body half across the velvet green of the grass. A thin thread of red, creeping from the wound in his breast, was losing itself in the sod.

One hand was doubled, as in a desperate effort at defence. His glasses were twisted under his shoulders. Death must have been nearly instantaneous. The dagger had reached his heart at the first thrust. One might have fancied an expression of overpowering amazement in the staring eyes. That was all. The weapon had caught him squarely on the left side. He had evidently whirled toward the assassin almost at the instant of the blow.

Whether in the second left him of life he had recognized his assailant, and the recognition had made the death-blow the quicker and the surer, were questions that only deepened the horror of the noon-day crime.

As though to emphasize the hour, the mahogany clock in Senator Duffield's library rang out its twelve monotonous chimes as John Dorrence, his valet, beat sharply on the door. The echo of the nervous tattoo was lost in an unanswering silence. Dorrence repeated his knock before he brought an impatient response from beyond the panels.

"Can you come, sir?" the valet burst out. "Something awful has happened, sir. It's, it's—"

The door was flung open. A ruddy-faced man with thick, white hair and grizzled moustache, and the hints of a nervous temperament showing in his eyes and voice, sprang into the hall. Somebody once remarked that Senator Duffield was Mark Twain's double. The Senator took the comparison as a compliment, perhaps because it was a woman who made it.

Dorrence seized his master by the sleeve, which loss of dignity did more to impress the Senator with the gravity of the situation than all of the servant's excitable words.

"Mr. Rennick, sir, has been stabbed, sir, on the lawn, and Miss Beth, sir—"

Senator Duffield staggered against the wall. The valet's alarm swerved to another channel.

"Shall I get the brandy, sir?"

"Brandy?" the Senator repeated vaguely. The next instant, as though grasping the situation anew, he sprang down the hall with the skirts of his frock coat flapping against his knees. At the door of the veranda, he whirled.

"Get the doctor on the 'phone, Dorrence—Redfield, if Scott is out. Let him know it's a matter of minutes! And, Dorrence—"

"Yes, sir!"

"Tell the telephone girl that, if this leaks to the newspapers, I will have the whole office discharged!"

A shifting group on the edge of the lawn, with that strange sense of awkwardness which sudden death brings, showed the scene of the tragedy.

The circle fell back as the Senator's figure appeared. On the grass, Rennick's body still lay where it had fallen—suggesting a skater who has ignominiously collapsed on the ice rather than a man stabbed to the heart. The group had been wondering at the fact in whispered monosyllables.

A kneeling girl was bending over the secretary's body. It was not until Senator Duffield had spoken her name twice that she glanced up. In her eyes was a grief so wild that for a moment he was held dumb.

"Come, Beth," he said, gently, "this is no place for you."

At once the white-faced girl became the central figure of the situation. If she heard him, she gave no sign. The Senator caught her shoulder and pushed her slowly away. One of the women-servants took her arm. Curiously enough, the two were the only members of the family that had been called to the scene.

The Senator swung on the group with a return of his aggressiveness.

"Some one, who can talk fast and to the point, tell me the story. Burke, you have a ready tongue. How did it happen?"

The groom—a much-tanned young fellow in his early twenties—touched his cap.

"I don't know, sir. No one knows. Mr. Rennick was lying here, stabbed, when we found him. He was already dead."

"But surely there was some cry, some sound of a scuffle?"

The groom shook his head. "If there was, sir, none of us heard it. We all liked Mr. Rennick, sir. I would have gone through fire and water if he needed my help. If there had been an outcry loud enough to reach the stable, I would have been there on the jump!"

"Do you mean to tell me that Rennick could have been struck down in the midst of fifteen or twenty people with no one the wiser? It's ridiculous, impossible!" Burke squared his shoulders, with an almost unconscious suggestion of dignity. "I am telling you the truth, sir!"

The Senator's glance dropped to his secretary's body and he looked up with a shudder. Then, as though with an effort, his eyes returned to the huddled form, and he stood staring down at the dead man, with a frown knitting his brow. Once he jerked his head toward the gardener with the curt question, "Who found him?" Jenkins shambled forward uneasily. "I did, sir. I hope you don't think I disturbed the body?"

The Senator shrugged his shoulders impatiently. He did not raise his head again until the sound of a motor in the driveway broke the tension. The surgeon had arrived. Almost at the same moment there was a cry from Jenkins.

The gardener stood perhaps a half a dozen yards from the body, staring at an object hidden in the grass at his feet. He stooped and raised it. It was a woman's slipper!

As a turn of his head showed him the eyes of the group turned in his direction, he walked across to Senator Duffield, holding his find at arm's length, as though its dainty outlines might conceal an adder's nest.

The slipper was of black suede, high-heeled and slender, tied with a broad, black ribbon. One end of the ribbon was broken and stained as though it had tripped its owner. On the thin sole were cakes of the peculiar red clay of the driveway.

It might have been unconscious magnetism that caused the Senator suddenly to turn his eyes in the direction of his daughter. She was swaying on the arm of the servant.

Throwing off the support of the woman, she took two quick steps forward, with her hand flung out as though to tear the slipper from him. And then, without a word, she fell prone on the grass.

II.

The telephone in my room must have been jangling a full moment before I struggled out of my sleep and raised myself to my elbow. It was with a feeling of distinct rebellion that I slipped into my kimono and slippers and shuffled across to the sputtering instrument in the corner. From eight in the morning until eight in the evening, I had been on racking duty in the Farragut poison trial, and the belated report of the wrangling jury, at an hour which made any sort of a meal impossible until after ten, had left me worn out physically and mentally. I glanced at my watch as I snapped the receiver to my ear. It lacked barely fifteen minutes of midnight. An unearthly hour to call a woman out of bed, even if she is past the age of sentimental dreams!

"Well?" I growled.

A laugh answered me at the other end of the wire. I would have flung the receiver back to the hook and myself back to bed had I not recognized the tones. There is only one person in the world, except the tyrant at our city editor's desk, who would arouse me at midnight. But I had thought this person separated from me by twelve hundred miles of ocean.

"Madelyn Mack!" I gasped.

The laughter ceased. "Madelyn Mack it is!" came back the answer, now reduced to a tone of decorous gravity. "Pardon my merriment, Nora. The mental picture of your huddled form—"

"But I thought you in Jamaica!" I broke in, now thoroughly awake.

"I was—until Saturday. Our steamer came out of quarantine at four o'clock this afternoon. As it develops, I reached here at the psychological moment."

I kicked a rocker to my side and dropped into it with a rueful glance at the rumpled sheets of the bed. With Madelyn Mack at the telephone at midnight, only one conclusion was possible; and such a conclusion shattered all thought of sleep.

"Have you read the evening dispatches from Boston, Nora?"

"I have read nothing—except the report of the Farragut jury!" I returned crisply. "Why?"

"If you had, you would perhaps divine the reason of my call. I have been retained in the Rennick murder case. I'm taking the one-thirty sleeper for Boston. I secured our berths just before I telephoned."

"Our berths!"

"I am taking you with me. Now that you are up, you may as well dress and ring for a taxicab. I will meet you at the Roanoke hotel."

"But," I protested, "don't you think—"

"Very well, if you don't care to go! That settles it!"

"Oh, I will be there!" I said with an air of resignation. "Ten minutes to dress, and fifteen minutes for the taxi!"

"I will add five minutes for incidentals," Madelyn replied and hung up the receiver.

The elevator boy at "The Occident," where I had my modest apartment, had become accustomed to the strange hours and strange visitors of a newspaper woman during my three years' residence. He opened the door with a grin of sympathy as the car reached my floor. As though to give more active expression to his feelings he caught up my bag and gave it a place of honor on his own stool.

"Going far?" he queried as I alighted at the main corridor.

"I may be back in twenty-four hours and I may not be back for twenty-four days," I answered cautiously—I knew Madelyn Mack!

As I waited for the whir of the taxicab, I appropriated the evening paper on the night clerk's desk. The Rennick murder case had been given a three-column head on the front page. If I had not been so absorbed in the Farragut trial, it could not have escaped me. I had not finished the head-lines, however, when the taxi, with a promptness almost uncanny, rumbled up to the curb.

I threw myself back against the cushions, switched on the electric light, and spread my paper over my knee, as the chauffeur turned off toward Fifth Avenue. The story was well written and had made much of a few facts. Trust my newspaper instinct to know that! I had expected a fantastic puzzle—when it could spur Madelyn into action within six hours after her landing—but I was hardly anticipating a problem such as I could read between rather than in the lines of type before me. Long before the "Roanoke" loomed into view, I had forgotten my lost sleep.

The identity of Raymond Rennick's assassin was as baffling as in the first moments of the discovery of the tragedy. There had been no arrests—nor hint of any. From the moment when the secretary had turned into the gate of the Duffield yard until the finding of his body, all trace of his movements had been lost as effectually as though the darkness of midnight had enveloped him, instead of the sunlight of noon. More than ten minutes could not have elapsed between his entrance into the grounds and the discovery of his murder—perhaps not more than five—but they had been sufficient for the assassin to effect a complete escape.

There was not even the shadow of a motive. Raymond Rennick was one of those few men who seemed to be without an enemy. In an official capacity, his conduct was without a blemish. In a social capacity, he was admittedly one of the most popular men in Brookline—among both sexes. Rumor had it, apparently on unquestioned authority, that the announcement of his engagement to Beth Duffield was to have been an event of the early summer. This fact was in my mind as I stared out into the darkness.

On a sudden impulse, I opened the paper again. From an inside page the latest photograph of the Senator's daughter, taken at a fashionable Boston studio, smiled up at me.

It was an excellent likeness as I remembered her at the inaugural ball the year before—a wisp of a girl, with a mass of black hair, which served to emphasize her frailness. I studied the picture with a frown. There was a sense of familiarity in its outlines, which certainly our casual meeting could not explain. Then, abruptly, my thoughts flashed back to the crowded court room of the afternoon—and I remembered.

In the prisoner's dock I saw again the figure of Beatrice Farragut, slender, fragile, her white face, her sombre gown, her eyes fixed like those of a frightened lamb on the jury which was to give her life—or death.

"She poison her husband?" had buzzed the whispered comments at my shoulders during the weary weeks of the trial.

"She couldn't harm a butterfly!" Like a mocking echo, the tones of the foreman had sounded the answering verdict of murder—in the first degree. And in New York this meant——

Why had Beatrice Farragut suggested Beth Duffield? Or was it Beth Duffield who had suggested—I crumpled the paper into a heap and tossed it from the window in disgust at my morbid imagination. B-u-r-r-h! And yet they say that a New York newspaper woman has no nerves!

A voice hailed us from the darkness and a white-gowned figure sprang out on to the walk. As the chauffeur brought the machine to a halt, Madelyn Mack caught my hands.

Her next two actions were thoroughly characteristic.

Whirling to the driver, she demanded shortly, "How soon can you make the Grand Central Station?"

The man hesitated. "Can you give me twenty minutes?"

"Just! We will leave here at one sharp. You will wait, please!"

Having thus disposed of the chauffeur—Madelyn never gave a thought to the matter of expense!—she seized my arm and pushed me through the entrance of the "Roanoke" as nonchalantly as though we had parted six hours before instead of six weeks.

"I hope you enjoyed Jamaica?" I ventured.

"Did you read the evening papers on the way over?" she returned as easily as though I had not spoken.

"One," I answered shortly. Madelyn's habit of ignoring my queries grated most uncomfortably at times.

"Then you know what has been published concerning the case?"

I nodded. "I imagine that you can add considerable."

"As a matter of fact, I know less than the reporters!" Madelyn threw open the door of her room. "You have interviewed Senator Duffield on several occasions, have you not, Nora?"

"You might say on several delicate occasions if you cared to!"

"You can tell me then whether the Senator is in the habit of polishing his glasses when he is in a nervous mood?"

A rather superior smile flashed over my face.

"I assure you that Senator Duffield never wears glasses on any occasion!"

Something like a chuckle came from Madelyn.

"Perhaps you can do as well on another question. You will observe in these newspapers four different photographs of the murdered secretary. Naturally, they bear many points of similarity—they were all taken in the last three years—but they contain one feature in common which puzzles me. Does it impress you in the same way?"

I glanced at the group of photographs doubtfully. Three of them were obviously newspaper "snap-shots," taken of the secretary while in the company of Senator Duffield. The fourth was a reproduction showing a conventional cabinet photograph. They showed a clean-shaven, well-built young man of thirty or thereabouts; tall, and I should say inclined to athletics. I turned from the newspapers to Madelyn with a shrug.

"I am afraid I don't quite follow you," I admitted ruefully. "There is nothing at all out of the ordinary in any of them that I can catch."

Madelyn carefully clipped the pictures and placed them under the front cover of her black morocco note-book. As she did so, a clock chimed the hour of one. We both pushed back our chairs.

As we stepped into the taxicab, Madelyn tapped my arm. "I wonder if Raymond Rennick polished his glasses when he was nervous?" she asked musingly.

III.

Boston, from the viewpoint of the South Station at half-past seven in the morning, suggests to me a rheumatic individual climbing stiffly out of bed. Boston distinctly resents anything happening before noon. I'll wager that nearly every important event that she has contributed to history occurred after lunch-time!

If Madelyn Mack had expected to have to find her way to the Duffield home without a guide, she was pleasantly disappointed. No less a person than the Senator himself was waiting us at the train-gate— a somewhat dishevelled Senator, it must be confessed, with the stubble of a day-old beard showing eloquently how his peace of mind and the routine of his habits had been shattered. As he shook hands with us he made an obvious attempt to recover something of his ease of manner.

"I trust that you had a pleasant night's rest," he ventured, as he led the way across the station to his automobile.

"Much pleasanter than you had, I fear," replied Madelyn.

The Senator sighed. "As a matter of fact, I found sleep hopeless; I spent most of the night with my cigar. The suggestion of meeting your train came as a really welcome relief."

As we stepped into the waiting motor, a leather-lunged newsboy thrust a bundle of heavy-typed papers into our faces. The Senator whirled with a curt dismissal on his tongue when Madelyn thrust a coin toward the lad and swept a handful of flapping papers into her lap.

"There is absolutely nothing new in the case, Miss Mack, I asure you," the Senator said impatiently. "The reporters have pestered me like so many leeches. The sight of a head-line makes me shiver."

Madelyn bent over her papers without comment. As I settled into the seat by her side, however, and the machine whirled around the corner, I saw that she was not even making a pretence of reading. I watched her with a frown as she turned the pages. There was no question of her interest, but it was not the type that held her attention. I doubted if she was perusing a line of the closely-set columns. It was not until she reached the last paper that I solved the mystery. It was the illustrations that she was studying!

When she finished the heap of papers, she began slowly and even more thoughtfully to go through them again. Now I saw that she was pondering the various photographs of Senator Duffield's family that the newspapers had published. I turned away from her bent form and tapping finger, but there was a magnetism in her abstraction that forced my eyes back to her in spite of myself. As my gaze returned to her, she thrust her gloved hand into the recesses of her bag and drew out her black morocco notebook. From its pages she selected the four newspaper pictures of the murdered secretary that she had offered me the night before. With a twinkle of satisfaction she grouped them about a large, black-bordered picture which stared up at her from the printed page in her lap.

Our ride to the Duffield gate was not a long one. In fact I was so absorbed by my furtive study of Madelyn Mack that I was started when the chauffeur slackened his speed, and I realized from a straightening of the Senator's bent shoulders that we were nearing our destination.

At the edge of the driveway, a quietly dressed man in a grey suit, who was strolling carelessly back and forth from the gate to the house, eyed us curiously as we passed, and touched his hat to the Senator. I knew at once he was a detective. (Trust a newspaper woman to "spot" a plain clothes man, even if he has left his police uniform at home!) Madelyn did not look up and the Senator made no comment.

As we stepped from the machine, a tall girl with severe, almost classical features and a profusion of nut-brown hair which fell away from her forehead without even the suggestion of a ripple, was awaiting us.

"My daughter, Maria," Senator Duffield announced formally.

Madelyn stepped forward with extended hand. It was evident that Miss Duffield had intended only a brief nod. For an instant she hesitated, with a barely perceptible flush. Then her fingers dropped limply into Madelyn Mack's palm. (I chuckled inwardly at the ill grace with which she did it!)

"This must be a most trying occasion for you," Madelyn said with a note of sympathy in her voice, which made me stare. Effusiveness of any kind was so foreign to her nature that I frowned as we followed our host into the wide front drawing room. As we entered by one door, a black-gowned, white-haired woman, evidently Mrs. Duffield, entered by the opposite door.

In spite of the reserve of the society leader, whose sway might be said to extend to three cities, she darted an appealing glance at Madelyn

Mack that melted much of the newspaper cynicism with which I was prepared to greet her. Madelyn crossed the room to her side and spoke a low sentence, that I did not catch, as she took her hand. I found myself again wondering at her unwonted friendliness. She was obviously exerting herself to gain the good will of the Duffield household. Why?

A trim maid, who stared at us as though we were museum freaks, conducted us to our rooms—adjoining apartments at the front of the third floor. The identity of Madelyn Mack had already been noised through the house, and I caught a saucer-eyed glance from a second servant as we passed down the corridor. If the atmosphere of suppressed curiosity was embarrassing my companion, however, she gave no sign of the fact. Indeed, we had hardly time to remove our hats when the breakfast gong rang.

The family was assembling in the old-fashioned dining-room when we entered. In addition to the members of the domestic circle whom I have already indicated, my attention was at once caught by two figures who entered just before us. One was a young woman whom it did not need a second glance to tell me was Beth Duffield. Her white face and swollen eyes were evidence enough of her overwrought condition, and I caught myself speculating why she had left her room.

Her companion was a tall, slender young fellow with just the faintest trace of a stoop in his shoulders. As he turned toward us, I saw a handsome, though self-indulgent face, to a close observer suggesting evidence of more dissipation than was good for its owner. And, if the newspaper stories of the doings of Fletcher Duffield were true, the facial index was a true one.—If I remember rightly, Senator Duffield's son more than once had made prim old Boston town rub her spectacled eyes at the tales of his escapades!

Fletcher Duffield bowed rather abstractedly as he was presented to us, but during the eggs and chops he brightened visibly, and put several curious questions to Madelyn as to her methods of work, which enlivened what otherwise would have been a rather dull half-hour.

As the strokes of nine rang through the room, my companion pushed her chair back.

"What time is the coroner's inquest, Senator?"

Mr. Duffield raised his eyebrows at the change in her attitude. "It is scheduled for eleven o'clock."

"And when do you expect Inspertor Taylor of headquarters?"

"In the course of an hour, I should say, perhaps less. His man, Martin, has been here since yesterday afternoon—you probably saw him as we drove into the yard. I can telephone Mr. Taylor, if you wish to see him sooner."

"That will hardly be necessary, thank you."

Madelyn walked across to the window. For a moment she stood peering out on to the lawn. Then she stooped, and her hand fumbled with the catch. The window swung open with the noiselessness of well-oiled hinges, and she stepped out on to the verandah, without so much as a glance at the group about the table.

I think the Senator and I rose from our chairs at the same instant. When we reached the window, Madelyn was half across the lawn. Perhaps twenty yards ahead of her towered a huge maple, rustling in the early morning breeze.

I realized that this was the spot where Raymond Rennick had met his death.

In spite of his nervousness, Senator Duffield did not forget his old-fashioned courtliness, which I believe had become second nature to him. Stepping aside with a slight bow, he held the window open for me, following at my shoulder. As we reached the lawn, I saw that the scene of the murder was in plain view from at least one of the principal rooms of the Duffield home.

Madelyn was leaning against the maple when we reached her. Senator Duffield said gravely, as he pointed to the gnarled trunk, "You are standing just at the point where the woman waited, Miss Mack."

"Woman?"

"I refer to the assassin," the Senator rejoined a trifle impatiently. "Judging by our fragmentary clues, she must have been hidden behind the trunk when poor Rennick appeared on the driveway. We found her slipper somewhat to the left of the tree—a matter of eight or ten feet, I should say."

"Oh!" said Madelyn listlessly. I fancied that she was somewhat annoyed that we had followed her.

"An odd clue, that slipper," the Senator continued with an obvious attempt to maintain the conversation. "If we were disposed to be fanciful, it might suggest the childhood legend of Cinderella." Madelyn did not answer. She stood leaning back against the tree with her eyes wandering about the yard. Once I saw her gaze flash down the driveway to the open gate, where the detective, Martin, stood watching us furtively.

"Nora," she said, without turning, "will you kindly walk six steps to your right?"

I knew better than to ask the reason for the request. With a shrug, I faced toward the house and came to a pause at the end of the stipulated distance.

"Is Miss Noraker standing where Mr. Rennick's body was found, Senator?"

"She will strike the exact spot, I think, if she takes two steps more."

I had hardly obeyed the suggestion when I caught the swift rustle of skirts behind me. I whirled to see Madelyn's lithe form darting toward me with her right hand raised as though it held a weapon.

"Good!" she cried. "I call you to witness, Senator, that I was fully six feet away when she turned! Now I want you to take Miss Noraker's place. The instant you hear me behind you—the *instant*, mind you—I want you to let me know." She walked back to the tree as the Senator reluctantly changed places with me. I could almost picture the murderess dashing upon her victim as Madelyn bent forward. The Senator turned his back to us with a rather ludicrous air of bewilderment.

My erratic friend had covered perhaps half of the distance between her and our host when he spun about with a cry of discovery. She paused with a long breath.

"Thank you, Senator. What first attracted your attention to me?"

"The rustle of your dress, of course!" Madelyn turned to me with the first smile of satisfaction I had seen since we entered the Duffield gate.

"Was the same true in your case, Nora?"

I nodded. "The fact that you are a woman hopelessly betrayed you. If you had not been hampered by petticoats—" Madelyn broke in upon my sentence with that peculiar freedom which she always reserves to herself. "There are two things I would like to ask of you, Senator, if I may."

"I am at your disposal, I assure you." "I would like to borrow a Boston directory, and the services of a messenger." We walked slowly up the driveway, Madelyn again relapsing into her preoccupied silence and Senator Duffield making no effort to induce her to speak.

IV.

We had nearly reached the verandah when there was the sound of a motor at the gate, and a red touring car swept into the yard. An elderly, cleanshaven man, in a long frock coat and a broad-brimmed felt hat, was sharing the front seat with the chauffeur. He sprang to the ground with extended hand as our host stepped forward to greet him. The two exchanged half a dozen low sentences at the side of the machine, and then Senator Duffield raised his voice as they approached us.

"Miss Mack, allow me to introduce my colleague, Senator Burroughs."

"I have heard of you, of course, Miss Mack," the Senator said genially, raising his broad-brimmed hat with a flourish. "I am very glad, indeed, that you are able to give us the benefit of your experience in this, er—unfortunate affair. I presume that it is too early to ask if you have developed a theory?"

"I wonder if you would allow me to reverse the question?" Madelyn responded as she took his hand.

"I fear that my detective ability would hardly be of much service to you, eh, Duffield?"

Our host smiled faintly as he turned to repeat to a servant Madelyn's request for a directory and a messenger. Senator Burroughs folded his arms as his chauffeur circled on toward the garage. There was an odd suggestion of nervousness in the whole group.—Or. was it fancy?

"Have you ever given particular study to the legal angle in your cases, Miss Mack?" The question came from Senator Burroughs as we ascended the steps.

"The legal angle? I am afraid I don't grasp your meaning."

The Senator's hand moved mechanically toward his cigar case. "I am a lawyer, and perhaps I argue unduly from a lawyer's viewpoint. We always work from the question of motive, Miss Mack. A professional detective, I believe—or, at least, the average professional detective—tries to find the criminal first and establish his motive afterward."

"Now, in a case such as this, Senator—"

"In a case such as this, Miss Mack, the trained legal mind would delve first for the motive in Mr. Rennick's assassination."

"And your legal mind, Senator, I presume, has delved for the motive. Has it found it?"

The Senator turned his unlighted cigar reflectively between his lips. "I have not found it! Eliminating the field of sordid passion and insanity, I divide the motives of the murderer under three heads—robbery, jealousy and revenge. In the present case, I eliminate the first possibility at the outset. There remain then only the two latter."

"You are interesting. You forget, however, a fourth motive—the strongest spur to crime in the human mind!"

Senator Burroughs took his cigar from his mouth.

"I mean the motive of—fear!" Madelyn said abruptly, as she swept into the house. When I followed her, Senator Burroughs had walked over to the railing and stood staring down at the ground below. He had tossed his cigar away.

In the room where we had breakfasted, one of the stable boys stood awkwardly awaiting Madelyn Mack's orders, while John Dorrence, the valet was just laying a city directory on the table.

"Nora," she said, as she turned to the boy, "will you kindly look up the list of packing houses?"

"Pick out the largest and give me the address," she continued, as I ran my finger through the closely typed pages. With a growing curiosity, I selected a firm whose prestige was advertised in heavy letters. Madelyn's fountain pen scratched a dozen lines across a sheet of her note-book, and she thrust it into an envelope and extended it to the stable lad.

As the youth backed from the room, Senator Duffield appeared at the window.

"I presume it will be possible for me to see Mr. Rennick's body, Senator?" Madelyn Mack asked.

Our host bowed.

"Also, I would like to look at his clothes—the suit he was wearing at the time of his death, I mean—and, when I am through, I want twenty or thirty minutes alone in his room. If Mr. Taylor should arrive before I am through, will you kindly let me know?"

"I can assure you Miss Mack, that the police have been through Mr. Rennick's apartment with a microscope."

"Then there can be no objection to my going through it with mine! By the way, Mr. Rennick's glasses—the pair that was found under his body—were packed with his clothes, were they not?"

"Certainly," the Senator responded.

I did not accompany Madelyn into the darkened room where the corpse of the murdered man was reposing. To my surprise, she rejoined me in less than five minutes.

"What did you find?" I queried as we ascended the stairs.

"A five-inch cut just above the sixth rib."

"That is what the newspapers said."

"You are mistaken. They said a three-inch cut. Have you ever tried to plunge a dagger through five inches of human flesh?"

"Certainly not."

Accustomed as I was to Madelyn Mack's eccentricities, I stood stock still and stared into her face.

"Oh, I'm not a murderess! I refer to my dissecting room experiences."

We had reached the upper hall when there was a quick movement at my shoulder, and I saw my companion's hand dart behind my waist. Before I could quite grasp the situation, she had caught my right arm in a grip of steel. For an instant I thought she was trying to force me back down the stairs. Then the force of her hold wrung a low cry of pain from my lips. She released me with a rueful apology.

"Forgive me, Nora! For a woman, I pride myself that I have a strong wrist!"

"Yes, I think you have!"

"Perhaps now you can appreciate what I mean when I say that even I haven't strength enough to inflict the wound that killed Raymond Rennick!"

"Then we must be dealing with an Amazon."

"Would Cinderella's missing slipper fit an Amazon?" she answered drily.

As she finished her sentence, we paused before a closed door which I rightly surmised led into the room of the murdered secretary. Madelyn's hand was on the knob when there was a step behind us, and Senator Duffield joined us with a rough bundle in his hands.

"Mr. Rennick's clothes," he explained. Madelyn nodded.

"Inspector Taylor left them in my care to hold until the inquest."

Madelyn flung the door open without any comment and led the way inside. Slipping the string from the bundle, she emptied the contents out on to the counterpane of the bed. They comprised the usual warm weather outfit of a well-dressed man, who evidently avoided the extremes of fashion, and she deftly sorted the articles into small neat piles. She glanced up with an expression of impatience.

"I thought you said they were here, Mr. Duffield!"

"What?"

"Mr. Rennick's glasses! Where are they?"

Senator Duffield fumbled in his pocket. "I beg your pardon, Miss Mack. I had overlooked them," he apologized, as he produced a thin paper parcel.

Madelyn carried it to the window and carefully unwrapped it.

"You will find the spectacles rather badly damaged, I fear. One lens is completely ruined."

Madelyn placed the broken glasses on the sill, and raised the blind to its full height. Then she dropped to her knees and whipped out her microscope. When she arose, her small, black-clad figure was tense with suppressed excitement.

A fat oak chiffonier stood in the corner nearest her. Crossing to its side, she rummaged among the articles that littered its surface, opened and closed the top drawer, and stepped back with an expression of annoyance. A writing table was the next point of her search, with results which I judged to be equally fruitless. She glanced uncertainly from the bed to the three chairs, the only other articles of furniture that the room contained. Then her eyes lighted again as they rested on the broad, carved mantel that spanned the empty fire-place.

It held the usual collection of bric-a-brac of a bachelor's room. At the end farthest from us, however, there was a narrow, red case, of which I caught only an indistinct view, when Madelyn's hand closed over it.

She whirled toward us. "I must ask you to leave me alone now, please!"

The Senator flushed at the peremptory command. I stepped into the hall and he followed me, with a shrug. He was closing the door when Madelyn raised her voice. "If Inspector Taylor is below, kindly send him up at once!"

"And what about the inquest, Miss Mack?"

"There will be no inquest—to-day!"

Senator Duffield led the way down stairs without a word. In the hall below, a ruddy-faced man, with grey hair, a thin grey beard and moustache, and a grey suit—suggesting an army officer in civilian clothes—

was awaiting us. I could readily imagine that Inspector Taylor was
something of a disciplinarian in the Boston police department. Also,
relying on Madelyn Mack's estimate, he was one of the three shrewdest
detectives on the American continent.

Senator Duffield hurried toward him with a suggestion of relief.
"Miss Mack is up-stairs, Inspector, and requested me to send you to her
the moment you arrived."

"Is she in Mr. Rennick's room?"

The Senator nodded. The Inspector hesitated as though about to ask
another question and then, as though thinking better of it, bowed and
turned to the stairs.

Inspector Taylor was one of those few policemen who had the
honor of being numbered among Madelyn Mack's personal friends,
and I fancied that he welcomed the news of her arrival.

Fletcher Duffield was chatting somewhat aimlessly with Senator Burroughs as we sauntered out into the yard again. None of the ladies of
the family were visible. The plain clothes man was still lounging discon-
solately in the vicinity of the gate. There was a sense of unrest in the
scene, a vague expectancy. Although no one voiced the suggestion, we
might all have been waiting to catch the first clap of distant thunder.

As Senator Duffield joined the men, I wandered across to the dining-
room window. I fancied the room was deserted, but I was mistaken. As
I faced about toward the driveway, a low voice caught my ear from
behind the curtains.

"You are Miss Mack's friend, are you not? No, don't turn around,
please!"

But I had already faced toward the open door. At my elbow was a
whitecapped maid—with her face almost as white as her cap—whom I
remembered to have seen at breakfast.

"Yes, I am Miss Mack's friend. What can I do for you?"

"I have a message for her. Will you see that she gets it?"

"Certainly."

"Tell her that I was at the door of Senator Duffield's library the night
before the murder."

My face must have expressed my bewilderment. For an instant I
fancied the girl was about to run from the room. I stepped through the
window and put my arm about her shoulders. She smiled faintly.

"I don't know much about the law, and evidence, and that sort of thing—and I'm afraid! You will take care of me, won't you?"

"Of course, I will, Anna. Your name is Anna, isn't it?"

The girl was rapidly recovering her self possession. "I thought you ought to know what happened Tuesday night. I was passing the door of the library—it was fairly late, about ten o'clock, I think—when I heard a man's voice inside the room. It was a loud angry voice like that of a person in a quarrel. Then I heard a second voice, lower and much calmer." "Did you recognize the speakers?" "They were Mr. Rennick and Senator Duffield!"

I caught my breath. "You said one of them was angry. Which was it?"

"Oh, it was the Senator! He was very much excited and worked up. Mr. Rennick seemed to be speaking very low." "What were they saying, Anna?" I tried to make my tones careless and indifferent, but they trembled in spite of myself.

"I couldn't catch what Mr. Rennick said. The Senator was saying some dreadful things. I remember he cried, 'You swindlers!' And then a bit later, 'I have evidence that should put you and your thieving crew behind the bars!' I think that is all. I was too bewildered to—"

A stir on the lawn interrupted the sentence. Madelyn Mack and Inspector Taylor had appeared. At the sound of their voices, the girl broke from my arm and darted toward the door.

Through the window, I heard the Inspector's heavy tones, as he announced curtly, "I am telephoning the coroner, Senator, that we are not ready for the inquest to-day. We must postpone it until to-morrow."

V.

The balance of the day passed without incident. In fact, I found the subdued quiet of the Duffield home becoming irksome as evening fell. I saw little of Madelyn Mack. She disappeared shortly after luncheon behind the door of her room, and I did not see her again until the dressing bell rang for dinner. Senator Duffield left for the city with Mr. Burroughs at noon, and his car did not bring him back until dark. The women of the family remained in their apartments during the entire day, nor could I wonder at the fact. A morbid crowd of curious sightseers was massed about the gates almost constantly, and it was necessary to send a call for two additional policeman to keep them back. In spite of the vigilance, frequent groups of newspaper men managed to slip into the grounds, and, after half a dozen experiences in frantically dodging a battery of cameras, I decided to stick to the shelter of the house.

It was with a feeling of distinct relief that I heard the door of Madelyn's room open and her voice called to me to enter. I found her stretched on a lounge before the window, with a mass of pillows under her head.

"Been asleep?" I asked.

"No—to tell the truth, I've been too busy."

"What? In this room!"

"This is the first time I've been here since noon!"

"Then where—"

"Nora, don't ask questions!"

I turned away with a shrug that brought a laugh from the lounge. Madelyn rose and shook out her skirts. I sat watching her as she walked across to the mirror and stood patting the great golden masses of her hair.

A low tap on the door interrupted her. Dorrence, the valet, stood outside as she opened it, extending an envelope. Madelyn fumbled it as she walked back. She let the envelope flutter to the floor and I saw that it contained only a blank sheet of paper. She thrust it into her pocket without explanation.

"How would you like a long motor ride, Nora?"

"For business or pleasure?"

"Pleasure! The day's work is finished." I don't know whether you agree with me or not, but I am strongly of the opinion that a whirl out under the elms of Cambridge, and then on to Concord and Lexington would be delightful in the moonlight. What do you say?"

The clock was hovering on the verge of midnight and the household had retired when we returned. Madelyn was in singularly cheery spirits. The low refrain which she was humming as the car swung into the grounds—"Schubert's Serenade," I think it was—ceased only when we stepped on to the verandah, and realized that we were entering the house of the dead.

I turned off my lights in silence, and glanced undecidedly from the bed to the rocker by the window. The cool night breeze beckoned me to the latter, and I drew the chair back a pace and cuddled down among the cushions. The lawn was almost silver under the flood of the moonlight, recalling vaguely the sweep of the ocean on a mid-summer night. Back and forth along the edge of the gate the figure of a man was pacing like a tired sentinel. It was the plain-clothes officer from headquarters. His figure suggested a state of siege. We might have been surrounded by a skulking enemy. Or was the enemy within, and the sentinel stationed to prevent his escape? I stumbled across to the bed and to sleep, with the question echoing oddly through my brain.

When I opened my eyes, the sun was throwing a yellow shaft of light across my bed, but it wasn't the sun that had awakened me. Madelyn was standing in the doorway, dressed, with an expression in her face which brought me to my elbow.

"What has happened now?"

"Burglars!"

"Burglars?" I repeated dully.

"I am going down to the library. Someone is making news for us fast, Nora. When will it be our turn?"

I dressed in record-breaking time, with my curiosity whetted by sounds of suppressed excitement which forced their way into the upper hall. The Duffield home not only was early astir, but was rudely jarred out of its customary routine.

When I descended, I found a nervous group of servants clustered about the door of the library. They stood aside to let me pass, with attitudes of uneasiness which I surmised would mean a whole-sale series of "notices" if the strange events in the usually well regulated household continued.

Behind the closed door of the library were Senator Duffield, his son Fletcher, and Madelyn Mack. It was easy to appreciate at a glance the unusual condition of the room. At the right, one of the long windows, partly raised, showed the small round hole of a diamond cutter just over the latch. It was obvious where the clandestine entrance and exit had been obtained. The most noticeable feature of the apartment, however, was a small, square safe in the corner, with its heavy lid swinging awkwardly ajar, and the rug below littered with a heap of papers, that had evidently been torn from its neatly tabulated series of drawers. The burglarious hands either had been very angry or very much in a hurry.

Even a number of unsealed envelopes had been ripped across, as though the pillager had been too impatient to extract their contents in the ordinary manner. To a man of Senator Duffield's methodical habits, it was easy to imagine that the scene had been a severe wrench.

Madelyn was speaking in her quick, incisive tones as I entered.

"Are you quite sure of that fact, Senator?" she asked sharply, as I closed the door and joined the trio.

"Quite sure, Miss Mack!"

"Then nothing is missing, absolutely nothing?"

"Not a single article, valuable or otherwise!"

"I presume then there were articles of more or less value in the safe?"

"There was perhaps four hundred dollars in loose bills in my private cash drawer, and, so far as I know, there is not a dollar gone."

"How about your papers and memoranda?"

The Senator shook his head. "There was nothing of the slightest use to a stranger. As a matter of fact, just two days ago, I took pains to destroy the only portfolio of valuable documents in the safe."

Madelyn stooped thoughtfully over the litter of papers on the rug. "You mean three evenings ago, don't you?"

"How on earth, Miss Mack—"

"You refer to the memoranda that you and Mr. Rennick were working on the night before his death, do you not?"

"Of course!" And then I saw Senator Duffield was staring at his curt questioner as though he had said something he hadn't meant to.

"I think you told me once before that the combination of your safe was known only to yourself and Mr. Rennick?" "You are correct."

"Then, to your knowledge, you are the only living person, who possesses this information at the present time?"

"That is the case. It was a rather intricate combination, and we changed it hardly a month ago."

Madelyn rose from the safe, glanced reflectively at a huge leather chair, and sank into its depths with a sigh.

"You say nothing has been stolen, Senator, that the burglar's visit yielded him nothing. For your peace of mind, I would like to agree with you, but I am sorry to inform you that you are mistaken."

"Surely, Miss Mack, you are hasty! I am confident that I have searched my possessions with the utmost care." "Nevertheless, you have been robbed!" Senator Duffield glanced down at her small lithe figure impatiently. "Then, perhaps, you will be good enough to tell me of what my loss consists?"

"I refer to the article for which your secretary was murdered! It was stolen from this room last night."

Had the point of a dagger pressed against Senator Dulfield's shoulders, he could not have bounded forward in greater consternation. His composure was shattered like a pane of glass crumbling.

He sprang toward the safe with a cry like a man in sudden fear or agony. Jerking back its door, he plunged his hand into its lower left compartment. When he straightened, he held a long, wax phonograph record.

His dismay had vanished in a quick blending of relief and anger, as his eyes swept from the cylinder to the grave figure of Madelyn Mack.

"I fail to appreciate your joke, Miss Mack—if you call it a joke to frighten a man without cause as you have me!"

"Have you examined the record in your hand, Senator?"

Fletcher Duffield and I stared at the two. There was a suggestion of tragedy in the scene as the impatience and irritation gradually faded from the Senator's face.

"It is a substitute!" he groaned. "A substitute! I have been tricked, victimized, robbed!"

He stood staring at the wax record as though it were a heated iron burning into his flesh. Suddenly it slipped from his fingers and was shattered on the floor.

But he did not appear to notice the fact as he burst out, "Do you realize that you are standing here inactive while the thief is escaping? I don't know how your wit surprised my secret, and don't care now, but you are throwing away your chances of stopping the burglar while he may be putting miles between himself and us! Are you made of ice, woman? Can't you appreciate what this means? In the name of heaven, Miss Mack—"

"The thief will not escape, Mr. Duffield!"

"It seems to me that he has already escaped."

"Let me assure you, Senator, that your missing property is as secure as though it were locked in your safe at this moment!"

"But do you realize that, once a hint of its nature is known, it will be almost worthless to me?"

"Better perhaps than you do,—so well that I pledge myself to return it to your hands within the next half hour!"

Senator Duffield took three steps forward until he stood so close to Madelyn that he could have reached over and touched her on the shoulder.

"I am an old man, Miss Mack, and the last two days have brought me almost to a collapse. If I have appeared unduly sharp, I tender you my apologies—but do not give me false hopes! Tell me frankly that you cannot encourage me. It will be a kindness. You will realize that I cannot blame you."

Senator Duffield's imperious attitude was so broken that I could hardly believe it possible that the same men who ruled a great political party, almost by the sway of his finger, was speaking. Madelyn caught his hand with a grasp of assurance.

"I will promise even more." She snapped open her watch "If you will return to this room at nine o'clock, not only will I restore your stolen property—but I will deliver the murderer of Raymond Rennick!"

"Rennick's murderer?" the Senator gasped.

Madelyn bowed. "In this room at nine o'clock."

I think I was the first to move toward the door. Fletcher Duffield hesitated a moment, staring at Madelyn, then he turned and hurried past me down the hall. His father followed more slowly. As he closed the door, I saw Madelyn standing where we had left her, leaning back against her chair, and staring at a woman's black slipper. It was the one which had been found by Raymond Rennick's dead body.

I made my way mechanically toward the dining-room, and was surprised to find that the members of the Duffield family were already at the table. With the exception of Madelyn, it was the same breakfast group as the morning before. In another house, this attempt to maintain the conventions in the face of tragedy might have seemed incongruous; but it was so thoroughly in keeping with the self-contained Duffield character that, after the first shock, I realized it was not at all surprising. I fancy that we all breathed a sigh of relief, however, when the meal was over.

We were rising from the table, when a folded note addressed to the Senator, was handed to the butler from the hall. He glanced through it hurriedly, and held up his hand for us to wait.

"This is from Miss Mack. She requests me to have all of the members of the family, and those servants who have furnished any evidence in connection with the, er—murder"—the Senator winced as he spoke the word—"to assemble in the library at nine o'clock. I think that we owe it both to ourselves and to her to obey her instructions to the letter. Perkins, will you kindly notify the servants?"

As it happened, Madelyn's audience in the library was increased by two spectators she had not named. The tooting of a motor sounded without, and the tall figure of Senator Burroughs met us as we were leaving the dining-room. Senator Duffield took his arm with a glance of relief, and explained the situation as he forced him to accompany us.

VI.

In the library, we found for the first time that Madelyn was not alone. Engaged in a low conversation with her, which ceased as we entered, was Inspector Taylor. He had evidently been designated as the spokesman of the occasion. "Is everybody here?" he asked.

"I think so," Senator Duffield replied. "There are really only five of the servants who count in the case."

Madelyn's eyes flashed over the circle. "Close the door, please, Mr. Taylor. I think you had better lock it also."

"There are fourteen persons in this room," she continued, "counting, of course, Inspector Taylor, Miss Noraker and myself. We may safely be said to be outside the case. There are then eleven persons here connected in some degree with the tragedy. It is in this list of eleven that I have searched for the murderer. I am happy to tell you that my search has been successful!"

Senator Duffield was the first to speak. "You mean to say, Miss Mack, that the murderer is in this room at the present time?"

"Correct."

"Then you accuse one of this group—"

"Of dealing the blow which killed your secretary, and, later, of plundering your safe."

Inspector Taylor moved quietly to a post between the two windows. Escape from the room was barred. I darted a stealthy glance around the circle in an effort to surprise a trace of guilt in the faces before me, and was startled to find my neighbors engaged in the same furtive occupation. Of the women of the family, the Senator's wife, had compressed her lips as though, as mistress of the house, she felt the need of maintaining her composure in any situation. Maria was toying with her bracelet, while Beth made no effort to conceal her agitation.

Senator Burroughs was studying the pattern of the carpet with a face as inscrutable as a mask. Fletcher Duffield was sitting back in his chair, his hands in his pockets. His father was leaning against the locked door, his eyes flashing from face to face. With the exception of Dorrence, the valet, and Perkins, the butler, who I do not think would have stirred out of their stolidness had the ceiling fallen, the servants were in an utter panic. Two of the maids were plainly bordering on hysterics.

Such was the group that faced Madelyn in the Duffield library. One of the number was a murderer, whom the next ten minutes were to brand as such. Which was it? Instinctively my eyes turned again toward the three women of the Duffield family, as Madelyn walked across to a portiere which screened a corner of the apartment.

Jerking it aside, she showed, suspended from a hook in the ceiling, a quarter of fresh veal.

On an adjoining stand was a long, thin-bladed knife, which might have been a dagger, ground to a razor-edge. Madelyn held it before her as she turned to us.

"This is the weapon which killed Mr. Rennick." I fancied I heard a gasp as she spoke. Although I whirled almost on the instant, however, I could detect no signs of it in the faces behind me.

"I propose to conduct a short experiment, which I assure you is absolutely necessary to my chain of reasoning," Madelyn continued. "You may or may not know that the body of a calf practically offers the same degree of resistance to a knife as the body of a man. Dead flesh, of course, is harder and firmer than living flesh, but I think that, adding the thickness of clothes, we may take it for granted that in the quarter of veal before us, we have a fair substitute for the body of Raymond Rennick. Now watch me closely, please!"

Drawing back her arm, she plunged her knife into the meat with a force which sent it spinning on its hook. She drew the knife out, and examined it reflectively.

"I have made a cut of only a little more than three and a half inches. The blow which killed Mr. Rennick penetrated at least five inches.

"Here we encounter a singularly striking feature of our case, involving a stratagem which I think I can safely say is the most unique in my experience. To all intents, it was a woman who killed Mr. Rennick. In fact, it has been taken for granted that he met his death at the hand of a female assassin. We must dispose of this conclusion at the outset, for the simple reason that it was physically impossible for a woman to have dealt the death blow!"

I chanced to be gazing directly at Fletcher Duffield as Madelyn made the statement. An expression of such relief flashed into his face that instinctively I turned about and followed the direction of his glance. His eyes were fixed on his sister, Beth.

Madelyn deposited the knife on the stand.

"Indeed, I may say there are few men—perhaps not one in ten—with a wrist strong enough to have dealt Mr. Rennick's death blow," she went on. "There is only one such person among the fourteen in this room at the present time.

"Again you will recall that the wound was delivered from the rear just as Mr. Rennick faced about in his own defence. Had he been attacked by a woman, he would have heard the rustle of her dress several feet before she possibly could have reached him. I think you will recall my demonstration of that fact yesterday morning, Mr. Duffield.

"Obviously then, it is a man whom we must seek if we would find the murderer of your secretary, and a man of certain peculiar characteristics. Two of these I can name now. He possessed a wrist developed to an extraordinary degree, and he owned feet as small and shapely as a woman's. Otherwise, the stratagem of wearing a woman's slippers and leaving one of them near the scene of the crime to divert suspicion from himself, would never have occurred to him!"

Again I thought I heard a gasp behind me, but its owner escaped me a second time.

"There was a third marked feature among the physical characteristics of the murderer. He was near-sighted—so much so that it was necessary for him to wear glasses of the kind known technically as a 'double lens.' Unfortunately for the assassin, when his victim fell, the latter caught the glasses in his hand, and they were broken under his body. The murderer may have been thrown into a panic, and feared to take the time to recover his spectacles; but it was a fatal blunder. Fortune, however, might have helped him even then in spite of this fact, for those who found the body fell into the natural error of considering the glasses to be the property of the murdered man. Had it not been for two minor details, this impression might never have been contradicted."

Madelyn held up a packet of newspaper illustrations. Several of them I recognized as the pictures of the murdered secretary that she had shown me at the "Roanoke." The others were also photographs of the same man.

"If Mr. Rennick hadn't been fond of having his picture taken, the fact that he never wore glasses on the street might not have been noticed. None of his pictures, not even the snap-shots, showed a man in spectacles. It is true that he did possess a pair, and it is here where those who discovered the crime went astray. But they were for reading purposes only, the kind termed a .125 lens, while those of his assailant were a .210 lens. To clinch the matter, I later found Mr. Rennick's own spectacles in his room where he had left them the evening before."

Madelyn held up the red leather case she had found on the mantel-piece, and tapped it musingly as she gave a slight nod to Inspector Taylor.

"We have now the following description of the murderer—a slenderly built man, with an unusual wrist, possibly an athlete at one time, who possesses a foot capable of squeezing into a woman's shoe, and who is handicapped by near-sightedness. Is there an individual in this room to whom this description applies?"

There was a new glitter in Madelyn's eyes as she continued.

"Through the co-operation of Inspector Taylor, I am enabled to answer this question. Mr. Taylor has traced the glasses of the assassin to the optician who gave the prescription for them. I am not surprised to find that the owner of the spectacles tallies with the owner of these other interesting articles."

With the words, she whisked from the stand at her elbow, the long, narrow-bladed dagger, and a pair of soiled, black suede slippers.

There was a suggestion of grotesque unreality about it all. It was much as though I had been viewing the denouement of a play from the snug vantage point of an orchestra seat, waiting for the lights to flare up and the curtain to ring down. A shriek ran through my ears, jarring me back to the realization that I was not a spectator, but a part of the play.

A figure darted toward the window. It was John Dorrence, the valet.

The next instant Inspector Taylor threw himself on the fleeing man's shoulders, and the two went to the floor.

"Can you manage him?" Madelyn called.

"Unless he prefers cold steel through his body to cold steel about his wrists," was the rejoinder.

"I think you may dismiss the other servants, Senator," Madelyn said. "I wish, however, that the family would remain a few moments."

As the door closed again, she continued, "I promised you also, Senator, the return of your stolen property. I have the honor to make that promise good."

From her stand, which was rapidly assuming the proportions of a conjurer's table, she produced a round, brown paper parcel.

"Before I unwrap this, have I your permission to explain its contents?"

"As you will, Miss Mack."

"Perhaps the most puzzling feature of the tragedy is the motive. It is this parcel which supplies us with the answer.

"Your secretary, Mr. Duffield, was an exceptional young man. Not only did he repeatedly resist bribery such as comes to few men, but he gave his life for his trust.

"At any time since this parcel came into his possession, he could have sold it for a fortune. Because he refused to sell it he was murdered for it. Perhaps every reader of the newspapers is more or less familiar with Senator Duffield's investigations of the ravages of a certain great Trust. A few days ago, the Senator came into possession of evidence against the combine of such a drastic nature that he realized it would mean nothing less than the annihilation of the monopoly, imprisonment for the chief officers, and a business sensation such as this country has seldom known.

"Once the officers of the Trust knew of his evidence, however, they would be forearmed in such a manner that its value would be largely destroyed. The evidence was a remarkable piece of detective work. It consisted of a phonographic record of a secret directors' meeting, laying bare the inmost depredations of the corporation."

Madelyn paused as the handcuffed valet showed signs of a renewed struggle. Inspector Taylor without comment calmly snapped a second pair of bracelets about his feet.

"The Trust was shrewd enough to appreciate the value of a spy in the Duffield home. Dorrence was engaged for the post, and from what I have learned of his character, he filled it admirably. How he stumbled on Senator Duffield's latest coup is immaterial. The main point is that he tried to bribe Mr. Rennick so persistently to betray his post that the latter threatened to expose him. Partly in the fear that he would carry out his threat, and partly in the hope that he carried memoranda which might lead to the discovery of the evidence that he sought, Dorrence planned and carried out the murder.

"In the secretary's pocket he discovered the combination of the safe, and made use of it last night. I found the stolen phonograph record this morning behind the register of the furnace pipe in Dorrence's room. I had already found that this was his cache, containing the dagger which killed Rennick, and the second of Cinderella's slippers. The pair was stolen some days ago from the room of Miss Beth Duffield."

The swirl of the day was finally over. Dorrence had been led to his cell; the coroner's jury had returned its verdict; and all that was mortal of Raymond Rennick had been laid in its last resting place. Madelyn and I had settled ourselves in the homeward bound Pullman as it rumbled out of the Boston station in the early dusk.

"There are two questions I want to ask," I said reflectively.

Madelyn looked up from her newspaper with a yawn.

"Why did John Dorrence bring you back a blank sheet of paper when you despatched him on your errand?"

"As a matter of fact, there was nothing else for him to bring back. Mr. Taylor kept him at police headquarters long enough to give me time to carry my search through his room. The message was a blind."

"And what was the quarrel that the servant girl, Anna, heard in the Duffield library?"

"It wasn't a quarrel, my dear girl. It was the Senator preparing the speech with which he intended to launch his evidence against the Trust. The Senator is in the habit of dictating his speeches to a phonograph. Some of them I am afraid, are rather fiery."

Arsène Lupin in Prison

Maurice Leblanc

THERE is no tourist worthy of the name who does not know the banks of the Seine, and has not noticed, in passing, the little feudal castle of the Malaquis, built upon a rock in the centre of the river. An arched bridge connects it with the shore. All around it, the calm waters of the great river play peacefully amongst the reeds, and the wagtails flutter over the moist crests of the stones.

The history of the Malaquis castle is stormy like its name, harsh like its outlines. It has passed through a long series of combats, sieges, assaults, rapines and massacres. A recital of the crimes that have been committed there would cause the stoutest heart to tremble. There are many mysterious legends connected with the castle, and they tell us of a famous subterranean tunnel that formerly led to the abbey of Jumieges and to the manor of Agnes Sorel, mistress of Charles VII.

In that ancient habitation of heroes and brigands, the Baron Nathan Cahorn now lived; or Baron Satan as he was formerly called on the Bourse, where he had acquired a fortune with incredible rapidity. The lords of Malaquis, absolutely ruined, had been obliged to sell the ancient castle at a great sacrifice. It contained an admirable collection of furniture, pictures, wood carvings, and faience. The Baron lived there alone, attended by three old servants. No one ever enters the place. No one had ever beheld the three Rubens that he possessed, his two Watteau, his Jean Goujon pulpit, and the many other treasures that he had acquired by a vast expenditure of money at public sales.

Baron Satan lived in constant fear, not for himself, but for the treasures that he had accumulated with such an earnest devotion and with so much perspicacity that the shrewdest merchant could not say that the Baron had ever erred in his taste or judgment. He loved them—his bibelots. He loved them intensely, like a miser; jealously, like a lover. Every day, at sunset, the iron gates at either end of the bridge and at the entrance to the court of honor are closed and barred. At the least touch on these gates, electric bells will ring throughout the castle.

One Thursday in September, a letter-carrier presented himself at the gate at the head of the bridge, and, as usual, it was the Baron himself who partially opened the heavy portal. He scrutinized the man as minutely as if he were a stranger, although the honest face and twinkling eyes of the postman had been familiar to the Baron for many years. The man laughed, as he said:

"It is only I, Monsieur le Baron. It is not another man wearing my cap and blouse."

"One can never tell," muttered the Baron.

The man handed him a number of newspapers, and then said:

"And now, Monsieur le Baron, here is something new."

"Something new?"

"Yes, a letter. A registered letter."

Living as a recluse, without friends or business relations, the baron never received any letters, and the one now presented to him immediately aroused within him a feeling of suspicion and distrust. It was like an evil omen. Who was this mysterious correspondent that dared to disturb the tranquility of his retreat?

"You must sign for it, Monsieur le Baron."

He signed; then took the letter, waited until the postman had disappeared beyond the bend in the road, and, after walking nervously to and fro for a few minutes, he leaned against the parapet of the bridge and opened the envelope. It contained a sheet of paper, bearing this heading: Prison de la Santé, Paris. He looked at the signature: Arsène Lupin. Then he read:

"*Monsieur Le Baron:*

"*There is, in the gallery in your castle, a picture of Philippe de Champaigne, of exquisite finish, which pleases me beyond measure. Your Rubens are also to my taste, as well as your smallest Watteau. In the salon to the right, I have noticed the Louis XIII cadence-table, the tapestries of Beauvais, the Empire gueridon signed 'Jacob,' and the Renaissance chest. In the salon to the left, all the cabinet full of jewels and miniatures.*

"For the present, I will content myself with those articles that can be conveniently removed. I will therefore ask you to pack them carefully and ship them to me, charges prepaid, to the station at Batignolles, within eight days, otherwise I shall be obliged to remove them myself during the night of 27 September; but, under those circumstances, I shall not content myself with the articles above mentioned.

"Accept my apologies for any inconvenience I may cause you, and believe me to be your humble servant,

"Arsène Lupin."

"P. S.—Please do not send the largest Watteau. Although you paid thirty thousand francs for it, it is only a copy, the original having been burned, under the Directoire by Barras, during a night of debauchery. Consult the memoirs of Garat.

"I do not care for the Louis XV chatelaine, as I doubt its authenticity."

That letter completely upset the baron. Had it borne any other signature, he would have been greatly alarmed—but signed by Arsène Lupin!

As an habitual reader of the newspapers, he was versed in the history of recent crimes, and was therefore well acquainted with the exploits of the mysterious burglar. Of course, he knew that Lupin had been arrested in America by his enemy Ganimard and was at present incarcerated in the Prison de la Santé. But he knew also that any miracle might be expected from Arsène Lupin. Moreover, that exact knowledge of the castle, the location of the pictures and furniture, gave the affair an alarming aspect. How could he have acquired that information concerning things that no one had ever seen?

The baron raised his eyes and contemplated the stern outlines of the castle, its steep rocky pedestal, the depth of the surrounding water, and shrugged his shoulders. Certainly, there was no danger. No one in the world could force an entrance to the sanctuary that contained his priceless treasures.

No one, perhaps, but Arsène Lupin! For him, gates, walls and drawbridges did not exist. What use were the most formidable obstacles or the most careful precautions, if Arsène Lupin had decided to effect an entrance?

That evening, he wrote to the Procurer of the Republique at Rouen. He enclosed the threatening letter and solicited aid and protection.

The reply came at once to the effect that Arsène Lupin was in custody in the Prison de la Santé, under close surveillance, with no opportunity to write such a letter, which was, no doubt, the work of some imposter. But, as an act of precaution, the Procurer had submitted the letter to an expert in handwriting, who declared that, in spite of certain resemblances, the writing was not that of the prisoner.

But the words "in spite of certain resemblances" caught the attention of the baron; in them, he read the possibility of a doubt which appeared to him quite sufficient to warrant the intervention of the law. His fears increased. He read Lupin's letter over and over again. "I shall be obliged to remove them myself." And then there was the fixed date: the night of 27 September.

To confide in his servants was a proceeding repugnant to his nature; but now, for the first time in many years, he experienced the necessity of seeking counsel with some one. Abandoned by the legal official of his own district, and feeling unable to defend himself with his own resources, he was on the point of going to Paris to engage the services of a detective.

Two days passed; on the third day, he was filled with hope and joy as he read the following item in the 'Réveil de Caudebec', a newspaper published in a neighboring town:

"We have the pleasure of entertaining in our city, at the present time, the veteran detective Mon. Ganimard who acquired a world-wide reputation by his clever capture of Arsène Lupin. He has come here for rest and recreation, and, being an enthusiastic fisherman, he threatens to capture all the fish in our river."

Ganimard! Ah, here is the assistance desired by Baron Cahorn! Who could baffle the schemes of Arsène Lupin better than Ganimard, the patient and astute detective? He was the man for the place.

The baron did not hesitate. The town of Caudebec was only six kilometers from the castle, a short distance to a man whose step was accelerated by the hope of safety.

After several fruitless attempts to ascertain the detective's address, the baron visited the office of the 'Réveil,' situated on the quai. There he found the writer of the article who, approaching the window, exclaimed:

"Ganimard? Why, you are sure to see him somewhere on the quai with his fishing-pole. I met him there and chanced to read his name engraved on his rod. Ah, there he is now, under the trees."

"That little man, wearing a straw hat?"

"Exactly. He is a gruff fellow, with little to say."

Five minutes later, the baron approached the celebrated Ganimard, introduced himself and sought to commence a conversation, but that was a failure. Then he broached the real object of his interview, and briefly stated his case. The other listened, motionless, with his attention riveted on his fishing-rod. When the baron had finished his story, the fisherman turned, with an air of profound pity, and said:

"Monsieur, it is not customary for thieves to warn people they are about to rob. Arsène Lupin, especially, would not commit such a folly."

"But—"

"Monsieur, if I had the least doubt, believe me, the pleasure of again capturing Arsène Lupin would place me at your disposal. But, unfortunately, that young man is already under lock and key."

"He may have escaped."

"No one ever escaped from the Santé."

"But, he—"

"He, no more than any other."

"Yet—"

"Well, if he escapes, so much the better. I will catch him again. Meanwhile, you go home and sleep soundly. That will do for the present. You frighten the fish."

The conversation was ended. The baron returned to the castle, reassured to some extent by Ganimard's indifference. He examined the bolts, watched the servants, and, during the next forty-eight hours, he became almost persuaded that his fears were groundless. Certainly, as Ganimard had said, thieves do not warn people they are about to rob.

The fateful day was close at hand. It was now the twenty-sixth of September and nothing had happened. But at three o'clock the bell rang. A boy brought this telegram:

"No goods at Batignolles station. Prepare everything for tomorrow night. Arsène."

This telegram threw the baron into such a state of excitement that he even considered the advisability of yielding to Lupin's demands.

However, he hastened to Caudebec. Ganimard was fishing at the same place, seated on a campstool. Without a word, he handed him the telegram.

"Well, what of it?" said the detective.

"What of it? But it is tomorrow."

"What is tomorrow?"

"The robbery! The pillage of my collections!"

Ganimard laid down his fishing-rod, turned to the baron, and exclaimed, in a tone of impatience:

"Ah! Do you think I am going to bother myself about such a silly story as that!"

"How much do you ask to pass tomorrow night in the castle?"

"Not a sou. Now, leave me alone."

"Name your own price. I am rich and can pay it."

This offer disconcerted Ganimard, who replied, calmly:

"I am here on a vacation. I have no right to undertake such work."

"No one will know. I promise to keep it secret."

"Oh! nothing will happen."

"Come! three thousand francs. Will that be enough?"

The detective, after a moment's reflection, said:

"Very well. But I must warn you that you are throwing your money out of the window."

"I do not care."

"In that case . . . but, after all, what do we know about this devil Lupin! He may have quite a numerous band of robbers with him. Are you sure of your servants?"

"My faith—"

"Better not count on them. I will telegraph for two of my men to help me. And now, go! It is better for us not to be seen together. Tomorrow evening about nine o'clock."

The following day—the date fixed by Arsène Lupin—Baron Cahorn arranged all his panoply of war, furbished his weapons, and, like a sentinel, paced to and fro in front of the castle. He saw nothing, heard nothing. At half-past eight o'clock in the evening, he dismissed his servants. They occupied rooms in a wing of the building, in a retired spot, well removed from the main portion of the castle. Shortly there-after, the baron heard the sound of approaching footsteps. It was Gani-mard and his two assistants—great, powerful fellows with immense hands, and necks like bulls. After asking a few questions relating to the location of the various entrances and rooms, Ganimard carefully closed and barricaded all the doors and windows through which one could gain access to the threatened rooms. He inspected the walls, raised the tapestries, and finally installed his assistants in the central gallery which was located between the two salons.

"No nonsense! We are not here to sleep. At the slightest sound, open the windows of the court and call me. Pay attention also to the water-side. Ten metres of perpendicular rock is no obstacle to those devils."

Ganimard locked his assistants in the gallery, carried away the keys, and said to the baron:

"And now, to our post."

He had chosen for himself a small room located in the thick outer wall, between the two principal doors, and which, in former years, had been the watchman's quarters. A peep-hole opened upon the bridge; another on the court. In one corner, there was an opening to a tunnel.

"I believe you told me, Monsieur le Baron, that this tunnel is the only subterranean entrance to the castle and that it has been closed up for time immemorial?"

"Yes."

"Then, unless there is some other entrance, known only to Arsène Lupin, we are quite safe."

He placed three chairs together, stretched himself upon them, lighted his pipe and sighed:

"Really, Monsieur le Baron, I feel ashamed to accept your money for such a sinecure as this. I will tell the story to my friend Lupin. He will enjoy it immensely."

The baron did not laugh. He was anxiously listening, but heard nothing save the beating of his own heart. From time to time, he leaned over the tunnel and cast a fearful eye into its depths. He heard the clock strike eleven, twelve, one.

Suddenly, he seized Ganimard's arm. The latter leaped up, awakened from his sleep.

"Do you hear?" asked the baron, in a whisper.

"Yes."

"What is it?"

"I was snoring, I suppose."

"No, no, listen."

"Ah! yes, it is the horn of an automobile."

"Well?"

"Well! it is very improbable that Lupin would use an automobile like a battering-ram to demolish your castle. Come, Monsieur le Baron, return to your post. I am going to sleep. Good-night."

That was the only alarm. Ganimard resumed his interrupted slumbers, and the baron heard nothing except the regular snoring of his companion. At break of day, they left the room. The castle was enveloped in a profound calm; it was a peaceful dawn on the bosom of a tranquil river. They mounted the stairs, Cahorn radiant with joy, Ganimard calm as usual. They heard no sound; they saw nothing to arouse suspicion.

"What did I tell you, Monsieur le Baron? Really, I should not have accepted your offer. I am ashamed."

He unlocked the door and entered the gallery. Upon two chairs, with drooping heads and pendent arms, the detective's two assistants were asleep.

"Tonnerre de nom d'un chien!" exclaimed Ganimard. At the same moment, the baron cried out:

"The pictures! The credence!"

He stammered, choked, with arms outstretched toward the empty places, toward the denuded walls where naught remained but the useless nails and cords. The Watteau, disappeared! The Rubens, carried away! The tapestries taken down! The cabinets, despoiled of their jewels!

"And my Louis XVI candelabra! And the Regent chandelier! . . . And my twelfth-century Virgin!"

He ran from one spot to another in wildest despair. He recalled the purchase price of each article, added up the figures, counted his losses, pell-mell, in confused words and unfinished phrases. He stamped with rage; he groaned with grief. He acted like a ruined man whose only hope is suicide.

If anything could have consoled him, it would have been the stupe-faction displayed by Ganimard. The famous detective did not move. He appeared to be petrified; he examined the room in a listless manner. The windows? . . . . closed. The locks on the doors? . . . . intact. Not a break in the ceiling; not a hole in the floor. Everything was in perfect order. The theft had been carried out methodically, according to a logical and inexorable plan.

"Arsène Lupin. . . . Arsène Lupin," he muttered.

Suddenly, as if moved by anger, he rushed upon his two assistants and shook them violently. They did not awaken.

"The devil!" he cried. "Can it be possible?"

He leaned over them and, in turn, examined them closely. They were asleep; but their response was unnatural.

"They have been drugged," he said to the baron.

"By whom?"

"By him, of course, or his men under his discretion. That work bears his stamp."

"In that case, I am lost—nothing can be done."

"Nothing," assented Ganimard.

"It is dreadful; it is monstrous."

"Lodge a complaint."

"What good will that do?"

"Oh; it is well to try it. The law has some resources."

"The law! Bah! it is useless. You represent the law, and, at this moment, when you should be looking for a clue and trying to discover something, you do not even stir."

"Discover something with Arsène Lupin! Why, my dear monsieur, Arsène Lupin never leaves any clue behind him. He leaves nothing to chance. Sometimes I think he put himself in my way and simply allowed me to arrest him in America."

"Then, I must renounce my pictures! He has taken the gems of my collection. I would give a fortune to recover them. If there is no other way, let him name his own price."

Ganimard regarded the baron attentively, as he said:

"Now, that is sensible. Will you stick to it?"

"Yes, yes. But why?"

"An idea that I have."

"What is it?"

"We will discuss it later—if the official examination does not succeed. But, not one word about me, if you wish my assistance."

He added, between his teeth:

"It is true I have nothing to boast of in this affair."

The assistants were gradually regaining consciousness with the bewildered air of people who come out of an hypnotic sleep. They opened their eyes and looked about them in astonishment. Ganimard questioned them; they remembered nothing.

"But you must have seen some one?"

"No."

"Can't you remember?"

"No, no."

"Did you drink anything?"

They considered a moment, and then one of them replied:

"Yes, I drank a little water."

"Out of that carafe?"

'Yes."

"So did I," declared the other.

Ganimard smelled and tasted it. It had no particular taste and no odor.

"Come," he said, "we are wasting our time here. One can't decide an Arsène Lupin problem in five minutes. But, morbleu! I swear I will catch him again."

The same day, a charge of burglary was duty performed by Baron Cahorn against Arsène Lupin, a prisoner in the Prison de la Santé.

The baron afterwards regretted making the charge against Lupin when he saw his castle delivered over to the gendarmes, the procureur, the judge d'instruction, the newspaper reporters and photographers, and a throng of idle curiosity-seekers.

The affair soon became a topic of general discussion, and the name of Arsène Lupin excited the public imagination to such an extent that the newspapers filled their columns with the most fantastic stories of his exploits which found ready credence amongst their readers.

But the letter of Arsène Lupin that was published in the 'Echo de France' (no one ever knew how the newspaper obtained it), that letter in which Baron Cahorn was impudently warned of the coming theft, caused considerable excitement. The most fabulous theories were advanced. Some recalled the existence of the famous subterranean tunnels, and that was the line of research pursued by the officers of the law, who searched the house from top to bottom, questioned every stone, studied the wainscoting and the chimneys, the window-frames and the girders in the ceilings. By the light of torches, they examined the immense cellars where the lords of Malaquis were wont to store their munitions and provisions. They sounded the rocky foundation to its very centre. But it was all in vain. They discovered no trace of a subterranean tunnel. No secret passage existed.

But the eager public declared that the pictures and furniture could not vanish like so many ghosts. They are substantial, material things and require doors and windows for their exits and their entrances, and so do the people that remove them. Who were those people? How did they gain access to the castle? And how did they leave it?

The police officers of Rouen, convinced of their own impotence, solicited the assistance of the Parisian detective force. Mon. Dudouis, chief of the Sûreté, sent the best sleuths of the iron brigade. He himself spent forty-eight hours at the castle, but met with no success. Then he sent for Ganimard, whose past services had proved so useful when all else failed.

Ganimard listened, in silence, to the instructions of his superior; then, shaking his head, he said:

"In my opinion, it is useless to ransack the castle. The solution of the problem lies elsewhere."

"Where, then?"

"With Arsène Lupin."

"With Arsène Lupin! To support that theory, we must admit his intervention."

"I do admit it. In fact, I consider it quite certain."

"Come, Ganimard, that is absurd. Arsène Lupin is in prison."

"I grant you that Arsène Lupin is in prison, closely guarded; but he must have fetters on his feet, manacles on his wrists, and gag in his mouth before I change my opinion."

"Why so obstinate, Ganimard?"

"Because Arsène Lupin is the only man in France of sufficient calibre to invent and carry out a scheme of that magnitude."

"Mere words, Ganimard."

"But true ones. Look! What are they doing? Searching for subterranean passages, stones swinging on pivots, and other nonsense of that kind. But Lupin doesn't employ such old-fashioned methods. He is a modern cracksman, right up to date."

"And how would you proceed?"

"I should ask your permission to spend an hour with him."

"In his cell?"

"Yes. During the return trip from America we became very friendly, and I venture to say that if he can give me any information without compromising himself he will not hesitate to save me from incurring useless trouble."

It was shortly after noon when Ganimard entered the cell of Arsène Lupin. The latter, who was lying on his bed, raised his head and uttered a cry of apparent joy.

"Ah! This is a real surprise. My dear Ganimard, here!"

"Ganimard himself."

"In my chosen retreat, I have felt a desire for many things, but my fondest wish was to receive you here."

"Very kind of you, I am sure."

"Not at all. You know I hold you in the highest regard."

"I am proud of it."

"I have always said: Ganimard is our best detective. He is almost,— you see how candid I am!—he is almost as clever as Sherlock Holmes. But I am sorry that I cannot offer you anything better than this hard stool. And no refreshments! Not even a glass of beer! Of course, you will excuse me, as I am here only temporarily."

Ganimard smiled, and accepted the proffered seat. Then the prisoner continued:

"Mon Dieu, how pleased I am to see the face of an honest man. I am so tired of those devils of spies who come here ten times a day to ransack my pockets and my cell to satisfy themselves that I am not preparing to escape. The government is very solicitous on my account."

"It is quite right."

"Why so? I should be quite contented if they would allow me to live in my own quiet way."

"On other people's money."

"Quite so. That would be so simple. But here, I am joking, and you are, no doubt, in a hurry. So let us come to business, Ganimard. To what do I owe the honor of this visit?

"The Cahorn affair," declared Ganimard, frankly.

"Ah! Wait, one moment. You see I have had so many affairs! First, let me fix in my mind the circumstances of this particular case. . . . Ah! yes, now I have it. The Cahorn affair, Malaquis castle, Seine-Inférieure. . . . Two Rubens, a Watteau, and a few trifling articles."

"Trifling!"

"Oh! ma foi, all that is of slight importance. But it suffices to know that the affair interests you. How can I serve you, Ganimard?"

"Must I explain to you what steps the authorities have taken in the matter?"

"Not at all, I have read the newspapers and I will frankly state that you have made very little progress."

"And that is the reason I have come to see you."

"I am entirely at your service."

"In the first place, the Cahorn affair was managed by you?"

"From A to Z."

"The letter of warning? the telegram?"

"All mine. I ought to have the receipts somewhere."

Arsène opened the drawer of a small table of plain white wood which, with the bed and stool, constituted all the furniture in his cell, and took therefrom two scraps of paper which he handed to Ganimard.

"Ah!" exclaimed the detective, in surprise, "I thought you were closely guarded and searched, and I find that you read the newspapers and collect postal receipts."

"Bah! these people are so stupid! They open the lining of my vest, they examine the soles of my shoes, they sound the walls of my cell, but they never imagine that Arsène Lupin would be foolish enough to choose such a simple hiding place."

Ganimard laughed, as he said:

"What a droll fellow you are! Really, you bewilder me. But, come now, tell me about the Cahorn affair."

"Oh! oh! not quite so fast! You would rob me of all my secrets; expose all my little tricks. That is a very serious matter."

"Was I wrong to count on your complaisance?"

"No, Ganimard, and since you insist—"

Arsène Lupin paced his cell two or three times, then, stopping before Ganimard, he asked:

"What do you think of my letter to the baron?"

"I think you were amusing yourself by playing to the gallery."

"Ah! playing to the gallery! Come, Ganimard, I thought you knew me better. Do I, Arsène Lupin, ever waste my time on such puerilities? Would I have written that letter if I could have robbed the baron without writing to him? I want you to understand that the letter was indispensable; it was the motor that set the whole machine in motion. Now, let us discuss together a scheme for the robbery of the Malaquis castle. Are you willing?"

"Yes, proceed."

"Well, let us suppose a castle carefully closed and barricaded like that of the Baron Cahorn. Am I to abandon my scheme and renounce the treasures that I covet, upon the pretext that the castle which holds them is inaccessible?"

"Evidently not."

"Should I make an assault upon the castle at the head of a band of adventurers as they did in ancient times?"

"That would be foolish."

"Can I gain admittance by stealth or cunning?"

"Impossible."

"Then there is only one way open to me. I must have the owner of the castle invite me to it."

"That is surely an original method."

"And how easy! Let us suppose that one day the owner receives a letter warning him that a notorious burglar known as Arsène Lupin is plotting to rob him. What will he do?"

"Send a letter to the Procureur."

"Who will laugh at him, because the said Arsène Lupin is actually in prison. Then, in his anxiety and fear, the simple man will ask the assistance of the first-comer, will he not?"

"Very likely."

"And if he happens to read in a country newspaper that a celebrated detective is spending his vacation in a neighboring town—"

"He will seek that detective."

"Of course. But, on the other hand, let us presume that, having foreseen that state of affairs, the said Arsène Lupin has requested one of his friends to visit Caudebec, make the acquaintance of the editor of the 'Réveil,' a newspaper to which the baron is a subscriber, and let said editor understand that such person is the celebrated detective—then, what will happen?"

"The editor will announce in the 'Réveil' the presence in Caudebec of said detective."

"Exactly, and one of two things will happen: either the fish—I mean Cahorn—will not bite, and nothing will happen; or, what is more likely, he will run and greedily swallow the bait. Thus, behold my Baron Cahorn imploring the assistance of one of my friends against me."

"Original, indeed!"

"Of course, the pseudo-detective at first refuses to give any assistance. On top of that comes the telegram from Arsène Lupin The frightened baron rushes once more to my friend and offers him a definite sum of money for his services. My friend accepts and summons two members of our band, who, during the night, whilst Cahorn is under the watchful eye of his protector, removes certain articles by way of the window and lowers them with ropes into a nice little launch chartered for the occasion. Simple, isn't it?"

"Marvelous! Marvelous!" exclaimed Ganimard. "The boldness of the scheme and the ingenuity of all its details are beyond criticism. But who is the detective whose name and fame served as a magnet to attract the baron and draw him into your net?"

"There is only one name could do it—only one."

"And that is?"

"Arsène Lupin's personal enemy—the most illustrious Ganimard."

"I?"

"Yourself, Ganimard. And, really, it is very funny. If you go there, and the baron decides to talk, you will find that it will be your duty to arrest yourself, just as you arrested me in America. Hein! the revenge is realty amusing: I cause Ganimard to arrest Ganimard."

Arsène Lupin laughed heartily. The detective, greatly vexed, bit his lips; to him the joke was quite devoid of humor. The arrival of a prison guard gave Ganimard an opportunity to recover himself. The man brought Arsène Lupin's luncheon, furnished by a neighboring restaurant.

After depositing the tray upon the table, the guard retired. Lupin broke his bread, ate a few morsels, and continued:

"But, rest easy, my dear Ganimard, you will not go to Malaquis. I can tell you something that will astonish you: the Cahorn affair is on the point of being settled."

"Excuse me; I have just seen the Chief of the Sureté."

"What of that? Does Mon. Dudouis know my business better than I do myself? You will learn that Ganimard—excuse me—that the pseudo-Ganimard still remains on very good terms with the baron. The latter has authorized him to negotiate a very delicate transaction with me, and, at the present moment, in consideration of a certain sum, it is probable that the baron has recovered possession of his pictures and other treasures. And on their return, he will withdraw his complaint. Thus, there is no longer any theft, and the law must abandon the case."

Ganimard regarded the prisoner with a bewildered air.

"And how do you know all that?"

"I have just received the telegram I was expecting."

"You have just received a telegram?"

"This very moment, my dear friend. Out of politeness, I did not wish to read it in your presence. But if you will permit me—"

"You are joking, Lupin."

"My dear friend, if you will be so kind as to break that egg, you will learn for yourself that I am not joking."

Mechanically, Ganimard obeyed, and cracked the egg-shell with the blade of a knife. He uttered a cry of surprise. The shell contained nothing but a small piece of blue paper. At the request of Arsène he unfolded it. It was a telegram, or rather a portion of a telegram from which the post-marks had been removed. It read as follows:

"Contract closed. Hundred thousand balls delivered. All well."

"One hundred thousand balls?" said Ganimard.

"Yes, one hundred thousand francs. Very little, but then, you know, these are hard times. . . . And I have some heavy bills to meet. If you only knew my budget. . . . living in the city comes very high."

Ganimard arose. His ill humor had disappeared. He reflected for a moment, glancing over the whole affair in an effort to discover a weak point; then, in a tone and manner that betrayed his admiration of the prisoner, he said:

"Fortunately, we do not have a dozen such as you to deal with; if we did, we would have to close up shop."

Arsène Lupin assumed a modest air, as he replied:

"Bah! a person must have some diversion to occupy his leisure hours, especially when he is in prison."

"What!" exclaimed Ganimard, "your trial, your defense, the examination—isn't that sufficient to occupy your mind?"

"No, because I have decided not to be present at my trial."

"Oh! oh!"

Arsène Lupin repeated, positively.

"I shall not be present at my trial."

"Really!"

"Ah! my dear monsieur, do you suppose I am going to rot upon the wet straw? You insult me. Arsène Lupin remains in prison just as long as it pleases him, and not one minute more."

"Perhaps it would have been more prudent if you had avoided getting there," said the detective, ironically.

"Ah! monsieur jests? Monsieur must remember that he had the honor to effect my arrest. Know then, my worthy friend, that no one, not even you, could have placed a hand upon me if a much more important event had not occupied my attention at that critical moment."

"You astonish me."

"A woman was looking at me, Ganimard, and I loved her. Do you fully understand what that means: to be under the eyes of a woman that one loves? I cared for nothing in the world but that. And that is why I am here."

"Permit me to say: you have been here a long time."

"In the first place, I wished to forget. Do not laugh; it was a delightful adventure and it is still a tender memory. Besides, I have been suffering from neurasthenia. Life is so feverish these days that it is necessary to take the 'rest cure' occasionally, and I find this spot a sovereign remedy for my tired nerves."

"Arsène Lupin, you are not a bad fellow, after all."

"Thank you," said Lupin. "Ganimard, this is Friday. On Wednesday next, at four o'clock in the afternoon, I will smoke my cigar at your house in the rue Pergolese."

"Arsène Lupin, I will expect you."

They shook hands like two old friends who valued each other at their true worth; then the detective stepped to the door.

"Ganimard!"

"What is it?" asked Ganimard, as he turned back.

"You have forgotten your watch."

"My watch?"

"Yes, it strayed into my pocket."

He returned the watch, excusing himself.

"Pardon me. . . . a bad habit. Because they have taken mine is no reason why I should take yours. Besides, I have a chronometer here that satisfies me fairly well."

He took from the drawer a large gold watch and heavy chain.

"From whose pocket did that come?" asked Ganimard.

Arsène Lupin gave a hasty glance at the initials engraved on the watch.

"J.B. . . . . Who the devil can that be? . . . . Ah! yes, I remember. Jules Bouvier, the judge who conducted my examination. A charming fellow! . . . ."

The Coin of Dionysius

Ernest Bramah

IT was eight o'clock at night and raining, scarcely a time when a business so limited in its clientele as that of a coin dealer could hope to attract any customer, but a light was still showing in the small shop that bore over its window the name of Baxter, and in the even smaller office at the back the proprietor himself sat reading the latest *Pall Mall*. His enterprise seemed to be justified, for presently the door bell gave its announcement, and throwing down his paper Mr. Baxter went forward.

As a matter of fact the dealer had been expecting someone and his manner as he passed into the shop was unmistakably suggestive of a caller of importance. But at the first glance towards his visitor the excess of deference melted out of his bearing, leaving the urbane, self-possessed shopman in the presence of the casual customer.

"Mr. Baxter, I think?" said the latter. He had laid aside his dripping umbrella and was unbuttoning overcoat and coat to reach an inner pocket. "You hardly remember me, I suppose? Mr. Carlyle—two years ago I took up a case for you——"

"To be sure. Mr. Carlyle, the private detective——"

"Inquiry agent," corrected Mr. Carlyle precisely.

"Well," smiled Mr. Baxter, "for that matter I am a coin dealer and not an antiquarian or a numismatist. Is there anything in that way that I can do for you?"

"Yes," replied his visitor; "it is my turn to consult you." He had taken a small wash-leather bag from the inner pocket and now turned something carefully out upon the counter. "What can you tell me about that?"

The dealer gave the coin a moment's scrutiny.

"There is no question about this," he replied. "It is a Sicilian tetradrachm of Dionysius."

"Yes, I know that—I have it on the label out of the cabinet. I can tell you further that it's supposed to be one that Lord Seastoke gave two hundred and fifty pounds for at the Brice sale in '94."

235

"It seems to me that you can tell me more about it than I can tell you," remarked Mr. Baxter. "What is it that you really want to know?"

"I want to know," replied Mr. Carlyle, "whether it is genuine or not."

"Has any doubt been cast upon it?"

"Certain circumstances raised a suspicion—that is all."

The dealer took another look at the tetradrachm through his magnifying glass, holding it by the edge with the careful touch of an expert. Then he shook his head slowly in a confession of ignorance.

"Of course I could make a guess——"

"No, don't," interrupted Mr. Carlyle hastily. "An arrest hangs on it and nothing short of certainty is any good to me."

"Is that so, Mr. Carlyle?" said Mr. Baxter, with increased interest. "Well, to be quite candid, the thing is out of my line. Now if it was a rare Saxon penny or a doubtful noble I'd stake my reputation on my opinion, but I do very little in the classical series."

Mr. Carlyle did not attempt to conceal his disappointment as he returned the coin to the bag and replaced the bag in the inner pocket.

"I had been relying on you," he grumbled reproachfully. "Where on earth am I to go now?"

"There is always the British Museum."

"Ah, to be sure, thanks. But will anyone who can tell me be there now?"

"Now? No fear!" replied Mr. Baxter. "Go round in the morning——"

"But I must know to-night," explained the visitor, reduced to despair again. "To-morrow will be too late for the purpose."

Mr. Baxter did not hold out much encouragement in the circumstances.

"You can scarcely expect to find anyone at business now," he remarked. "I should have been gone these two hours myself only I happened to have an appointment with an American millionaire who fixed his own time." Something indistinguishable from a wink slid off Mr. Baxter's right eye. "Offmunson he's called, and a bright young pedigree-hunter has traced his descent from Offa, King of Mercia. So he—quite naturally—wants a set of Offas as a sort of collateral proof."

"Very interesting," murmured Mr. Carlyle, fidgeting with his watch. "I should love an hour's chat with you about your millionaire customers—some other time. Just now—look here, Baxter, can't you give me a line of introduction to some dealer in this sort of thing who happens to live in town? You must know dozens of experts."

"Why, bless my soul, Mr. Carlyle, I don't know a man of them away from his business," said Mr. Baxter, staring. "They may live in Park Lane or they may live in Petticoat Lane for all I know. Besides, there aren't so many experts as you seem to imagine. And the two best will very likely quarrel over it. You've had to do with 'expert witnesses,' I suppose?"

"I don't want a witness; there will be no need to give evidence. All I want is an absolutely authoritative pronouncement that I can act on. Is there no one who can really say whether the thing is genuine or not?"

Mr. Baxter's meaning silence became cynical in its implication as he continued to look at his visitor across the counter. Then he relaxed.

"Stay a bit; there is a man—an amateur—I remember hearing wonderful things about some time ago. They say he really does know."

"There you are," explained Mr. Carlyle, much relieved. "There always is someone. Who is he?"

"Funny name," replied Baxter. "Something Wynn or Wynn something." He craned his neck to catch sight of an important motor-car that was drawing to the kerb before his window. "Wynn Carrados! You'll excuse me now, Mr. Carlyle, won't you? This looks like Mr. Offmunson."

Mr. Carlyle hastily scribbled the name down on his cuff.

"Wynn Carrados, right. Where does he live?"

"Haven't the remotest idea," replied Baxter, referring the arrangement of his tie to the judgment of the wall mirror. "I have never seen the man myself. Now, Mr. Carlyle, I'm sorry I can't do any more for you. You won't mind, will you?"

Mr. Carlyle could not pretend to misunderstand. He enjoyed the distinction of holding open the door for the transatlantic representative of the line of Offa as he went out, and then made his way through the muddy streets back to his office. There was only one way of tracing a private individual at such short notice—through the pages of the directories, and the gentleman did not flatter himself by a very high estimate of his chances.

Fortune favoured him, however. He very soon discovered a Wynn Carrados living at Richmond, and, better still, further search failed to unearth another. There was, apparently, only one householder at all events of that name in the neighbourhood of London. He jotted down the address and set out for Richmond.

The house was some distance from the station, Mr. Carlyle learned. He took a taxicab and drove, dismissing the vehicle at the gate. He prided himself on his power of observation and the accuracy of the deductions which resulted from it—a detail of his business. "It's nothing more than using one's eyes and putting two and two together," he would modestly declare, when he wished to be deprecatory rather than impressive, and by the time he had reached the front door of "The Turrets" he had formed some opinion of the position and tastes of the man who lived there.

A man-servant admitted Mr. Carlyle and took in his card—his private card with the bare request for an interview that would not detain Mr. Carrados for ten minutes. Luck still favoured him; Mr. Carrados was at home and would see him at once. The servant, the hall through which they passed, and the room into which he was shown, all contributed something to the deductions which the quietly observant gentleman was half unconsciously recording.

"Mr. Carlyle," announced the servant.

The room was a library or study. The only occupant, a man of about Carlyle's own age, had been using a typewriter up to the moment of his visitor's entrance. He now turned and stood up with an expression of formal courtesy.

"It's very good of you to see me at this hour," apologised the caller.

The conventional expression of Mr. Carrados's face changed a little.

"Surely my man has got your name wrong?" he explained. "Isn't it Louis Calling?"

The visitor stopped short and his agreeable smile gave place to a sudden flash of anger or annoyance.

"No sir," he replied stiffly. "My name is on the card which you have before you."

"I beg your pardon," said Mr. Carrados, with perfect good-humour. "I hadn't seen it. But I used to know a Calling some years ago—at St. Michael's."

"St. Michael's!" Mr. Carlyle's features underwent another change, no less instant and sweeping than before. "St. Michael's! Wynn Carrados? Good heavens! it isn't Max Wynn—old 'Winning' Wynn?"

"A little older and a little fatter—yes," replied Carrados. "*I have* changed my name you see."

"Extraordinary thing meeting like this," said his visitor, dropping into a chair and staring hard at Mr. Carrados. "I have changed more than my name. How did you recognize me?"

"The voice," replied Carrados. "It took me back to that little smoke-dried attic den of yours where we——"

"My God!" exclaimed Carlyle bitterly, "don't remind me of what we were going to do in those days." He looked round the well-furnished, handsome room and recalled the other signs of wealth that he had noticed. "At all events, you seem fairly comfortable, Wynn."

"I am alternately envied and pitied," replied Carrados, with a placid tolerance of circumstance that seemed characteristic of him. "Still, as you say, I am fairly comfortable."

"Envied, I can understand. But why are you pitied?"

"Because I am blind," was the tranquil reply.

"Blind!" exclaimed Mr. Carlyle, using his own eyes superlatively. "Do you mean—literally blind?"

"Literally. . . . I was riding along a bridle-path through a wood about a dozen years ago with a friend. He was in front. At one point a twig sprang back—you know how easily a thing like that happens. It just flicked my eye—nothing to think twice about."

"And that blinded you?"

"Yes, ultimately. It's called amaurosis."

"I can scarcely believe it. You seem so sure and self-reliant. Your eyes are full of expression—only a little quieter than they used to be. I believe you were typing when I came. . . . Aren't you having me?"

"You miss the dog and the stick?" smiled Carrados. "No; it's a fact."

"What an awful affliction for you, Max. You were always such an impulsive, reckless sort of fellow—never quiet. You must miss such a fearful lot."

"Has anyone else recognized you?" asked Carrados quietly.

"Ah, that was the voice, you said," replied Carlyle.

"Yes; but other people heard the voice as well. Only I had no blundering, self-confident eyes to be hoodwinked."

"That's a rum way of putting it," said Carlyle. "Are your ears never hoodwinked, may I ask?"

"Not now. Nor my fingers. Nor any of my other senses that have to look out for themselves."

"Well, well," murmured Mr. Carlyle, cut short in his sympathetic emotions. "I'm glad you take it so well. Of course, if you find it an advantage to be blind, old man——" He stopped and reddened. "I beg your pardon," he concluded stiffly.

"Not an advantage perhaps," replied the other thoughtfully. "Still it has compensations that one might not think of. A new world to explore, new experiences, new powers awakening; strange new perceptions ; life in the fourth dimension. But why do you beg my pardon, Louis?"

"I am an ex-solicitor, struck off in connexion with the falsifying of a trust account, Mr. Carrados," replied Carlyle, rising.

"Sit down, Louis," said Carrados suavely. His face, even his incredibly living eyes, beamed placid good-nature. "The chair on which you will sit, the roof above you, all the comfortable surroundings to which you have so amiably alluded, are the direct result of falsifying a trust account. But do I call you 'Mr. Carlyle' in consequence? Certainly not, Louis."

"I did not falsify the account," cried Carlyle hotly. He sat down however, and added more quietly: "But why do I tell you all this? I have never spoken of it before."

"Blindness invites confidence," replied Carrados. "We are out of the running—human rivalry ceases to exist. Besides, why shouldn't you? In my case the account *was* falsified."

"Of course that's all bunkum, Max," commented Carlyle. "Still, I appreciate your motive."

"Practically everything I possess was left to me by an American cousin, on the condition that I took the name of Carrados. He made his fortune by an ingenious conspiracy of doctoring the crop reports and unloading favourably in consequence. And I need hardly remind you that the receiver is equally guilty with the thief."

"But twice as safe. I know something of that, Max. . . . Have you any idea what my business is?"

"You shall tell me," replied Carrados.

"I run a private inquiry agency. When I lost my profession I had to do something for a living. This occurred. I dropped my name, changed my appearance and opened an office. I knew the legal side down to the ground and I got a retired Scotland Yard man to organize the outside work."

"Excellent!" cried Carrados. "Do you unearth many murders?"

"No," admitted Mr. Carlyle; "our business lies mostly on the conventional lines among divorce and defalcation."

"That's a pity," remarked Carrados. "Do you know, Louis, I always had a secret ambition to be a detective myself. I have even thought lately that I might still be able to do something at it if the chance came my way. That makes you smile?"

"Well, certainly, the idea——"

"Yes, the idea of a blind detective—the blind tracking the alert—"

"Of course, as you say, certain facilities are no doubt quickened," Mr. Carlyle hastened to add considerately, "but, seriously, with the exception of an artist, I don't suppose there is any man who is more utterly dependent on his eyes."

Whatever opinion Carrados might have held privately, his genial exterior did not betray a shadow of dissent. For a full minute he continued to smoke as though he derived an actual visual enjoyment from the blue sprays that travelled and dispersed across the room. He had already placed before his visitor a box containing cigars of a brand which that gentleman keenly appreciated but generally regarded as unattainable, and the matter-of-fact ease and certainty with which the blind man had brought the box and put it before him had sent a questioning flicker through Carlyle's mind.

"You used to be rather fond of art yourself, Louis," he remarked presently. "Give me your opinion of my latest purchase—the bronze lion on the cabinet there." Then, as Carlyle's gaze went about the room, he added quickly: "No, not that cabinet—the one on your left."

Carlyle shot a sharp glance at his host as he got up, but Carrados's expression was merely benignly complacent. Then he strolled across to the figure.

"Very nice," he admitted. "Late Flemish, isn't it?"

"No, It is a copy of Vidal's 'Roaring Lion.'"

"Vidal?"

"A French artist." The voice became indescribably flat. "He, also, had the misfortune to be blind, by the way."

"You old humbug, Max!" shrieked Carlyle, "you've been thinking that out for the last five minutes." Then the unfortunate man bit his lip and turned his back towards his host.

"Do you remember how we used to pile it up on that obtuse ass Sanders, and then roast him?" asked Carrados, ignoring the half-smothered exclamation with which the other man had recalled himself.

"Yes," replied Carlyle quietly. "This is very good," he continued, addressing himself to the bronze again. "How ever did he do it?"

"With his hands."

"Naturally. But, I mean, how did he study his model?"

"Also with his hands. He called it 'seeing near.'"

"Even with a lion—handled it?"

"In such cases he required the services of a keeper, who brought the animal to bay while Vidal exercised his own particular gifts. . . . You don't feel inclined to put me on the track of a mystery, Louis?"

Unable to regard this request as anything but one of old Max's unquenchable pleasantries, Mr. Carlyle was on the point of making a suitable reply when a sudden thought caused him to smile knowingly. Up to that point, he had, indeed, completely forgotten the object of his visit. Now that he remembered the doubtful Dionysius and Baxter's recommendation he immediately assumed that some mistake had been made. Either Max was not the Wynn Carrados he had been seeking or else the dealer had been misinformed; for although his host was wonderfully expert in the face of his misfortune, it was inconceivable that he could decide the genuineness of a coin without seeing it. The opportunity seemed a good one of getting even with Carrados by taking him at his word.

"Yes," he accordingly replied, with crisp deliberation, as he re-crossed the room; "yes, I will, Max. Here is the clue to what seems to be a rather remarkable fraud." He put the tetradrachm into his host's hand. "What do you make of it?"

For a few seconds Carrados handled the piece with the delicate manipulation of his finger-tips while Carlyle looked on with a self-appreciative grin. Then with equal gravity the blind man weighed the coin in the balance of his hand. Finally he touched it with his tongue.

"Well?" demanded the other.

"Of course I have not much to go on, and if I was more fully in your confidence I might come to another conclusion——"

"Yes, yes," interposed Carlyle, with amused encouragement.

"Then I should advise you to arrest the parlourmaid, Nina Brun, communicate with the police authorities of Padua for particulars of the career of Helene Brunesi, and suggest to Lord Seastoke that he should return to London to see what further depredations have been made in his cabinet."

Mr. Carlyle's groping hand sought and found a chair, on to which he dropped blankly. His eyes were unable to detach themselves for a single moment from the very ordinary spectacle of Mr. Carrados's mildly benevolent face, while the sterilized ghost of his now forgotten amusement still lingered about his features.

"Good heavens!" he managed to articulate, "how do you know?"

"Isn't that what you wanted of me?" asked Carrados suavely.

"Don't humbug, Max," said Carlyle severely. "This is no joke." An undefined mistrust of his own powers suddenly possessed him in the presence of this mystery. "How do you come to know of Nina Brun and Lord Seastoke?"

"You are a detective, Louis," replied Carrados. "How does one know these things? By using one's eyes and putting two and two together."

Carlyle groaned and flung out an arm petulantly.

"Is it all bunkum, Max? Do you really see all the time—though that doesn't go very far towards explaining it."

"Like Vidal, I see very well—at close quarters," replied Carrados, lightly running a forefinger along the inscription on the tetradrachm. "For longer range I keep another pair of eyes. Would you like to test them?"

Mr. Carlyle's assent was not very gracious; it was, in fact, faintly sulky. He was suffering the annoyance of feeling distinctly unimpressive in his own department; but he was also curious.

"The bell is just behind you, if you don't mind," said his host. "Parkinson will appear. You might take note of him while he is in."

The man who had admitted Mr. Carlyle proved to be Parkinson.

"This gentleman is Mr. Carlyle, Parkinson," explained Carrados the moment the man entered. "You will remember him for the future?"

Parkinson's apologetic eye swept the visitor from head to foot, but so lightly and swiftly that it conveyed to that gentleman the comparison of being very deftly dusted.

"I will endeavour to do so, sir," replied Parkinson, turning again to his master.

"I shall be at home to Mr. Carlyle whenever he calls. That is all."

"Very well, sir."

"Now, Louis," remarked Mr. Carrados briskly, when the door had closed again, "you have had a good opportunity of studying Parkinson. What is he like?"

"In what way?"

"I mean as a matter of description. I am a blind man—I haven't seen my servant for twelve years—what idea can you give me of him? I asked you to notice."

"I know you did, but your Parkinson is the sort of man who has very little about him to describe. He is the embodiment of the ordinary. His height is about average——"

"Five feet nine," murmured Carrados. "Slightly above the mean."

"Scarcely noticeably so. Clean-shaven. Medium brown hair. No particularly marked features. Dark eyes. Good teeth."

"False," interposed Carrados. "The teeth—not the statement."

"Possibly," admitted Mr. Carlyle. "I am not a dental expert and I had no opportunity of examining Mr. Parkinson's mouth in detail. But what is the drift of all this?"

"His clothes?"

"Oh, just the ordinary evening dress of a valet. There is not much room for variety in that."

"You noticed, in fact, nothing special by which Parkinson could be identified?"

"Well, he wore an unusually broad gold ring on the little finger of the left hand."

"But that is removable. And yet Parkinson has an ineradicable mole—a small one, I admit—on his chin. And you a human sleuth-hound. Oh, Louis!"

"At all events," retorted Carlyle, writhing a little under this good-humoured satire, although it was easy enough to see in it Carrados's affectionate intention—"at all events, I dare say I can give as good a description of Parkinson as he can give of me."

"That is what we are going to test. Ring the bell again."

"Seriously?"

"Quite. I am trying my eyes against yours. If I can't give you fifty out of a hundred I'll renounce my private detectorial ambition for ever."

"It isn't quite the same," objected Carlyle, but he rang the bell.

"Come in and close the door, Parkinson," said Carrados when the man appeared. "Don't look at Mr. Carlyle again—in fact, you had better stand with your back towards him, he won't mind. Now describe to me his appearance as you observed it."

Parkinson tendered his respectful apologies to Mr. Carlyle for the liberty he was compelled to take, by the deferential quality of his voice.

"Mr. Carlyle, sir, wears patent leather boots of about size seven and very little used. There are five buttons, but on the left boot one button—the third up—is missing, leaving loose threads and not the more usual metal fastener. Mr. Carlyle's trousers, sir, are of a dark material, a dark grey line of about a quarter of an inch width on a darker ground. The bottoms are turned permanently up and are, just now, a little muddy, if I may say so."

"Very muddy," interposed Mr. Carlyle generously. "It is a wet night, Parkinson."

"Yes, sir; very unpleasant weather. If you will allow me, sir, I will brush you in the hall. The mud is dry now, I notice. Then, sir," continued Parkinson, reverting to the business in hand, "there are dark green cashmere hose. A curb-pattern key-chain passes into the left-hand trouser pocket."

From the visitor's nether garments the photographic-eyed Parkinson proceeded to higher ground, and with increasing wonder Mr. Carlyle listened to the faithful catalogue of his possessions. His fetter-and-link albert of gold and platinum was minutely described. His spotted blue ascot, with its gentlemanly pearl scarfpin, was set forth, and the fact that the buttonhole in the left lapel of his morning coat showed signs of use was duly noted. What Parkinson saw he recorded, but he made no deductions. A handkerchief carried in the cuff of the right sleeve was simply that to him and not an indication that Mr. Carlyle was, indeed, left-handed.

But a more delicate part of Parkinson's undertaking remained. He approached it with a double cough.

"As regards Mr. Carlyle's personal appearance, sir——"

"No, enough!" cried the gentleman concerned hastily. "I am more than satisfied. You are a keen observer, Parkinson."

"I have trained myself to suit my master's requirements, sir," replied the man. He looked towards Mr. Carrados, received a nod and withdrew.

Mr. Carlyle was the first to speak.

"That man of yours would be worth five pounds a week to me, Max," he remarked thoughtfully. "But, of course——"

"I don't think that he would take it," replied Carrados, in a voice of equally detached speculation. "He suits me very well. But you have the chance of using his services—indirectly."

"You still mean that—seriously?"

"I notice in you a chronic disinclination to take me seriously, Louis. It is really—to an Englishman—almost painful. Is there something inherently comic about me or the atmosphere of The Turrets?"

"No, my friend," replied Mr. Carlyle, "but there is something essentially prosperous. That is what points to the improbable. Now what is it?"

"It might be merely a whim, but it is more than that," replied Carrados. "It is, well, partly vanity, partly *ennui,* partly"—certainly there was something more nearly tragic in his voice than comic now—"partly hope."

Mr. Carlyle was too tactful to pursue the subject.

"Those are three tolerable motives," he acquiesced. "I'll do anything you want, Max, on one condition."

"Agreed. And it is?"

"That you tell me how you knew so much of this affair." He tapped the silver coin which lay on the table near them. "I am not easily flabbergasted," he added.

"You won't believe that there is nothing to explain—that it was purely second-sight?"

"No," replied Carlyle tersely: "I won't."

"You are quite right. And yet the thing is very simple."

"They always are—when you know," soliloquised the other. "That's what makes them so confoundedly difficult when you don't."

"Here is this one then. In Padua, which seems to be regaining its old reputation as the birthplace of spurious antiques, by the way, there lives an ingenious craftsman named Pietro Stelli. This simple soul, who possesses a talent not inferior to that of Cavino at his best, has for many years turned his hand to the not unprofitable occupation of forging rare

Greek and Roman coins. As a collector and student of certain Greek colonials and a specialist in forgeries I have been familiar with Stelli's workmanship for years. Latterly he seems to have come under the influence of an international crook called—at the moment—Dompierre, who soon saw a way of utilizing Stelli's genius on a royal scale. Helene Brunesi, who in private life is—and really is, I believe—Madame Dompierre, readily lent her services to the enterprise."

"Quite so," nodded Mr. Carlyle, as his host paused.

"You see the whole sequence, of course?"

"Not exactly—not in detail," confessed Mr. Carlyle.

"Dompierre's idea was to gain access to some of the most celebrated cabinets of Europe and substitute Stelli's fabrications for the genuine coins. The princely collection of rarities that he would thus amass might be difficult to dispose of safely, but I have no doubt that he had matured his plans. Helene, in the person of Nina Brun, an Anglicised French parlourmaid—a part which she fills to perfection—was to obtain wax impressions of the most valuable pieces and to make the exchange when the counterfeits reached her. In this way it was obviously hoped that the fraud would not come to light until long after the real coins had been sold, and I gather that she has already done her work successfully in general houses. Then, impressed by her excellent references and capable manner, my housekeeper engaged her, and for a few weeks she went about her duties here. It was fatal to this detail of the scheme, however, that I have the misfortune to be blind. I am told that Helene has so innocently angelic a face as to disarm suspicion, but I was incapable of being impressed and that good material was thrown away. But one morning my material fingers—which, of course, knew nothing of Helene's angelic face—discovered an unfamiliar touch about the surface of my favourite Euclideas, and, although there was doubtless nothing to be seen, my critical sense of smell reported that wax had been recently pressed against it. I began to make discreet inquiries and in the meantime my cabinets went to the local bank for safety. Helene countered by receiving a telegram from Angiers, calling her to the death-bed of her aged mother. The aged mother succumbed; duty compelled Helene to remain at the side of her stricken patriarchal father, and doubtless The Turrets was written off the syndicate's operations as a bad debt."

"Very interesting," admitted Mr. Carlyle; "but at the risk of seeming obtuse"—his manner had become delicately chastened—"I must say that I fail to trace the inevitable connexion between Nina Brun and this particular forgery—assuming that it is a forgery."

"Set your mind at rest about that, Louis," replied Carrados. "It is a forgery, and it is a forgery that none but Pietro Stelli could have achieved. That is the essential connexion. Of course, there are accessories. A private detective coming urgently to see me with a notable tetradrachm in his pocket, which he announces to be the clue to a remarkable fraud—well, really, Louis, one scarcely needs to be blind to see through that."

"And Lord Seastoke? I suppose you happened to discover that Nina Brun had gone there?"

"No, I cannot claim to have discovered that, or I should certainly have warned him at once when I found out—only recently—about the gang. As a matter of fact, the last information I had of Lord Seastoke was a line in yesterday's *Morning Post* to the effect that he was still at Cairo. But many of these pieces——" He brushed his finger almost lovingly across the vivid chariot race that embellished the reverse of the coin, and broke off to remark: "You really ought to take up the subject, Louis. You have no idea how useful it might prove to you some day."

"I really think I must," replied Carlyle grimly. "Two hundred and fifty pounds the original of this cost, I believe."

"Cheap, too; it would make five hundred pounds in New York to-day. As I was saying, many are literally unique. This gem by Kimon is—here is his signature, you see; Peter is particularly good at lettering—and as I handled the genuine tetradrachm about two years ago, when Lord Seastoke exhibited it at a meeting of our society in Albemarle Street, there is nothing at all wonderful in my being able to fix the locale of your mystery. Indeed, I feel that I ought to apologize for it all being so simple."

"I think," remarked Mr. Carlyle, critically examining the loose threads on his left boot, "that the apology on that head would be more appropriate from me."

The Divination of the Zagury Capsules

Headon Hill

ON the first floor of one of the handsome buildings that are rapidly
replacing "Old London" in the streets running from the Strand to
the Embankment was a suite of offices, bearing on the outer door the
words "Confidential Advice," and below, in smaller letters, "Mark
Poignand, Manager." The outer offices, providing accommodation for
a couple of up-to-date clerks and a lady typist, were resplendent with
brass-furnished counters and cathedral-glass partitions; and the private
room in the rear, used by the manager, was fitted up in the quietly luxurious style of a club smoking-room. But even this latter did not form the
innermost sanctum of all, for at its far corner a locked door led into a
still more private chamber, which was never entered by any of the inferior staff, and but rarely by the manager himself. In this room—strange
anomaly within earshot of the thronging traffic of the Strand—a little
wizened old Hindoo mostly sat cross-legged, playing with a basket of
cobras, and chewing betel-nut from morning to night. Now and again
he would be called on to lay aside his occupations for a brief space, and
these intervals were quickly becoming a factor to be reckoned with by
those who desired to envelop their doings in darkness.

Mark Poignand, though the younger son of a good family, possessed
only a modest capital, bringing him an income of under three hundred
a year, and after his success in the matter of the Afghan Kukhri, he was
taken with the idea of entering professionally on the field of "private
investigation." He was shrewd enough to see that without Kala Persad's
aid his journey to India would have ended in failure, and he determined to utilise the snake-charmer's instinctive faculty as the mainstay
of the new undertaking. He had no difficulty in working upon the old
man's sense of gratitude to induce him to go to England, and all that
remained was to sell out a portion of his capital and establish himself in
good style as a private investigator, with Kala Persad installed in the

back room. A rumour had got about that he had successfully conducted a delicate mission to India, and this, in conjunction with the novelty of such a business being run by a young man not unknown in society, brought him clients from the start.

At first Mark felt some anxiety as to the outcome of his experiment, but by compelling himself with an effort to be true to the system he had drawn up, he found that his first few unimportant cases worked out with the best results. Briefly, his system was this:—When an inquiry was placed in his hands, he would lay the facts as presented to him before Kala Persad, and would then be guided in future operations by his follower's suspicions. On one or two occasions he had nearly failed through a tendency to prefer his own judgment to the snake-charmer's instinct, but he had been able to retrace his steps in time to prove the correctness of Kala Persad's original solution, and to save the credit of the office. It devolved upon himself entirely to procure evidence and discover how the mysteries were brought about, and in this he found ample scope for his ingenuity, for Kala Persad was profoundly ignorant of the methods adopted by those whom he suspected. It was more than half the battle, however, to start with the weird old man's finger pointed, so far unerringly, at the right person, and Mark Poignand recognised that without the oracle of the back room he would have been nowhere. Some of Kala Persad's indications pointed in directions into which his own wildest flights of fancy would never have led him.

It was not till Poignand had been in practice for nearly three months that a case was brought to him involving the capital charge—a case of such terrible interest to one of our oldest noble families that its unravelling sent clients thronging to the office, and assured the success of the enterprise. One murky, fog-laden morning in December he was sitting in the private room, going through the day's correspondence, when the clerk brought him a lady's visiting card, engraved with the name of "Miss Lascelles."

"What like is she?" asked Poignand.

"Well-dressed, young, and, as far as I can make out under her thick veil, good-looking," replied the clerk. "I should judge from her voice that she is anxious and agitated."

"Very well," replied Poignand; "show her in when I ring." And the other having retired, he rose and went to the back wall, where an oil painting, heavily framed, and tilted at a considerable angle, was hung. Behind the picture was a sliding panel, which he shot back, leaving an opening about a foot square into the inner room.

"Ho! there, Kala Persad," he called through. "A lady is here with a secret; are you ready?"

As soon as a wheezy voice on the other side had chuckled "Ha, Sahib!" in reply, Poignand readjusted the picture, but left the aperture open. Settling himself in his chair, he touched a bell, and the next moment was rising to receive his client—a tall, graceful girl, clad in expensive mourning. Directly the clerk had left the room, she raised her veil, displaying a face winningly beautiful, but intensely pale, and marked with the traces of recent grief. Her nervousness was so painfully evident that Poignand hastened to reassure her.

"I hope you will try and treat me as though I were a private friend," he said. "If you can bring yourself to give me your entire confidence, I have no doubt that I can serve you, but it is necessary that you should state your case with the utmost fulness."

His soothing tones had the desired effect. "I have every confidence in you," was the reply, given in a low, sweet voice. "It is not that that troubles me, but the fearful peril threatening the honour, and perhaps the life, of one very dear to me. I was tempted to come to you, Mr. Poignand, because of the marvellous insight which enabled you to recover the Duchess of Gainsborough's jewel-case the other day. It seemed almost as though you could read the minds of persons you have not even seen, and, Heaven knows, there is a secret in some dark mind somewhere that I must uncover."

"Let me have the details as concisely as possible, please," said Poignand, pushing his own chair back a little, so as to bring the sound of her voice more in line with the hidden opening.

"You must know then," Miss Lascelles began, "that I live with my father, who is a retired general of the Indian army, at The Briary—a house on the outskirts of Beechfield, in Buckinghamshire. I am engaged to be married to the second son of Lord Bradstock—the Honble. Harry Furnival, as he is called by courtesy. The matter which

I want you to investigate is the death of Lord Bradstock's eldest son, Leonard Furnival, which took place last week."

"Indeed!" exclaimed Poignand; "I saw the death announced in the paper, but there was no hint of anything wrong. I gathered that the death arose from natural causes."

"So it was believed at the time," replied Miss Lascelles, "but owing to circumstances that have since occurred, the body was exhumed on the day after the funeral. As the result of an autopsy held yesterday, Leonard's death is now attributed to poison, and an inquest has been ordered for to-morrow. In the meanwhile, by some cruel combination of chances, Harry is suspected of having given the poison to the brother whom he loved so well, in order to clear the way for his own succession; and the terrible part of it all is that his father, and others who ought to stand by him in his need, share in that suspicion. He has not the slightest wish to go away or to shirk inquiry, but he believes that he is already watched by the police, and that he will certainly be arrested after the inquest to-morrow.

"I must go back a little, so as to make you understand exactly what is known to have happened, and also what is supposed to have happened at Bradstock Hall, which is a large mansion, standing about a mile and a half from the small country town of Beechfield. For the last twelve months of his life, or, to speak more correctly, for the last ten months but two, Leonard was given up as in a hopeless consumption, from which he could not possibly recover. At the commencement of his illness, which arose from a chill caught while out shooting, he was attended by Dr. Youle, of Beechfield. Almost from the first the doctor gave Lord Bradstock to understand that his eldest son's lungs were seriously affected, and that his recovery was very doubtful. As time went on, Dr. Youle became confirmed in his view, and, despite the most constant attention, the invalid gradually declined till, about two months ago, Lord Bradstock determined to have a second medical opinion. Though Dr. Youle was very confident that he had diagnosed and treated the case correctly, he consented to meet Dr. Lucas, the other Beechfield medical man, in consultation. After a careful examination Dr. Lucas entirely disagreed with Dr. Youle as to the nature of the disease, being of the opinion that the trouble arose from pneumonia, which should yield to the proper treatment for that malady. This meant, of course, that if he was right there was still a prospect of the patient's recovery, and so buoyed up was Lord Bradstock with hope that he installed Dr. Lucas in the place of Dr. Youle, who was very angry at the doubt cast on his treatment. The new *regimen* worked well for some weeks, and Leonard began to gain ground, very slowly, but still so decidedly that Dr. Lucas was hopeful of getting him downstairs by the early spring.

"Imagine then the consternation of every one when, one morning last week, the valet, on going into the room, found the poor fellow so much worse that Dr. Lucas had to be hurriedly sent for, and only arrived in time to see his patient die. Death was immediately preceded by the spitting of blood and by violent paroxysms of coughing, and these being more or less symptoms of both the maladies that had been in turn treated, no one thought of foul play for an instant. Discussion of the case was confined to the fact that Dr. Youle was now proved to have been right and Dr. Lucas wrong.

"The first hint of anything irregular came from Dixon, the valet, on Monday last, the day of the funeral. After the ceremony, he was clearing away from the sick-room the last sad traces of Leonard's illness, when, among the medicine bottles and appliances, he came across a small box of gelatine capsules, which he remembered to have seen Mr. Harry Furnival give to his brother the day before the latter's death. Thinking that they had been furnished by Dr. Lucas, and there being a good many left in the box, he put them aside with a stethoscope and one or two things which the doctor had left, and later in the day took them over to his house at Beechfield. The moment Dr. Lucas saw the capsules he disclaimed having furnished them, or even having prescribed anything of the kind, and expressed surprise at Dixon's statement that he had seen Harry present the box to his brother. Recognising them as a freely advertised patent specific, he was curious to test their composition, and, having opened one with this purpose in view, he at once made the most dreadful discovery. Instead of its original filling—probably harmless, whatever it may have been—the capsule contained a substance which he believed to be a fatal dose of a vegetable poison—little known in this country, but in common use among the natives of Madagascar—called tanghin. Turning again to one of the entire capsules, he found slight traces of the gelatine case having been melted and re-sealed.

"I cannot blame him for the course he took. It was his duty to report the discovery, and apart from this he was naturally anxious to follow up a theory which would prove his own opinion, and not Dr. Youle's, to have been right. For if Leonard Furnival had really died by poison, it was still likely that, given a fair chance, he might have verified his, Dr. Lucas', prediction of recovery. The necessary steps were taken, and the examination of the body, conducted by the Home Office authorities, proved Dr. Lucas to be right in both points. Not only was it shown that Leonard Furnival undoubtedly died from the effects of the poison, but it was clearly demonstrated that he was recovering from the pneumonia for which Dr. Lucas was treating him."

"You have stated the case admirably, Miss Lascelles," said Poignand. "There is yet one important point left, though. How does Mr. Harry Furnival account for his having provided the deceased with these capsules?"

"He admits that he procured them for his brother at his request, and he indignantly denies that he tampered with them," was the reply. "It seems that Leonard was attracted some months ago by the advertisement of a patent medicine known as the 'Zagury Capsules,' which profess to be a sleep-producing tonic. Not liking to incur the professional ridicule of his medical man, he induced his brother to procure them for him. This first occurred when Dr. Youle was in attendance, and being under the impression that they did him some good, he continued to take them while in Dr. Lucas' care. Harry was in the habit of purchasing them quite openly at the chemist's in Beechfield as though for himself, but he says that before humouring his brother he took the precaution of asking Dr. Youle if the capsules were harmless, and received an affirmative reply. Unfortunately Dr. Youle, though naturally anxious to refute the poison theory, has forgotten the circumstance, both he and Dr. Lucas having been successively ignorant of the use of the capsules."

"You say that Lord Bradstock believes in his son's guilt?" asked Poignand.

"He has not said so in so many words," replied Miss Lascelles, "but he refuses to see him till the matter is cleared up. Lord Bradstock is a very stern man, and Leonard was always his favourite. My dear father and I are the only ones to refuse to listen to the rumours against Harry that are flying about Beechfield. We know that Harry could no more have committed a crime than Lord Bradstock himself, and papa would have come with me here to-day were he not laid up with gout. And now, Mr. Poignand, can you help us? It is almost too much to expect you to do anything in time to prevent an arrest, but—but will you try?"

The circumstances demanded a guarded answer. "Indeed I will," said Poignand. "It is not my custom to give a definite opinion till I have had an opportunity to look into a case, but I shall go down to Beechfield presently—it is only an hour's run, I think—and I will call upon you later in the day. I trust by then to be able to report progress."

At his request, Miss Lascelles added a few particulars about the persons living at Bradstock Hall on the day of the death—besides Lord Bradstock and his two sons, there were only the servants—and took her leave, being anxious to catch the next train home. Poignand waited till her cab wheels sounded in the street below, then rose hastily, and, having first closed the sliding panel, passed into the room beyond. He looked thoughtful and worried, for he could not, rack his brains as he would, see any other solution to the puzzle than the one he was called upon to refute. It was true that the details of which he was so far in possession were of the broadest, but every one of them pointed to Harry Fumival—the admittedly secret purchaser of the capsule—as the only person who could have given them their deadly attributes. And then, to back up that admission, there loomed up, in the way of a successful issue, the damning supplement of a powerful motive. The tenant of the back room, he fully expected, would confirm his own impression— that they were called on to champion a lost cause.

There was nothing at first sight as he entered the plainly furnished apartment either to reassure or to dash his hopes. Kala Persad despised the two chairs that had been provided for his accommodation, and spent most of his time squatting or reclining on the Indian *charpoy* which had been unearthed for him from some East-end opium den. He was sitting on the edge of it now, with his skinny brown hands stretched out to the warmth of a glowing fire, for Miss Lascelles' story had kept him at the panel long enough to induce shivering; and if there was one thing that made him repent his bargain, it was the cold of an English winter. At his feet, like-minded with their owner, the cobras squirmed and twisted in the basket which had first excited Poignand's curiosity on the midnight solitudes of the Sholapur road.

"Well?" said Poignand; "do you know enough English by this time to have understood what the lady said, or must I repeat it?"

The old man raised his filmy eyes, and regarded the other with a puckering of the leathery brows that might have meant anything from contempt to deep reverence.

"Words—seprit words—tell Kala Persad nothing, Sahib," he said. "All words together—what you call one burra jumble—help Kala Persad to pick kernel from the nut. Mem Sahib ishpoke many things no use, but I understand enough to read secret. Why!"—with infinite scorn—"the secret read itself."

Poignand's heart sank within him.

"I was afraid it was rather too clear a case for us to be of any use," he said.

The snake-charmer, as though he had not heard, went on to recapitulate the heads of the story in little snappy jerks. "One old burra Lord Sahib, big estates; two son, one very sick. First one *hakim* (doctor) try to cure—no use. Then other *hakim;* no use too—sick man die. Other son bring physic, poison physic, give him brother. Servant man find poison after dead. Old lord angry, says his son common *budmash* murderer; but missee Mem Sahib, betrothed of Harry, she say no, and come buy wisdom of Kala Persad. You not think that plain enough, sahib?"

"Uncommonly so," said Poignand dejectedly. "It is pretty clear that the Mem Sahib, as you call her, wants us to undertake a job not exactly in our line of business. If we are to satisfy her, we shall have to prove that a guilty man is innocent."

"Yah! Yah-ah-ah-ah!" Kala Persad drawled, hugging himself, and rocking to and fro in delight. And before Poignand could divine his intention, he had leaped from the *charpoy* to hiss with his betel-stained lips an emphatic sentence into the ear of his employer, who first started back in astonishment, then listened gravely. Having thus unburdened himself, Kala Persad returned to the warmth of the fire, nodding and mouthing and muttering, much as when his wizened face had peered from among the bushes in Major Merwood's garden. The old man was excited; the jungle-instinct of pursuit was strong upon him, and he began to croon weird noises to his cobras.

Poignand looked at the red-turbaned, huddled figure almost in awe; then went slowly back into his own room.

"It is marvellous," he muttered to himself. "As usual! the solution is the very last thing one would have thought of, and yet when once presented in shape is distinctly possible. It is on the cards that he may be wrong, but I will fight it out on that line."

*   *   *

Early in the afternoon of the same day there was some commotion at the Beechfield railway station, on the arrival of a London train, through the station-master being called to a first-class compartment in which a gentleman had been taken suddenly ill. The passenger, who was booked through to the North, was, at his own request, removed from the train to the adjacent Railway Hotel, where he was deposited, weak and shivering all over with ague, in the landlord's private room at the back of the bar. The administration of some very potent brown brandy caused him to recover sufficiently to give some account of himself, and to inquire if medical skill was within the capabilities of Beechfield. He was an officer in the army, it appeared—Captain Hawke, of the 24th Lancers—and was home on sick leave from India, where he had contracted the intermittent fever that was his present trouble.

"I ought to have known better than to travel on one of the days when this infernal scourge was due," he said; "but having done so, I must make the best of it. Are there any doctors in the place who are not absolute duffers?"

The landlord, anxious for the medical credit of Beechfield, informed his guest that there was a choice of two qualified practitioners. "Dr. Youle is the old-established man, sir, and accounted clever by some. Dr. Lucas is younger, and lately set up, though he is getting on better since his lordship took him up at the Hall."

"I don't care who took him up," replied Captain Hawke irascibly. "Which was the last to lose a patient? that will be as good a test as anything."

"Well, sir, I suppose, in a manner of speaking, Dr. Lucas was," said the landlord, "seeing that the Honourable Leonard died under his care; but people are saying that Mr. Harry—"

"That will do," interposed the invalid, with military testiness; "don't worry me with your Toms and Harrys. Send for the other man— Youle, or whatever his name is."

The subservient landlord, much impressed with the captain's imperious petulance, which bespoke an ability and willingness to pay for the best, went out to execute the errand in person. The moment his broad back had disappeared into the outer regions, Captain Hawke, doubtless under the influence of the brown brandy, grew so much better that he sat up and looked about him. The bar-parlour in which he found himself was partly separated from the private bar by a glass partition, having a movable window that had been left open. The customers were thus both audible and visible to the belated traveller, who, strangely enough for a dapper young captain of Lancers, evinced a furtive interest in their personality and conversation. The first was chiefly of the country tradesman type, while the latter consisted of the " 'E done it, sure enough" style of argument, usual in such places when rustic stolidity is startled by the commission of some serious crime.

"There was two 'tecs from Scotland Yard watching the Hall all night. 'Tain't no use his trying to bolt," said the local butcher.

"They do say as how the warrant's made out already," put in another; "only they won't lock him up till to-morrow, owing to wanting his evidence at the inquest. Terrible hard on his lordship, ain't it?"

"That be so," added a third worthy; "the old lord was always partial to Leonard—natural like, perhaps, seeing as he was the heir. But whatever ailed Master Harry to go and do such a thing licks me. He was always a nice-spoken lad, and open as the day, to my thinking."

"These rustics have got hold of a foregone conclusion, apparently," said the sufferer from ague to himself, as footsteps sounded in the passage, and he sank wearily down on the sofa again.

The next moment the landlord re-entered, accompanied by a stout and rather tall man, whom he introduced as Dr. Youle. The doctor's age might have been forty-five, and his figure, just tending to middle-aged stoutness, was encased in the regulation black frock-coat of his profession. There was nothing about him to suggest even a remote connection with the tragedy that was engrossing the town. In fact, the expression of his broad face, taken as a whole, was that of one on good terms with himself and with all the world; though it is a question whether the large, not to say "hungry" mouth, if studied separately, did not discount the value of its perpetual smile. He entered with the mingled air of importance and genial respect which the occasion demanded.

The captain's manner to the doctor differed from his manner to the landlord. Leaving medical skill out of the question, he recognised that he had a gentleman and a man of some local position to deal with, and he modified his petulance accordingly. The landlord had already told the doctor the history of his arrival, so that it only remained to describe his sensations and the nature of his ailment. The latter, indeed, was more or less apparent; for the shivering was still sufficiently violent to shake the horse-hair sofa on which he lay.

"The surgeon of my regiment used to give me some stuff that relieved this horrid trembling instantly," said the captain; "but I never could get him to part with the prescription. However, I daresay, doctor, that you know of something equally efficacious."

"Yes, I flatter myself that I can improve matters in that direction," was the reply. "My house is quite close, and I will run over and fetch you a draught. You are, of course, aware that the ague is of an intermittent character, recurring every other day till it subsides?"

"I know it only too well," replied Captain Hawke. "I shall be as fit as a fiddle to-morrow, probably only to relapse the next day into another of these attacks. I do not know how you are situated domestically, doctor; but I was wondering whether you could take me in, and look after me for a few days till I get over this bout. I am nervous about myself, and, without any disparagement to the hospitality of our friend here, I should feel happier under medical supervision."

Dr. Youle's hungry mouth showed by its eager twitching that the prospect of a resident patient, even for a day or two, was by no means distasteful to him. "I shall be only too pleased to look after you," he said. "I shall be much occupied to-morrow—rather unpleasantly employed as a witness at an inquest; but, as you say, you will most likely be feeling better then, and not so much in need of my services. If you really wish the arrangement, you had better have a closed fly and come over at once. I will run on ahead, and prepare a draught for you."

The landlord, not best pleased with the abstraction of his guest, went to order a carriage, and a quarter of an hour later Captain Hawke, with his luggage, was driven to the doctor's residence—a prim, red-brick house in the middle of the sleepy High Street. Dr. Youle was waiting on the doorstep to receive his patient, and at once conducted him to a small back room on the ground floor, evidently the surgery.

"Drink this," he said, handing the invalid a glass of roaming liquid, "and then if you will sit quietly in the easy chair while I see about your things, I don't doubt that I shall find you better. The effect is almost instantaneous."

But the doctor himself could hardly have foreseen with what rapidity his words were to be verified. He had no sooner closed the door than Captain Hawke sprang to his feet, all traces of shivering gone, and applied himself to the task of searching the room. One wall was fitted with shelves laden with bottles containing liquids, and these obtained the eccentric invalid's first attention. Rapidly scanning the labels, he passed along the shelves apparently without satisfying his quest, for he came to the end without putting his hand to bottle or jar. Pausing for a moment to listen to the doctor's voice in the distance directing the flyman with the luggage, he recommenced his search by examining a range of drawers that formed a back to the mixing dresser, and which, also systematically labelled, were found to contain dry drugs. Here again nothing held his attention, and he was turning away with vexed impatience on his face, when, at the very end of the row, and lower than the others, he espied a drawer ticketted "Miscellaneous." Pulling it open, he saw that it was three parts filled with medicine corks, scarlet string, and sealing wax, all heaped together in such confusion that it was impossible to take in the details of the medley at a glance. Removing the string and sealing wax, the inquisitive captain ran his fingers lightly through the bulk of the corks, till they closed on some hard substance hidden from view. When he withdrew his hand it held a small package, which, after one flash of eager scrutiny, he transferred to his pocket.

Even now, however, though he drew a long breath of relief, it seemed that the search was not yet complete; for, after carefully rearranging and closing the drawer, he tried the door of a corner cupboard, only to find it locked. He had just drawn a bunch of peculiar-looking keys from his pocket, when the voice of the doctor bidding the flyman a cheery "Good-day!" caused him to glide quietly back to the armchair. The next moment his host entered, rubbing his hands, and smiling professionally.

"Your mixture has done wonders, doctor," the captain said. "I am another man already, and my experience tells me that I am safe for another forty-eight hours. By the way, I was so seedy when they hauled me out of the train that I don't even know where I am. What place is this?"

"This is Beechfield in Buckinghamshire, about an hour from town," said the doctor. "An old-fashioned country centre, you know."

"Beechfield, by Jove!" exclaimed Captain Hawke, with an air of mingled surprise and pleasure. "Well, that is a curious coincidence, for an old friend of my father's lives, or lived, somewhere about here, I believe—General Lascelles—do you know him?"

"Yes, I know the General," replied Dr. Youle, a little absently: then added, "He has a nice little place, called The Elms, a hundred yards or so beyond the top of the High Street."

"Well, I feel so much better that I will stroll out and see the General," said Hawke. "I will take care to be back in time to have the pleasure of dining with you—at half-past seven, I think you said?"

"Yes, that is the hour," replied the doctor thoughtfully; "but are you sure you are wise in venturing out? Besides, you will find the General and his daughter in some distress. They are interested—"

"All the more reason that I go and cheer them up. What is wrong with them?" snapped the patient.

"They are interested in the inquest on poor young Furnival, which I told you was to be held to-morrow. It is possible that you may hear me spoken of in connection with the case, though their view of it ought to be identical with mine—that death was due to natural causes. I believe the whole thing is a cock-and-bull story, got up by an impudent young practitioner here to account for his losing his patient, as I knew he would from the first. The wonder is that the Home Office analysts should back him up in pretending to discern a poison about which hardly anything is known."

The captain had risen, his face wearing a look of infinite boredom. "My dear doctor," he said, "you can't expect me to concern myself with the matter; I've quite enough to do to worry about my own ailments. I only want to see the General to chat about old times, not about local inquests. Will you kindly show me your front door, and point out the direction I should take to reach The Elms?"

Dr. Youle smiled, with perhaps a shade of relief at the invalid's self-absorption, and led the way out of the room. The captain followed him into the passage for a few paces, then, with an exclamation about a forgotten handkerchief, darted back into the surgery, and, quick as lightning, undid the catch that fastened the window, being at his host's heels again almost before the latter had noticed his absence. In another minute, duly instructed in the route, he started walking swiftly through the shadows of the early winter twilight towards the end of the town.

But apparently the immediate desire to visit his "father's old friend" had passed away. Taking the first by-way that ran at right angles to the High Street, he passed thence into a lane that brought him to the back of Dr. Youle's house, where he disappeared among the foliage of the garden. It was a long three-quarters of an hour before he crept cautiously into the lane again, and even then The Elms was not his first destination. Not till he had paid two other rather lengthy visits—one of them to the Beechfield chemist—did he find himself ushered into the presence of General and Miss Lascelles. A distinguished-looking young man, dressed, like father and daughter, in deep mourning, was with them in the fire-lit library, and evinced an equal agitation on the entrance of Dr. Youle's resident patient. The conversation, however, did not turn on bygone associations and mutual reminiscences. Miss Lascelles sprang forward with outstretched hands and glistening eyes,—

"Oh, Mr. Poignand!" she cried; "I can see that you have news for us—good news, too, I think?"

"Yes," was the reply; "I hold the real murderer of Leonard Furnival in the hollow of my hand, which means, of course, that the other absurd charge is demolished."

★   ★   ★

Dr. Youle, who was a bachelor, had ordered his cook to prepare a dainty little repast in honour of the guest, and as the dinner hour approached, and "the captain" had not returned, he began to get anxious about the fish. On the stroke of seven, however, the front door bell rang, and the laggard was admitted, looking so flushed and heated that, when they were seated in the cosy dining-room, the doctor ventured on a remonstrance.

"I have been interested," was the explanation, "very deeply interested, by what I heard at the Lascelles' about this poisoning case—so much so that I was obliged to stay and hear it out. It seems that the stuff employed was tanghin, the poison which the natives of Madagascar use in their trials by ordeal. Have you ever seen a trial by ordeal, doctor?"

It was the host's turn now to be bored by the subject. He shook his head absently, and passed the sherry decanter.

"It is an admirable institution for keeping down the population," persisted the other. "Whenever a man is suspected of a crime, he has to eat half a dozen of these berries, on the supposition that if he is innocent they will do him no harm. Needless to say, the poison fails to discriminate between the stomachs of good and bad men, and the accused is always proved guilty. It must be a terrible thing to be proved guilty when you are innocent, Dr. Youle."

Some change of tone caused the doctor to look up and catch his guest's eye. The two men stared steadily at each other for the space of ten seconds, then the doctor winced a little and said,—

"What have I to do with Madagascar poisons and innocent men? Tanghin is hardly known in this country, and cannot be procured at the wholesale druggists. I have never even seen it."

The sound of a bell ringing somewhere in the kitchen premises reached them, and Poignand pushed his chair back from the table as he replied,—

"Not even seen it, eh? Strange, then, that a supply of the berries, and a tincture distilled from them, should have been discovered in that corner cupboard in your surgery. Strange, too, that a box of the Zagury capsules, in which vehicle the poison was administered to Leonard Furnival, should have been found among your medicine corks, stamped with the rubber stamp of Hollings, the Beechfield chemist, though he swears he never supplied you with any capsules. Stranger still that Hollings should remember—now that it has been called to his mind—your apparently aimless lingering in his shop on the day before the death, and the fidgety movements now revealed as the legerdemain by which you substituted your poisoned packet for the one the chemist had lying ready on the counter against Mr. Harry Furnival's call. It is no use, Dr. Youle; you would have been wiser to have destroyed such fatal evidences. Your wicked sacrifice of a valuable life, in order to prove your mistaken treatment right at the expense of your successful rival, is as clear as noonday. Ah! here is the inspector."

As he spoke, two or three men entered the room, and one of them—the detective who had been detailed to watch Harry Furnival—quietly effected the arrest. The wretched culprit, broken down completely by Mark Poignand's unofficial "bluff," blustered a little at first, but quickly weakened, and saved further trouble by a full admission, almost on the exact lines of the accusation. Knowing, by his previous observations, and from the question asked him by Harry, that Leonard Furnival was in the habit of taking the patent capsules, he had bought a box in London, and, after replacing the original contents with poison, had watched his chance to change the boxes. His motive was to injure, and put in the wrong, the rising young practitioner who had supplanted him, and whose toxicological knowledge, by a curious irony of fate, was the first link in the chain of detection. The tanghin berries he had procured from a firm of Madagascar merchants, by passing himself off as the representative of a well-known wholesale druggist, who, at the trial, disclaimed all knowledge of him and all dealings in the fatal drug.

Poignand's working out of the case was regarded as masterly; but he knew very well that unless he had started on the presupposition of Youle's guilt, he should never have come upon the truth. When he got back to the office, he went straight through to the inner room, where the shrunken, red-turbaned figure was playing with the cobras by the fire.

"Now tell me, how did you suspect the doctor?" asked Poignand, after outlining the events which had led to a successful issue.

"Sahib," said Kala Persad gravely, "what else was there of hatred, of injury, of revenge in the story the pretty Missee Mem Sahib told? Where there is a wound on the black heart of man, there is the place to look for crime."

The Dead Hand

R. Austin Freeman

I. How It Happened

ABOUT Half-Past Eight on a fine, sunny June morning, a small yacht crept out of Sennen Cove, near the Land's End, and headed for the open sea. On the shelving beach of the cove two women and a man, evidently visitors (or "foreigners," to use the local term), stood watching her departure with valedictory waving of cap or handkerchief, and the boatman who had put the crew on board, aided by two of his comrades, was hauling his boat up above the tide-mark.

A light, northerly breeze filled the yacht's sails and drew her gradually seaward. The figures of her crew dwindled to the size of dolls, shrank with the increasing distance to the magnitude of insects, and at last, losing all individuality, became mere specks merged in the form of the fabric that bore them.

On board the receding craft two men sat in the little cockpit. They formed the entire crew, for the *Sandhopper* was only a ship's lifeboat, timbered and decked, of light draught and, in the matter of spars and canvas, what the art critics would call "reticent."

Both men, despite the fineness of the weather, wore yellow oilskins and sou'westers, and that was about all they had in common. In other respects they made a curious contrast—the one small, slender, sharp-featured, dark almost to swarthiness, and restless and quick in his movements; the other large, massive, red-faced, blue-eyed, with the rounded outlines suggestive of ponderous strength; a great ox of a man, heavy, stolid, but much less unwieldy than he looked.

The conversation incidental to getting the yacht under way had ceased, and silence had fallen on the occupants of the cockpit. The big man grasped the tiller and looked sulky, which was probably his usual aspect, and the small man watched him furtively.

265

The land was nearly two miles distant when the latter broke the silence.

"Joan Haygarth has come on wonderfully the last few months; getting quite a fine-looking girl. Don't you think so, Purcell?"

"Yes," answered Purcell, "and so does Phil Rodney."

"You're right," agreed the other. "She isn't a patch on her sister, though, and never will be. I was looking at Maggie as we came down the beach this morning and thinking what a handsome girl she is. Don't you agree with me?"

Purcell stooped to look under the boom, and answered without turning his head:

"Yes, she's all right."

"All right!" exclaimed the other. "Is that the way—"

"Look here, Varney," interrupted Purcell. "I don't want to discuss my wife's looks with you or any other man. She'll do for me or I shouldn't have married her."

A deep, coppery flush stole into Varney's cheeks. But he had brought the rather brutal snub on himself and apparently had the fairness to recognise the fact, for he mumbled an apology and relapsed into silence.

When next he spoke he did so with a manner diffident and uneasy, as though approaching a disagreeable or difficult subject.

"There's a little matter, Dan, that I've been wanting to speak to you about when we got a chance of a private talk."

He glanced rather anxiously at his stolid companion, who grunted, and then, without removing his gaze from the horizon ahead, replied: "You've a pretty fair chance now, seeing that we shall be bottled up together for another five or six hours. And it's fairly private unless you bawl loud enough to be heard at the Longships."

It was not a gracious invitation. But if Varney resented the rebuff he showed no sign of annoyance, for reasons which appeared when he opened his subject.

"What I wanted to say," he resumed, "was this. We're both doing pretty well now on the square. You must be positively piling up the shekels, and I can earn a decent living, which is all I want. Why shouldn't we drop this flash note business?"

Purcell kept his blue eye fixed on the horizon and appeared to ignore the question; but after an interval and without moving a muscle he said gruffly: "Go on," and Varney continued:

"The lay isn't what it was, you know. At first it was all plain sailing. The notes were 1st-class copies and not a soul suspected anything until they were presented at the bank. Then the murder was out, and the next little trip that I made was a very different affair. Two or three of the notes were queried quite soon after I had changed them, and I had to be precious fly, I can tell you, to avoid complications. And now that the second batch has come in to the Bank, the planting of fresh specimens is going to be harder still. There isn't a money-changer on the Continent of Europe that isn't keeping his weather eyeball peeled, to say nothing of the detectives that the Bank people have sent abroad."

He paused and looked appealingly at his companion. But Purcell, still minding his helm, only growled "Well?"

"Well, I want to chuck it, Dan. When you've had a run of luck and pocketed your winnings it is time to stop play."

"You've come into some money, then, I take it?" said Purcell.

"No, I haven't. But I can make a living now by safe and respectable means, and I'm sick of all this scheming and dodging with the gaol everlastingly under my lee."

"The reason I asked," said Purcell, "is that there is a trifle outstanding. You hadn't forgotten that, I suppose?"

"No, I hadn't forgotten it, but I thought that perhaps you might be willing to let me down a bit easily."

The other man pursed up his thick lips and continued to gaze stonily over the bow.

"Oh, that's what you thought?" he said; and then, after a pause: "I fancy you must have lost sight of some of the facts when you thought that. Let me just remind you how the case stands. To begin with, you start your career with a little playful embezzlement, you blue the proceeds and you are mug enough to be found out. Then I come in. I compound the affair with old Marston for a couple of thousand, and practically clean myself out of every penny I possess, and he consents to regard your temporary absence in the light of a holiday.

"Now, why do I do this? Am I a philanthropist? Devil a bit. I'm a man of business. Before I ladle out that two thousand, I make a business contract with you. I have discovered how to make a passable imitation of the Bank of England paper; you are a skilled engraver and a plausible scamp. I am to supply you with paper blanks, you are to engrave plates, print the notes, and get them changed. I am to take two-thirds of the proceeds; and, although I have done the most difficult part of the work, I agree to regard my share of the profits as constituting repayment of the loan.

"Our contract amounts to this: I lend you two thousand without security—with an infernal amount of insecurity, in fact—you 'promise, covenant, and agree, as the lawyers say, to hand me back ten thousand in instalments, being the products of our joint industry. It is a verbal contract which I have no means of enforcing, but I trust you to keep your word, and up to the present you have kept it. You have paid me a little over four thousand. Now you want to cry off and leave the balance unpaid. Isn't that the position?"

"Not exactly," said Varney. "I'm not crying off the debt; I only want time. Look here, Dan; I'm making about three fifty a year now. That isn't much, but I'll manage to let you have a hundred a year out of it. What do you say to that?"

Purcell laughed scornfully. "A hundred a year to pay off six thousand! That'll take just sixty years: and as I'm now forty-three, I shall be exactly a hundred and three years of age when the last instalment is paid. I think, Varney, you'll admit that a man of a hundred and three is getting past his prime."

"Well, I'll pay you something down to start. I've saved about eighteen hundred pounds out of the note business. You can have that now, and I'll pay off as much I can at a time until I'm clear. Remember, that if I should happen to get clapped in chokee for twenty years or so, you won't get anything. And, I tell you, it's getting a risky business."

"I'm willing to take the risk," said Purcell.

"I daresay you are," Varney retorted passionately, "because it's my risk. If I am grabbed, it's my racket. You sit out. It's I who passed the notes, and I'm known to be a skilled engraver. That'll be good enough for them. They won't trouble about who made the paper."

"I hope not," said Purcell.

"Of course they wouldn't; and you know I shouldn't give you away."

"Naturally. Why should you? Wouldn't do you any good."

"Well, give me a chance, Dan," Varney pleaded. "This business is getting on my nerves. I want to be quit of it. You've had four thousand; that's a hundred per cent. You haven't done so badly."

"I didn't expect to do badly. I took a big risk. I gambled two thousand for ten."

"Yes; and you got me out of the way while you put the screw on poor old Haygarth to make his daughter marry you."

It was an indiscreet thing to say, but Purcell's stolid indifference to his danger and distress had ruffled Varney's temper.

Purcell, however, was unmoved. "I don't know," he said, "what you mean by getting you out of the way. You were never in the way. You were always hankering after Maggie, but I could never see that she wanted you."

"Well, she certainly didn't want *you,*" Varney retorted. "And, for that matter, I don't much think she wants you now."

For the first time Purcell withdrew his eye from the horizon to turn it on his companion. And an evil eye it was, set in the great, sensual face, now purple with anger.

"What the devil do you mean?" he exclaimed furiously; "you infernal, sallow-faced, little whipper-snapper! If you mention my wife's name again I'll knock you on the head and pitch you overboard."

Varney's face flushed darkly, and for a moment he was inclined to try the wager a battle. But the odds were impossible, and if Varney was not a coward, neither was he a fool. But the discussion was at an end. Nothing was to be hoped for now. These indiscreet words had rendered further pleading impossible.

The silence that settled down in the yacht and the aloofness that encompassed the two men were conducive to reflection. Each ignored the presence of the other. When the course was altered southerly, Purcell slacked out the sheets with his own hand as he put up the helm. He might have been sailing singlehanded. And Varney watched him askance, but made no move; sitting hunched up on the locker, nursing a slowly-matured hatred and thinking his thoughts.

Very queer thoughts they were. He was following out the train of events that might have happened, pursuing them to their possible consequences. Supposing Purcell had carried out his threat? Well, there would have been a pretty tough struggle, for Varney was no weakling. But a struggle with that solid fifteen stone of flesh could end only one way. No, there was no doubt; he would have gone overboard.

And what then? Would Purcell have gone back to Sennen Cove, or sailed alone into Penzance? In either case, he would have had to make up some sort of story; and no one could have contradicted him whether the story was believed or not. But it would have been awkward for Purcell.

Then there was the body. That would have been washed up sooner or later, as much of it as the lobsters had left. Well, lobsters don't eat clothes or bones, and a dent in the skull might take some accounting for. Very awkward this—for Purcell. He would probably have had to clear out; to make a bolt for it, in short.

The mental picture of this great bully fleeing in terror from the vengeance of the law gave Varney appreciable pleasure. Most of his life he had been borne down by the moral and physical weight of this domineering brute. At school, Purcell had fagged him; he had even bullied him up at Cambridge; and now he had fastened on for ever, like the Old Man of the Sea. And Purcell always got the best of it. When he, Varney, had come back from Italy after that unfortunate little affair, behold! the girl whom they had both wanted (and who had wanted neither of them) had changed from Maggie Haygarth into Maggie Purcell. And so it was even unto this day. Purcell, a prosperous stockjobber now, spent a part of his secret leisure making, in absolute safety, these accursed paper blanks; which he, Varney, must risk his liberty to change into money. Yes, it was quite pleasant to think of Purcell sneaking from town to town, from country to country, with the police at his heels.

But in these days of telegraphs and extradition there isn't much chance for a fugitive. Purcell would have been caught to a certainty; and he would have been hanged; no doubt of it. The imagined picture of the execution gave him quite a lengthy entertainment. Then his errant thoughts began to spread out in search of other possibilities. For, after all, it was not an absolute certainty that Purcell could have got him overboard. There was just the chance that Purcell might have gone overboard himself. That would have been a very different affair.

Varney settled himself composedly to consider the new and interesting train of consequences that would thus have been set going. They were more agreeable to contemplate than the others, because they did not include his own demise. The execution scene made no appearance in this version. The salient fact was that his oppressor would have vanished; that the intolerable burden of his servitude would have been lifted for ever; that he would have been free.

It was mere idle speculation to while away a dull hour with an uncongenial companion, and he let his thoughts ramble at large. One moment he was dreamily wondering whether Maggie would ever have listened to him, ever have come to care for him; the next, he was back in the yacht's cabin, where hung from a hook on the bulkhead the revolver that the Rodneys used to practise at floating bottles. It was usually loaded, he knew, but, if not, there was a canvas bag full of cartridges in the starboard locker. Again, he found himself dreaming of the home that he would have had, a home very different from the cheerless lodgings in which he moped at present; and then his thoughts had flitted back to the yacht's hold, and were busying themselves with the row of half-hundredweights that rested on the timbers on either side of the kelson.

When Varney had thus brought his mental picture, so to speak, to a finish, its completeness surprised him. It was so simple, so secure. He had actually planned out the scheme of a murder, and he found himself wondering whether many murders passed undetected. They well might if murders were as easy and as safe as this—a dangerous reflection for an injured and angry man. And at this critical point his meditations were interrupted by Purcell, continuing the conversation as if there had been no pause:

"So you can take it from me, Varney, that I expect you to stick to your bargain. I paid down my money, and I'm going to have my pound of flesh."

It was a brutal thing to say, and it was brutally said. But more than that, it was inopportune—or opportune, as you will; for it came as a sort of infernal doxology to the devil's anthem that had been, all unknown, ringing in Varney's soul.

Purcell had spoken without looking round. That was his unpleasant habit. Had he looked at his companion, he might have been startled. A change in Varney's face might have given him pause; a warm flush, a sparkle of the eye, a look of elation, of settled purpose, deadly, inexorable—the look of a man who has made a fateful resolution.

It was so simple, so secure! That was the burden of the song that echoed in Varney's brain.

He glanced over the sea. They had opened the south coast now, and he could see, afar off, a fleet of black-sailed luggers heading east. They wouldn't be in his way. Nor would the big four-master that was creeping away to the west, for she was hull down already, and other ships there were none.

There was one hindrance, though. Dead ahead the Wolf Rock Lighthouse rose from the blue water, its red-and-white ringed tower looking like some gaudily painted toy. The keepers of lonely lighthouses have a natural habit of watching the passing shipping through their glasses, and it was possible that one of their telescopes might be pointed at the yacht at this very moment. That was a complication.

Suddenly there came down the wind a sharp report like the firing of a gun, quickly followed by a second. It was the explosive signal from the Longships Lighthouse; but when they looked round there was no lighthouse to be seen—the dark-blue, heaving water faded away at the foot of an advancing wall of vapour.

Purcell cursed fluently. A pretty place, this, to be caught in, in a fog! And then, as his eye lighted on his companion, he demanded angrily: "What the devil are you grinning at?"

For Varney, drunk with suppressed excitement, snapped his fingers at rocks and shoals; he was thinking only of the lighthouse keeper's telescope and of the revolver that hung on the bulkhead. He must make some excuse presently to go below and secure that revolver.

But no excuse was necessary. The opportunity came of itself. After a hasty glance at the vanishing land and another at the compass, Purcell put up the helm to gybe the yacht round on to an easterly course.

As she came round, the single headsail that she carried in place of jib and foresail shivered for a few seconds, and then filled suddenly on the opposite tack. And at this moment the halyards parted with a loud snap; the end of the rope flew through the blocks, and, in an instant, the sail was down and its upper half trailing in the water alongside.

Purcell swore volubly, but kept an eye to business. "Run below, Varney," said he, "and fetch up that coil of new rope out of the starboard locker while I had the sail on board. And look alive. We don't want to drift down on to the Wolf."

Varney obeyed with silent alacrity and a curious feeling of elation. It was going to be even easier and safer than he had thought. He slipped through the hatch into the cabin, quietly took the revolver from its hook, and examined the chambers.

Finding them all loaded, he cocked the hammer and slipped the weapon carefully into the inside breast pocket of his oilskin coat. Then he took the coil of rope from the locker and went on deck.

As he emerged from the hatch, he perceived that the yacht was already enveloped in fog, which drifted past in steamy clouds, and that she had come up head to wind. Purcell was kneeling on the forecastle, tugging at the sail, which had caught under the forefoot, and punctuating his efforts with deep-voiced curses.

Varney stole silently along the deck, steadying himself by mast and shroud, softly laid down the coil of rope, and approached. Purcell was quite engrossed with his task; his back was towards Varney, his face over the side, intent on the entangled sail. It was a chance in a thousand.

With scarcely a moment's hesitation, Varney stooped forward, steadying himself with a hand on the little windlass, and softly drawing forth the revolver, pointed it at the back of Purcell's head at the spot where the back seam of his sou'wester met the brim.

The report rang out but weak and flat in that open space, and a cloud of smoke mingled with the fog; but it blew away immediately, and showed Purcell almost unchanged in posture, crouching on the sail, with his chin resting on the little rim of bulwark, while behind him his murderer, as if turned into bronze, still stood stooping forward, one hand grasping the windlass, the other still pointing the revolver.

Thus the two figures remained for some seconds motionless like some horrible waxworks, until the little yacht, lifting to the swell, gave a more than usually lively curvet; when Purcell rolled over on to his back, and Varney relaxed the rigidity of his posture like a golf-player who has watched his ball drop.

Purcell was dead. That was the salient fact. The head wagged to and fro as the yacht pitched and rolled, the limp arms and legs seemed to twitch, the limp body to writhe uneasily. But Varney was not disturbed. Lifeless things will move on an unsteady deck. He was only interested to notice how the passive movements produced the illusion of life. But it was only illusion. Purcell was dead. There was no doubt of that.

The double report from the Longships came down the wind, and then, as if in answer, a prolonged, deep bellow. That was the fog-horn of the lighthouse on the Wolf Rock, and it sounded surprisingly near. But, of course, these signals were meant to be heard at a distance. Then a stream of hot sunshine, pouring down on deck, startled him, and made him hurry. The body must be got overboard before the fog lifted.

With an uneasy glance at the clear sky overhead, he hastily cast off the broken halyard from its cleat and cut off a couple of fathoms. Then he hurried below, and, lifting the trap in the cabin floor, hoisted out one of the iron half-hundredweights with which the yacht was ballasted.

As he stepped on deck with the weight in his hand, the sun was shining overhead; but the fog was still thick below, and the horn sounded once more from the Wolf. And again it struck him as surprisingly near.

He passed the length of rope that he had cut off twice round Purcell's body, hauled it tight, and secured it with a knot. Then he made the ends fast to the handle of the iron weight.

Not much fear of Purcell drifting ashore now. That weight would hold him as long as there was anything to hold. But it had taken some time to do, and the warning bellow from the Wolf seemed to draw nearer and nearer. He was about to heave the body over when his eye fell on the dead man's sou'wester, which had fallen off when the body rolled over.

That hat must be got rid of, for Purcell's name was worked in silk on the lining and there was an unmistakeable bullet-hole through the back. It must be destroyed, or, which would be simpler and quicker, lashed securely on the dead man's head.

Hurriedly, Varney ran aft and descended to the cabin. He had noticed a new ball of spunyarn in the locker when he had fetched the rope. This would be the very thing.

He was back again in a few moments with the ball in his hand, unwinding it as he came, and without wasting time he knelt down by the body and fell to work.

And every half minute the deep-voiced growl of the Wolf came to him out of the fog, and each time it sounded nearer and yet nearer.

By the time he had made the sou'wester secure the dead man's face and chin were encased in a web of spunyarn that made him look like some old-time, grotesque-vizored Samurai warrior.

Varney rose to his feet. But his task was not finished yet. There was Purcell's suit-case. That must be sunk, too, and there was something in it that had figured in the detailed picture that his imagination had drawn. He ran to the cockpit where the suit-case lay, and having tried its fastenings and found it unlocked, he opened it and took out a letter that lay on top of the other contents. This he tossed through the hatch into the cabin, and, having closed and fastened the suit-case, he carried it forward and made it fast to the iron weight with half a dozen turns of spunyarn.

That was really all, and indeed it was time. As he rose once more to his feet the growl of the foghorn burst out, as it seemed, right over the stern of the yacht, and she was drifting stern foremost, who could say how fast. Now, too, he caught a more ominous sound, which he might have heard sooner had he listened—the wash of water, the boom of breakers bursting on a rock.

A sudden revulsion came over him. He burst into a wild, sardonic laugh. And had it come to this, after all? Had he schemed and laboured only to leave himself alone on an unmanageable craft drifting down to shipwreck and certain death? Had he taken all this thought and care to secure Purcell's body, when his own might be resting beside it on the sea-bottom within an hour?

But the reverie was brief. Suddenly, from the white void over his very head, as it seemed, there issued a stunning, thunderous roar that shook the deck under his feet. The water around him boiled into a foamy chaos, the din of bursting waves was in his ears, the yacht plunged and wallowed amidst clouds of spray, and for an instant a dim, gigantic shadow loomed through the fog and was gone. In that moment his nerve had come back. Holding on with one hand to the windlass he dragged the body to the edge of the forecastle, hoisted the weight outboard, and then, taking advantage of a heavy lurch, gave the corpse a vigorous shove. There was a rattle and a hollow splash, and corpse and weight and suit-case had vanished into the seething water.

He clung to the swinging mast and waited. Breathlessly he told out the allotted seconds until once again the invisible Titan belched forth his thunderous warning. But this time the roar came over the yacht's bow. She had drifted past the rock then. The danger was over, and Purcell would have to go down to Davy Jones' locker companionless after all.

Very soon the water around ceased to boil and tumble, and as the yacht's wild plunging settled down once more into the normal rise and fall on the long swell, Varney turned his attention to the refitting of the halyard. But what was this on the creamy, duck sail? A pool of blood and two gory imprints of his own left hand! That wouldn't do at all. He would have to clear that away before he could hoist the sail, which was annoying, as the yacht was helpless without her headsail, and was evidently drifting out to sea.

He fetched a bucket, a swab, and a scrubbing-brush, and set to work. The bulk of the large bloodstain cleared off pretty completely after he had drenched the sail with a bucketfull or two and given it a good scrubbing. But the edge of the stain where the heat of the deck had dried it remained like a painted boundary on a map, and the two hand-prints—which had also dried, though they faded to a pale buff—continued clearly visible.

Varney began to grow uneasy. If those stains would not come out—especially the hand-prints—it would be very awkward, they would take so much explaining. He decided to try the effect of marine soap, and fetched a cake from the cabin; but even this did not obliterate the stains completely, though it turned them a faint, greenish brown, very unlike the colour of blood. So he scrubbed on until at last the hand-prints faded away entirely, and the large stain was reduced to a faint green, wavy line, and that was the best he could do—and quite good enough, for if that faint line should ever be noticed no one would suspect its origin.

He put away the bucket and proceeded with the refitting. The sea had disengaged the sail from the forefoot, and he hauled it on board without difficulty. Then there was the reeving of the new halyard, a trouble-some business involving the necessity of his going aloft, where his weight—small man as he was—made the yacht roll most infernally, and set him swinging to and fro like the bob of a metronome. But he was a smart yachtsman and active, though not powerful, and a few minutes' strenuous exertion ended in his sliding down the shrouds with the new halyard running fairly through the upper block. A vigorous haul or two at the new, hairy rope sent the head of the dripping sail aloft, and the yacht was once more under control.

The rig of the *Sandhopper* was not smart, but it was handy. She carried a short bow-sprit to accommodate the single headsail and a relatively large mizzen, of which the advantage was, that by judicious management of the mizzen-sheet the yacht would sail with very little attention to the helm. Of this advantage Varney was keenly apprecia-tive just now, for he had several things to do before entering port. He wanted refreshment, he wanted a wash, and the various traces of recent events had to be removed. Also, there was that letter to be attended to. So that it was convenient to be able to leave the helm in charge of a lashing for a minute now and again.

When he had washed, he put the kettle on the spirit stove, and while it was heating busied himself in cleaning the revolver, flinging the empty cartridge-case overboard, and replacing it with a cartridge from the bag in the locker. Then he picked up the letter that he had taken from Purcell's suit-case and examined it. It was addressed to "Joseph Penfield, Esq., George Yard, Lombard Street," and was unstamped, though the envelope was fastened up. He affixed a stamp from his pocket-book, and when the kettle began to boil, he held the envelope in the steam that issued from the spout. Very soon the flap of the enve-lope loosened and curled back, when he laid it aside to mix himself a mug of hot grog, which, together with the letter and a biscuit-tin, he took out into the cockpit. The fog was still dense, and the hoot of a steamer's whistle from somewhere to the westward caused him to reach the foghorn out of the locker, and blow a long blast on it. As if in answer to his treble squeak came the deep bass note from the Wolf, and unconsciously he looked round. He turned automatically, as one does towards a sudden noise, not expecting to see anything but fog, and what he did see startled him not a little.

For there was the lighthouse—or half of it, rather—standing up above the fog-bank, clear, distinct, and hardly a mile away. The gilded vane, the sparkling lantern, the gallery, and the upper half of the red and white ringed tower, stood sharp against the pallid sky; but the lower half was invisible. It was a strange apparition—like half a lighthouse suspended in mid-air—and uncommonly disturbing, too. It raised a very awkward question. If he could see the lantern, the light-keepers could see him. But how long had the lantern been clear of the fog?

Thus he meditated as, with one hand on the tiller, he munched his biscuit and sipped his grog. Presently he picked up the stamped enve-lope and drew from it a letter and a folded document, both of which he tore into fragments and dropped overboard. Then, from his pocket-book, he took a similar but unaddressed envelope from which he drew out the contents, and very curious those contents were.

There was a letter, brief and laconic, which he read over thoughtfully. "These," it ran, "are all I have by me, but they will do for the present, and when you have planted them I will let you have a fresh supply." There was no date and no signature, but the rather peculiar hand-writing was similar to that on the envelope addressed to Joseph Penfield, Esq.

The other contents consisted of a dozen sheets of blank paper, each of the size of a Bank of England note. But they were not quite blank, for each bore an elaborate water-mark, identical with that of a twenty-pound banknote. They were, in fact, the "paper blanks" of which Purcell had spoken. The envelope with its contents had been slipped into his hand by Purcell, without remark, only three days ago.

Varney refolded the "blanks," enclosed them within the letter, and slipped letter and "blanks" together into the stamped envelope, the flap of which he licked and reclosed.

"I should like to see old Penfield's face when he opens that envelope," was his reflection as, with a grim smile, he put it away in his pocket-book. "And I wonder what he will do," he added, mentally; "however, I shall see before many days are over."

Varney looked at his watch. He was to meet Jack Rodney on Penzance Pier at a quarter to three. He would never do it at this rate, for when he opened Mount's Bay, Penzance would be right in the wind's eye. That would mean a long beat to windward. Then Rodney would be there first, waiting for him. Deuced awkward, this. He would have to account for his being alone on board; would have to invent some lie about having put Purcell ashore at Mousehole or Newlyn. But a lie is a very pernicious thing. Its effects are cumulative. You never know when you have done with it. Now, if he had reached Penzance before Rodney he need have said nothing about Purcell—for the present, at any rate, and that would have been so much safer.

When the yacht was about abreast of Lamorna Cove, though some seven miles to the south, the breeze began to draw ahead and the fog cleared off quite suddenly. The change of wind was unfavourable for the moment, but when it veered round yet a little more until it blew from east-north-east, Varney brightened up considerably. There was still a chance of reaching Penzance before Rodney arrived; for now, as soon as he had fairly opened Mount's Bay, he could head straight for his destination and make it on a single board.

Between two and three hours later the *Sandhopper* entered Penzance Harbour, and, threading her way among an assemblage of luggers and small coasters, brought up alongside the Albert Pier at the foot of a vacant ladder. Having made the yacht fast to a couple of rings, Varney divested himself of his oilskins, locked the cabin scuttle, and climbed the ladder. The change of wind had saved him after all, and, as he strode away along the pier, he glanced complacently at his watch. He still had nearly half an hour to the good.

He seemed to know the place well and to have a definite objective, for he struck out briskly from the foot of the pier into Market Jew Street, and from thence by a somewhat zig-zag route to a road which eventually brought him out about the middle of the Esplanade. Continuing westward, he entered the Newlyn Road along which he walked rapidly for about a third of a mile, when he drew up opposite a small letter-box which was let into a wall. Here he stopped to read the tablet on which was printed the hours of collection, and then, having glanced at his watch, he walked on again, but at a less rapid pace.

When he reached the outskirts of Newlyn he turned and began slowly to retrace his steps, looking at his watch from time to time with a certain air of impatience. Presently a quick step behind him caused him to look round. The newcomer was a postman, striding along, bag on shoulder, with the noisy tread of a heavily-shod man, and evidently collecting letters. Varney let him pass; watched him halt at the little letterbox, unlock the door, gather up the letters and stow them in his bag; heard the clang of the iron door, and finally saw the man set forth again on his pilgrimage. Then he brought forth his pocket-book and, drawing from it the letter addressed to Joseph Penfield, Esq., stepped up to the letter-box. The tablet now announced that the next collection would be at 8.30 p.m. Varney read the announcement with a faint smile, glanced again at his watch, which indicated two minutes past four, and dropped the letter into the box.

As he walked up the pier, with a large paper bag under his arm, he became aware of a tall man, who was doing sentry-go before a Gladstone bag, that stood on the coping opposite the ladder, and who, observing his approach, came forward to meet him.

"Here you are, then, Rodney," was Varney's rather unoriginal greeting.

"Yes," replied Rodney, "and here I've been for nearly half an hour. Purcell gone?"

"Bless you, yes; long ago," answered Varney.

"I didn't see him at the station. What train was he going by?"

"I don't know. He said something about taking Falmouth on the way; had some business or other there. But I expect he's gone to have a feed at one of the hotels. We got hung up in a fog—that's why I'm so late; I've been up to buy some prog."

"Well," said Rodney, "bring it on board. It's time we were under way. As soon as we are outside, I'll take charge and you can go below and stoke up at your ease."

The two men descended the ladder and proceeded at once to hoist the sails and cast off the shore-ropes. A few strokes of an oar sent them clear of the lee of the pier, and in five minutes the yacht *Sandhopper* was once more outside, heading south with a steady breeze from east-north-east.

II. The Unravelling of the Mystery

Romance lurks in unsuspected places. We walk abroad amidst scenes made dull by familiarity, and let our thoughts ramble far away beyond the commonplace. In fancy we thread the ghostly aisles of some tropical forest; we linger on the white beach of some lonely coral island, where the cocoa-nut palms, shivering in the sea-breeze, patter a refrain to the song of the surf; we wander by moonlight through the narrow streets of some southern city, and hear the thrum of the guitar rise to the shrouded balcony; and behold! all the time Romance is at our very doors.

★   ★   ★

It was on a bright afternoon early in March, that I sat beside my friend Thorndyke on one of the lower benches of the lecture theatre of the Royal College of Surgeons. Not a likely place this to encounter Romance, and yet there it was, if we had only known it, lying unnoticed at present on the green baize cover of the lecturer's table. But, for the moment, we were thinking of nothing but the lecture.

The theatre was nearly full. It usually was when Professor D'Arcy lectured; for that genial *savant* had the magnetic gift of infusing his own enthusiasm into the lecture, and so into his audience, even when, as on this occasion, his subject lay on the outside edge of medical science. To-day he was lecturing on marine worms, standing before the great blackboard with a bunch of coloured chalks in either hand, talking with easy eloquence—mostly over his shoulder—while he covered the black surface with those delightful drawings that added so much to the charm of his lectures.

I watched his flying fingers with fascination, dividing my attention between him and a young man on the bench below me, who was frantically copying the diagrams in a large note-book, assisted by an older friend, who sat by him and handed him the coloured pencils as he needed them.

The latter part of the lecture dealt with those beautiful sea-worms that build themselves tubes to live in; worms like the *Serpula,* that make their shelly or stony tubes by secretion from their own bodies; or, like the *Sabella* or *Terbella,* build them up with sand-grains, little stones, or frag-ments of shell.

When the lecture came to an end, we trooped down into the arena to look at the exhibits and exchange a few words with the genial pro-fessor. Thorndyke knew him very well, and was welcomed with a warm handshake and a facetious question.

"What are you doing here, Thorndyke?" asked Professor D'Arcy. "Is it possible that there are medico-legal possibilities even in a marine worm?"

"Oh, come!" protested Thorndyke, "don't make me such a hide-bound specialist. May I have no rational interest in life? Must I live for ever in the witness-box, like a marine worm in its tube?"

"I suspect you don't get very far out of your tube," said the profes-sor, with a smile at my colleague. "And that reminds me that I have something in your line. What do you make of this? Let us hear you extract its history."

Here, with a mischievous twinkle, he handed Thorndyke a small, round object, which my friend inspected curiously as it lay in the palm of his hand.

"In the first place," said he, "it is a cork; the cork of a small jar."

"Right," said the professor—"full marks. What else?"

"The cork has been saturated with paraffin wax."

"Right again."

"Then some Robinson Crusoe seems to have used it as a button, judging by the two holes in it, and an end of what looks like cat-gut."

"Yes."

"Finally, a marine worm of some kind—a *Terebella,* I think—has built a tube on it."

"Quite right. And now tell us the history of the cork or button."

"I should like to know something more about the worm first," said Thorndyke.

"The worm," said Professor D'Arcy, "is *Terebella Rufescens.* It lives, unlike most other species, on a rocky bottom, and in a depth of water of not less than ten fathoms."

It was at this point that Romance stepped in. The young man whom I had noticed working so strenuously at his notes had edged up alongside, and was staring at the object in Thorndyke's hand, not with mere interest or curiosity, but with the utmost amazement and horror. His expression was so remarkable that we all, with one accord, dropped our conversation to look at him.

"Might I be allowed to examine that specimen?" he asked; and when Thorndyke handed it to him, he held it close to his eyes, scrutinising it with frowning astonishment, turned it over and over, and felt the frayed ends of cat-gut between his fingers. Finally, he beckoned to his friend, and the two whispered together for a while, and watching them I saw the second man's eyebrows lift, and the same expression of horrified surprise appear on his face. Then the younger man addressed the professor.

"Would you mind telling me where you got this specimen, sir?"

The professor was quite interested. "It was sent to me," he said, "by a friend, who picked it up on the beach at Morte Hoe, on the coast of North Cornwall."

The two young men looked significantly at one another, and, after a brief pause, the older one asked: "Is this specimen of much value, sir?"

"No," replied the professor; "it is only a curiosity. There are several specimens of the worm in our collection. But why do you ask?"

"Because I should like to acquire it. I can't give you particulars—I am a lawyer, I may explain—but, from what my brother tells me it appears that this object has a bearing on—er—on a case in which we are both interested. A very important bearing, I may add, on a very important case."

The professor was delighted. "There, now, Thorndyke," he chuckled. "What did I tell you? The medico-legal worm has arrived. I told you it was something in your line, and now you've been forestalled. Of course," he added, turning to the lawyer, "you are very welcome to this specimen. I'll give you a box to carry it in, with some cotton wool."

The specimen was duly packed in its box, and the latter deposited in the lawyer's pocket; but the two brothers did not immediately leave the theatre. They stood apart, talking earnestly together, until Thorndyke and I had taken our leave of the professor, when the lawyer advanced and addressed my colleague.

"I don't suppose you remember me, Dr. Thorndyke," he began; but my friend interrupted him.

"Yes, I do. You are Mr. Rodney. You were junior to Brooke in *Jelks v. Partington.* Can I be of any assistance to you?"

"If you would be so kind," replied Rodney. "My brother and I have been talking this over, and we think we should like to have your opinion on the case. The fact is, we both jumped to a conclusion at once, and now we've got what the Yankees call 'cold feet.' We think that we may have jumped too soon. Let me introduce my brother, Dr. Philip Rodney."

We shook hands, and, making our way out of the theatre, presently emerged from the big portico into Lincoln's Inn Fields.

"If you will come and take a cup of tea at my chambers in Old Buildings," said Rodney, "we can give you the necessary particulars. There isn't so very much to tell, after all. My brother identifies the cork or button, and that seems to be the only plain fact that we have. Tell Dr. Thorndyke how you identified it, Phil."

"It is a simple matter," said Philip Rodney. "I went out in a boat to do some dredging with a friend named Purcell. We both wore our oilskins as the sea was choppy and there was a good deal of spray blowing about; but Purcell had lost the top button of his, so that the collar kept blowing open and letting the spray down his neck. We had no spare buttons or needles or thread on board, but it occurred to me that I could rig up a jury button with a cork from one of my little collecting jars; so I took one out, bored a couple of holes through it with a pipe-cleaner, and threaded a piece of cat-gut through the holes."

"Why cat-gut?" asked Thorndyke.

"Because I happened to have it. I play the fiddle, and I generally have a bit of a broken string in my pocket; usually an E string—the E strings are always breaking, you know. Well, I had the end of an E string in my pocket then, so I fastened the button on with it. I bored two holes in the coat, passed the ends of the string through, and tied a reef-knot. It was as strong as a house."

"You have no doubt that it is the same cork?"

"None at all. First there is the size, which I know from having ordered the corks separately from the jars. Then I paraffined them myself after sticking on the blank labels. The label is there still, protected by the wax. And lastly there is the cat-gut; the bit that is left is obviously part of an E string."

"Yes," said Thorndyke, "the identification seems to be unimpeachable. Now let us have the story."

"We'll have some tea first," said Rodney. "This is my burrow." As he spoke, he dived into the dark entry of one of the ancient buildings on the south side of the little square, and we followed him up the crabbed, time-worn stairs, so different from our own lordly staircase in King's Bench Walk. He let us into his chambers, and, having offered us each an armchair, said: "My brother will spin you the yarn while I make the tea. When you have heard him you can begin the examination-in-chief. You understand that this is a confidential matter and that we are dealing with it professionally?"

"Certainly," replied Thorndyke, "we quite understand that." And thereupon Philip Rodney began his story.

"One morning last June two men started from Sennen Cove, on the west coast of Cornwall, to sail to Penzance in a little yacht that belongs to my brother and me. One of them was Purcell, of whom I spoke just now, and the other was a man named Varney. When they started, Purcell was wearing the oilskin coat with this button on it. The yacht arrived at Penzance at about four in the afternoon. Purcell went ashore alone to take the train to London or Falmouth, and was never seen again dead or alive. The following day Purcell's solicitor, a Mr. Penfield, received a letter from him bearing the Penzance postmark and the hour 8.45 p.m. The letter was evidently sent by mistake—put into the wrong envelope—and it appears to have been a highly compromising document. Penfield refuses to give any particulars, but thinks that the letter fully accounts for Purcell's disappearance—thinks, in fact, that Purcell has bolted.

"It was understood that Purcell was going to London from Penzance, but he seems to have told Varney that he intended to call in at Falmouth. Whether or not he went to Falmouth we don't know. Varney saw him go up the ladder on to the pier, and there all traces of him vanished. Varney thinks he may have discovered the mistake about the letter and got on board some outward-bound ship at Falmouth; but that is only surmise. Still, it is highly probable; and when my brother and I saw that button at the museum, we remembered the suggestion and instantly jumped to the conclusion that poor Purcell had gone overboard."

"And then," said Rodney, handing us our tea-cups, "when we came to talk it over we rather tended to revise our conclusion."

"Why?" asked Thorndyke.

"Well, there are several other possibilities. Purcell may have found a proper button on the yacht and cut off the cork and thrown it overboard—we must ask Varney if he did—or the coat itself may have gone over or been lost or given away, and so on."

On this Thorndyke made no comment, stirring his tea slowly with an air of deep preoccupation. Presently he looked up and asked, "Who saw the yacht start?"

"I did," said Philip. "I and Mrs. Purcell and her sister and some fishermen on the beach. Purcell was steering, and he took the yacht right out to sea, outside the Longships. A sea fog came down soon after, and we were rather anxious, because the Wolf Rock lay right to leeward of the yacht."

"Did anyone besides Varney see Purcell at Penzance?"

"Apparently not. But we haven't asked. Varney's statement seemed to settle that question. He couldn't very well have been mistaken, you know," Philip added with a smile.

"Besides," said Rodney, "if there were any doubt, there is the letter. It was posted in Penzance after eight o'clock at night. Now I met

Varney on the pier at a quarter-past four, and we sailed out of Penzance a few minutes later to return to Sennen."

"Had Varney been ashore?" asked Thorndyke.

"Yes, he had been up to the town buying some provisions."

"But you said Purcell went ashore alone."

"Yes, but there's nothing in that. Purcell was not a genial man. It was the sort of thing he would do."

"And that is all that you know of the matter?" Thorndyke asked, after a few moments' reflection.

"Yes. But we might see if Varney can remember anything more, and we might try if we can squeeze any more information out of old Penfield."

"You won't," said Thorndyke. "I know Penfield and I never trouble to ask him questions. Besides, there is nothing to ask at present. We have an item of evidence that we have not fully examined. I suggest that we exhaust that, and meanwhile keep our own counsel most completely."

Rodney looked dissatisfied. "If," said he, "the item of evidence that you refer to is the button, it seems to me that we have got all that we are likely to get out of it. We have identified it, and we know that it has been thrown up on the beach at Morte Hoe. What more can we learn from it?"

"That remains to be seen," replied Thorndyke. "We may learn nothing, but, on the other hand, we may be able to trace the course of its travels and learn its recent history. It may give us a hint as to where to start a fresh inquiry."

Rodney laughed sceptically. "You talk like a clairvoyant, as if you had the power to make this bit of cork break out into fluent discourse. Of course, you can look at the thing and speculate and guess, but surely the common sense of the matter is to ask a plain question of the man who probably knows. If it turns out that Varney saw Purcell throw the button overboard, or can tell us how it got into the sea, all your speculations will have been useless. I say, let us ask Varney first, and if he knows nothing, it will be time to start guessing."

But Thorndyke was calmly obdurate. "We are not going to guess, Rodney; we are going to investigate. Let me have the button for a couple of days. If I learn nothing from it, I will return it to you, and you can then refresh your legal soul with verbal testimony. But give scientific methods a chance first."

With evident reluctance Rodney handed him the little box. "I have asked your advice," he said rather ungraciously, "so I suppose I must take it; but your methods appeal more to the sporting than the business instincts."

"We shall see," said Thorndyke, rising with a satisfied air. "But, meanwhile, I stipulate that you make no communication to anybody."

"Very well," said Rodney; and we took leave of the two brothers.

As we walked down Chancery Lane, I looked at Thorndyke, and detected in him an air of purpose for which I could not quite account. Clearly, he had something in view.

"It seems to me," I said tentatively, "that there was something in what Rodney said. Why shouldn't the button just have been thrown overboard?"

He stopped and looked at me with humorous reproach, "Jervis!" he exclaimed, "I am ashamed of you. You are as bad as Rodney. You have utterly lost sight of the main fact, which is a most impressive one. Here is a cork button. Now an ordinary cork, if immersed long enough, will soak up water until it is water-logged, and then sink to the bottom. But this one is impregnated with paraffin wax. It can't get water-logged, and it can't sink. It would float for ever."

"Well?"

"But it *has* sunk. It has been lying at the bottom of the sea for months, long enough for a *Terebella* to build a tube on it. And we have D'Arcy's statement that it has been lying in not less than ten fathoms of water. Then, at last, it has broken loose and risen to the surface and drifted ashore. Now, I ask you, what has held it down at the bottom of the sea? Of course, it may have been only the coat, weighted by something in the pocket; but there is a much more probable suggestion."

"Yes, I see," said I.

"I suspect you don't—altogether," he rejoined, with a malicious smile. And in the end it turned out that he was right.

The air of purpose that I noted was not deceptive. No sooner had we reached our chambers, then he fell to work as if with a definite object. Standing by the window, he scrutinised the button, first with the naked eye, and then with a lens, and finally laying it on the stage of the microscope, examined the worm-tube by the light of a condenser with a two-inch objective. And the result seemed to please him amazingly.

His next proceeding was to detach, with a fine pair of forceps, the largest of the tiny fragments of stone of which the worm-tube was built. This fragment he cemented on a slide with Canada balsam; and, fetching form the laboratory a slip of Turkey stone, he proceeded to grind the little fragment to a flat surface. Then he melted the balsam, turned the fragment over, and repeated the grinding process until the little fragment was ground down to a thin film or plate, when he applied fresh balsam and a cover-glass. The specimen was now ready for examination; and it was at this point that I suddenly remembered I had an appointment at six o'clock.

It had struck half-past seven when I returned, and a glance round the room told me that the battle was over—and won. The table was littered with trays of mineralogical sections and open books of reference relating to geology and petrology, and one end was occupied by an outspread geological chart of the British Isles. Thorndyke sat in his armchair, smiling with a bland contentment, and smoking a Trichinopoly cheroot.

"Well," I said cheerfully, "what's the news?"

"He removed the cheroot, blew out a cloud of smoke, and replied in a single word:

"Phonolite."

"Thank you," I said. "Brevity is the soul of wit. But would you mind amplifying the joke to the dimensions of intelligibility?"

"Certainly," he replied gravely. "I will endeavour to temper the wind to the shorn lamb. You noticed, I suppose, that the fragments of rock of which that worm-tube was built are all alike?"

"All the same kind of rock? No, I did not."

"Well, they are, and I have spent a strenuous hour identifying that rock. It is the peculiar, resonant, volcanic rock known as phonolite or clink-stone."

"That is very interesting," said I. "And now I see the object of your researches. You hope to get a hint as to the locality where the button has been lying."

"I hoped, as you say, to get a hint, but I have succeeded beyond my expectations. I have been able to fix the locality exactly."

"Have you really?" I exclaimed. "How on earth did you manage that?"

"By a very singular chance," he replied. "It happens that phonolite occurs in two places only in the neighbourhood of the British Isles. One is inland and may be disregarded. The other is the Wolf Rock."

"The rock of which Philip Rodney was speaking?"

"Yes. He said, you remember, that he was afraid that the yacht might drift down on it in the fog. Well, this Wolf Rock is a very remarkable structure. It is what is called a 'volcanic neck,' that is, it is a mass of altered lava that once filled the funnel of a volcano. The volcano has disappeared, but this cast of the funnel remains standing up from the bottom of the sea like a great column. It is a single mass of phonolite, and thus entirely different in composition from the seabed around or anywhere near these islands. But, of course, immediately at its base, the sea-bottom must be covered with decomposed fragments which have fallen from its sides, and it is from these fragments that our *Terebella* has built its tube. So, you see, we can fix the exact locality in which that button has been lying all the months that the tube was building, and we now have a point of departure for fresh investigations."

"But," I said, "this is a very significant discovery, Thorndyke. Shall you tell Rodney?"

"Certainly I shall. But there are one or two questions that I shall ask him first. I have sent him a note inviting him to drop in to-night with his brother, so we had better run round to the club and get some dinner. I said nine o'clock."

It was a quarter to nine when we had finished dinner, and ten minutes later we were back in our chambers. Thorndyke made up the fire, placed the chairs hospitably round the hearth, and laid on the table the notes that he had taken at the late interview. Then the Treasury clock struck nine, and within less than a minute our two guests arrived.

"I should apologise," said Thorndyke, as we shook hands, "for my rather peremptory message, but I thought it best to waste no time."

"You certainly have wasted no time," said Rodney, "if you have already extracted its history from the button. Do you keep a tame medium on the premises, or are you a clairvoyant yourself?"

"There is our medium," replied Thorndyke, indicating the microscope standing on a side-table under its bell glass. "The man who uses it becomes to some extent a clairvoyant. But I should like to ask you one or two questions if I may."

Rodney made no secret of his disappointment. "We had hoped," said he, "to hear answers rather than questions. However, as you please."

"Then," said Thorndyke, quite unmoved by Rodney's manner, "I will proceed; and I will begin with the yacht in which Purcell and Varney travelled from Sennen to Penzance. I understand that the yacht belongs to you and was lent by you to these two men?"

Rodney nodded, and Thorndyke then asked: "Has the yacht ever been out of your custody on any other occasion?"

"No," replied Rodney, "excepting on this occasion, one or both of us have always been on board."

Thorndyke made a note of the answer and proceeded: "When you resumed possession of the yacht, did you find her in all respects as you had left her?"

"My dear sir," Rodney exclaimed impatiently, "may I remind you that we are inquiring—if we are inquiring about anything—into the disappearance of a man who was seen to go ashore from this yacht and who certainly never came on board again? The yacht is out of it altogether."

"Nevertheless," said Thorndyke, "I should be glad if you would answer my question."

"Oh, very well," Rodney replied irritably. "Then we found her substantially as we had left her."

"Meaning by 'substantially'?—"

"Well, they had had to rig a new jib halyard. The old one had parted."

"Did you find the old one on board?"

"Yes; in two pieces, of course."

"Was the whole of it there?"

"I suppose so. We never measured the pieces. But really, sir, these questions seem extraordinarily irrelevant."

"They are not," said Thorndyke. "You will see that presently. I want to know if you missed any rope, cordage, or chain."

Here Philip interposed. "There was some spun-yarn missing. They opened a new ball and used up several yards. I meant to ask Varney what they used it for."

Thorndyke jotted down a note and asked: "Was there any of the ironwork missing? Any anchor, chain, or any other heavy object?"

Rodney shook his head impatiently, but again Philip broke in.

"You are forgetting the ballast-weight, Jack. You see," he continued, addressing Thorndyke, "the yacht is ballasted with half-hundredweights, and, when we came to take out the ballast to lay her up for the winter, we found one of the weights missing. I have no idea when it disappeared, but there was certainly one short, and neither of us had taken it out."

"Can you," asked Thorndyke, "fix any date on which all the ballast-weights were in place?"

"Yes, I think I can. A few days before Purcell went to Penzance we beached the yacht—she is only a little boat—to give her a scrape. Of course, we had to take out the ballast, and when we launched her again I helped to put it back. I am certain all the weights were there then."

Here Jack Rodney, who had been listening with ill-concealed impatience, remarked:

"This is all very interesting, sir, but I cannot conceive what bearing it has on the movements of Purcell after he left the yacht."

"It has a most direct and important bearing," said Thorndyke. "Perhaps I had better explain before we go any further. Let me begin by pointing out that this button has been lying for many months at the bottom of the sea at a depth of not less than ten fathoms. That is proved by the worm-tube which has been built on it. Now, as this button is a waterproofed cork, it could not have sunk by itself; it has been sunk by some body to which it was attached, and there is evidence that that body was a very heavy one."

"What evidence is there of that?" asked Rodney.

"There is the fact that it has been lying continuously, in one place. A body of moderate weight, as you know, moves about the sea-bottom impelled by currents and tide-streams, but this button has been lying unmoved in one place."

"Indeed," said Rodney with manifest scepticism. "Perhaps you can point out the spot where it has been lying."

"I can," Thorndyke replied. "That button, Mr. Rodney, has been lying all these months at the base of the Wolf Rock."

The two brothers started very perceptibly. They stared at Thorndyke, they looked at one another, and then the lawyer challenged the statement.

"You make this assertion very confidently," he said. "Can you give us any evidence to support it?"

Thorndyke's reply was to produce the button, the section, the test-specimens, the microscope, and the geological chart. In great detail, and with his incomparable lucidity, he assembled the facts, and explained their connection, evolving the unavoidable conclusion.

The different effect of the demonstration on the two men interested me greatly. To the lawyer, accustomed to dealing with verbal and documentary evidence, it manifestly appeared as a far-fetched, rather fantastic argument, ingenious, amusing, and entirely unconvincing. On Philip, the doctor, it made a profound impression. Accustomed to acting on inferences from facts of his own observing, he gave full weight to each item of evidence, and I could see that his mind was already stretching out to the, as yet unstated, corollaries.

The lawyer was the first to speak. "What inference," he asked, "do you wish us to draw from this very ingenious theory of yours?"

"The inference," Thorndyke replied impassively, "I leave to you; but perhaps it would help you if I recapitulate the facts."

"Perhaps it would," said Rodney.

"Then," said Thorndyke, "I will take them in order. This is the case of a man who was seen to start on a voyage for a given destination in company with one other person. His start out to sea was witnessed by a number of persons. From that moment he was never seen again by any person excepting his one companion. He is said to have reached his destination, but his arrival there rests upon the unsupported verbal testimony of one person, the said companion. Thereafter he vanished utterly, and since then has made no sign of being alive, although there are several persons with whom he could have safely communicated.

"Some eight months later a portion of this man's clothing is found. It bears evidence of having been lying at the bottom of the sea for many months, so that it must have sunk to its resting place within a very short time of the man's disappearance. The place where it has been lying is one over, or near, which the man must have sailed in the yacht. It has been moored to the bottom by some very heavy object; and a very heavy object has disappeared from the yacht. That heavy object had apparently not disappeared when the yacht started, and was not seen on the yacht afterwards. The evidence goes to show that the disappearance of that object coincided in time with the disappearance of the man; and a quantity of cordage disappeared, certainly, on that day. Those are the facts in our possession at present, Mr. Rodney, and I think the inference emerges automatically."

There was a brief silence, during which the two brothers cogitated profoundly and with very disturbed expressions. Then Rodney spoke.

"I am bound to admit, Dr. Thorndyke, that, as a scheme of circumstantial evidence, this is extremely ingenious and complete. It is impossible to mistake your meaning. But you would hardly expect us to charge a highly respectable gentleman of our acquaintance with having murdered his friend and made away with the body, on a—well—a rather far-fetched theory."

"Certainly not," replied Thorndyke. "But, on the other hand, with this body of circumstantial evidence before us, it is clearly imperative that some further investigations should be made before we speak of the matter to any human soul."

Rodney agreed somewhat grudgingly. "What do you suggest?" he asked.

"I suggest that we thoroughly overhaul the yacht in the first place. Where is she now?"

"Under a tarpaulin in a yard at Battersea. The gear and stores are in a disused workshop in the yard."

"When could we look over her?"

"To-morrow morning, if you like," said Rodney.

"Very well," said Thorndyke. "We will call for you at nine, if that will suit."

It suited perfectly, and the arrangement was accordingly made. A few minutes later the two brothers took their leave, but as they were shaking hands, Philip said suddenly:

"There is one little matter that occurs to me. I have only just remembered it, and I don't suppose it is of any consequence, but it is as well to mention everything. You remember my brother saying that one of the jib halyards broke that day?"

"Yes."

"Well, of course, the jib came down and went partly overboard. Now, the next time I hoisted the sail, I noticed a small stain on it; a greenish stain like that of mud, only it wouldn't wash out, and it is there still. I meant to ask Varney about it. Stains of that kind on the jib usually come from a bit of mud on the fluke of the anchor, but the anchor was quite clean when I examined it, and besides, it hadn't been down on that day. I thought I'd better tell you about it."

"I'm glad you did," said Thorndyke. "We will have a look at that stain to-morrow. Good-night" Once more he shook hands, and then, re-entering the room, stood for quite a long time with his back to the fire, thoughtfully examining the toes of his boots.

We started forth next morning for our rendezvous considerably earlier than seemed necessary. But I made no comment, for Thorndyke was in that state of extreme taciturnity which characterised him whenever he was engaged on an absorbing case with an insufficiency of evidence. I knew that he was turning over and over the facts that he had, and searching for new openings; but I had no clue to the trend of his thoughts until, passing the gateway of Lincoln's Inn, he walked briskly up Chancery Lane into Holborn, and finally halted outside a wholesale druggist's.

"I shan't be more than a few minutes," said he; "are you coming in?"

I was, most emphatically. Questions were forbidden at this stage, but there was no harm in keeping one's ears open; and when I heard his order I was the richer by a distinct clue to his next movements. Tincture of Guiacum and Ozonic Ether formed a familiar combination, and the size of the bottles indicated the field of investigation.

We found the brothers waiting for us at Lincoln's Inn. They both looked rather hard at the parcel that I was now carrying, and especially at Thorndyke's green canvas-covered research case; but they made no comment, and we set forth at once on the rather awkward cross-country journey to Battersea. Very little was said on the way, but I noticed that both men took our quest more seriously than I had expected, and I judged that they had been talking the case over.

Our journey terminated at a large wooden gate on which Rodney knocked loudly with his stick; whereupon a wicket was opened, and, after a few words of explanation, we passed through into a large yard. Crossing this, we came to a wharf, beyond which was a small stretch of unreclaimed shore, and here, drawn well above high-water mark, a small, double-ended yacht stood on chocks under a tarpaulin cover.

"This is the yacht," said Rodney. "The gear and loose fittings are stored in the workshop behind us. Which will you see first?"

"Let us look at the gear," said Thorndyke, and we turned to the disused workshop into which Rodney admitted us with a key from his pocket. I looked curiously about the long, narrow interior with its prosaic contents, so little suggestive of tragedy or romance. Overhead the yacht's spars rested on the tie-beams, from which hung bunches of blocks; on the floor a long row of neatly-painted half-hundredweights, a pile of chain-cable, two anchors, a stove, and other oddments such as water breakers, buckets, mops, etc., and on the long benches at the side, folded sails, locker cushions, side-light lanterns, the binnacle, the cabin lamp, and other more delicate fittings. Thorndyke, too, glanced round inquisitively, and, depositing his case on the bench, asked, "Have you still got the broken jib halyard of which you were telling me?"

"Yes," said Rodney, "it is here under the bench." He drew out a coil of rope, and flinging it on the floor, began to uncoil it, when it separated into two lengths.

"Which are the broken ends?" Thorndyke asked.

"It broke near the middle," said Rodney, "where it chafed on the cleat when the sail was hoisted. This is the one end, you see, frayed out like a brush in breaking, and the other—" He picked up the second half and, passing it rapidly through his hands, held up the end. He did not finish the sentence, but stood with a frown of surprise staring at the rope in his hands.

"This is queer," he said, after a pause, "The broken end has been cut off. Did you cut it off, Phil?"

"No," replied Philip. "It is just as I took it from the locker, where, I suppose, you or Varney stowed it."

"The question is," said Thorndyke, "how much has it been cut off? Do you know the original length of the rope?"

"Yes. Forty-two feet. It is not down in the inventory, but I remember working it out. Let us see how much there is here."

He laid the two lengths of rope along the floor and we measured them with Thorndyke's spring tape. The combined length was exactly thirty-one feet.

"So," said Thorndyke, "there are eleven feet missing, without allowing for the lengthening of the rope by stretching. That is a very important fact."

"What made you suspect that part of the halyard might be missing as well as the spunyarn?" Philip asked.

"I did not think," replied Thorndyke, "that a yachtsman would use spunyarn to lash a half-handredweight to a corpse. I suspected that the spunyarn was used for something else. By the way, I see you have a revolver there. Was that on board at the time?"

"Yes," said Rodney. "It was hanging on the cabin bulkhead. Be careful. I don't think it has been unloaded."

Thorndyke opened the breech of the revolver, and dropping the cartridges into his hand, peered down the barrel and into each chamber separately.

"It is quite clean inside," he remarked. Then, glancing at the ammunition in his hand, "I notice," said he, "that these cartridges are not all alike. There is one Curtis and Harvey, and five Eleys."

Philip looked with a distinctly startled expression at the little heap of cartridges in Thorndyke's hand, and picking out the odd one, examined it with knitted brows.

"When did you fire the revolver last, Jack?" he asked, looking up at his brother.

"On the day when we potted at those champagne bottles," was the reply.

Philip raised his eyebrows. "Then," said he, "this is a very remarkable affair. I distinctly remember on that occasion, when we had sunk all the bottles, reloading the revolver with Eleys, and that there were then three cartridges left over in the bag. When I had loaded I opened the new box of Curtis and Harvey's, upped them into the bag and threw the box overboard."

"Did you clean the revolver?" asked Thorndyke.

"No, I didn't. I mean to do it later, but forgot to."

"But," said Thorndyke, "it has undoubtedly been cleaned, and very thoroughly. Shall we check the cartridges in the bag? There ought to be forty-nine Curtis and Harvey's and three Eley's if what you tell us is correct."

Philip searched among the raffle on the bench and produced a small linen bag. Untying the string, he shot out on the bench a heap of cartridges which he counted one by one. There were fifty-two in all, and three of them were Eley's.

"Then," said Thorndyke, "it comes to this: since you used that revolver it has been used by someone else. That someone fired only a single shot, after which he carefully cleaned the barrel and reloaded. Incidentally, he seems to have known where the cartridge bag was kept, but did not know about the change in the make of the cartridges. You notice," he added, looking at Rodney, "that the circumstantial evidence accumulates."

"I do, indeed," Rodney replied gloomily. "Is there anything else that you wish to examine?"

"Yes. There is the sail. You spoke of a stain on the jib. Shall we see if we can make anything of that?"

"I don't think you will make much of it," said Philip. "It is very faint. However, you shall see it." He picked out one of the bundles of white duck, and, while he was unfolding it, Thorndyke dragged an empty bench into the middle of the floor under the skylight. Over this the sail was spread so that the mysterious mark was in the middle of the bench. It was very inconspicuous; just a faint, grey-green, wavy line like the representation of an island on a map. We all looked at it attentively for a few moments, and then Thorndyke said, "Would you mind if I made a further stain on the sail? I should like to apply some re-agents."

"Of course, you must do what is necessary," said Rodney. "The evidence is more important than the sail."

Accordingly Thorndyke unpacked our parcel, and as the two bottles emerged, Philip read the labels with evident surprise, remarking:

"I shouldn't have thought the Guiacum test would have been of any use after all these months."

"It will act, I think, if the pigment is there," said Thorndyke; and as he spoke he poured a quantity of the tincture—which he had ordered diluted to our usual working strength—on the middle of the stained area. The pool of liquid rapidly spread considerably beyond the limits of the stain, growing paler as it extended. Then Thorndyke cautiously dropped small quantities of the Ether at various points around the stained area and watched closely as the two liquids mingled in the fabric of the sail. Gradually the Ether spread towards the stain, and, first at one point and then at another, approached and finally crossed the wavy grey line, and at each point the same change occurred; first, the faint grey line turned into a strong blue line, and then the colour extended to the enclosed space, until the entire area of the stain stood out, a conspicuous blue patch.

Philip and Thorndyke looked at one another significantly, and the latter said, "You understand the meaning of this reaction, Mr. Rodney; this is a bloodstain, and a very carefully washed bloodstain."

"So I supposed," Rodney replied, and for a while we were all silent.

There was something very dramatic and solemn in the sudden appearance of this staring blue patch on the sail, with the sinister message that it brought. But what followed was more dramatic still. As we stood silently regarding the blue stain, the mingled liquids continued to spread: and suddenly, at the extreme edge of the wet area, we became aware of a new spot of blue. At first a mere speck, it grew slowly as the liquid spread over the canvas into a small oval, and then a second spot appeared by its side.

At this point Thorndyke poured out a fresh charge of the tincture, and when it had soaked into the cloth, cautiously applied a sprinkling of Ether. Instantly the blue spots began to elongate, fresh spots and patches appeared, and as they ran together there sprang out of the blank surface the clear impression of a hand—a left hand, complete in all its details excepting the third finger, which was represented by an oval spot at some two-thirds of its length.

The dreaded significance of this apparition and the uncanny and mysterious manner of its emergence from the white surface impressed us so that for a while none of us spoke. At length I ventured to remark on the absence of the impression of the third finger.

"I think," said Thorndyke, "that the impression is there. That spot looks like the mark of a finger-tip, and its position rather suggests a finger with a stiff joint."

As he made this statement, both brothers simultaneously uttered a smothered exclamation.

Thorndyke looked up at them sharply. "What is it?" he asked.

The two men looked at one another with an expression of awe. Then Rodney said in a hushed voice, hardly above a whisper, "Varney, the man who was with Purcell on the yacht—he has a stiff joint on the third finger of his left hand."

There was nothing more to say. The case was complete. The key-stone had been laid in the edifice of circumstantial evidence. The investigation was at an end.

After an interval of silence, during which Thorndyke was busily writing up his notes, Rodney asked, "What is to be done now? Shall I swear an information?"

Thorndyke shook his head. No man was more expert in accumulating circumstantial evidence; none was more loth to rely on it.

"A murder charge," said he, "should be supported by proof of death and, if possible, by production of the body."

"But the body is at the bottom of the sea!"

"True. But we know its whereabouts. It is a small area, with the light-house as a landmark. If that area were systematically worked over with a trawl or dredge, or better still, with a creeper, there should be a very good chance of recovering the body, or, at least, the clothing and the weight."

Rodney reflected for a few moments. "I think you are right," he said at length. "The thing is practicable, and it is our duty to do it. I suppose you couldn't come down and help us?"

"Not now. But in a few days the spring vacation will commence, and then Jervis and I could join you, if the weather were suitable." "Thank you both," replied Rodney. "We will make the arrangements, and let you know when we are ready."

★   ★   ★

It was quite early on a bright April morning when the two Rodneys, Thorndyke, and I steamed out of Penzance Harbour in a small open launch. The sea was very calm for the time of year, the sky was of a warm blue, and a gentle breeze stole out of the north-east. Over the launch's side hung a long spar, secured to a tow-rope by a bridle, and to the spar were attached a number of creepers—lengths of chain fitted with rows of hooks. The outfit further included a spirit compass, provided with sights, a sextant, and a hand-lead.

"It's lucky we didn't run up against Varney in the town," Philip remarked, as the harbour dwindled in the distance.

"Varney!" exclaimed Thorndyke. "Do you mean that he lives at Penzance?"

"He keeps rooms there, and spends most of his spare time down in this part. He was always keen on sea-fishing, and he's keener than ever now. He keeps a boat of his own, too. It's queer, isn't it, if what we think is true?"

"Very," said Thorndyke; and by his meditative manner I judge that circumstances afforded him matter for curious speculation.

As we passed abreast of the Land's End, and the solitary lighthouse rose ahead on the verge of the horizon, we began to overtake the scattered members of a fleet of luggers, home with lowered mainsails and hand-lines down, others with their black sails set, heading for a more distant fishing-ground. Threading our way among them, we suddenly became aware that one of the smaller luggers was heading so as to close in on us. Rodney, observing this, was putting over the helm to avoid her when a seafaring voice from the little craft hailed us.

"Launch ahoy there! Gentleman aboard wants to speak to you."

We looked at one another significantly and in some confusion; and meanwhile our solitary "hand"—seaman, engineer, and fireman combined—without waiting for orders, shut off steam. The lugger closed in rapidly and of a sudden there appeared, holding on by the mainstay, a small dark fellow who hailed us cheerfully: "Hullo, you fellows! Whither away? What's your game?"

"God!" exclaimed Philip. "It's Varney. Sheer off, Jack! Don't let him come alongside."

"But it was too late. The launch had lost way and failed to answer the helm. The lugger sheered in, sweeping abreast of us within a foot; and, as she crept past, Varney sprang lightly from her gunwale and dropped neatly on the side bench in our stern sheets.

"Where are you off to?" he asked. "You can't be going out to fish in this baked-potato can?"

"No," faltered Rodney, "we're not. We're going to do some dredging—or rather—"

Here Thorndyke came to his assistance. "Marine worms," said he, "are the occasion of this little voyage. There seem to be some very uncommon ones on the bottom at the base of the Wolf Rock. I have seen some in a collection, and I want to get a few more if I can."

It was a skillfully-worded explanation, and I could see that, for the time, Varney accepted it. But from the moment when the Wolf Rock was mentioned all his vivacity of manner died out. In an instant he had become grave, thoughtful, and a trifle uneasy.

The introductions over, he reverted to the subject. He questioned us closely, especially as to our proposed methods. And it was impossible to evade his questions. There were the creepers in full view; there was the compass and the sextant; and presently these appliances would have to be put in use. Gradually, as the nature of our operations dawned on him, his manner changed more and more. A horrible pallor overspread his face, and a terrible restlessness took possession of him.

Rodney, who was navigating, brought the launch to within a quarter of a mile of the rock, and then, taking cross-bearings on the lighthouse and a point of land, directed us to lower the creepers.

It was a most disagreeable experience for us all. Varney, pale and clammy, fidgeted about the boat, now silent and moody, now almost hysterically boisterous. Thorndyke watched him furtively and, I think, judged by his manner how near we were to the object of our search.

Calm as the day was, the sea was breaking heavily over the rock, and as we worked in closer the water around boiled and eddied in an unpleasant and even dangerous manner. The three keepers in the gallery of the lighthouse watched us through their glasses, and one of them bellowed to us through a megaphone to keep further away.

"What do you say?" asked Rodney. "It's a bit risky here, with the rock right under our lee. Shall we try another side?"

"Better try one more cast this side," said Thorndyke; and he spoke so definitely that we all, including Varney, looked at him curiously. But no one answered, and the creepers were dropped for a fresh cast still nearer the rock. We were then north of the lighthouse, and headed south so as to pass the rock on its east side. As we approached, the man with the megaphone bawled out fresh warnings, and continued to roar at us until we were abreast of the rock in a wild tumble of confused waves.

At this moment Philip, who held the towline with a single turn round a cleat, said that he felt a pull, but that it seemed as if the creepers had broken away. As soon, therefore, as we were out of the backwash into smooth water, we hauled in the linen to examine the creepers.

I looked over the side eagerly, for something new in Thorndyke's manner impressed me. Varney, too, who had hitherto taken little notice of the creepers, now knelt on the side bench, gazing earnestly into the clear water, when the tow-rope was rising.

At length the beam came in sight, and below it, on one of the creepers, a yellowish object, dimly seen through the wavering water.

"There's somethin' on this time," said the engineer, craning over the side. He shut off steam, and, with the rest of us, watched the incoming creeper. I looked at Varney, kneeling on the bench apart from us, not fidgeting now, but still rigid, pale as wax, and staring with dreadful fascination at the slowly-rising object.

Suddenly the engineer uttered an exclamation. "Why, 'tis a sou'wester, and all laced about wi' spuny'n. Surely 'tis—Hi! steady, sir! My God!"

There was a heavy splash, and as Rodney rushed forward for the boat-hook I saw Varney rapidly sinking head first through the clear, blue-green water, dragged down by the hand-lead that he had hitched to his waist. By the time Rodney was back he was far out of reach; but for a long time, as it seemed, we could see him sinking, sinking, growing paler, more shadowy, more shapeless, but always steadily following the lead sinker, until at last he faded from our sight into the darkness of the ocean.

Not until he had vanished did we haul on board the creeper with its dreadful burden. Indeed, we never hauled it on board; for as Philip, with an unsteady hand, unhooked the sou'wester hat from the creeper, the encircling coils of spunyarn slipped, and from inside the hat a skull dropped into the water and sank. We watched it grow green and pallid and small, until it vanished, as Varney had vanished. Then Philip turned and flung the hat down in the bottom of the boat. Thorndyke picked it up and unwound the spunyarn.

"Do you identify it?" he asked, and then, as he turned it over, he added, "But I see it identifies itself." He held it towards me, and I read in embroidered letters on the silk lining, "Dan Purcell."

The Mystery of the Felwyn Tunnel

L. T. Meade and Robert Eustace

I WAS making experiments of some interest at South Kensington, and hoped that I had perfected a small but not unimportant discovery, when, on returning home one evening in late October in the year 1893, I found a visiting card on my table. On it were inscribed the words, "Mr. Geoffrey Bainbridge." This name was quite unknown to me, so I rang the bell and inquired of my servant who the visitor had been. He described him as a gentleman who wished to see me on most urgent business, and said further that Mr. Bainbridge intended to call again later in the evening. It was with both curiosity and vexation that I awaited the return of the stranger. Urgent business with me generally meant a hurried rush to one part of the country or the other. I did not want to leave London just then; and when at half-past nine Mr. Geoffrey Bainbridge was ushered into my room, I received him with a certain coldness which he could not fail to perceive. He was a tall, well-dressed, elderly man. He immediately plunged into the object of his visit.

"I hope you do not consider my unexpected presence an intrusion, Mr. Bell," he said. "But I have heard of you from our mutual friends, the Greys of Uplands. You may remember once doing that family a great service."

"I remember perfectly well," I answered more cordially. "Pray tell me what you want; I shall listen with attention."

"I believe you are the one man in London who can help me," he continued, "I refer to a matter especially relating to your own particular study. I need hardly say that whatever you do will not be unrewarded."

"That is neither here nor there," I said; "but before you go any further, allow me to ask one question. Do you want me to leave London at present?"

He raised his eyebrows in dismay.

"I certainly do," he answered.

"Very well; pray proceed with your story."

He looked at me with anxiety.

"In the first place," he began, "I must tell you that I am chairman of the Lytton Vale Railway Company in Wales, and that it is on an important matter connected with our line that I have come to consult you. When I explain to you the nature of the mystery, you will not wonder, I think, at my soliciting your aid."

"I will give you my closest attention," I answered; and then I added, impelled to say the latter words by a certain expression on his face, "if I can see my way to assisting you I shall be ready to do so."

"Pray accept my cordial thanks," he replied. "I have come up from my place at Felwyn to-day on purpose to consult you. It is in that neighbourhood that the affair has occurred. As it is essential that you should be in possession of the facts of the whole matter, I will go over things just as they happened."

I bent forward and listened attentively.

"This day fortnight," continued Mr. Bainbridge, "our quiet little village was horrified by the news that the signalman on duty at the mouth of the Felwyn Tunnel had been found dead under the most mysterious circumstances. The tunnel is at the end of a long cutting between Llanlys and Felwyn stations. It is about a mile long, and the signal-box is on the Felwyn side. The place is extremely lonely, being six miles from the village across the mountains. The name of the poor fellow who met his death in this mysterious fashion was David Pritchard. I have known him from a boy, and he was quite one of the steadiest and most trustworthy men on the line. On Tuesday evening he went on duty at six o'clock; on Wednesday morning the day-man who had come to relieve him was surprised not to find him in the box. It was just getting daylight, and the 6.30 local was coming down, so he pulled the signals and let her through. Then he went out, and, looking up the line towards the tunnel, saw Pritchard lying beside the line close to the mouth of the tunnel. Roberts, the day-man, ran up to him and found, to his horror, that he was quite dead. At first Roberts naturally supposed that he had been cut down by a train, as there was a wound at the back of the head; but he was not lying on the metals. Roberts ran back to the box and telegraphed through to Felwyn Station. The message was sent on to the village, and at half-past seven o'clock the police inspector came up to my house with the news. He and I, with the local doctor, went off at once to the tunnel.

We found the dead man lying beside the metals a few yards away from the mouth of the tunnel, and the doctor immediately gave him a careful examination. There was a depressed fracture at the back of the skull, which must have caused his death; but how he came by it was not so clear. On examining the whole place most carefully, we saw, further, that there were marks on the rocks at the steep side of the embankment as if some one had tried to scramble up them. Why the poor fellow had attempted such a climb, God only knows. In doing so he must have slipped and fallen back on to the line, thus causing the fracture of the skull. In no case could he have gone up more than eight or ten feet, as the banks of the cutting run sheer up, almost perpendicularly, beyond that point for more than a hundred and fifty feet. There are some sharp boulders beside the line, and it was possible that he might have fallen on one of these and so sustained the injury. The affair must have occurred some time between 11.45 p.m. and 6 a.m., as the engine-driver of the express at 11.45 p.m. states that the line was signalled clear, and he also caught sight of Pritchard in his box as he passed."

"This is deeply interesting," I said; "pray proceed."

Bainbridge looked at me earnestly; he then continued:—

"The whole thing is shrouded in mystery. Why should Pritchard have left his box and gone down to the tunnel? Why, having done so, should he have made a wild attempt to scale the side of the cutting, an impossible feat at any time? Had danger threatened, the ordinary course of things would have been to run up the line towards the signal-box. These points are quite unexplained. Another curious fact is that death appears to have taken place just before the day-man came on duty, as the light at the mouth of the tunnel had been put out, and it was one of the night signalman's duties to do this as soon as daylight appeared; it is possible, therefore, that Pritchard went down to the tunnel for that purpose. Against this theory, however, and an objection that seems to nullify it, is the evidence of Dr. Williams, who states that when he examined the body his opinion was that death had taken place some hours before. An inquest was held on the following day, but before it took place there was a new and most important development. I now come to what I consider the crucial point in the whole story.

"For a long time there had been a feud between Pritchard and another man of the name of Wynne, a platelayer on the line. The

object of their quarrel was the blacksmith's daughter in the neighbouring village—a remarkably pretty girl and an arrant flirt. Both men were
madly in love with her, and she played them off one against the other.
The night but one before his death Pritchard and Wynne had met
at the village inn, had quarrelled in the bar—Lucy, of course, being
the subject of their difference. Wynne was heard to say (he was a man
of powerful build and subject to fits of ungovernable rage) that he
would have Pritchard's life. Pritchard swore a great oath that he would
get Lucy on the following day to promise to marry him. This oath, it
appears, he kept, and on his way to the signal-box on Tuesday evening
met Wynne, and triumphantly told him that Lucy had promised to be
his wife. The men had a hand-to-hand fight on the spot, several
people from the village being witnesses of it. They were separated
with difficulty, each vowing vengeance on the other. Pritchard went
off to his duty at the signal-box and Wynne returned to the village to
drown his sorrows at the public-house.

"Very late that same night Wynne was seen by a villager going in the
direction of the tunnel. The man stopped him and questioned him. He
explained that he had left some of his tools on the line, and was on his
way to fetch them. The villager noticed that he looked queer and
excited, but not wishing to pick a quarrel thought it best not to question him further. It has been proved that Wynne never returned home
that night, but came back at an early hour on the following morning,
looking dazed and stupid. He was arrested on suspicion, and at the
inquest the verdict was against him."

"Has he given any explanation of his own movements?" I asked.

"Yes; but nothing that can clear him. As a matter of fact, his tools
were nowhere to be seen on the line, nor did he bring them home with
him. His own story is that being considerably the worse for drink, he
had fallen down in one of the fields and slept there till morning."

"Things took black against him," I said.

"They do; but listen, I have something more to add. Here comes a
very queer feature in the affair. Lucy Ray, the girl who had caused the
feud between Pritchard and Wynne, after hearing the news of
Pritchard's death, completely lost her head, and ran frantically about the
village declaring that Wynne was the man she really loved, and that she
had only accepted Pritchard in a fit of rage with Wynne for not himself

bringing matters to the point. The case looks very bad against Wynne, and yesterday the magistrate committed him for trial at the coming assizes. The unhappy Lucy Ray and the young man's parents are in a state bordering on distraction."

"What is your own opinion with regard to Wynne's guilt?" I asked.

"Before God, Mr. Bell, I believe the poor fellow is innocent, but the evidence against him is very strong. One of the favourite theories is that he went down to the tunnel and extinguished the light, knowing that this would bring Pritchard out of his box to see what was the matter, and that he then attacked him, striking the blow which fractured the skull."

"Has any weapon been found about, with which he could have given such a blow?"

"No; nor has anything of the kind been discovered on Wynne's person; that fact is decidedly in his favour."

"But what about the marks on the rocks?" I asked.

"It is possible that Wynne may have made them in order to divert suspicion by making people think that Pritchard must have fallen, and so killed himself. The holders of this theory base their belief on the absolute want of cause for Pritchard's trying to scale the rock. The whole thing is the most absolute enigma. Some of the country folk have declared that the tunnel is haunted (and there certainly has been such a rumour current among them for years). That Pritchard saw some apparition, and in wild terror sought to escape from it by climbing the rocks, is another theory, but only the most imaginative hold it."

"Well, it is a most extraordinary case," I replied.

'Yes, Mr. Bell, and I should like to get your opinion of it. Do you see your way to elucidate the mystery?"

"Not at present; but I shall be happy to investigate the matter to my utmost ability."

"But you do not wish to leave London at present?"

"That is so; but a matter of such importance cannot be set aside. It appears, from what you say, that Wynne's life hangs more or less on my being able to clear away the mystery?"

"That is indeed the case. There ought not to be a single stone left unturned to get at the truth, for the sake of Wynne. Well, Mr. Bell, what do you propose to do?"

"To see the place without delay," I answered.

"That is right; when can you come?"

"Whenever you please."

"Will you come down to Felwyn with me to-morrow? I shall leave Paddington by the 7.10, and if you will be my guest I shall be only too pleased to put you up."

"That arrangement will suit me admirably," I replied. "I will meet you by the train you mention, and the affair shall have my best attention."

"Thank you," he said, rising. He shook hands with me and took his leave.

The next day I met Bainbridge at Paddington Station, and we were soon flying westward in the luxurious private compartment that had been reserved for him I could see by his abstracted manner and his long lapses of silence that the mysterious affair at Felwyn Tunnel was occupying all his thoughts.

It was two o'clock in the afternoon when the train slowed down at the little station of Felwyn. The station-master was at the door in an instant to receive us.

"I have some terribly bad news for you, sir," he said, turning to Bainbridge as we alighted; "and yet in one sense it is a relief, for it seems to clear Wynne."

"What do you mean?" cried Bainbridge. 'Bad news? Speak out at once!"

'Well, sir, it is this: there has been another death at Felwyn signal-box. John Davidson, who was on duty last night, was found dead at an early hour this morning in the very same place where we found poor Pritchard."

"Good God!" cried Bainbridge, starting back, "what an awful thing! What, in the name of Heaven, does it mean, Mr. Bell? This is too fearful. Thank goodness you have come down with us."

"It is as black a business as I ever heard of, sir," echoed the station-master; "and what we are to do I don't know. Poor Davidson was found dead this morning, and there was neither mark nor sign of what killed him—that is the extraordinary part of it. There's a perfect panic abroad, and not a signalman on the line will take duty to-night. I was quite in despair, and was afraid at one time that the line would have to be closed, but at last it occurred to me to wire to Lytton Vale, and they are sending down an inspector. I expect him by a special every moment. I believe this is he coming now," added the station-master, looking up the line.

There was the sound of a whistle down the valley, and in a few moments a single engine shot into the station, and an official in uniform stepped on to the platform.

"Good-evening, sir," he said, touching his cap to Bainbridge; "I have just been sent down to inquire into this affair at the Felwyn Tunnel, and though it seems more of a matter for a Scotland Yard detective than one of ourselves, there was nothing for it but to come. All the same, Mr. Bainbridge, I cannot say that I look forward to spending tonight alone at the place."

'You wish for the services of a detective, but you shall have some one better," said Bainbridge, turning towards me. "This gentleman, Mr. John Bell, is the man of all others for our business. I have just brought him down from London for the purpose."

An expression of relief flitted across the inspector's face.

"I am very glad to see you, sir," he said to me, "and I hope you will be able to spend the night with me in the signal-box. I must say I don't much relish the idea of tackling the thing single-handed; but with your help, sir, I think we ought to get to the bottom of it somehow. I am afraid there is not a man on the line who will take duty until we do. So it is most important that the thing should be cleared, and without delay."

I readily assented to the inspector's proposition, and Bainbridge and I arranged that we should call for him at four o'clock at the village inn and drive him to the tunnel.

We then stepped into the wagonette which was waiting for us, and drove to Bainbridge's house.

Mrs. Bainbridge came out to meet us, and was full of the tragedy. Two pretty girls also ran to greet their father, and to glance inquisitively at me. I could see that the entire family was in a state of much excitement.

"Lucy Ray has just left, father," said the elder of the girls. "We had much trouble to soothe her; she is in a frantic state."

"You have heard, Mr. Bell, all about this dreadful mystery?" said Mrs. Bainbridge as she led me towards the dining-room.

"Yes," I answered; "your husband has been good enough to give me every particular."

"And you have really come here to help us?"

"I hope I may be able to discover the cause," I answered.

"It certainly seems most extraordinary," continued Mrs. Bainbridge. "My dear," she continued, turning to her husband, "you can easily imagine the state we were all in this morning when the news of the second death was brought to us."

"For my part," said Ella Bainbridge, "I am sure that Felwyn Tunnel is haunted. The villagers have thought so for a long time, and this second death seems to prove it, does it not?" Here she looked anxiously at me.

"I can offer no opinion," I replied, "until I have sifted the matter thoroughly."

"Come, Ella, don't worry Mr. Bell," said her father; "if he is as hungry as I am, he must want his lunch."

We then seated ourselves at the table and commenced the meal. Bainbridge, although he professed to be hungry, was in such a state of excitement that he could scarcely eat. Immediately after lunch he left me to the care of his family and went into the village.

"It is just like him," said Mrs. Bainbridge; "he takes these sort of things to heart dreadfully. He is terribly upset about Lucy Ray, and also about the poor fellow Wynne. It is certainly a fearful tragedy from first to last."

"Well, at any rate," I said, "this fresh death will upset the evidence against Wynne."

"I hope so, and there is some satisfaction in the fact. Well, Mr. Bell, I see you have finished lunch; will you come into the drawing-room?"

I followed her into a pleasant room overlooking the valley of the Lytton.

By-and-by Bainbridge returned, and soon afterwards the dog-cart came to the door. My host and I mounted, Bainbridge took the reins, and we started off at a brisk pace.

"Matters get worse and worse," he said the moment we were alone. "If you don't clear things up to-night, Bell, I say frankly that I cannot imagine what will happen."

We entered the village, and as we rattled down the ill-paved streets I was greeted with curious glances on all sides. The people were standing about in groups, evidently talking about the tragedy and nothing else. Suddenly, as our trap bumped noisily over the paving-stones, a girl darted out of one of the houses and made frantic motions to Bainbridge to stop the horse. He pulled the mare nearly up on her haunches, and the girl came up to the side of the dog-cart.

"You have heard it?" she said, speaking eagerly and in a gasping voice. "The death which occurred this morning will clear Stephen Wynne, won't it, Mr. Bainbridge?—it will, you are sure, are you not?"

"It looks like it, Lucy, my poor girl," he answered. "But there, the whole thing is so terrible that I scarcely know what to think."

She was a pretty girl with dark eyes, and under ordinary circumstances must have had the vivacious expression of face and the brilliant complexion which so many of her countrywomen possess. But now her eyes were swollen with weeping and her complexion more or less disfigured by the agony she had gone through. She looked piteously at Bainbridge, her lips trembling. The next moment she burst into tears.

"Come away, Lucy," said a woman who had followed her out of the cottage; "Fie—for shame! don't trouble the gentlemen; come back and stay quiet."

"I can't, mother, I can't," said the unfortunate girl. "If they hang him, I'll go clean off my head. Oh, Mr. Bainbridge, do say that the second death has cleared him!"

"I have every hope that it will do so, Lucy," said Bainbridge, "but now don't keep us, there's a good girl; go back into the house. This gentleman has come down from London on purpose to look into the whole matter. I may have good news for you in the morning."

The girl raised her eyes to my face with a look of intense pleading. "Oh, I have been cruel and a fool, and I deserve everything," she gasped; "but, sir, for the love of Heaven, try to clear him."

I promised to do my best.

Bainbridge touched up the mare, she bounded forward, and Lucy disappeared into the cottage with her mother.

The next moment we drew up at the inn where the Inspector was waiting, and soon afterwards were bowling along between the high banks of the country lanes to the tunnel. It was a cold, still afternoon; the air was wonderfully keen, for a sharp frost had held the countryside in its grip for the last two days. The sun was just tipping the hills to westward when the trap pulled up at the top of the cutting. We hastily alighted, and the Inspector and I bade Bainbridge good-bye. He said that he only wished that he could stay with us for the night, assured us that little sleep would visit him, and that he would be back at the cutting at an early hour on the following morning; then the noise of his horse's feet was heard fainter and fainter as he drove back over the frost-bound roads. The Inspector and I ran along the little path to the wicket-gate in the fence, stamping our feet on the hard ground to restore circulation after our cold drive. The next moment we were looking down upon the scene of the mysterious deaths, and a weird and lonely place it looked. The tunnel was at one end of the rock cutting, the sides of which ran sheer down to the line for over a hundred and fifty feet. Above the tunnel's mouth the hills rose one upon the other. A more dreary place it would have been difficult to imagine. From a little clump of pines a delicate film of blue smoke rose straight up on the still air. This came from the chimney of the signal-box.

As we started to descend the precipitous path the Inspector sang out a cheery "Hullo!" The man on duty in the box immediately answered. His voice echoed and reverberated down the cutting, and the next moment he appeared at the door of the box. He told us that he would be with us immediately, but we called back to him to stay where he was, and the next instant the Inspector and I entered the box.

"The first thing to do," said Henderson the Inspector, "is to send a message down the line to announce our arrival."

This he did, and in a few moments a crawling goods train came panting up the cutting. After signalling her through we descended the wooden flight of steps which led from the box down to the line and walked along the metals towards the tunnel till we stood on the spot where poor Davidson had been found dead that morning. I examined the ground and all around it most carefully. Everything tallied exactly with the description I had received. There could be no possible way of approaching the spot except by going along the line, as the rocky sides of the cutting were inaccessible.

"It is a most extraordinary thing, sir," said the signalman whom we had come to relieve. "Davidson had neither mark nor sign on him— there he lay stone dead and cold, and not a bruise nowhere; but Pritchard had an awful wound at the back of the head. They said he got it by climbing the rocks—here, you can see the marks for yourself, sir. But now, is it likely that Pritchard would try to climb rocks like these, so steep as they are?"

"Certainly not," I replied.

"Then how do you account for the wound, sir?" asked the man with an anxious face.

"I cannot tell you at present," I answered.

"And you and Inspector Henderson are going to spend the night in the signal-box?"

'Yes."

A horrified expression crept over the signalman's face.

"God preserve you both," he said; "I wouldn't do it—not for fifty pounds. It's not the first time I have heard tell that Felwyn Tunnel is haunted. But, there, I won't say any more about that. It's a black business, and has given trouble enough. There's poor Wynne, the same thing as convicted of the murder of Pritchard; but now they say that Davidson's death will clear him. Davidson was as good a fellow as you would come across this side of the country, but for the matter of that, so was Pritchard. The whole thing is terrible—it upsets one, that it do, sir."

"I don't wonder at your feelings," I answered; 'but now, see here, I want to make a most careful examination of everything. One of the theories is that Wynne crept down this rocky side and fractured Pritchard's skull. I believe such a feat to be impossible. On examining these rocks I see that a man might climb up the side of the tunnel as far as from eight to ten feet, utilising the sharp projections of rock for the purpose; but it would be out of the question for any man to come down the cutting. No; the only way Wynne could have approached Pritchard was by the line itself. But, after all, the real thing to discover is this," I continued: "what killed Davidson? Whatever caused his death is, beyond doubt, equally responsible for Pritchard's. I am now going into the tunnel."

Inspector Henderson went in with me. The place struck damp and chill. The walls were covered with green, evil-smelling fungi, and through the brickwork the moisture was oozing and had trickled down in long lines to the ground. Before us was nothing but dense darkness.

When we re-appeared the signalman was lighting the red lamp on the post, which stood about five feet from the ground just above the entrance to the tunnel.

"Is there plenty of oil?" asked the Inspector.

"Yes, sir, plenty," replied the man. "Is there anything more I can do for either of you gentlemen?" he asked, pausing, and evidently dying to be off.

"Nothing," answered Henderson; "I will wish you good-evening."

"Good-evening to you both," said the man. He made his way quickly up the path and was soon lost to sight.

Henderson and I then returned to the signal-box.

By this time it was nearly dark.

"How many trains pass in the night?" I asked of the Inspector.

"There's the 10.20 down express," he said, "it will pass here at about 10.40; then there's the 11.45 up, and then not another train till the 6.30 local to-morrow morning. We shan't have a very lively time," he added.

I approached the fire and bent over it, holding out my hands to try and get some warmth into them.

"It will take a good deal to persuade me to go down to the tunnel, whatever I may see there," said the man "I don't think, Mr. Bell, I am a coward in any sense of the word, but there's something very uncanny about this place, right away from the rest of the world. I don't wonder one often hears of signalmen going mad in some of these lonely boxes. Have you any theory to account for these deaths, sir?"

"None at present," I replied.

"This second death puts the idea of Pritchard being murdered quite out of court," he continued.

"I am sure of it," I answered.

"And so am I, and that's one comfort," continued Henderson. "That poor girl, Lucy Ray, although she was to be blamed for her conduct, is much to be pitied now; and as to poor Wynne himself, he protests his innocence through thick and thin. He was a wild fellow, but not the sort to take the life of a fellow-creature. I saw the doctor this afternoon while I was waiting for you at the inn, Mr. Bell, and also the police sergeant. They both say they do not know what Davidson died of. There was not the least sign of violence on the body."

"Well, I am as puzzled as the rest of you," I said. 'I have one or two theories in my mind, but none of them will quite fit the situation."

The night was piercingly cold, and, although there was not a breath of wind, the keen and frosty air penetrated into the lonely signal-box.

We spoke little, and both of us were doubtless absorbed by our own thoughts and speculations. As to Henderson, he looked distinctly uncomfortable, and I cannot say that my own feelings were too pleasant. Never had I been given a tougher problem to solve, and never had I been so utterly at my wits' end for a solution.

Now and then the Inspector got up and went to the telegraph instrument, which intermittently clicked away in its box. As he did so he made some casual remark and then sat down again. After the 10.40 had gone through, there followed a period of silence which seemed almost oppressive. All at once the stillness was broken by the whirr of the electric bell, which sounded so sharply in our ears that we both started. Henderson rose.

"That's the 11.45 coming," he said, and, going over to the three long levers, he pulled two of them down with a loud clang. The next moment, with a rush and a scream, the express tore down the cutting, the carriage lights streamed past in a rapid flash, the ground trembled, a few sparks from the engine whirled up into the darkness, and the train plunged into the tunnel.

"And now," said Henderson, as he pushed back the levers, "not another train till daylight. My word, it is cold!"

It was intensely so. I piled some more wood on the fire and, turning up the collar of my heavy ulster, sat down at one end of the bench and leant my back against the wall. Henderson did likewise; we were neither of us inclined to speak. As a rule, whenever I have any night work to do, I am never troubled with sleepiness, but on this occasion I felt unaccountably drowsy. I soon perceived that Henderson was in the same condition.

"Are you sleepy?" I asked of him.

"Dead with it, sir," was his answer; "but there's no fear, I won't drop off."

I got up and went to the window of the box. I felt certain that if I sat still any longer I should be in a sound sleep. This would never do. Already it was becoming a matter of torture to keep my eyes open. I began to pace up and down; I opened the door of the box and went out on the little platform.

"What's the matter, sir?" inquired Henderson, jumping up with a start.

"I cannot keep awake," I said.

"Nor can I," he answered, "and yet I have spent nights and nights of my life in signal-boxes and never was the least bit drowsy; perhaps it's the cold."

'Perhaps it is," I said; "but I have been out on as freezing nights before, and—"

The man did not reply; he had sat down again; his head was nodding.

I was just about to go up to him and shake him, when it suddenly occurred to me that I might as well let him have his sleep out. I soon heard him snoring, and he presently fell forward in a heap on the floor. By dint of walking up and down, I managed to keep from dropping off myself, and in torture which I shall never be able to describe, the night wore itself away. At last, towards morning, I awoke Henderson.

"You have had a good nap," I said; "but never mind, I have been on guard and nothing has occurred."

"Good God! have I been asleep?" cried the man.

"Sound," I answered.

"Well, I never felt anything like it," he replied. 'Don't you find the air very close, sir?"

"No," I said; "it is as fresh as possible; it must be the cold."

"I'll just go and have a look at the light at the tunnel," said the man; "it will rouse me."

He went on to the little platform, whilst I bent over the fire and began to build it up. Presently he returned with a scared took on his face. I could see by the light of the oil lamp which hung on the wall that he was trembling.

"Mr. Bell," he said, "I believe there is somebody or something down at the mouth of the tunnel now." As he spoke he clutched me by the arm "Go and look," he said; "whoever it is, it has put out the light."

"Put out the light?" I cried. "Why, what's the time?"

Henderson pulled out his watch.

"Thank goodness, most of the night is gone," he said; "I didn't know it was so late, it is half-past five."

"Then the local is not due for an hour yet?" I said.

"No; but who should put out the light?" cried Henderson.

I went to the door, flung it open, and looked out. The dim outline of the tunnel was just visible looming through the darkness, but the red light was out.

"What the dickens does it mean, sir?" gasped the Inspector. "I know the lamp had plenty of oil in it. Can there be any one standing in front of it, do you think?"

We waited and watched for a few moments, but nothing stirred.

"Come along," I said, "let us go down together and see what it is."

"I don't believe I can do it, sir; I really don't!"

"Nonsense," I cried. "I shall go down alone if you won't accompany me. Just hand me my stick, will you?"

"For God's sake, be careful, Mr. Bell. Don't go down, whatever you do. I expect this is what happened before, and the poor fellows went down to see what it was and died there. There's some devilry at work, that's my belief."

"That is as it may be," I answered shortly, "but we certainly shall not find out by stopping here. My business is to get to the bottom of this, and I am going to do it. That there is danger of some sort, I have very little doubt; but danger or not, I am going down."

"If you'll be warned by me, sir, you'll just stay quietly here."

"I must go down and see the matter out," was my answer. "Now listen to me, Henderson. I see that you are alarmed, and I don't wonder. Just stay quietly where you are and watch, but if I call come at once. Don't delay a single instant. Remember I am putting my life into your hands. If I call 'Come,' just come to me as quick as you can, for I may want help. Give me that lantern."

He unhitched it from the wall, and taking it from him, I walked cautiously down the steps on to the line. I still felt curiously, unaccountably drowsy and heavy. I wondered at this, for the moment was such a critical one as to make almost any man wide awake. Holding the lamp high above my head, I walked rapidly along the line. I hardly knew what I expected to find. Cautiously along the metals I made my way, peering right and left until I was close to the fatal spot where the bodies had been found. An uncontrollable shudder passed over me. The next moment, to my horror, without the slightest warning, the light I was carrying went out, leaving me in total darkness. I started back, and stumbling against one of the loose boulders reeled against the wall and nearly fell. What was the matter with me? I could hardly stand. I felt giddy and faint, and a horrible sensation of great tightness seized me across the chest. A loud ringing noise sounded in my ears. Struggling madly for breath, and with the fear of impending death upon me, I turned and tried to run from a danger I could neither understand nor grapple with. But before I had taken two steps my legs gave way from under me, and uttering a loud cry I fell insensible to the ground.

Out of an oblivion which, for all I knew, might have lasted for moments or centuries, a dawning consciousness came to me. I knew that I was lying on hard ground; that I was absolutely incapable of realising, nor had I the slightest inclination to discover, where I was. All I wanted was to lie quite still and undisturbed. Presently I opened my eyes.

Some one was bending over me and looking into my face.

"Thank God, he is not dead," I heard in whispered tones. Then, with a flash, memory returned to me.

"What has happened?" I asked.

"You may well ask that, sir," said the Inspector gravely. "It has been touch and go with you for the last quarter of an hour; and a near thing for me too."

I sat up and looked around me. Daylight was just beginning to break, and I saw that we were at the bottom of the steps that led up to the signal-box. My teeth were chattering with the cold and I was shivering like a man with ague.

"I am better now," I said; "just give me your hand."

I took his arm, and holding the rail with the other hand staggered up into the box and sat down on the bench.

"Yes, it has been a near shave," I said; "and a big price to pay for solving a mystery."

"Do you mean to say you know what it is?" asked Henderson eagerly.

"Yes," I answered, "I think I know now; but first tell me how long was I unconscious?"

"A good bit over half an hour, sir, I should think. As soon as I heard you call out I ran down as you told me, but before I got to you I nearly fainted. I never had such a horrible sensation in my life. I felt as weak as a baby, but I just managed to seize you by the arms and drag you along the line to the steps, and that was about all I could do."

"Well, I owe you my life," I said; "just hand me that brandy flask, I shall be the better for some of its contents."

I took a long pull. Just as I was laying the flask down Henderson started from my side.

"There," he cried, "the 6.30 is coming." The electric bell at the instrument suddenly began to ring. "Ought I to let her go through, sir?" he inquired.

"Certainly," I answered. "That is exactly what we want. Oh, she will be all right."

"No danger to her, sir?"

"None, none; let her go through."

He pulled the lever and the next moment the train tore through the cutting.

"Now I think it will be safe to go down again," I said. "I believe I shall be able to get to the bottom of this business."

Henderson stared at me aghast.

"Do you mean that you are going down again to the tunnel?" he gasped.

"Yes," I said; "give me those matches. You had better come too. I don't think there will be much danger now; and there is daylight, so we can see what we are about."

The man was very loth to obey me, but at last I managed to persuade him. We went down the line, walking slowly, and at this moment we both felt our courage revived by a broad and cheerful ray of sunshine.

"We must advance cautiously," I said, "and be ready to run back at a moment's notice."

"God knows, sir, I think we are running a great risk," panted poor Henderson; "and if that devil or whatever else it is should happen to be about—why, daylight or no daylight—"

"Nonsense! man," I interrupted; "if we are careful, no harm will happen to us now. Ah! and here we are!" We had reached the spot where I had fallen. "Just give me a match, Henderson."

He did so, and I immediately lit the lamp. Opening the glass of the lamp, I held it close to the ground and passed it to and fro. Suddenly the flame went out.

"Don't you understand now?" I said, looking up at the Inspector.

"No, I don't, sir," he replied with a bewildered expression.

Suddenly, before I could make an explanation, we both heard shouts from the top of the cutting, and looking up I saw Bainbridge hurrying down the path. He had come in the dog-cart to fetch us.

"Here's the mystery," I cried as he rushed up to us, "and a deadlier scheme of Dame Nature's to frighten and murder poor humanity I have never seen."

As I spoke I lit the lamp again and held it just above a tiny fissure in the rock. It was at once extinguished.

"What is it?" said Bainbridge, panting with excitement.

"Something that nearly finished *me*," I replied. "Why, this is a natural escape of choke damp. Carbonic acid gas—the deadliest gas imaginable, because it gives no warning of its presence, and it has no smell. It must have collected here during the hours of the night when no train was passing, and gradually rising put out the signal light. The constant rushing of the trains through the cutting all day would temporarily disperse it."

As I made this explanation Bainbridge stood like one electrified, while a curious expression of mingled relief and horror swept over Henderson's face.

"An escape of carbonic acid gas is not an uncommon phenomenon in volcanic districts," I continued, "as I take this to be; but it is odd what should have started it. It has sometimes been known to follow earthquake shocks, when there is a profound disturbance of the deep strata."

"It is strange that you should have said that," said Bainbridge, when he could find his voice.

"What do you mean?"

"Why, that about the earthquake. Don't you remember, Henderson," he added, turning to the Inspector, "we had felt a slight shock all over South Wales about three weeks back?"

"Then that, I think, explains it," I said. "It is evident that Pritchard really did climb the rocks in a frantic attempt to escape from the gas and fell back on to these boulders. The other man was cut down at once, before he had time to fly."

"But what is to happen now?" asked Bainbridge. "Will it go on for ever? How are we to stop it?"

"The fissure ought to be drenched with lime water, and then filled up; but all really depends on what is the size of the supply and also the depth. It is an extremely heavy gas, and would lie at the bottom of a cutting like water. I think there is more here just now than is good for us," I added.

"But how," continued Bainbridge, as we moved a few steps from the fatal spot, "do you account for the interval between the first death and the second?"

"The escape must have been intermittent. If wind blew down the cutting, as probably was the case before this frost set in, it would keep the gas so diluted that its effects would not be noticed. There was enough down here this morning, before that train came through, to poison an army. Indeed, if it had not been for Henderson's promptitude, there would have been another inquest—on myself."

I then related my own experience.

"Well, this clears Wynne, without doubt," said Bainbridge; "but alas! for the two poor fellows who were victims. Bell, the Lytton Vale Railway Company owe you unlimited thanks; you have doubtless saved many lives, and also the Company, for the line must have been closed if you had not made your valuable discovery. But now come home with me to breakfast. We can discuss all those matters later on."

The Angel of the Lord

Melville Davisson Post

I ALWAYS thought my father took a long chance, but somebody had to take it and certainly I was the one least likely to be suspected. It was a wild country. There were no banks. We had to pay for the cattle, and somebody had to carry the money. My father and my uncle were always being watched. My father was right, I think.

"Abner," he said, "I'm going to send Martin. No one will ever suppose that we would trust this money to a child."

My uncle drummed on the table and rapped his heels on the floor. He was a bachelor, stern and silent. But he could talk . . . and when he did, he began at the beginning and you heard him through; and what he said—well, he stood behind it.

"To stop Martin," my father went on, "would be only to lose the money; but to stop you would be to get somebody killed."

I knew what my father meant. He meant that no one would undertake to rob Abner until after he had shot him to death.

I ought to say a word about my Uncle Abner. He was one of those austere, deeply religious men who were the product of the Reformation. He always carried a Bible in his pocket and he read it where he pleased. Once the crowd at Roy's Tavern tried to make sport of him when he got his book out by the fire; but they never tried it again. When the fight was over Abner paid Roy eighteen silver dollars for the broken chairs and the table—and he was the only man in the tavern who could ride a horse. Abner belonged to the church militant, and his God was a war lord.

So that is how they came to send me. The money was in greenbacks in packages. They wrapped it up in newspaper and put it into a pair of saddlebags, and I set out. I was about nine years old. No, it was not as bad as you think. I could ride a horse all day when I was nine years old—most any kind of a horse. I was tough as whit'-leather, and I knew the country I was going into. You must not picture a little boy rolling a hoop in the park.

It was an afternoon in early autumn. The clay roads froze in the night; they thawed out in the day and they were a bit sticky. I was to stop at Roy's Tavern, south of the river, and go on in the morning. Now and then I passed some cattle driver, but no one overtook me on the road until almost sundown; then I heard a horse behind me and a man came up. I knew him. He was a cattleman named Dix. He had once been a shipper, but he had come in for a good deal of bad luck. His partner, Alkire, had absconded with a big sum of money due the grazers. This had ruined Dix; he had given up his land, which wasn't very much, to the grazers. After that he had gone over the mountain to his people, got together a pretty big sum of money and bought a large tract of grazing land. Foreign claimants had sued him in the courts on some old title and he had lost the whole tract and the money that he had paid for it. He had married a remote cousin of ours and he had always lived on her lands, adjoining those of my Uncle Abner.

Dix seemed surprised to see me on the road.

"So it's you, Martin," he said; "I thought Abner would be going into the upcountry."

One gets to be a pretty cunning youngster, even at this age, and I told no one what I was about.

"Father wants the cattle over the river to run a month," I returned easily, "and I'm going up there to give his orders to the grazers."

He looked me over, then he rapped the saddlebags with his knuckles. "You carry a good deal of baggage, my lad."

I laughed. "Horse feed," I said. "You know my father! A horse must be fed at dinner time, but a man can go till he gets it."

One was always glad of any company on the road, and we fell into an idle talk. Dix said he was going out into the Ten Mile country; and I have always thought that was, in fact, his intention. The road turned south about a mile our side of the tavern. I never liked Dix; he was of an apologetic manner, with a cunning, irresolute face.

A little later a man passed us at a gallop. He was a drover named Marks, who lived beyond my Uncle Abner, and he was riding hard to get in before night. He hailed us, but he did not stop; we got a shower of mud and Dix cursed him. I have never seen a more evil face. I suppose it was because Dix usually had a grin about his mouth, and when that sort of face gets twisted there's nothing like it.

After that he was silent. He rode with his head down and his fingers plucking at his jaw, like a man in some perplexity. At the crossroads he stopped and sat for some time in the saddle, looking before him. I left him there, but at the bridge he overtook me. He said he had concluded to get some supper and go on after that.

Roy's Tavern consisted of a single big room, with a loft above it for sleeping quarters. A narrow covered way connected this room with the house in which Roy and his family lived. We used to hang our saddles on wooden pegs in this covered way. I have seen that wall so hung with saddles that you could not find a place for another stirrup. But tonight Dix and I were alone in the tavern. He looked cunningly at me when I took the saddle-bags with me into the big room and when I went with them up the ladder into the loft. But he said nothing—in fact, he had scarcely spoken. It was cold; the road had begun to freeze when we got in. Roy had lighted a big fire. I left Dix before it. I did not take off my clothes, because Roy's beds were mattresses of wheat straw covered with heifer skins—good enough for summer but pretty cold on such a night, even with the heavy, hand-woven coverlet in big white and black checks.

I put the saddle-bags under my head and lay down. I went at once to sleep, but I suddenly awaked. I thought there was a candle in the loft, but it was a gleam of light from the fire below, shining through a crack in the floor. I lay and watched it, the coverlet pulled up to my chin. Then I began to wonder why the fire burned so brightly. Dix ought to be on his way some time and it was a custom for the last man to rake out the fire. There was not a sound. The light streamed steadily through the crack.

Presently it occurred to me that Dix had forgotten the fire and that I ought to go down and rake it out. Roy always warned us about the fire when he went to bed. I got up, wrapped the great coverlet around me, went over to the gleam of light and looked down through the crack in the floor. I had to lie out at full length to get my eye against the board. The hickory logs had turned to great embers and glowed like a furnace of red coals.

Before this fire stood Dix. He was holding out his hands and turning himself about as though he were cold to the marrow; but with all that chill upon him, when the man's face came into the light I saw it covered with a sprinkling of sweat.

I shall carry the memory of that face. The grin was there at the mouth, but it was pulled about; the eyelids were drawn in; the teeth were clamped together. I have seen a dog poisoned with strychnine look like that.

I lay there and watched the thing. It was as though something potent and evil dwelling within the man were in travail to re-form his face upon its image. You cannot realize how that devilish labor held me— the face worked as though it were some plastic stuff, and the sweat oozed through. And all the time the man was cold; and he was crowding into the fire and turning himself about and putting out his hands. And it was as though the heat would no more enter in and warm him than it will enter in and warm the ice.

It seemed to scorch him and leave him cold—and he was fearfully and desperately cold! I could smell the singe of the fire on him, but it had no power against this diabolic chill. I began myself to shiver, although I had the heavy coverlet wrapped around me.

The thing was a fascinating horror; I seemed to be looking down into the chamber of some abominable maternity. The room was filled with the steady red light of the fire. Not a shadow moved in it. And there was silence. The man had taken off his boots and he twisted before the fire without a sound. It was like the shuddering tales of possession or transformation by a drug. I thought the man would burn himself to death. His clothes smoked. How could he be so cold?

Then, finally, the thing was over! I did not see it for his face was in the fire. But suddenly he grew composed and stepped back into the room. I tell you I was afraid to look! I do not know what thing I expected to see there, but I did not think it would be Dix.

Well, it was Dix; but not the Dix that any of us knew. There was a certain apology, a certain indecision, a certain servility in that other Dix, and these things showed about his face. But there was none of these weaknesses in this man.

His face had been pulled into planes of firmness and decision; the slack in his features had been taken up; the furtive moving of the eye was gone. He stood now squarely on his feet and he was full of courage. But I was afraid of him as I have never been afraid of any human creature in this world! Something that had been servile in him, that had skulked behind disguises, that had worn the habiliments of subterfuge, had now come forth; and it had molded the features of the man to its abominable courage.

Presently he began to move swiftly about the room. He looked out at the window and he listened at the door; then he went softly into the covered way. I thought he was going on his journey; but then he could not be going with his boots there beside the fire. In a moment he returned with a saddle blanket in his hand and came softly across the room to the ladder.

Then I understood the thing that he intended, and I was motionless with fear. I tried to get up, but I could not. I could only lie there with my eye strained to the crack in the floor. His foot was on the ladder, and I could already feel his hand on my throat and that blanket on my face, and the suffocation of death in me, when far away on the hard road I heard a horse!

He heard it, too, for he stopped on the ladder and turned his evil face about toward the door. The horse was on the long hill beyond the bridge, and he was coming as though the devil rode in his saddle. It was a hard, dark night. The frozen road was like flint; I could hear the iron of the shoes ring. Whoever rode that horse rode for his life or for something more than his life, or he was mad. I heard the horse strike the bridge and thunder across it. And all the while Dix hung there on the ladder by his hands and listened. Now he sprang softly down, pulled on his boots and stood up before the fire, his face—this new face—gleaming with its evil courage. The next moment the horse stopped.

I could hear him plunge under the bit, his iron shoes ripping the frozen road; then the door leaped back and my Uncle Abner was in the room. I was so glad that my heart almost choked me and for a moment I could hardly see—everything was in a sort of mist.

Abner swept the room in a glance, then he stopped.

"Thank God!" he said; "I'm in time." And he drew his hand down over his face with the fingers hard and close as though he pulled something away.

"In time for what?" said Dix.

Abner looked him over. And I could see the muscles of his big shoulders stiffen as he looked. And again he looked him over. Then he spoke and his voice was strange.

"Dix," he said, "is it you?"

"Who would it be but me?" said Dix.

"It might be the devil," said Abner. "Do you know what your face looks like?"

"No matter what it looks like!" said Dix.

"And so," said Abner, "we have got courage with this new face."

Dix threw up his head.

"Now, look here, Abner," he said, "I've had about enough of your big manner. You ride a horse to death and you come plunging in here; what the devil's wrong with you?"

"There's nothing wrong with me," replied Abner, and his voice was low. "But there's something damnably wrong with you, Dix."

"The devil take you," said Dix, and I saw him measure Abner with his eye. It was not fear that held him back; fear was gone out of the creature; I think it was a kind of prudence.

Abner's eyes kindled, but his voice remained low and steady.

"Those are big words," he said.

"Well," cried Dix, "get out of the door then and let me pass!"

"Not just yet," said Abner; "I have something to say to you."

"Say it then," cried Dix, "and get out of the door."

"Why hurry?" said Abner. "It's a long time until daylight, and I have a good deal to say."

"You'll not say it to me," said Dix. "I've got a trip to make tonight; get out of the door."

Abner did not move. "You've got a longer trip to make tonight than you think, Dix," he said; "but you're going to hear what I have to say before you set out on it."

I saw Dix rise on his toes and I knew what he wished for. He wished for a weapon; and he wished for the bulk of bone and muscle that would have a chance against Abner. But he had neither the one nor the other. And he stood there on his toes and began to curse—low, vicious, withering oaths, that were like the swish of a knife.

Abner was looking at the man with a curious interest.

"It is strange," he said, as though speaking to himself, "but it explains the thing. While one is the servant of neither, one has the courage of neither; but when he finally makes his choice he gets what his master has to give him."

Then he spoke to Dix.

"Sit down!" he said; and it was in that deep, level voice that Abner used when he was standing close behind his words. Every man in the hills knew that voice; one had only a moment to decide after he heard it. Dix knew that, and yet for one instant he hung there on his toes, his eyes shimmering like a weasel's, his mouth twisting. He was not afraid! If he had had the ghost of a chance against Abner he would have taken it. But he knew he had not, and with an oath he threw the saddle blanket into a corner and sat down by the fire.

Abner came away from the door then. He took off his great coat. He put a log on the fire and he sat down across the hearth from Dix. The new hickory sprang crackling into flames. For a good while there was silence; the two men sat at either end of the hearth without a word. Abner seemed to have fallen into a study of the man before him. Finally he spoke:

"Dix," he said, "do you believe in the providence of God?"

Dix flung up his head.

"Abner," he cried, "if you are going to talk nonsense I promise you upon my oath that I will not stay to listen."

Abner did not at once reply. He seemed to begin now at another point.

"Dix," he said, "you've had a good deal of bad luck. . . . Perhaps you wish it put that way."

"Now, Abner," he cried, "you speak the truth; I have had hell's luck."

"Hell's luck you have had," replied Abner. "It is a good word. I accept it. Your partner disappeared with all the money of the grazers on the other side of the river; you lost the land in your lawsuit; and you are to-night without a dollar. That was a big tract of land to lose. Where did you get so great a sum of money?"

"I have told you a hundred times," replied Dix. "I got it from my people over the mountains. You know where I got it."

"Yes," said Abner. "I know where you got it, Dix. And I know another thing. But first I want to show you this," and he took a little penknife out of his pocket. "And I want to tell you that I believe in the providence of God, Dix."

"I don't care a fiddler's damn what you believe in," said Dix.

"But you do care what I know," replied Abner.

"What do you know?" said Dix.

"I know where your partner is," replied Abner.

I was uncertain about what Dix was going to do, but finally he answered with a sneer.

"Then you know something that nobody else knows."

"Yes," replied Abner, "there is another man who knows."

"Who?" said Dix.

"You," said Abner.

Dix leaned over in his chair and looked at Abner closely.

"Abner," he cried, "you are talking nonsense. Nobody knows where Alkire is. If I knew I'd go after him."

"Dix," Abner answered, and it was again in that deep, level voice, "if I had got here five minutes later you would have gone after him. I can promise you that, Dix.

"Now, listen! I was in the upcountry when I got your word about the partnership; and I was on my way back when at Big Run I broke a stirrup-leather. I had no knife and I went into the store and bought this one; then the storekeeper told me that Alkire had gone to see you. I didn't want to interfere with him and I turned back. . . . So I did not become your partner. And so I did not disappear. . . . What was it that prevented? The broken stirrup-leather? The knife? In old times, Dix, men were so blind that God had to open their eyes before they could see His angel in the way before them. . . . They are still blind, but they ought not to be that blind. . . . Well, on the night that Alkire disappeared I met him on his way to your house. It was out there at the bridge. He had broken a stirrup-leather and he was trying to fasten it with a nail. He asked me if I had a knife, and I gave him this one. It was beginning to rain and I went on, leaving him there in the road with the knife in his hand."

Abner paused; the muscles of his great iron jaw contracted.

"God forgive me," he said; "it was His angel again! I never saw Alkire after that."

"Nobody ever saw him after that," said Dix. "He got out of the hills that night."

"No," replied Abner; "it was not in the night when Alkire started on his journey; it was in the day."

"Abner," said Dix, "you talk like a fool. If Alkire had traveled the road in the day somebody would have seen him."

"Nobody could see him on the road he traveled," replied Abner.

"What road?" said Dix.

"Dix," replied Abner, "you will learn that soon enough."

Abner looked hard at the man.

"You saw Alkire when he started on his journey," he continued; "but did you see who it was that went with him?"

"Nobody went with him," replied Dix; "Alkire rode alone."

"Not alone," said Abner; "there was another."

"I didn't see him," said Dix.

"And yet," continued Abner, "you made Alkire go with him."

I saw cunning enter Dix's face. He was puzzled, but he thought Abner off the scent.

"And I made Alkire go with somebody, did I? Well, who was it? Did you see him?"

"Nobody ever saw him."

"He must be a stranger."

"No," replied Abner, "he rode the hills before we came into them."

"Indeed!" said Dix. "And what kind of a horse did he ride?"

"White!" said Abner.

Dix got some inkling of what Abner meant now, and his face grew livid.

"What are you driving at?" he cried. "You sit here beating around the bush. If you know anything, say it out; let's hear it. What is it?"

Abner put out his big sinewy hand as though to thrust Dix back into his chair.

"Listen!" he said. "Two days after that I wanted to get out into the Ten Mile country and I went through your lands; I rode a path through the narrow valley west of your house. At a point on the path where there is an apple tree something caught my eye and I stopped. Five minutes later I knew exactly what had happened under that apple tree. . . . Someone had ridden there; he had stopped under that tree; then something happened and the horse had run away—I knew that by the tracks of a horse on this path. I knew that the horse had a rider and that it had stopped under this tree, because there was a limb cut from the tree at a certain height. I knew the horse had remained there, because the small twigs of the apple limb had been pared off, and they lay in a heap on the path. I knew that something had frightened the horse and that it had run away, because the sod was torn up where it had jumped. . . . Ten minutes later I knew that the rider had not been in the saddle when the horse jumped; I knew what it was that had frightened the horse; and I knew that the thing had occurred the day before. Now, how did I know that?

"Listen! I put my horse into the tracks of that other horse under the tree and studied the ground. Immediately I saw where the weeds beside the path had been crushed, as though some animal had been lying down there, and in the very center of that bed I saw a little heap of fresh earth. That was strange, Dix, that fresh earth where the animal had been lying down! It had come there after the animal had got up, or else it would have been pressed flat. But where had it come from?

"I got off and walked around the apple tree, moving out from it in an ever-widening circle. Finally I found an ant heap, the top of which had been scraped away as though one had taken up the loose earth in his hands. Then I went back and plucked up some of the earth. The under clods of it were colored as with red paint. . . . No, it wasn't paint.

"There was a brush fence some fifty yards away. I went over to it and followed it down.

"Opposite the apple tree the weeds were again crushed as though some animal had lain there. I sat down in that place and drew a line with my eye across a log of the fence to a limb of the apple tree. Then I got on my horse and again put him in the tracks of that other horse under the tree; the imaginary line passed through the pit of my stomach! . . . I am four inches taller than Alkire."

It was then that Dix began to curse. I had seen his face work while Abner was speaking and that spray of sweat had reappeared. But he kept the courage he had got.

"Lord Almighty, man!" he cried. "How prettily you sum it up! We shall presently have Lawyer Abner with his brief. Because my renters have killed a calf; because one of their horses frightened at the blood has bolted, and because they cover the blood with earth so the other horses traveling the path may not do the like; straightway I have shot Alkire out of his saddle. . . . Man! What a mare's nest! And now, Lawyer Abner, with your neat little conclusions, what did I do with

Alkire after I had killed him? Did I cause him to vanish into the air with a smell of sulphur or did I cause the earth to yawn and Alkire to descend into its bowels?"

"Dix," replied Abner, "your words move somewhat near the truth."

"Upon my soul," cried Dix, "you compliment me. If I had that trick of magic, believe me, you would be already some distance down."

Abner remained a moment silent.

"Dix," he said, "what does it mean when one finds a plot of earth resodded?"

"Is that a riddle?" cried Dix. "Well, confound me, if I don't answer it! You charge me with murder and then you fling in this neat conundrum. Now, what could be the answer to that riddle, Abner? If one had done a murder this sod would overlie a grave and Alkire would be in it in his bloody shirt. Do I give the answer?"

"You do not," replied Abner.

"No!" cried Dix. "Your sodded plot no grave, and Alkire not within it waiting for the trump of Gabriel! Why, man, where are your little damned conclusions?"

"Dix," said Abner, "you do not deceive me in the least; Alkire is not sleeping in a grave."

"Then in the air," sneered Dix, "with the smell of sulphur?"

"Nor in the air," said Abner.

"Then consumed with fire, like the priests of Baal?"

"Nor with fire," said Abner.

Dix had got back the quiet of his face; this banter had put him where he was when Abner entered. "This is all fools' talk," he said; "if I had killed Alkire, what could I have done with the body? And the horse! What could I have done with the horse? Remember, no man has ever seen Alkire's horse any more than he has seen Alkire—and for the reason that Alkire rode him out of the hills that night. Now, look here, Abner, you have asked me a good many questions. I will ask you one. Among your little conclusions do you find that I did this thing alone or with the aid of others?"

"Dix," replied Abner, "I will answer that upon my own belief you had no accomplice."

"Then," said Dix, "how could I have carried off the horse? Alkire I might carry; but his horse weighed thirteen hundred pounds!"

"Dix," said Abner, "no man helped you do this thing; but there were men who helped you to conceal it."

"And now," cried Dix, "the man is going mad! Who could I trust with such work, I ask you? Have I a renter that would not tell it when he moved on to another's land, or when he got a quart of cider in him? Where are the men who helped me?"

"Dix," said Abner, "they have been dead these fifty years."

I heard Dix laugh then, and his evil face lighted as though a candle were behind it. And, in truth, I thought he had got Abner silenced.

"In the name of Heaven!" he cried. "With such proofs it is a wonder that you did not have me hanged."

"And hanged you should have been," said Abner.

"Well," cried Dix, "go and tell the sheriff, and mind you lay before him those little, neat conclusions: How from a horse track and the place where a calf was butchered you have reasoned on Alkire's murder, and to conceal the body and the horse you have reasoned on the aid of men who were rotting in their graves when I was born; and see how he will receive you!"

Abner gave no attention to the man's flippant speech. He got his great silver watch out of his pocket, pressed the stem and looked. Then he spoke in his deep, even voice.

"Dix," he said, "it is nearly midnight; in an hour you must be on your journey, and I have something more to say. Listen! I knew this thing had been done the previous day because it had rained on the night that I met Alkire, and the earth of this ant heap had been disturbed after that. Moreover, this earth had been frozen, and that showed a night had passed since it had been placed there. And I knew the rider of that horse was Alkire because, beside the path near the severed twigs lay my knife, where it had fallen from his hand. This much I learned in some fifteen minutes; the rest took somewhat longer.

"I followed the track of the horse until it stopped in the little valley below. It was easy to follow while the horse ran, because the sod was torn; but when it ceased to run there was no track that I could follow. There was a little stream threading the valley, and I began at the wood and came slowly up to see if I could find where the horse had crossed. Finally I found a horse track and there was also a man's track, which meant that you had caught the horse and were leading it away. But where?

"On the rising ground above there was an old orchard where there had once been a house. The work about that house had been done a hundred years. It was rotted down now. You had opened this orchard into the pasture. I rode all over the face of this hill and finally I entered this orchard. There was a great, flat, moss-covered stone lying a few steps from where the house had stood. As I looked I noticed that the moss growing from it into the earth had been broken along the edges of the stone, and then I noticed that for a few feet about the stone the ground had been resodded. I got down and lifted up some of this new sod. Under it the earth had been soaked with that . . . red paint.

"It was clever of you, Dix, to resod the ground; that took only a little time and it effectually concealed the place where you had killed the horse; but it was foolish of you to forget that the broken moss around the edges of the great flat stone could not be mended."

"Abner!" cried Dix. "Stop!" And I saw that spray of sweat, and his face working like kneaded bread, and the shiver of that abominable chill on him.

Abner was silent for a moment and then he went on, but from another quarter.

"Twice," said Abner, "the Angel of the Lord stood before me and I did not know it; but the third time I knew it. It is not in the cry of the wind, nor in the voice of many waters that His presence is made known to us. That man in Israel had only the sign that the beast under him would not go on. Twice I had as good a sign, and tonight, when Marks broke a stirrup-leather before my house and called me to the door and asked me for a knife to mend it, I saw and I came."

The log that Abner had thrown on was burned down, and the fire was again a mass of embers; the room was filled with that dull red light. Dix had got on to his feet, and he stood now twisting before the fire, his hands reaching out to it, and that cold creeping in his bones, and the smell of the fire on him.

Abner rose. And when he spoke his voice was like a thing that has dimensions and weight.

"Dix," he said, "you robbed the grazers; you shot Alkire out of his saddle; and a child you would have murdered!"

And I saw the sleeve of Abner's coat begin to move, then it stopped. He stood staring at something against the wall. I looked to see what the thing was, but I did not see it. Abner was looking beyond the wall, as though it had been moved away.

And all the time Dix had been shaking with that hellish cold, and twisting on the hearth and crowding into the fire. Then he fell back, and he was the Dix I knew—his face was slack; his eye was furtive; and he was full of terror.

It was his weak whine that awakened Abner. He put up his hand and brought the fingers hard down over his face, and then he looked at this new creature, cringing and beset with fears.

"Dix," he said, "Alkire was a just man; he sleeps as peacefully in that abandoned well under his horse as he would sleep in the churchyard. My hand has been held back; you may go. Vengeance is mine, I will repay, saith the Lord."

"But where shall I go, Abner?" the creature wailed; "I have no money and I am cold."

Abner took out his leather wallet and flung it toward the door.

"There is money," he said—"a hundred dollars—and there is my coat. Go! But if I find you in the hills to-morrow, or if I ever find you, I warn you in the name of the living God that I will stamp you out of life!"

I saw the loathsome thing writhe into Abner's coat and seize the wallet and slip out through the door; and a moment later I heard a horse. And I crept back on to Roy's heifer skin.

When I came down at daylight my Uncle Abner was reading by the fire.

Bibliography

Allen, Grant. "The Great Ruby Robbery," *The Strand Magazine*, London, 1892.

Barr, Robert. "The Absent-Minded Coterie," *The Triumphs of Eugene Valmont*, 1906.

Boothby, Guy. "The Duchess of Wiltshire's Diamonds," *Pearson's Magazine*, London, February 1897.

Bramah, Ernest. "The Coin of Dionysus," *Max Carrados*, Methuen & Co, London, 1914.

Chesterton, G. K. "The Hammer of God," (as "The Bolt from the Blue"), *The Saturday Evening Post,* Indianapolis, Indiana, November 1910.

Freeman, R. Austin. "The Dead Hand," *Pearson's Magazine*, London, October-November 1912.

Futrelle, Jacques. "The Problem of the Stolen Rubens," *The Thinking Machine*, Dodd, Mead and Company, New York, 1907.

Hill, Headon. "The Divination of the Zagury Capsules," *The Divination of Kala Persad*, Ward, Lock & Bowden, Ltd., 1895.

Hume, Fergus. "The Green-Stone God and the Stockbroker," *The Dwarf's Chamber and Other Stories*, Ward, Lock & Bowden, Ltd., London, 1896.

Leblanc, Maurice. "Arsène Lupin in Prison" ("Arsène Lupin en prison"), *Je sais tout*, Paris, No. 11, 15 December 1905.

Meade, L. T., and Eustace, Robert. "The Mystery of the Felwyn Tunnel," *A Master of Mysteries*, Ward, Lock & Company, Ltd., London, 1898.

Morrison, Arthur. "The Lenton Croft Robberies," *The Strand Magazine*, London, Volume VII, January-June 1894.

Orczy, Baroness. "The Ninescore Mystery," *Lady Molly of Scotland Yard*, Cassell and Company, London, 1910.

Pirkis, Catherine L. "The Murder at Troyte's Hill," *The Ludgate Monthly*, London, March 1893.

Post, Melville Davisson. "The Angel of the Lord," *The Saturday Evening Post*, Indianapolis, Indiana, 1911.

Weir, Hugh C. "Cinderella's Slipper," *Maclean's*, Toronto, September 1914.